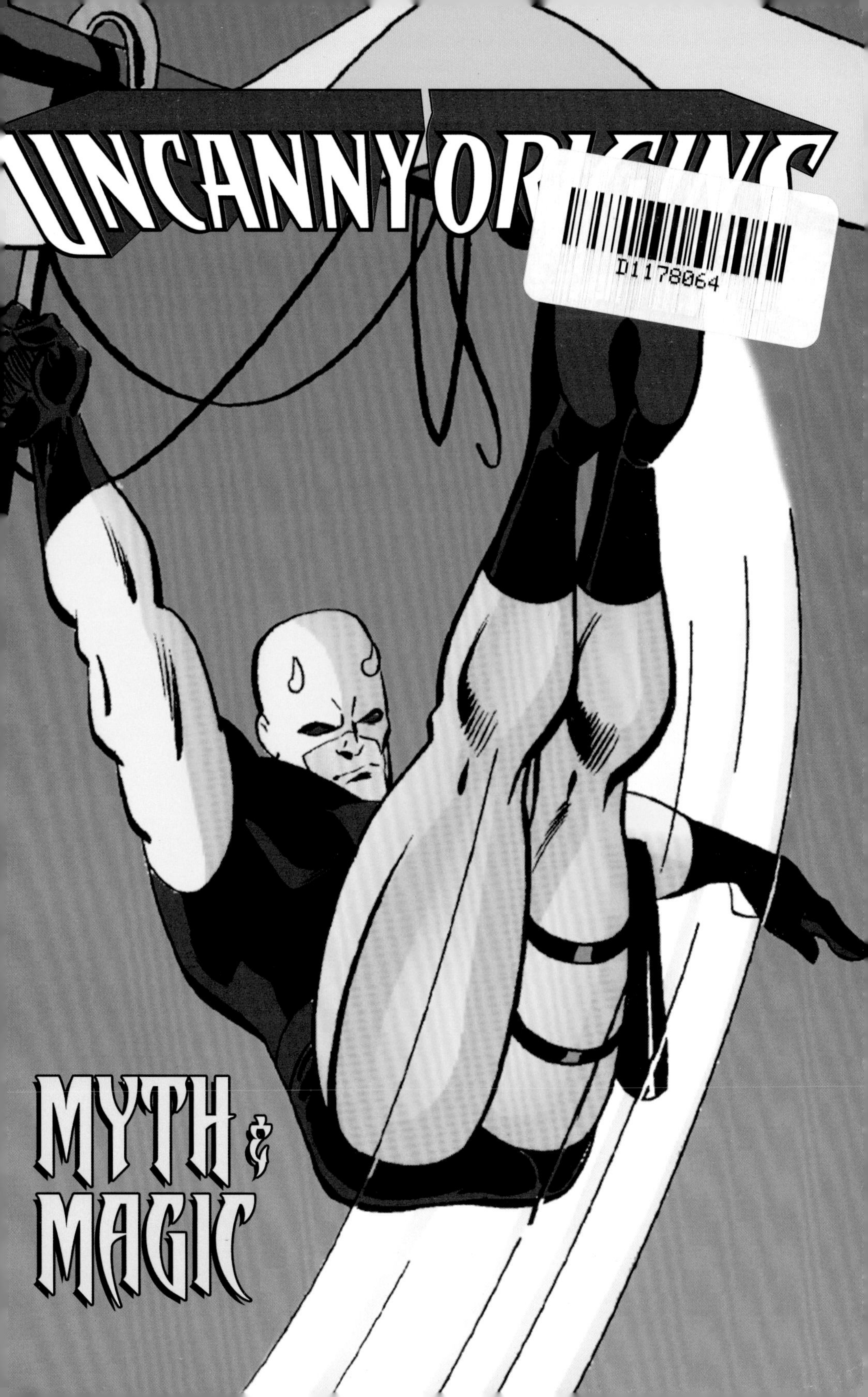
UNCANNY OR
D1178064
MYTH & MAGIC

UNCANNY ORIGINS
MYTH & MAGIC

BILL ROSEMANN, JIM ALEXANDER, LYSA HAWKINS, GLENN HERDLING, LEN WEIN & BOB BUDIANSKY
WRITERS

MARC CAMPOS & M.C. WYMAN
WRITERS

MARC CAMPOS & RALPH CABRERA
WRITERS

SCOTT ROCKWELL, BOB SHAREN & KGM GRAPHICS
COLORISTS

JACK MORELLI & JOHN COSTANZA
LETTERERS

PAUL TUTRONE
ASSISTANT EDITOR

JOE ANDREANI WITH TERRY KAVANAGH, BOBBIE CHASE & MATT HICKS
EDITORS

M.C. WYMAN & RALPH CABRERA
FRONT COVER ARTISTS

COLLECTION EDITOR **MARK D. BEAZLEY**
ASSISTANT EDITOR **CAITLIN O'CONNELL**
ASSOCIATE MANAGING EDITOR **KATERI WOODY**
ASSOCIATE MANAGER, DIGITAL ASSETS **JOE HOCHSTEIN**
SENIOR EDITOR, SPECIAL PROJECTS **JENNIFER GRÜNWALD**

VP PRODUCTION & SPECIAL PROJECTS **JEFF YOUNGQUIST**
RESEARCH & LAYOUT **JEPH YORK**
PRODUCTION **JOE FRONTIRRE**
BOOK DESIGNER **ADAM DEL RE**
SVP PRINT, SALES & MARKETING **DAVID GABRIEL**

DIRECTOR, LICENSED PUBLISHING **SVEN LARSEN**
EDITOR IN CHIEF **C.B. CEBULSKI**
CHIEF CREATIVE OFFICER **JOE QUESADA**
PRESIDENT **DAN BUCKLEY**
EXECUTIVE PRODUCER **ALAN FINE**

UNCANNY ORIGINS: MYTH & MAGIC. Contains material originally published in magazine form as UNCANNY ORIGINS (1996) #8-14. First printing 2019. ISBN 978-1-302-92043-2. Published by MARVEL WORLDWIDE, INC., a subsidiary of MARVEL ENTERTAINMENT, LLC. OFFICE OF PUBLICATION: 135 West 50th Street, New York, NY 10020. © 2019 MARVEL No similarity between any of the names, characters, persons, and/or institutions in this magazine with those of any living or dead person or institution is intended, and any such similarity which may exist is purely coincidental. **Printed in Canada.** DAN BUCKLEY, President, Marvel Entertainment; JOHN NEE, Publisher; JOE QUESADA, Chief Creative Officer; TOM BREVOORT, SVP of Publishing; DAVID BOGART, Associate Publisher & SVP of Talent Affairs; DAVID GABRIEL, VP of Print & Digital Publishing; JEFF YOUNGQUIST, VP of Production & Special Projects; DAN CARR, Executive Director of Publishing Technology; ALEX MORALES, Director of Publishing Operations; DAN EDINGTON, Managing Editor; SUSAN CRESPI, Production Manager; STAN LEE, Chairman Emeritus. For information regarding advertising in Marvel Comics or on Marvel.com, please contact Vit DeBellis, Custom Solutions & Integrated Advertising Manager, at vdebellis@marvel.com. For Marvel subscription inquiries, please call 888-511-5480. **Manufactured between 10/25/2019 and 11/26/2019 by SOLISCO PRINTERS, SCOTT, QC, CANADA.**

10 9 8 7 6 5 4 3 2 1

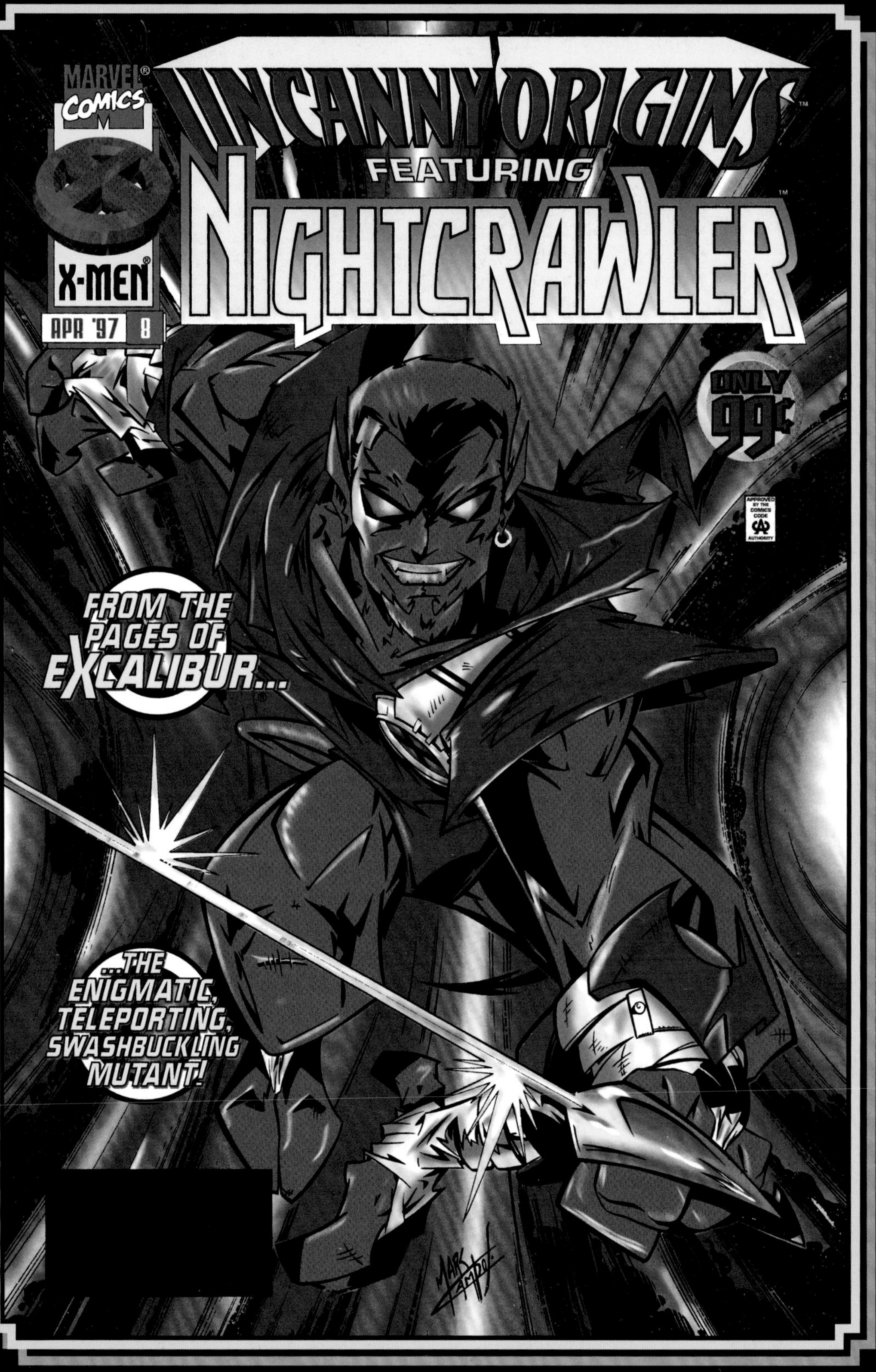
MARVEL COMICS
UNCANNY ORIGINS
FEATURING
NIGHTCRAWLER
X-MEN
APR '97 8
ONLY 99¢
APPROVED BY THE COMICS CODE AUTHORITY
FROM THE PAGES OF EXCALIBUR...
...THE ENIGMATIC, TELEPORTING, SWASHBUCKLING MUTANT!

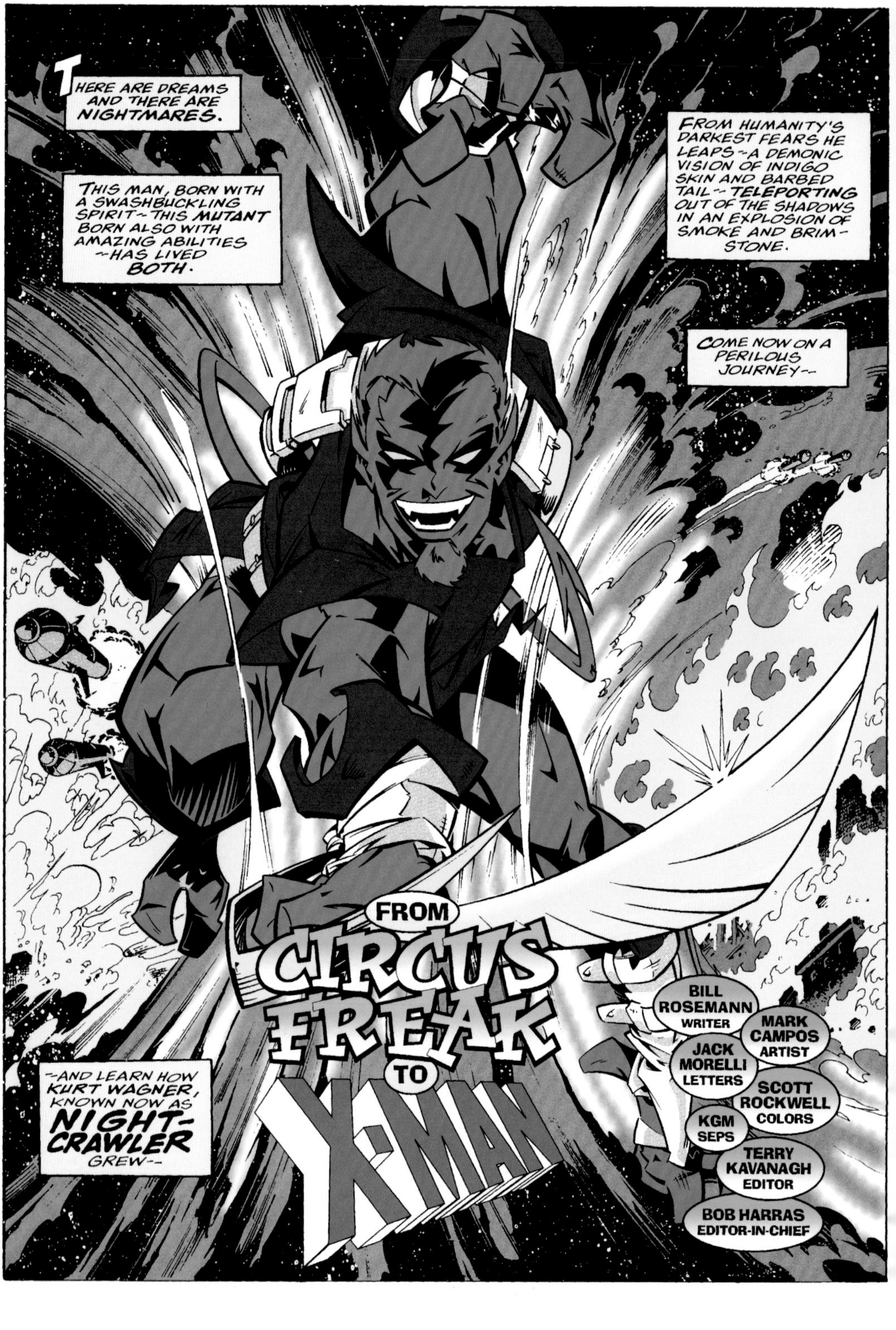
THERE ARE DREAMS AND THERE ARE NIGHTMARES.
THIS MAN, BORN WITH A SWASHBUCKLING SPIRIT-- THIS MUTANT BORN ALSO WITH AMAZING ABILITIES --HAS LIVED BOTH.
FROM HUMANITY'S DARKEST FEARS HE LEAPS--A DEMONIC VISION OF INDIGO SKIN AND BARBED TAIL--TELEPORTING OUT OF THE SHADOWS IN AN EXPLOSION OF SMOKE AND BRIM-STONE.
COME NOW ON A PERILOUS JOURNEY--
--AND LEARN HOW KURT WAGNER, KNOWN NOW AS NIGHT-CRAWLER GREW--
FROM CIRCUS FREAK TO X-MAN
BILL ROSEMANN WRITER
MARK CAMPOS ARTIST
JACK MORELLI LETTERS
SCOTT ROCKWELL COLORS
KGM SEPS
TERRY KAVANAGH EDITOR
BOB HARRAS EDITOR-IN-CHIEF

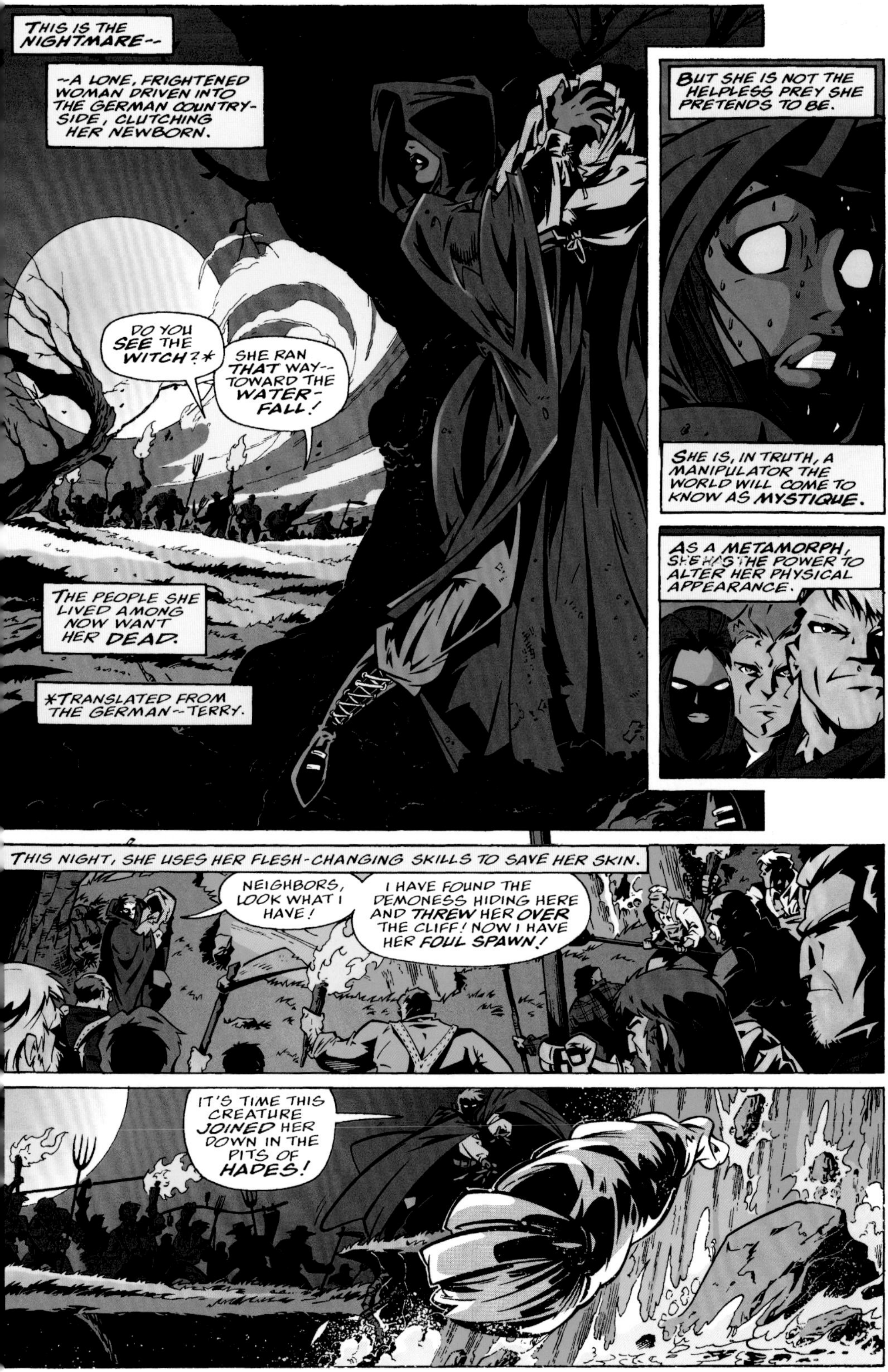
THIS IS THE NIGHTMARE--
--A LONE, FRIGHTENED WOMAN DRIVEN INTO THE GERMAN COUNTRYSIDE, CLUTCHING HER NEWBORN.
DO YOU SEE THE WITCH?*
SHE RAN THAT WAY--TOWARD THE WATERFALL!
THE PEOPLE SHE LIVED AMONG NOW WANT HER DEAD.
*TRANSLATED FROM THE GERMAN--TERRY.
BUT SHE IS NOT THE HELPLESS PREY SHE PRETENDS TO BE.
SHE IS, IN TRUTH, A MANIPULATOR THE WORLD WILL COME TO KNOW AS MYSTIQUE.
AS A METAMORPH, SHE HAS THE POWER TO ALTER HER PHYSICAL APPEARANCE.
THIS NIGHT, SHE USES HER FLESH-CHANGING SKILLS TO SAVE HER SKIN.
NEIGHBORS, LOOK WHAT I HAVE!
I HAVE FOUND THE DEMONESS HIDING HERE AND THREW HER OVER THE CLIFF! NOW I HAVE HER FOUL SPAWN!
IT'S TIME THIS CREATURE JOINED HER DOWN IN THE PITS OF HADES!

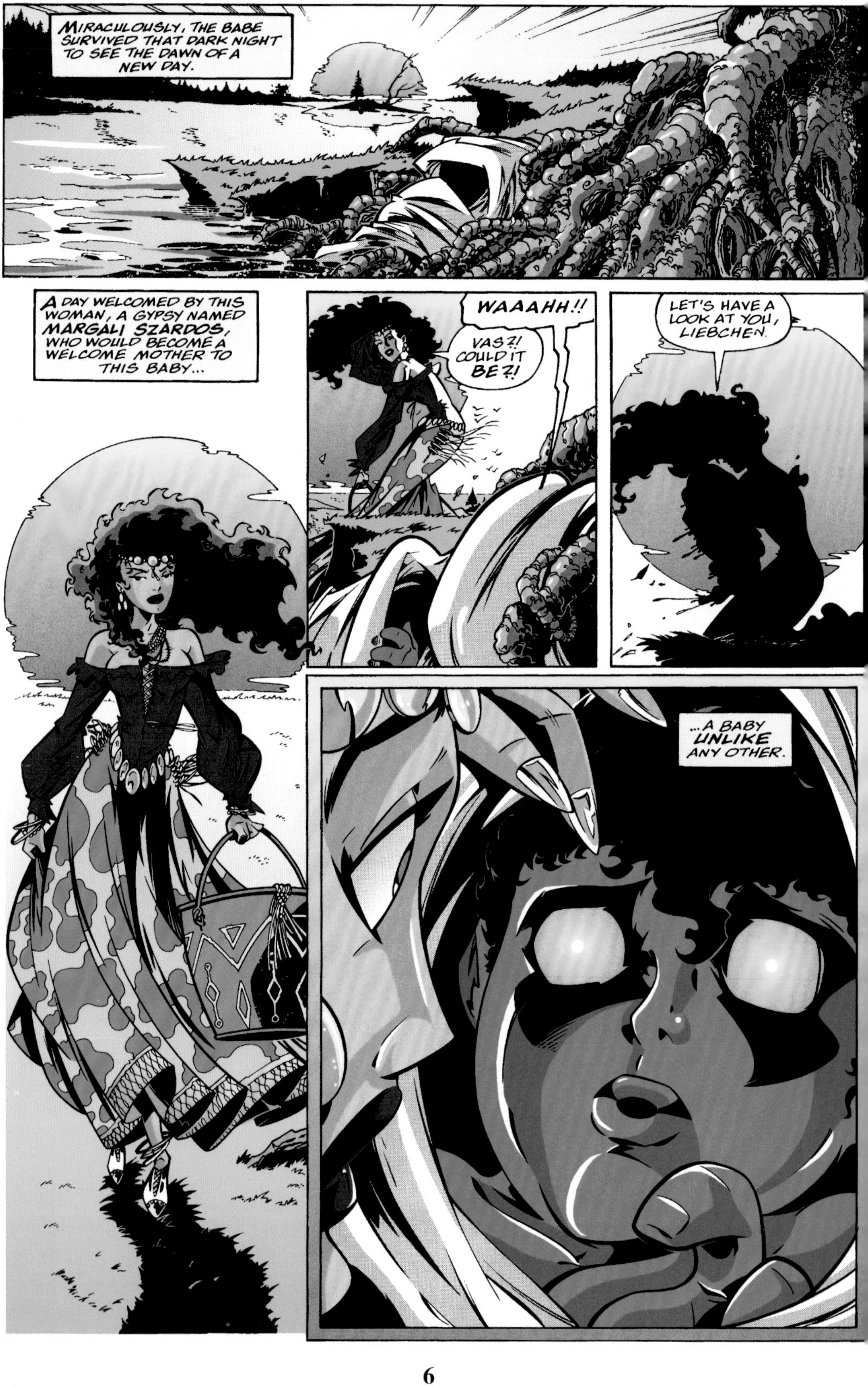
MIRACULOUSLY, THE BABE SURVIVED THAT DARK NIGHT TO SEE THE DAWN OF A NEW DAY.
A DAY WELCOMED BY THIS WOMAN, A GYPSY NAMED MARGALI SZARDOS, WHO WOULD BECOME A WELCOME MOTHER TO THIS BABY...
WAAAHH!!
VAS?! COULD IT BE?!
LET'S HAVE A LOOK AT YOU, LIEBCHEN.
...A BABY UNLIKE ANY OTHER.

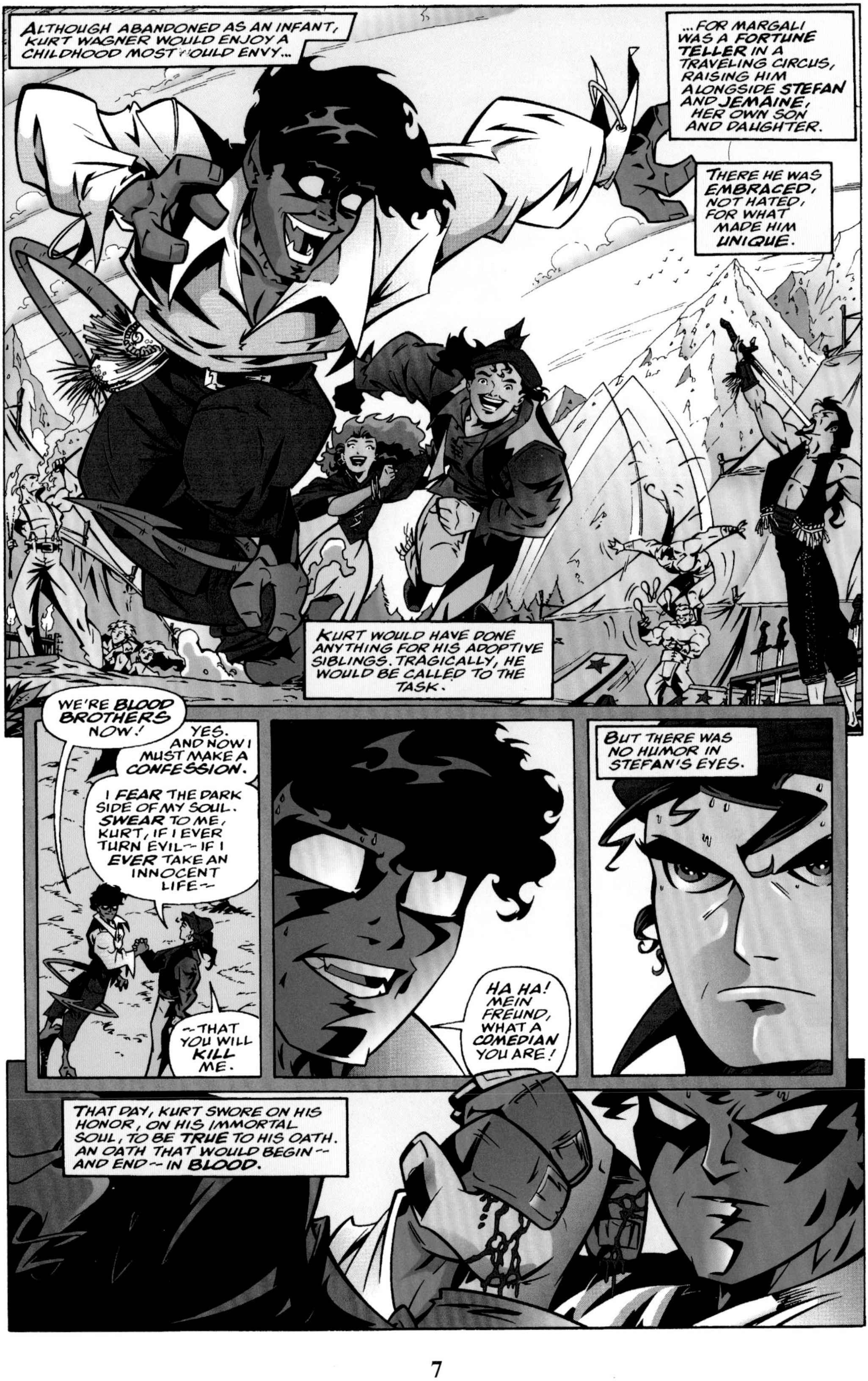

ALTHOUGH ABANDONED AS AN INFANT, KURT WAGNER WOULD ENJOY A CHILDHOOD MOST WOULD ENVY...
...FOR MARGALI WAS A FORTUNE TELLER IN A TRAVELING CIRCUS, RAISING HIM ALONGSIDE STEFAN AND JEMAINE, HER OWN SON AND DAUGHTER.
THERE HE WAS EMBRACED, NOT HATED, FOR WHAT MADE HIM UNIQUE.
KURT WOULD HAVE DONE ANYTHING FOR HIS ADOPTIVE SIBLINGS. TRAGICALLY, HE WOULD BE CALLED TO THE TASK.
WE'RE BLOOD BROTHERS NOW!
YES. AND NOW I MUST MAKE A CONFESSION.
I FEAR THE DARK SIDE OF MY SOUL. SWEAR TO ME, KURT, IF I EVER TURN EVIL-- IF I EVER TAKE AN INNOCENT LIFE--
--THAT YOU WILL KILL ME.
HA HA! MEIN FREUND, WHAT A COMEDIAN YOU ARE!
BUT THERE WAS NO HUMOR IN STEFAN'S EYES.
THAT DAY, KURT SWORE ON HIS HONOR, ON HIS IMMORTAL SOUL, TO BE TRUE TO HIS OATH. AN OATH THAT WOULD BEGIN-- AND END-- IN BLOOD.

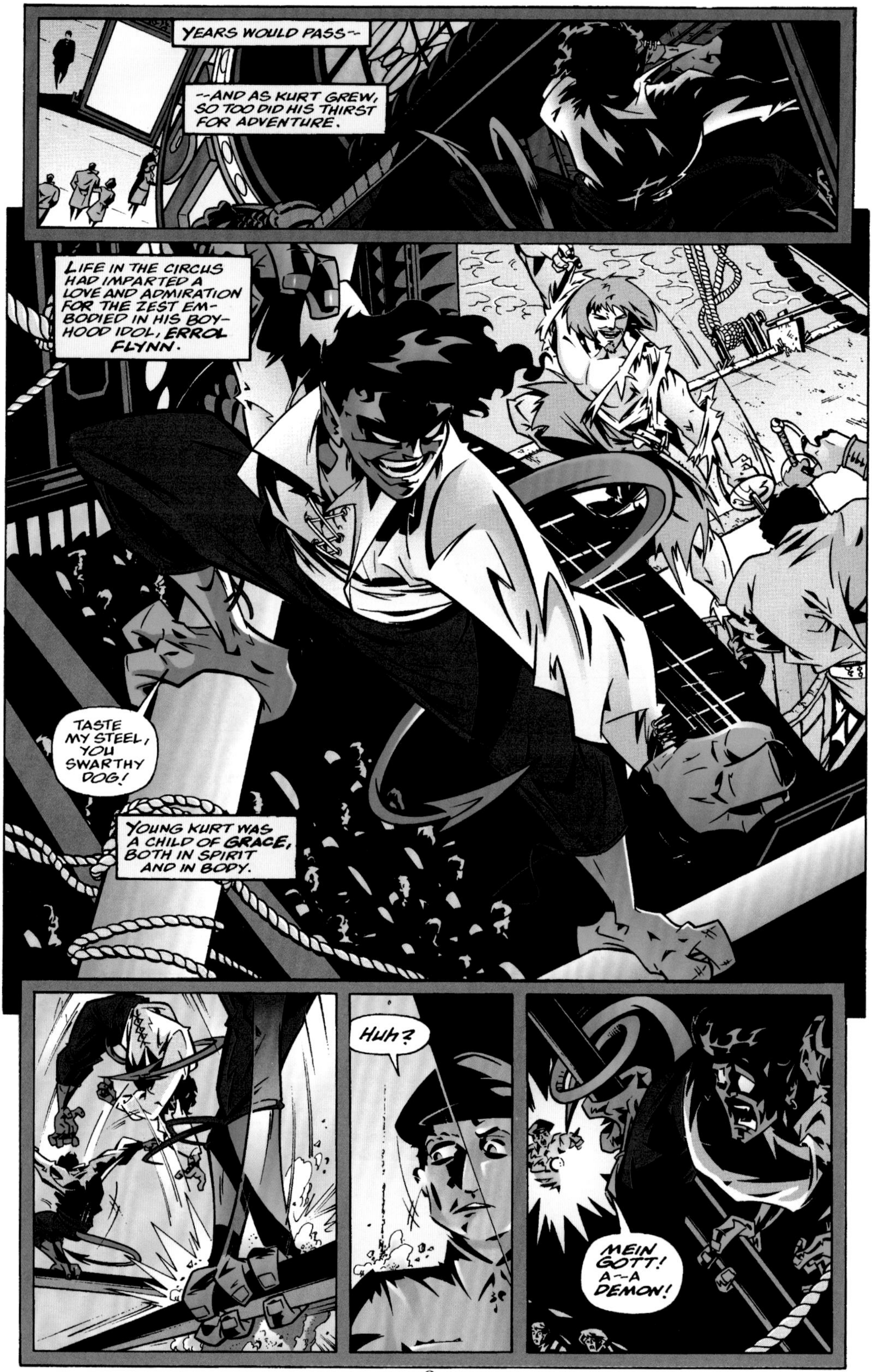
YEARS WOULD PASS--
--AND AS KURT GREW, SO TOO DID HIS THIRST FOR ADVENTURE.
LIFE IN THE CIRCUS HAD IMPARTED A LOVE AND ADMIRATION FOR THE ZEST EMBODIED IN HIS BOYHOOD IDOL, ERROL FLYNN.
TASTE MY STEEL, YOU SWARTHY DOG!
YOUNG KURT WAS A CHILD OF GRACE, BOTH IN SPIRIT AND IN BODY.
Huh?
MEIN GOTT! A--A DEMON!

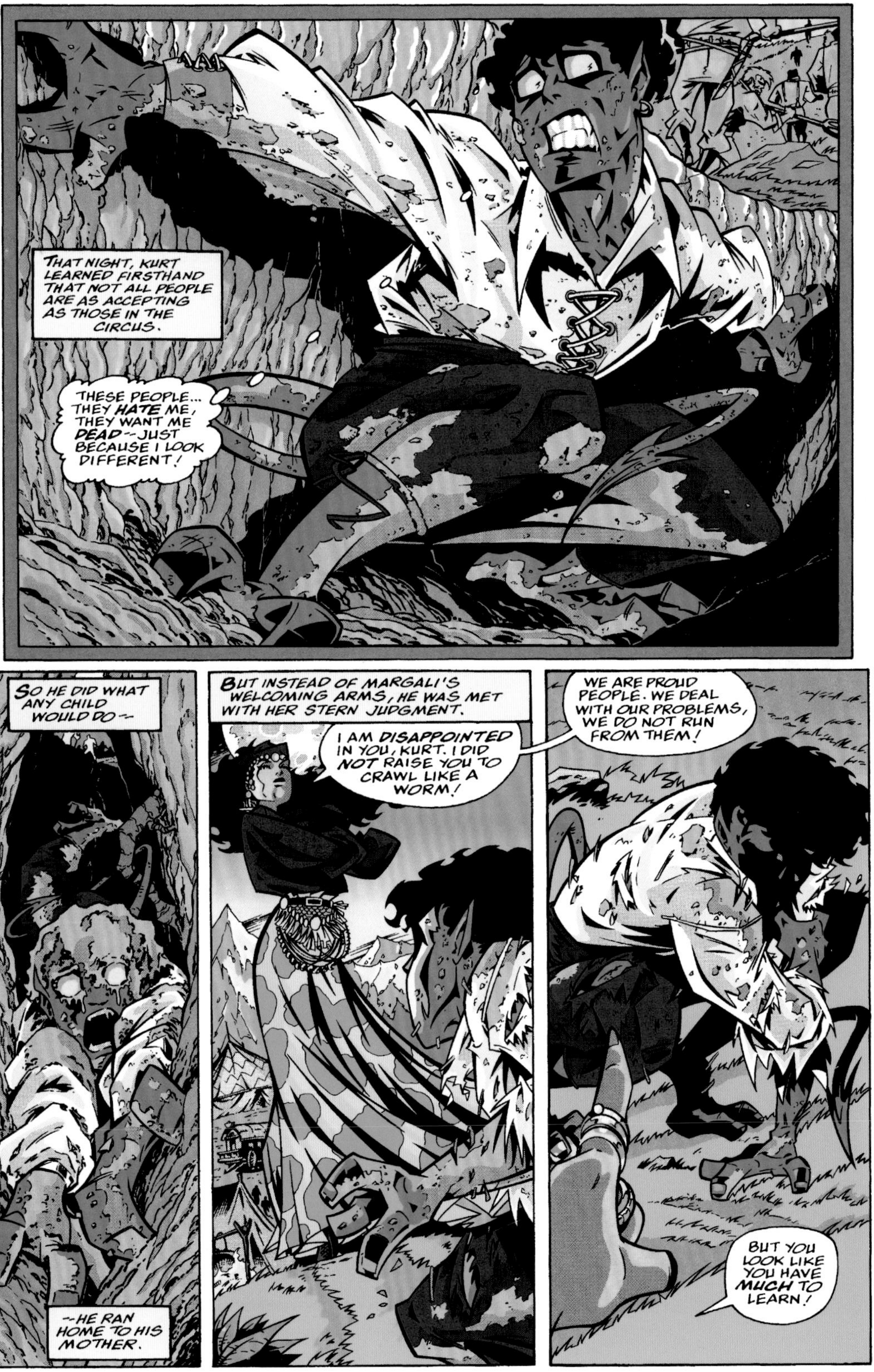

THAT NIGHT, KURT LEARNED FIRSTHAND THAT NOT ALL PEOPLE ARE AS ACCEPTING AS THOSE IN THE CIRCUS.
THESE PEOPLE... THEY HATE ME, THEY WANT ME DEAD--JUST BECAUSE I LOOK DIFFERENT!
SO HE DID WHAT ANY CHILD WOULD DO--
--HE RAN HOME TO HIS MOTHER.
BUT INSTEAD OF MARGALI'S WELCOMING ARMS, HE WAS MET WITH HER STERN JUDGMENT.
I AM DISAPPOINTED IN YOU, KURT. I DID NOT RAISE YOU TO CRAWL LIKE A WORM!
WE ARE PROUD PEOPLE. WE DEAL WITH OUR PROBLEMS, WE DO NOT RUN FROM THEM!
BUT YOU LOOK LIKE YOU HAVE MUCH TO LEARN!

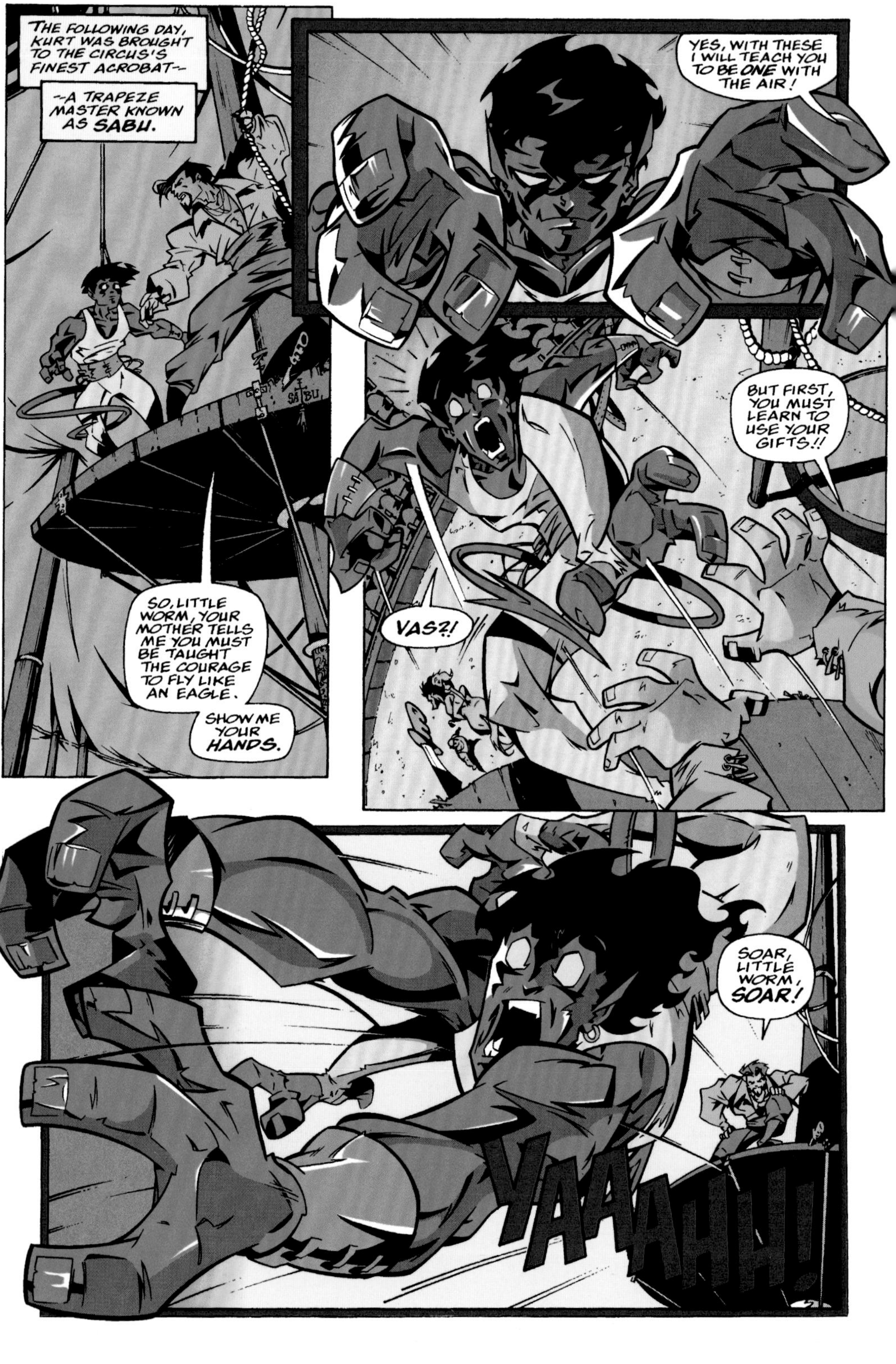
THE FOLLOWING DAY, KURT WAS BROUGHT TO THE CIRCUS'S FINEST ACROBAT--
--A TRAPEZE MASTER KNOWN AS SABU.
SABU
SO, LITTLE WORM, YOUR MOTHER TELLS ME YOU MUST BE TAUGHT THE COURAGE TO FLY LIKE AN EAGLE.
SHOW ME YOUR HANDS.
YES, WITH THESE I WILL TEACH YOU TO BE ONE WITH THE AIR!
BUT FIRST, YOU MUST LEARN TO USE YOUR GIFTS!!
VAS?!
SOAR, LITTLE WORM, SOAR!
YAAAHH!

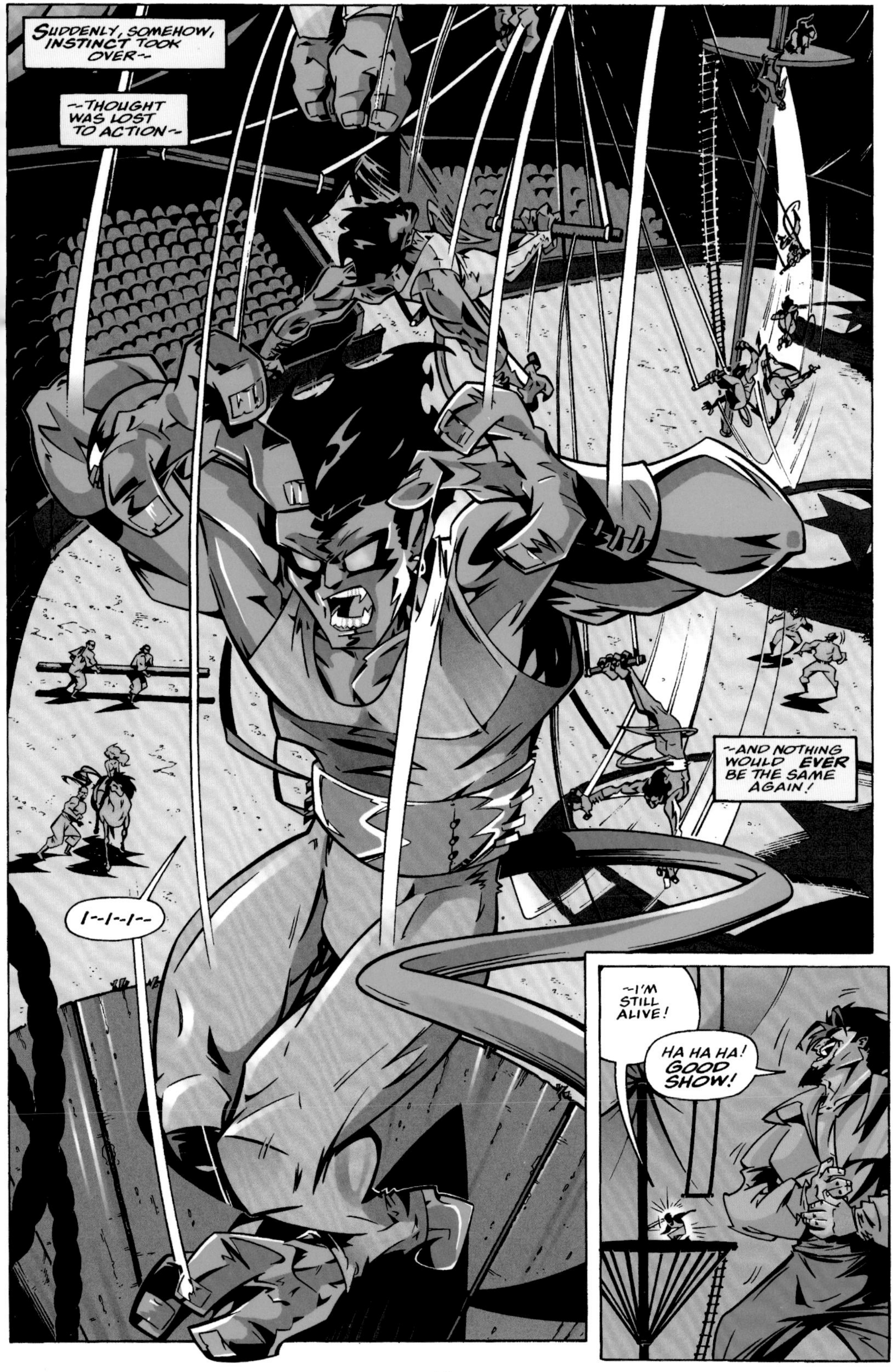
SUDDENLY, SOMEHOW, INSTINCT TOOK OVER--
--THOUGHT WAS LOST TO ACTION--
--AND NOTHING WOULD EVER BE THE SAME AGAIN!
I--I--I--
--I'M STILL ALIVE!
HA HA HA! GOOD SHOW!

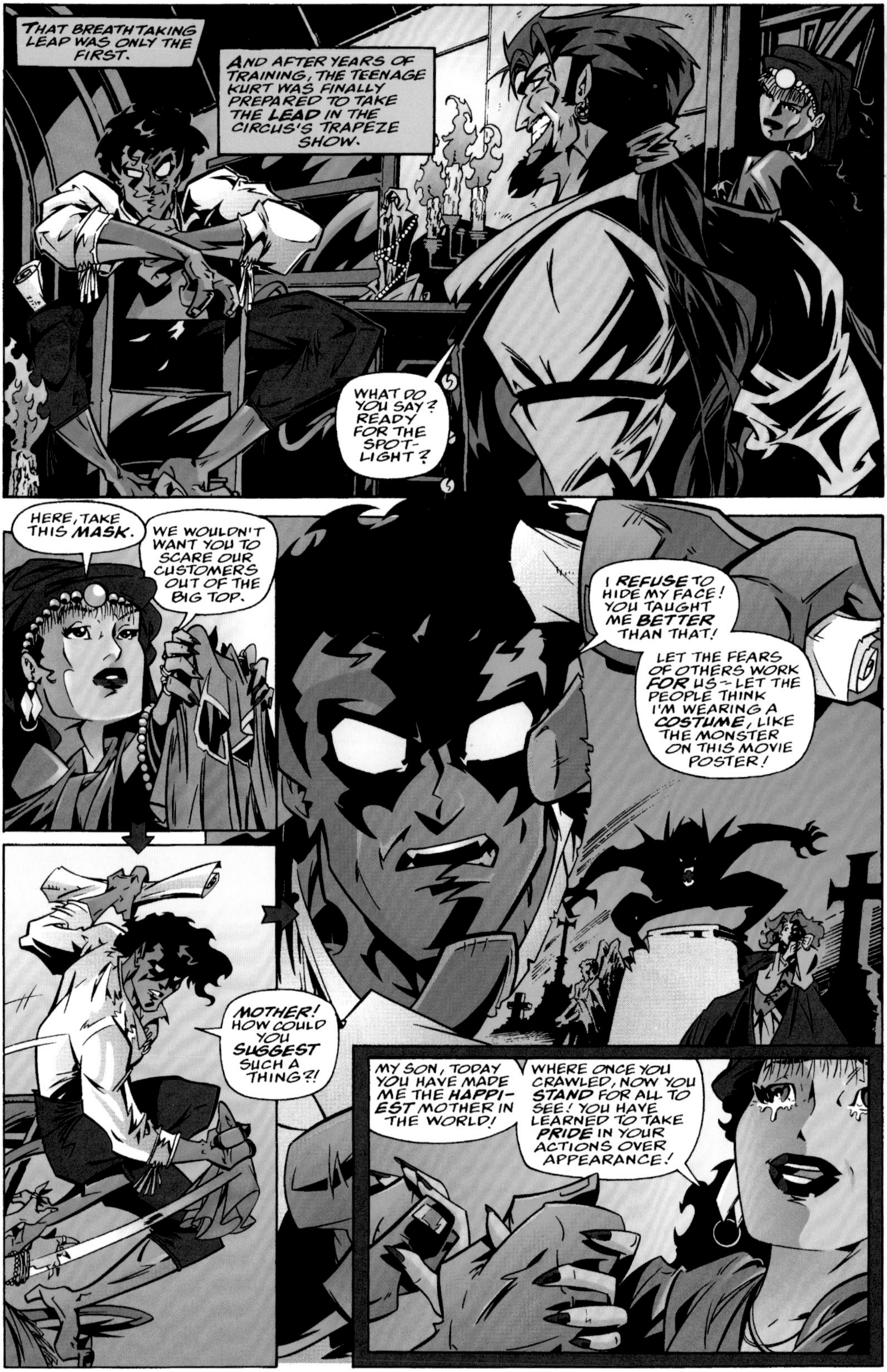

THAT BREATHTAKING LEAP WAS ONLY THE FIRST.
AND AFTER YEARS OF TRAINING, THE TEENAGE KURT WAS FINALLY PREPARED TO TAKE THE LEAD IN THE CIRCUS'S TRAPEZE SHOW.
WHAT DO YOU SAY? READY FOR THE SPOT-LIGHT?
HERE, TAKE THIS MASK.
WE WOULDN'T WANT YOU TO SCARE OUR CUSTOMERS OUT OF THE BIG TOP.
I REFUSE TO HIDE MY FACE! YOU TAUGHT ME BETTER THAN THAT!
LET THE FEARS OF OTHERS WORK FOR US-- LET THE PEOPLE THINK I'M WEARING A COSTUME, LIKE THE MONSTER ON THIS MOVIE POSTER!
MOTHER! HOW COULD YOU SUGGEST SUCH A THING?!
MY SON, TODAY YOU HAVE MADE ME THE HAPPI-EST MOTHER IN THE WORLD!
WHERE ONCE YOU CRAWLED, NOW YOU STAND FOR ALL TO SEE! YOU HAVE LEARNED TO TAKE PRIDE IN YOUR ACTIONS OVER APPEARANCE!

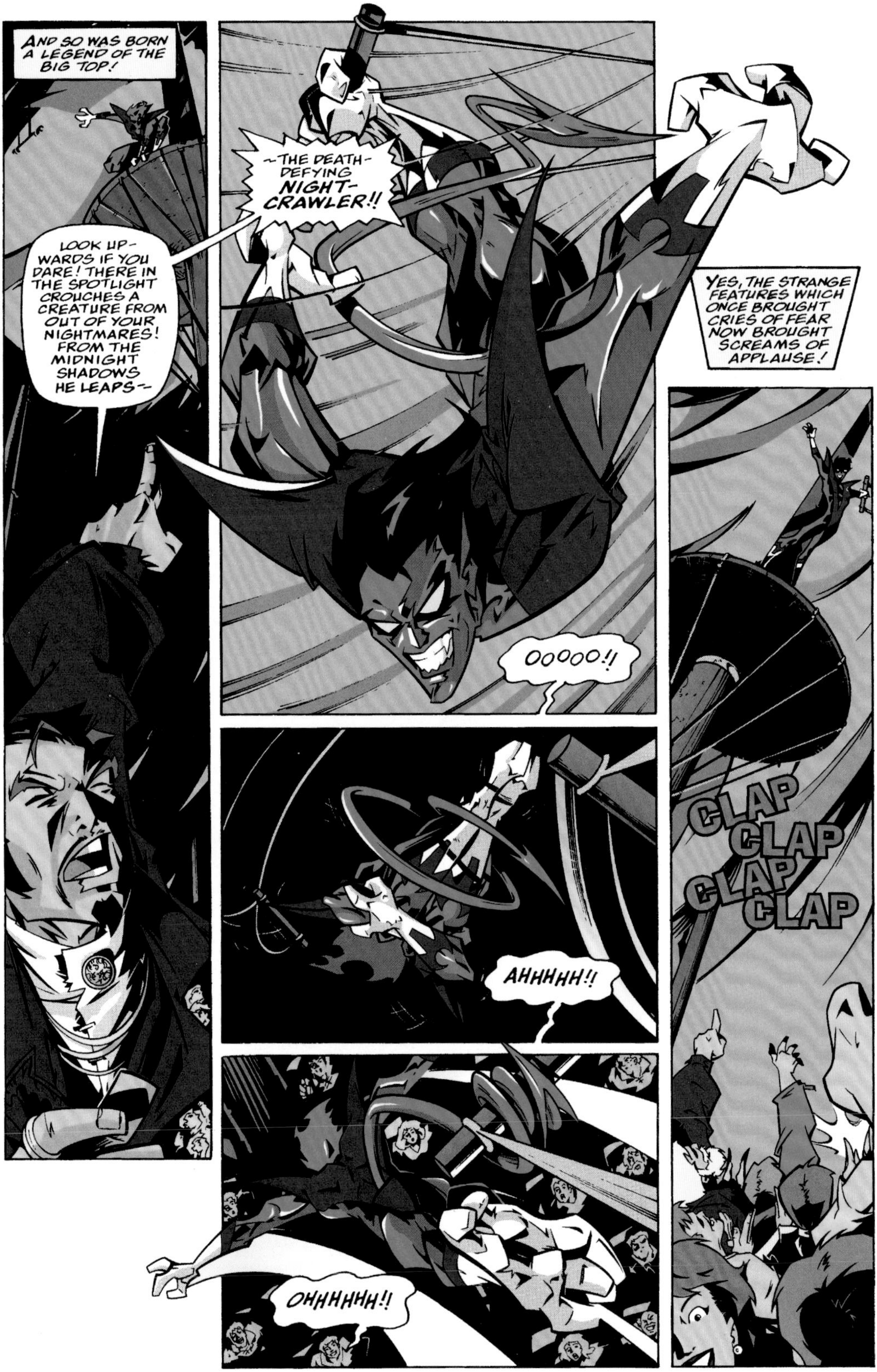
AND SO WAS BORN A LEGEND OF THE BIG TOP!
LOOK UP-WARDS IF YOU DARE! THERE IN THE SPOTLIGHT CROUCHES A CREATURE FROM OUT OF YOUR NIGHTMARES! FROM THE MIDNIGHT SHADOWS HE LEAPS--
--THE DEATH-DEFYING NIGHT-CRAWLER!!
OOOOO!!
AHHHHH!!
OHHHHHH!!
YES, THE STRANGE FEATURES WHICH ONCE BROUGHT CRIES OF FEAR NOW BROUGHT SCREAMS OF APPLAUSE!
CLAP
CLAP
CLAP
CLAP

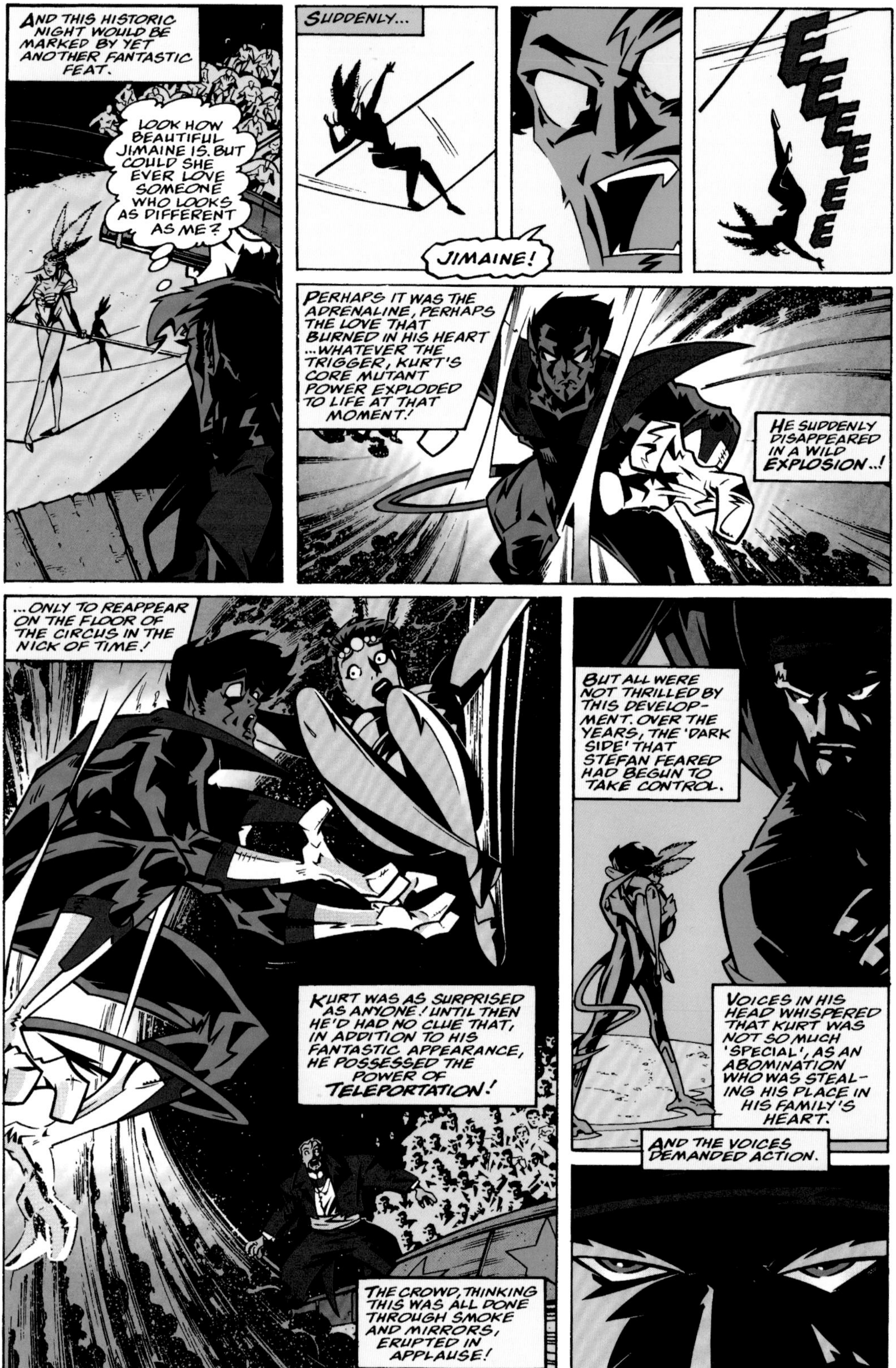
AND THIS HISTORIC NIGHT WOULD BE MARKED BY YET ANOTHER FANTASTIC FEAT.
LOOK HOW BEAUTIFUL JIMAINE IS. BUT COULD SHE EVER LOVE SOMEONE WHO LOOKS AS DIFFERENT AS ME?
SUDDENLY...
JIMAINE!
EEEEEEEE
PERHAPS IT WAS THE ADRENALINE, PERHAPS THE LOVE THAT BURNED IN HIS HEART ...WHATEVER THE TRIGGER, KURT'S CORE MUTANT POWER EXPLODED TO LIFE AT THAT MOMENT!
HE SUDDENLY DISAPPEARED IN A WILD EXPLOSION..!
...ONLY TO REAPPEAR ON THE FLOOR OF THE CIRCUS IN THE NICK OF TIME!
KURT WAS AS SURPRISED AS ANYONE! UNTIL THEN HE'D HAD NO CLUE THAT, IN ADDITION TO HIS FANTASTIC APPEARANCE, HE POSSESSED THE POWER OF TELEPORTATION!
THE CROWD, THINKING THIS WAS ALL DONE THROUGH SMOKE AND MIRRORS, ERUPTED IN APPLAUSE!
BUT ALL WERE NOT THRILLED BY THIS DEVELOPMENT. OVER THE YEARS, THE 'DARK SIDE' THAT STEFAN FEARED HAD BEGUN TO TAKE CONTROL.
VOICES IN HIS HEAD WHISPERED THAT KURT WAS NOT SO MUCH 'SPECIAL', AS AN ABOMINATION WHO WAS STEALING HIS PLACE IN HIS FAMILY'S HEART.
AND THE VOICES DEMANDED ACTION.

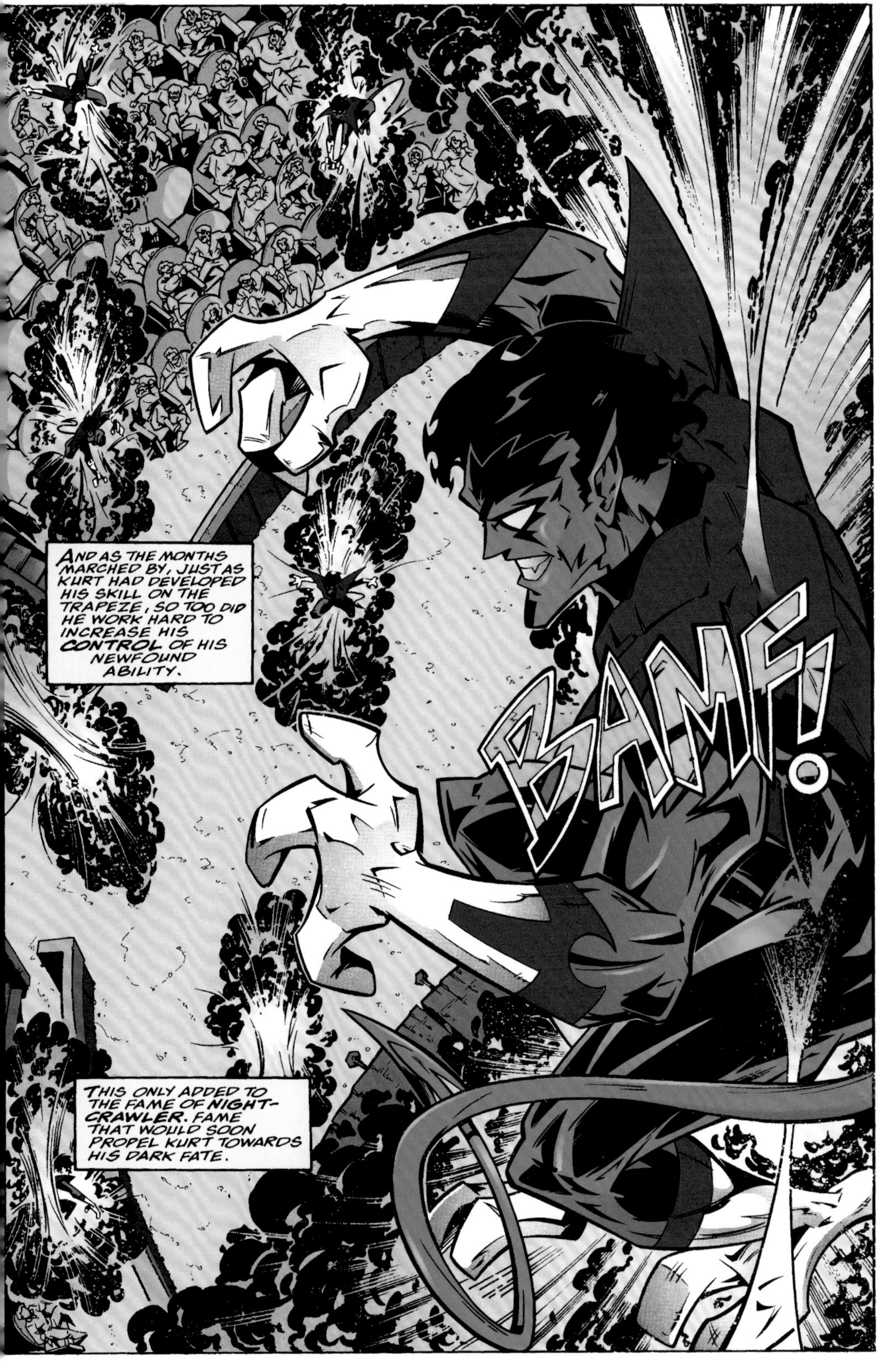
AND AS THE MONTHS MARCHED BY, JUST AS KURT HAD DEVELOPED HIS SKILL ON THE TRAPEZE, SO TOO DID HE WORK HARD TO INCREASE HIS CONTROL OF HIS NEWFOUND ABILITY.
BAMF!
THIS ONLY ADDED TO THE FAME OF NIGHT-CRAWLER. FAME THAT WOULD SOON PROPEL KURT TOWARDS HIS DARK FATE.

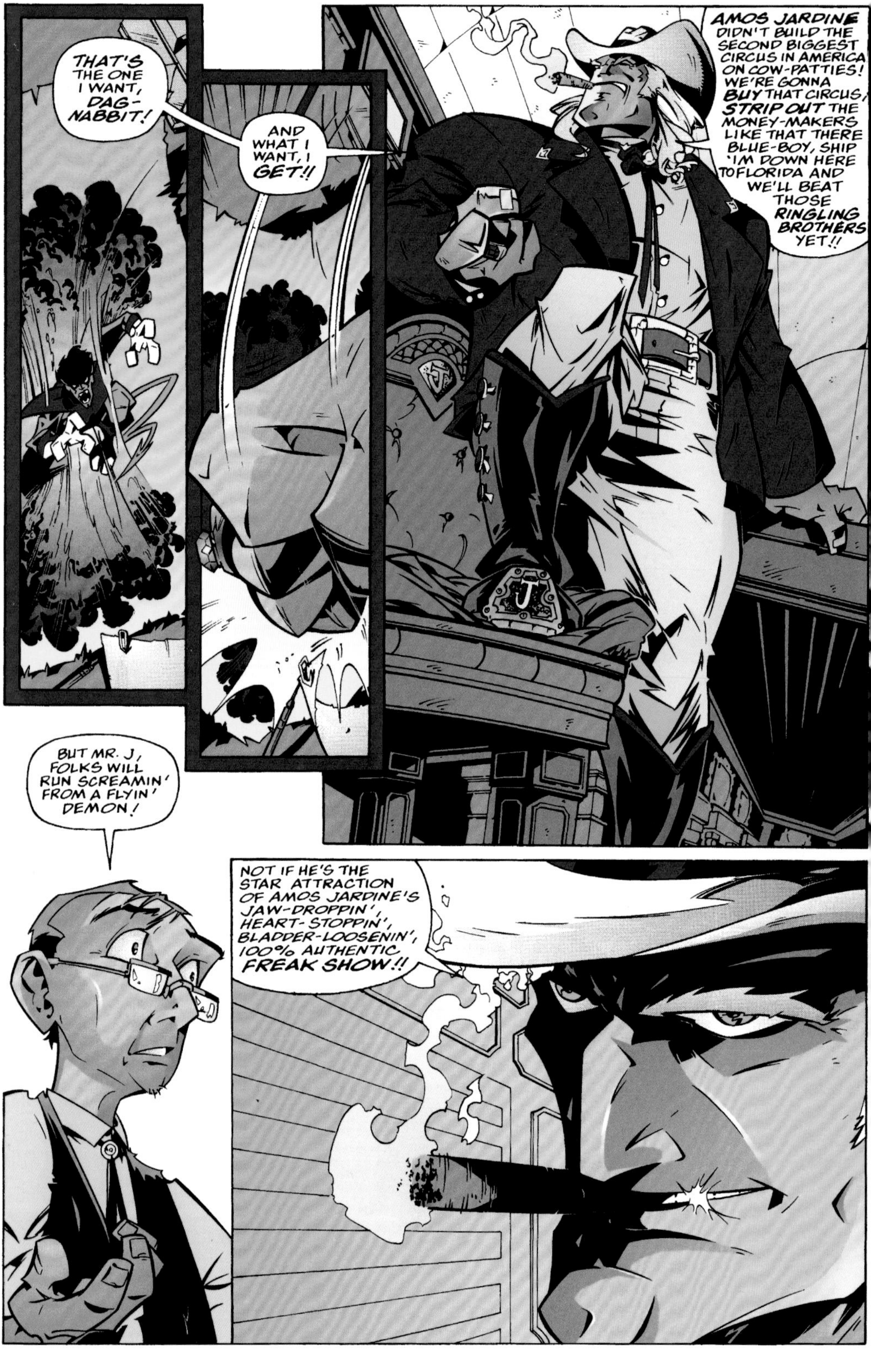
THAT'S THE ONE I WANT, DAG-NABBIT!
AND WHAT I WANT, I GET!!
AMOS JARDINE DIDN'T BUILD THE SECOND BIGGEST CIRCUS IN AMERICA ON COW-PATTIES! WE'RE GONNA BUY THAT CIRCUS, STRIP OUT THE MONEY-MAKERS LIKE THAT THERE BLUE-BOY, SHIP 'IM DOWN HERE TO FLORIDA AND WE'LL BEAT THOSE RINGLING BROTHERS YET!!
BUT MR. J, FOLKS WILL RUN SCREAMIN' FROM A FLYIN' DEMON!
NOT IF HE'S THE STAR ATTRACTION OF AMOS JARDINE'S JAW-DROPPIN', HEART-STOPPIN', BLADDER-LOOSENIN', 100% AUTHENTIC FREAK SHOW!!

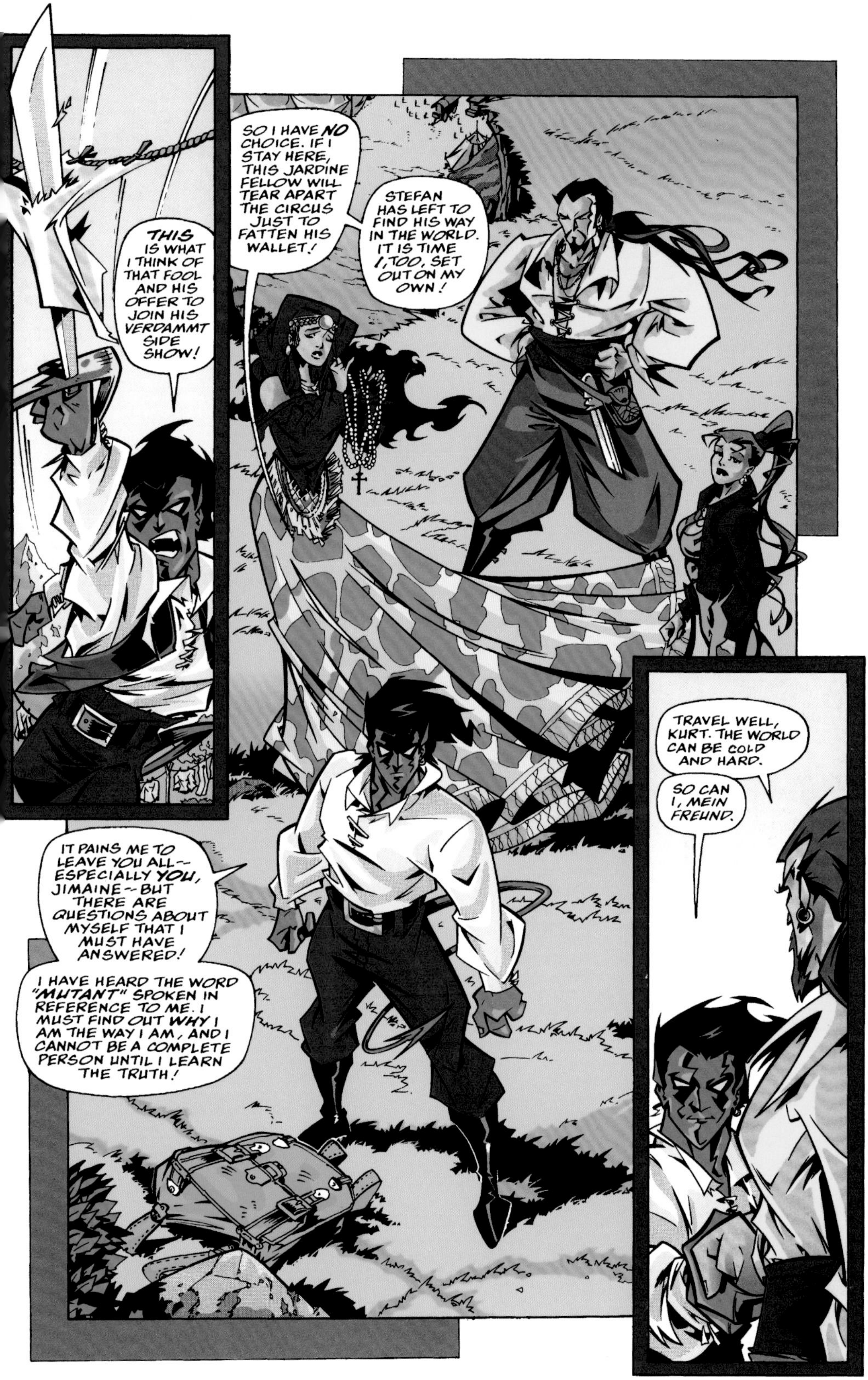
THIS IS WHAT I THINK OF THAT FOOL AND HIS OFFER TO JOIN HIS VERDAMMT SIDE SHOW!
SO I HAVE NO CHOICE. IF I STAY HERE, THIS JARDINE FELLOW WILL TEAR APART THE CIRCUS JUST TO FATTEN HIS WALLET!
STEFAN HAS LEFT TO FIND HIS WAY IN THE WORLD. IT IS TIME I, TOO, SET OUT ON MY OWN!
IT PAINS ME TO LEAVE YOU ALL-- ESPECIALLY YOU, JIMAINE--BUT THERE ARE QUESTIONS ABOUT MYSELF THAT I MUST HAVE ANSWERED!
I HAVE HEARD THE WORD "MUTANT" SPOKEN IN REFERENCE TO ME. I MUST FIND OUT WHY I AM THE WAY I AM, AND I CANNOT BE A COMPLETE PERSON UNTIL I LEARN THE TRUTH!
TRAVEL WELL, KURT. THE WORLD CAN BE COLD AND HARD.
SO CAN I, MEIN FREUND.

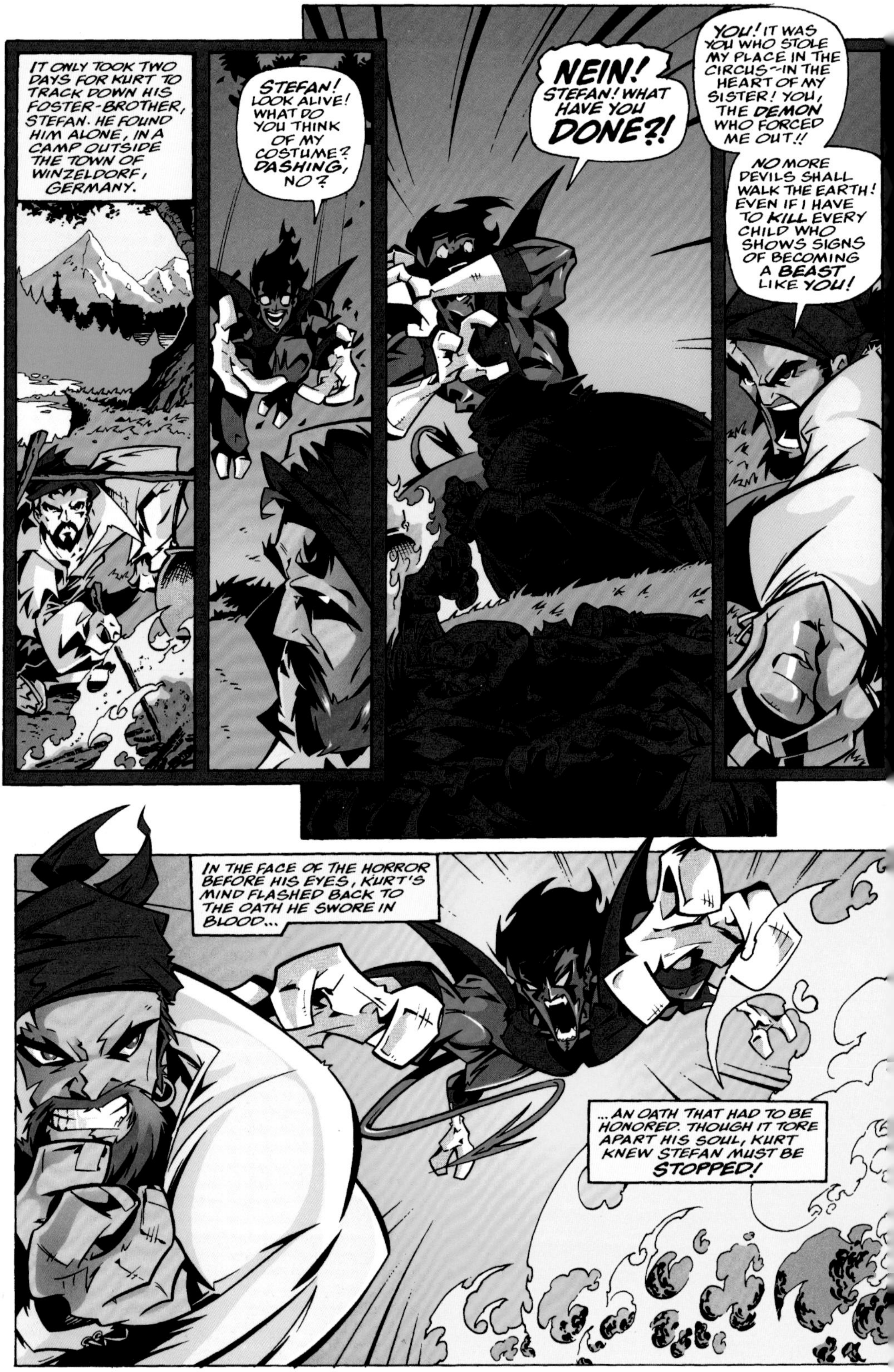

IT ONLY TOOK TWO DAYS FOR KURT TO TRACK DOWN HIS FOSTER-BROTHER, STEFAN. HE FOUND HIM ALONE, IN A CAMP OUTSIDE THE TOWN OF WINZELDORF, GERMANY.
STEFAN! LOOK ALIVE! WHAT DO YOU THINK OF MY COSTUME? DASHING, NO?
NEIN! STEFAN! WHAT HAVE YOU DONE?!
YOU! IT WAS YOU WHO STOLE MY PLACE IN THE CIRCUS--IN THE HEART OF MY SISTER! YOU, THE DEMON WHO FORCED ME OUT!!
NO MORE DEVILS SHALL WALK THE EARTH! EVEN IF I HAVE TO KILL EVERY CHILD WHO SHOWS SIGNS OF BECOMING A BEAST LIKE YOU!
IN THE FACE OF THE HORROR BEFORE HIS EYES, KURT'S MIND FLASHED BACK TO THE OATH HE SWORE IN BLOOD...
...AN OATH THAT HAD TO BE HONORED. THOUGH IT TORE APART HIS SOUL, KURT KNEW STEFAN MUST BE STOPPED!

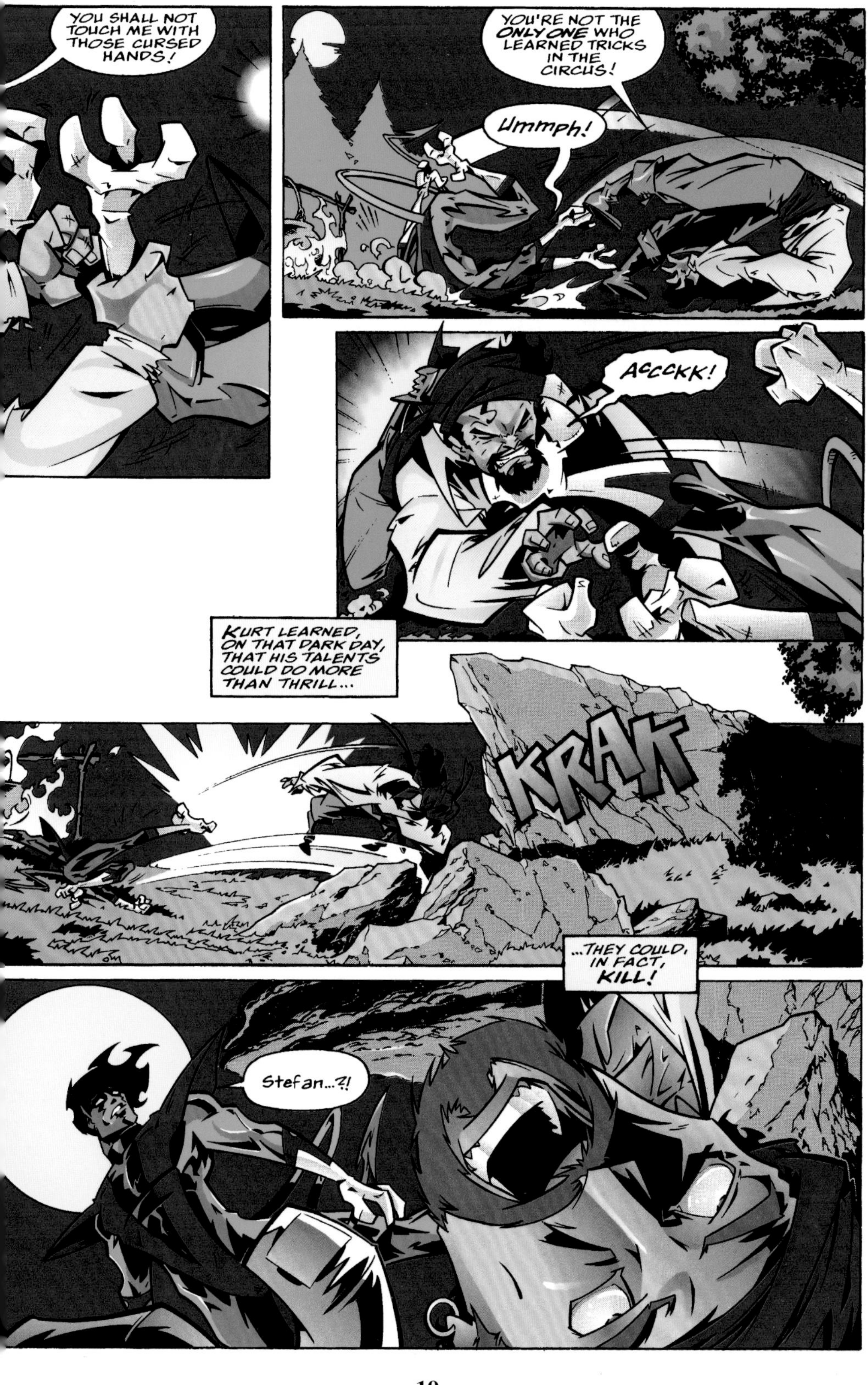
YOU SHALL NOT TOUCH ME WITH THOSE CURSED HANDS!
YOU'RE NOT THE ONLY ONE WHO LEARNED TRICKS IN THE CIRCUS!
Ummph!
ACCCKK!
KURT LEARNED, ON THAT DARK DAY, THAT HIS TALENTS COULD DO MORE THAN THRILL...
KRAK
...THEY COULD, IN FACT, KILL!
Stefan...?!

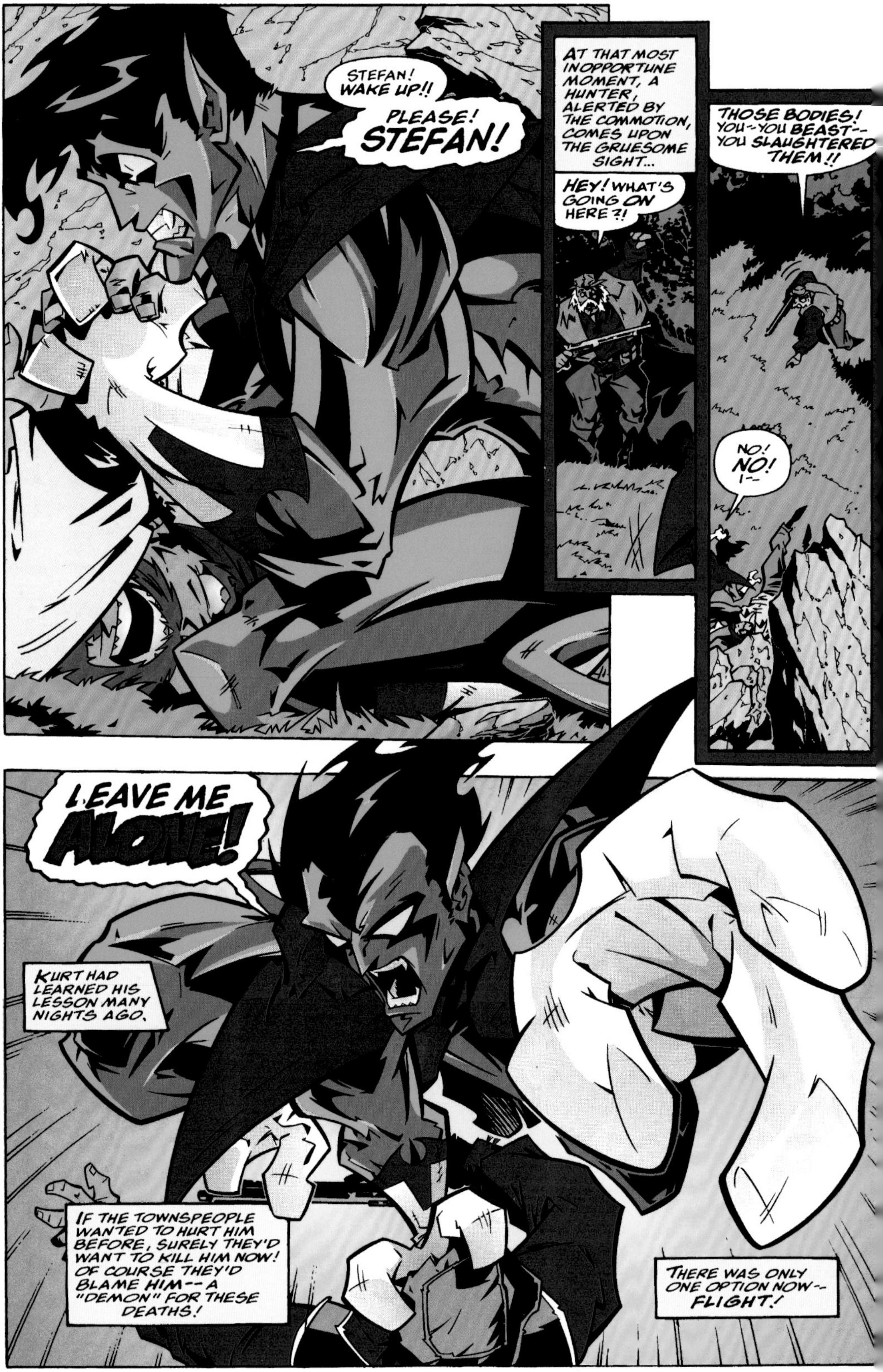
STEFAN! WAKE UP!!
PLEASE! STEFAN!
AT THAT MOST INOPPORTUNE MOMENT, A HUNTER, ALERTED BY THE COMMOTION, COMES UPON THE GRUESOME SIGHT...
HEY! WHAT'S GOING ON HERE?!
THOSE BODIES! YOU--YOU BEAST--YOU SLAUGHTERED THEM!!
NO! NO! I--
LEAVE ME ALONE!
KURT HAD LEARNED HIS LESSON MANY NIGHTS AGO.
IF THE TOWNSPEOPLE WANTED TO HURT HIM BEFORE, SURELY THEY'D WANT TO KILL HIM NOW! OF COURSE THEY'D BLAME HIM--A "DEMON" FOR THESE DEATHS!
THERE WAS ONLY ONE OPTION NOW--FLIGHT!

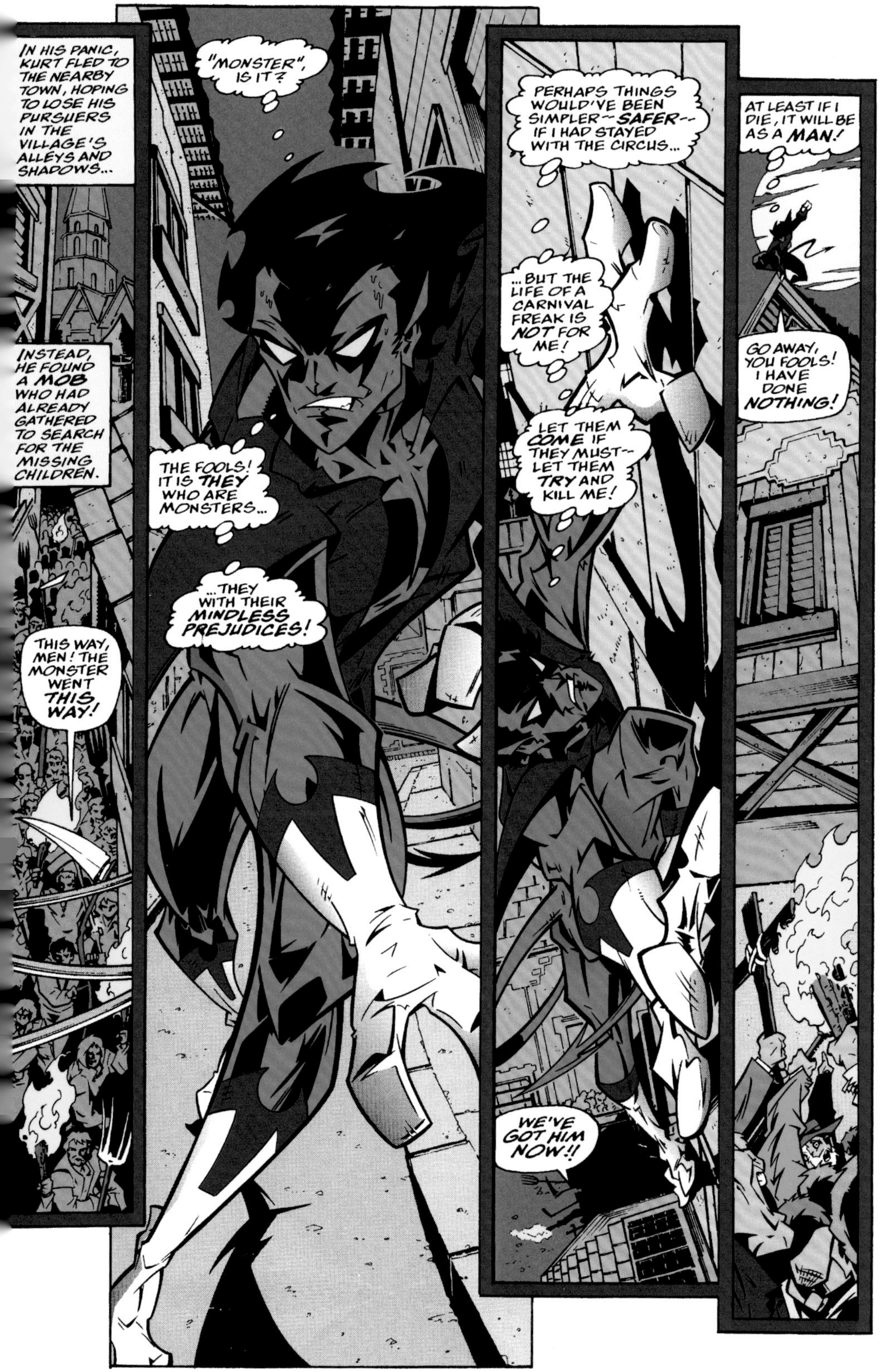
IN HIS PANIC, KURT FLED TO THE NEARBY TOWN, HOPING TO LOSE HIS PURSUERS IN THE VILLAGE'S ALLEYS AND SHADOWS...
INSTEAD, HE FOUND A MOB WHO HAD ALREADY GATHERED TO SEARCH FOR THE MISSING CHILDREN.
THIS WAY, MEN! THE MONSTER WENT THIS WAY!
"MONSTER", IS IT?
THE FOOLS! IT IS THEY WHO ARE MONSTERS...
...THEY WITH THEIR MINDLESS PREJUDICES!
PERHAPS THINGS WOULD'VE BEEN SIMPLER--SAFER--IF I HAD STAYED WITH THE CIRCUS...
...BUT THE LIFE OF A CARNIVAL FREAK IS NOT FOR ME!
LET THEM COME IF THEY MUST--LET THEM TRY AND KILL ME!
WE'VE GOT HIM NOW!!
AT LEAST IF I DIE, IT WILL BE AS A MAN!
GO AWAY, YOU FOOLS! I HAVE DONE NOTHING!

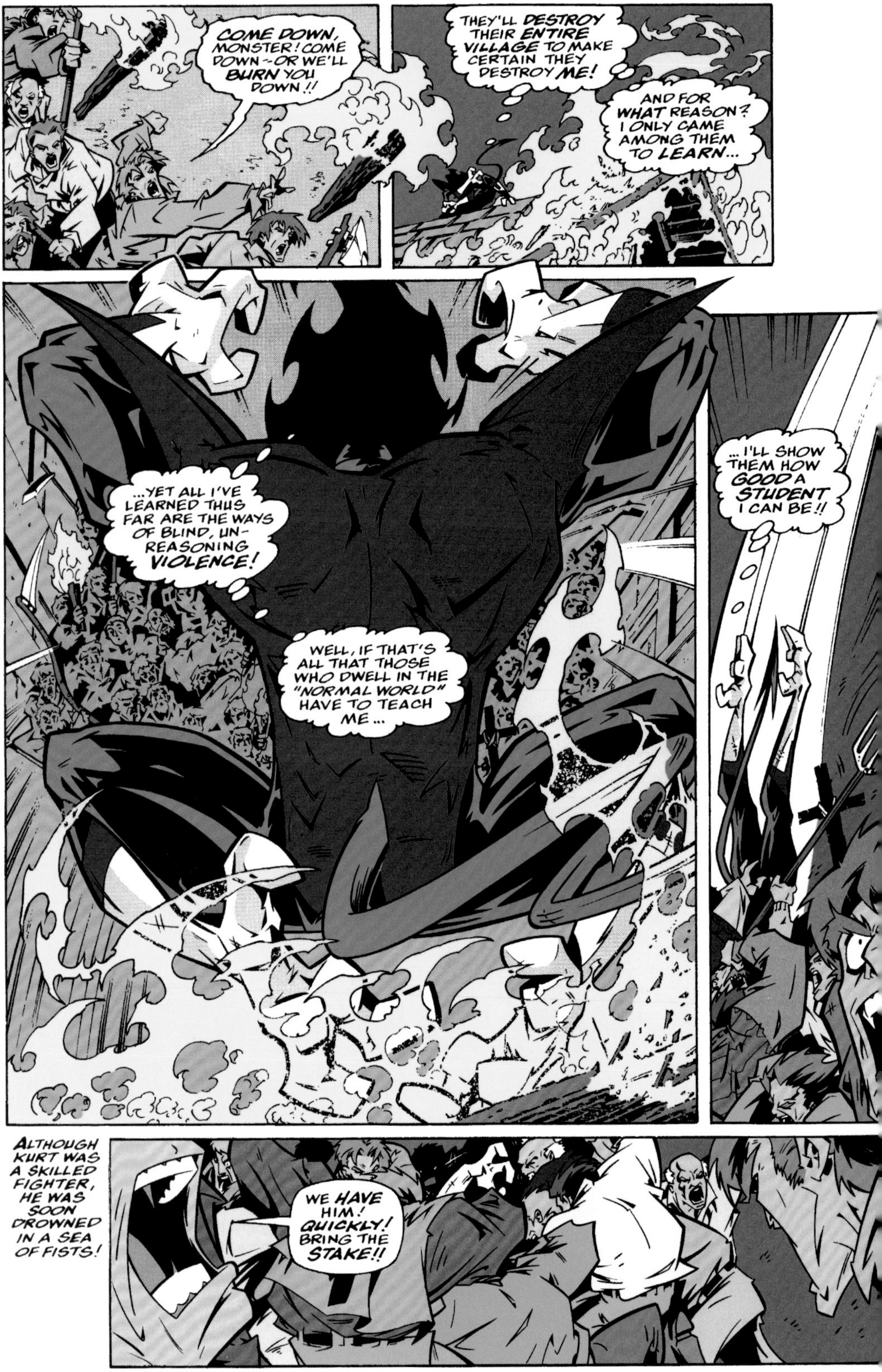
COME DOWN, MONSTER! COME DOWN--OR WE'LL BURN YOU DOWN!!
THEY'LL DESTROY THEIR ENTIRE VILLAGE TO MAKE CERTAIN THEY DESTROY ME!
AND FOR WHAT REASON? I ONLY CAME AMONG THEM TO LEARN...
...YET ALL I'VE LEARNED THUS FAR ARE THE WAYS OF BLIND, UN-REASONING VIOLENCE!
WELL, IF THAT'S ALL THAT THOSE WHO DWELL IN THE "NORMAL WORLD" HAVE TO TEACH ME...
...I'LL SHOW THEM HOW GOOD A STUDENT I CAN BE!!
ALTHOUGH KURT WAS A SKILLED FIGHTER, HE WAS SOON DROWNED IN A SEA OF FISTS!
WE HAVE HIM! QUICKLY! BRING THE STAKE!!

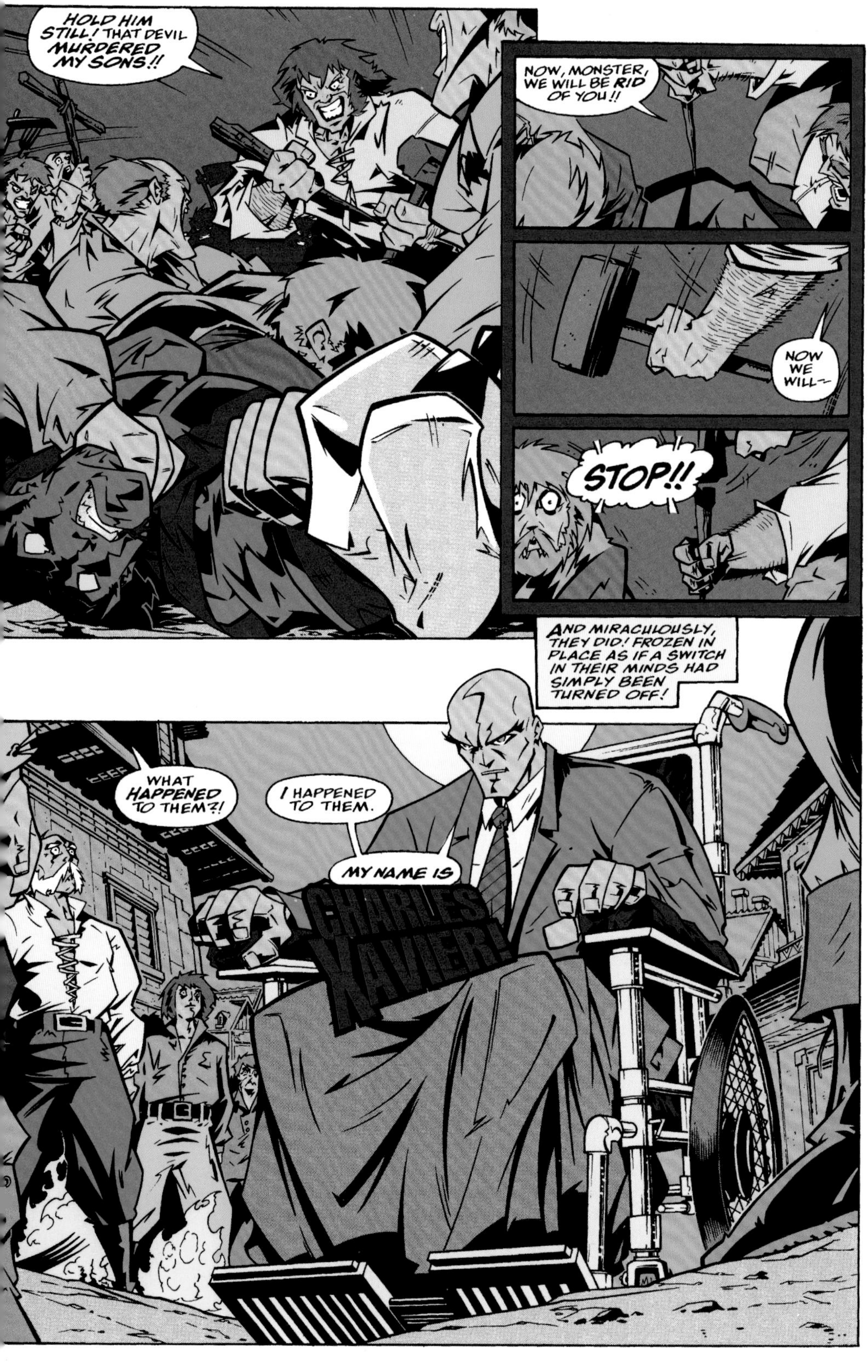
HOLD HIM STILL! THAT DEVIL MURDERED MY SONS!!
NOW, MONSTER, WE WILL BE RID OF YOU!!
NOW WE WILL—
STOP!!
AND MIRACULOUSLY, THEY DID! FROZEN IN PLACE AS IF A SWITCH IN THEIR MINDS HAD SIMPLY BEEN TURNED OFF!
WHAT HAPPENED TO THEM?!
I HAPPENED TO THEM.
MY NAME IS
CHARLES XAVIER!

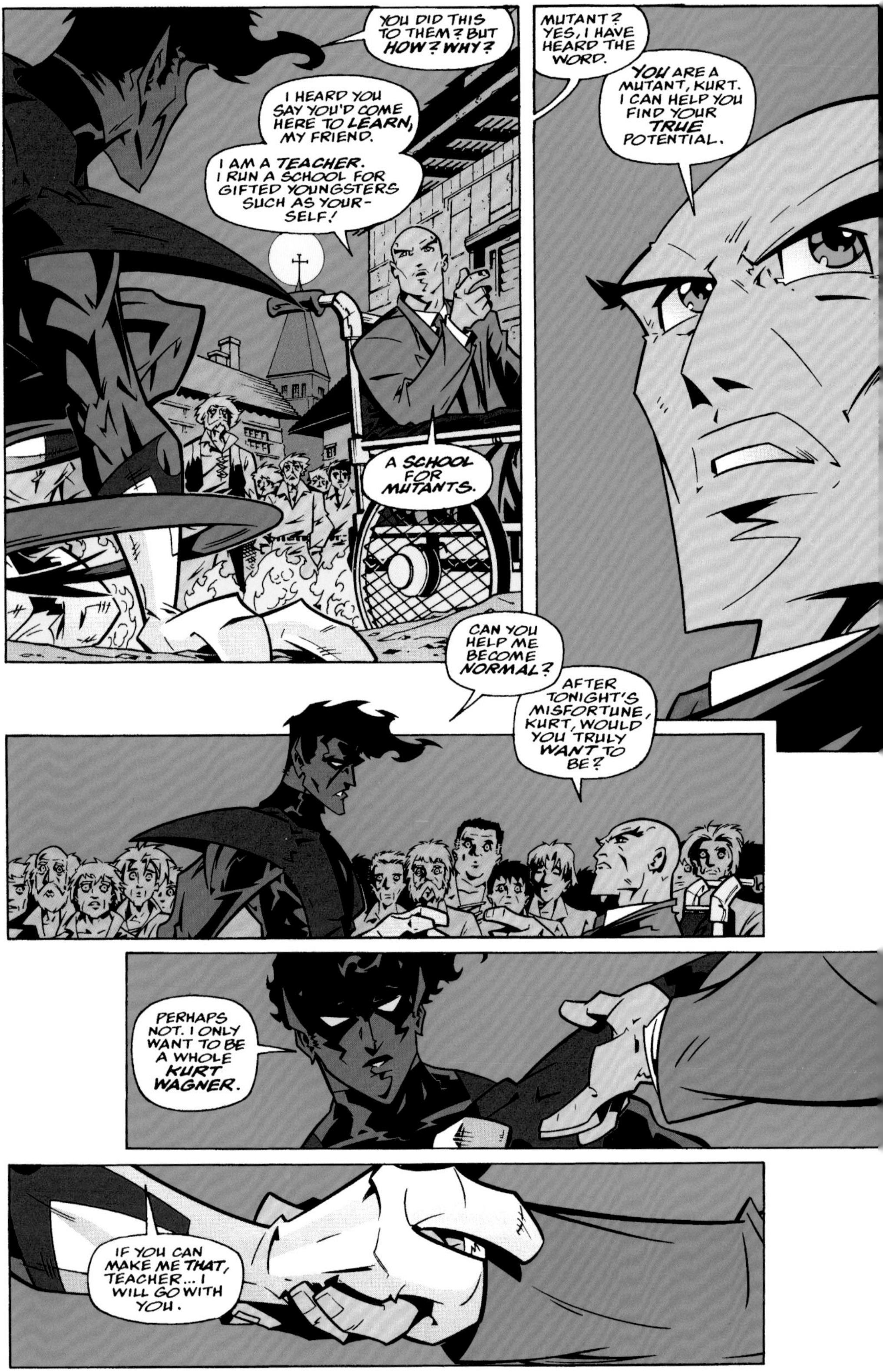

YOU DID THIS TO THEM? BUT HOW? WHY?
I HEARD YOU SAY YOU'D COME HERE TO LEARN, MY FRIEND.
I AM A TEACHER. I RUN A SCHOOL FOR GIFTED YOUNGSTERS SUCH AS YOURSELF!
A SCHOOL FOR MUTANTS.
MUTANT? YES, I HAVE HEARD THE WORD.
YOU ARE A MUTANT, KURT. I CAN HELP YOU FIND YOUR TRUE POTENTIAL.
CAN YOU HELP ME BECOME NORMAL?
AFTER TONIGHT'S MISFORTUNE, KURT, WOULD YOU TRULY WANT TO BE?
PERHAPS NOT. I ONLY WANT TO BE A WHOLE KURT WAGNER.
IF YOU CAN MAKE ME THAT, TEACHER... I WILL GO WITH YOU.

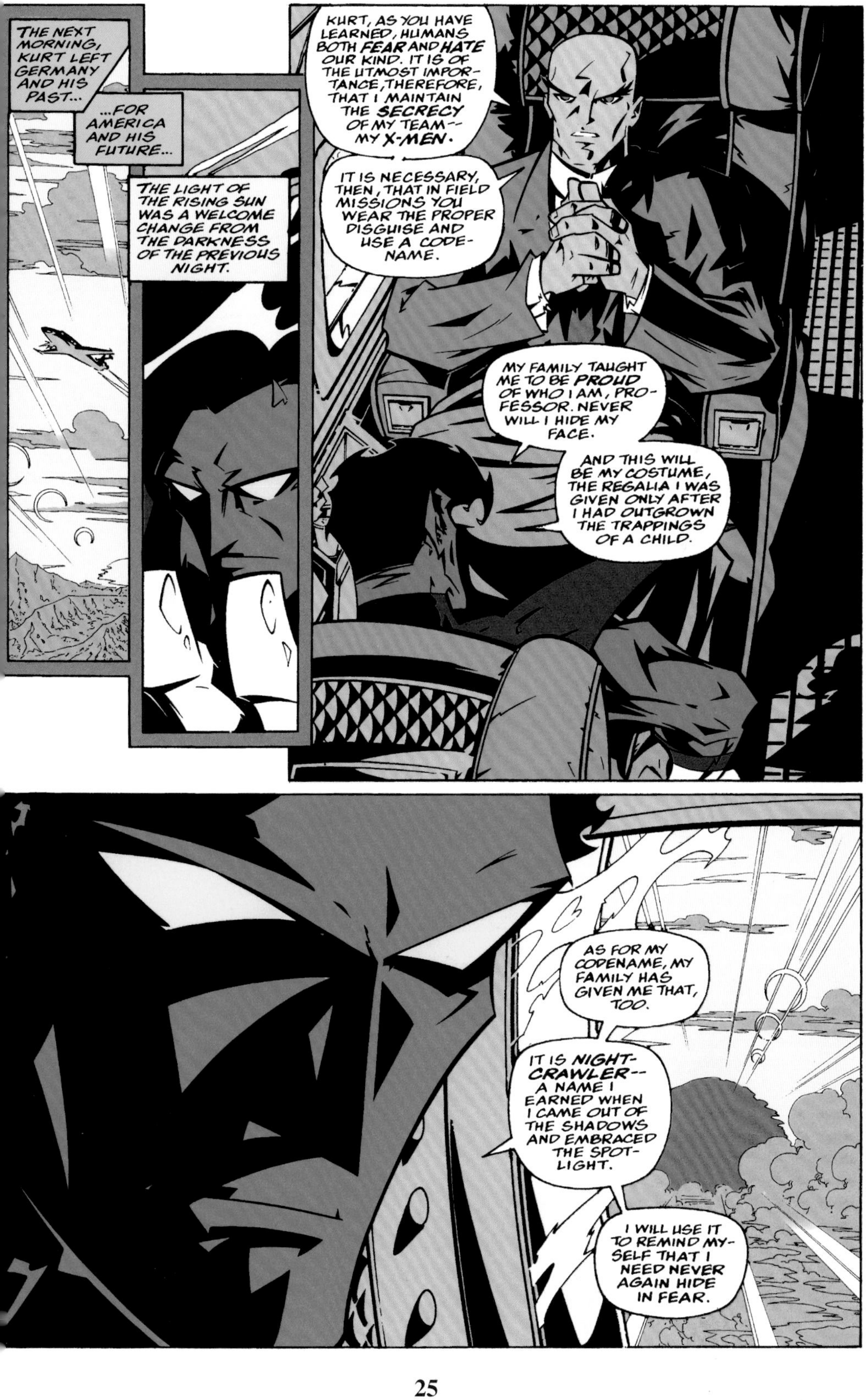
THE NEXT MORNING, KURT LEFT GERMANY AND HIS PAST...
...FOR AMERICA AND HIS FUTURE...
THE LIGHT OF THE RISING SUN WAS A WELCOME CHANGE FROM THE DARKNESS OF THE PREVIOUS NIGHT.
KURT, AS YOU HAVE LEARNED, HUMANS BOTH FEAR AND HATE OUR KIND. IT IS OF THE UTMOST IMPORTANCE, THEREFORE, THAT I MAINTAIN THE SECRECY OF MY TEAM-- MY X-MEN.
IT IS NECESSARY, THEN, THAT IN FIELD MISSIONS YOU WEAR THE PROPER DISGUISE AND USE A CODE-NAME.
MY FAMILY TAUGHT ME TO BE PROUD OF WHO I AM, PROFESSOR. NEVER WILL I HIDE MY FACE.
AND THIS WILL BE MY COSTUME, THE REGALIA I WAS GIVEN ONLY AFTER I HAD OUTGROWN THE TRAPPINGS OF A CHILD.
AS FOR MY CODENAME, MY FAMILY HAS GIVEN ME THAT, TOO.
IT IS NIGHTCRAWLER-- A NAME I EARNED WHEN I CAME OUT OF THE SHADOWS AND EMBRACED THE SPOTLIGHT.
I WILL USE IT TO REMIND MYSELF THAT I NEED NEVER AGAIN HIDE IN FEAR.

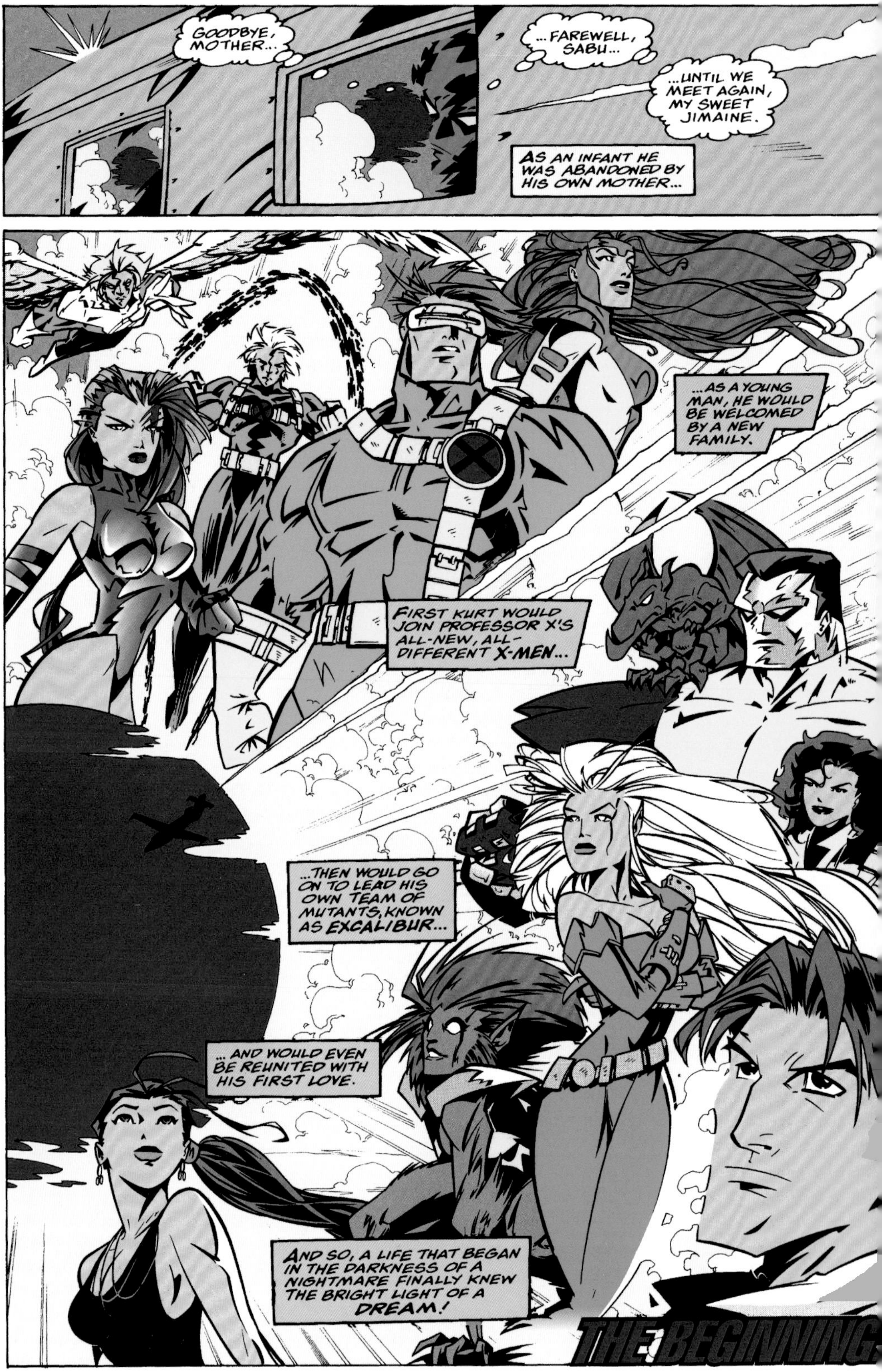
GOODBYE, MOTHER...
...FAREWELL, SABU...
...UNTIL WE MEET AGAIN, MY SWEET JIMAINE.
AS AN INFANT HE WAS ABANDONED BY HIS OWN MOTHER...
...AS A YOUNG MAN, HE WOULD BE WELCOMED BY A NEW FAMILY.
FIRST KURT WOULD JOIN PROFESSOR X'S ALL-NEW, ALL-DIFFERENT X-MEN...
...THEN WOULD GO ON TO LEAD HIS OWN TEAM OF MUTANTS, KNOWN AS EXCALIBUR...
...AND WOULD EVEN BE REUNITED WITH HIS FIRST LOVE.
AND SO, A LIFE THAT BEGAN IN THE DARKNESS OF A NIGHTMARE FINALLY KNEW THE BRIGHT LIGHT OF A DREAM!
THE BEGINNING

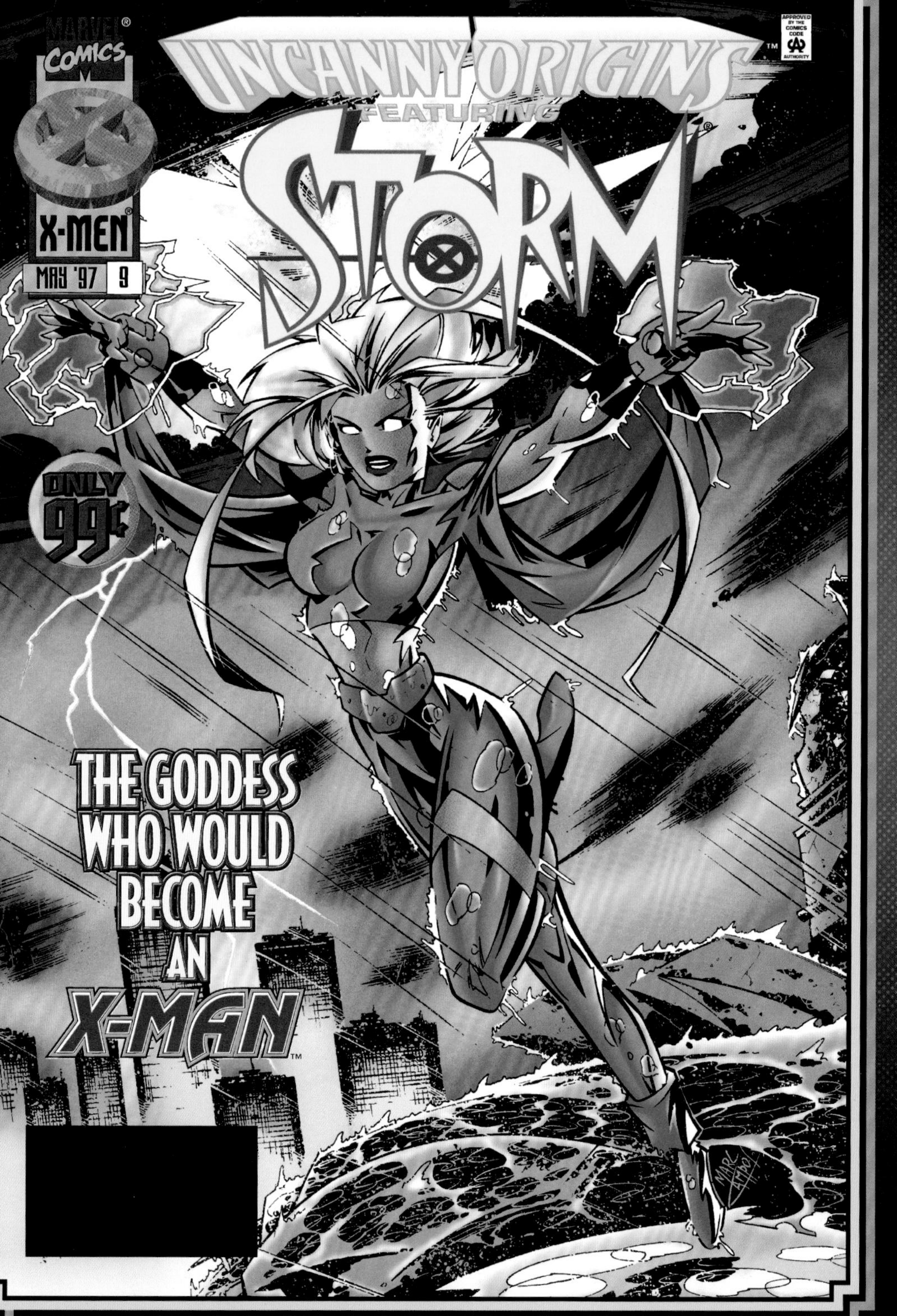

MARVEL COMICS
X-MEN
MAY '97 9
UNCANNY ORIGINS
FEATURING
STORM
APPROVED BY THE COMICS CODE AUTHORITY
ONLY 99¢
THE GODDESS WHO WOULD BECOME AN X-MAN

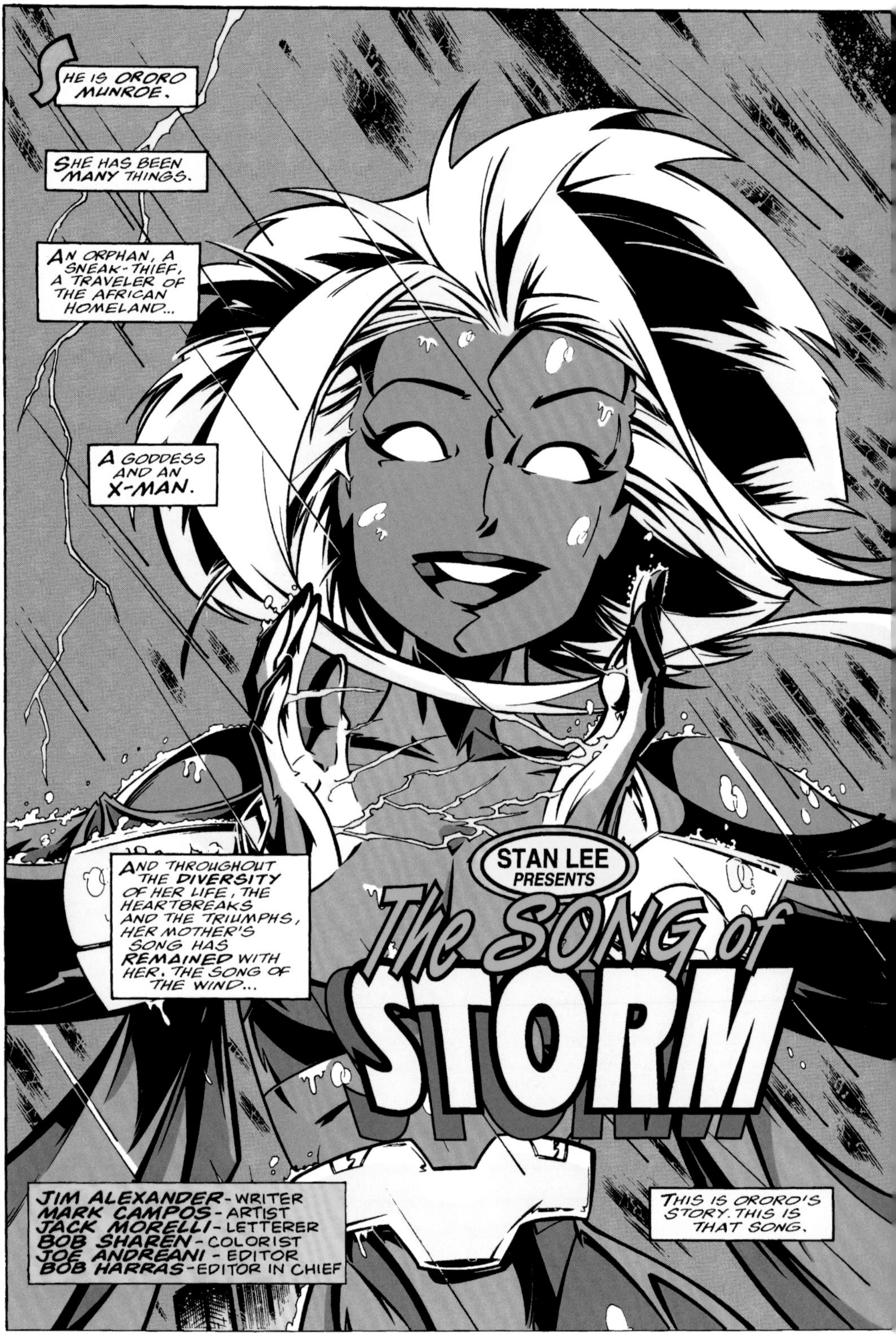
SHE IS ORORO MUNROE.
SHE HAS BEEN MANY THINGS.
AN ORPHAN, A SNEAK-THIEF, A TRAVELER OF THE AFRICAN HOMELAND...
A GODDESS AND AN X-MAN.
AND THROUGHOUT THE DIVERSITY OF HER LIFE, THE HEARTBREAKS AND THE TRIUMPHS, HER MOTHER'S SONG HAS REMAINED WITH HER. THE SONG OF THE WIND...
STAN LEE PRESENTS
The SONG of STORM
JIM ALEXANDER - WRITER
MARK CAMPOS - ARTIST
JACK MORELLI - LETTERER
BOB SHAREN - COLORIST
JOE ANDREANI - EDITOR
BOB HARRAS - EDITOR IN CHIEF
THIS IS ORORO'S STORY. THIS IS THAT SONG.

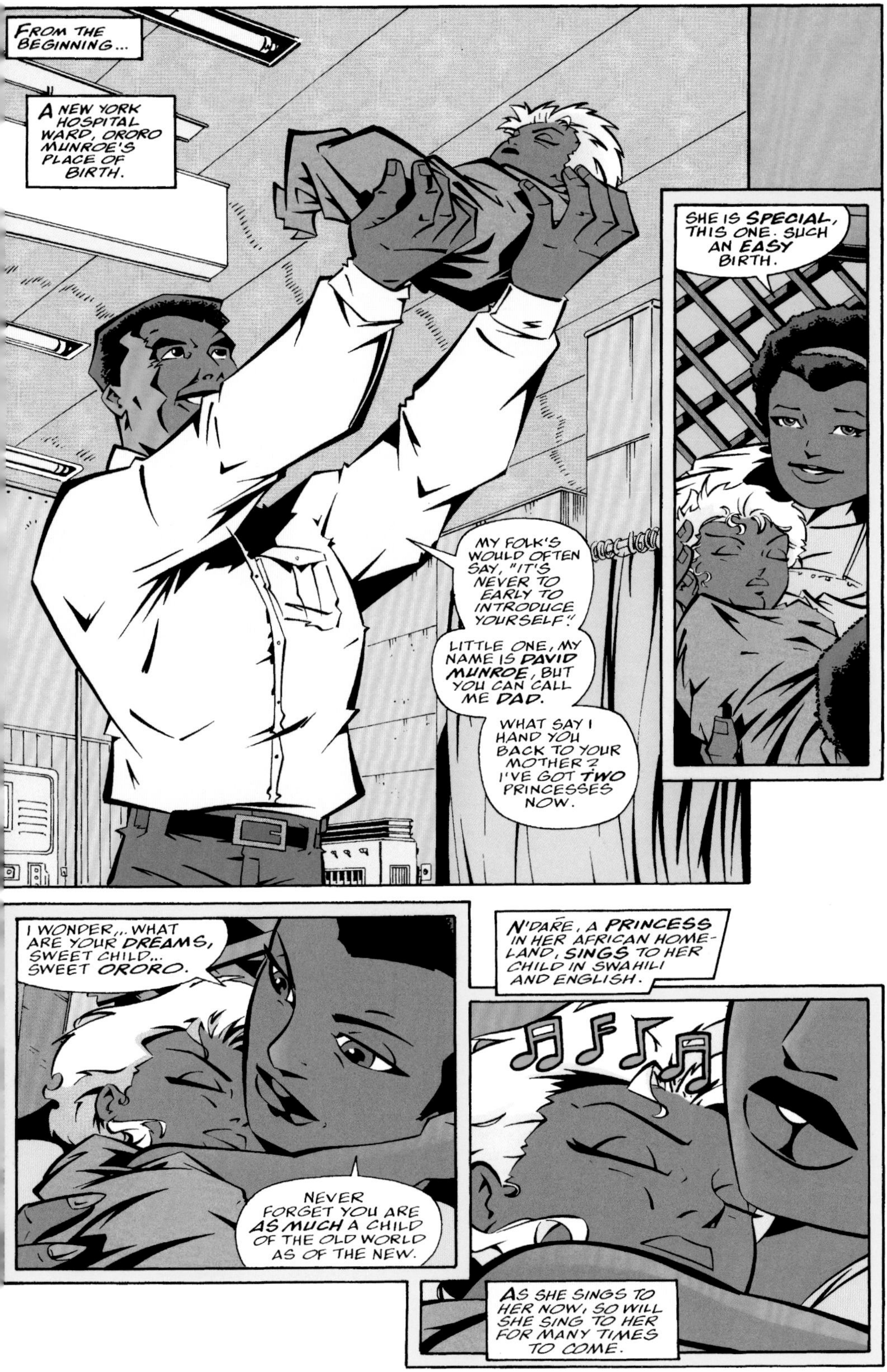
FROM THE BEGINNING...
A NEW YORK HOSPITAL WARD, ORORO MUNROE'S PLACE OF BIRTH.
SHE IS SPECIAL, THIS ONE. SUCH AN EASY BIRTH.
MY FOLK'S WOULD OFTEN SAY, "IT'S NEVER TO EARLY TO INTRODUCE YOURSELF."
LITTLE ONE, MY NAME IS DAVID MUNROE, BUT YOU CAN CALL ME DAD.
WHAT SAY I HAND YOU BACK TO YOUR MOTHER? I'VE GOT TWO PRINCESSES NOW.
I WONDER... WHAT ARE YOUR DREAMS, SWEET CHILD... SWEET ORORO.
NEVER FORGET YOU ARE AS MUCH A CHILD OF THE OLD WORLD AS OF THE NEW.
N'DARE, A PRINCESS IN HER AFRICAN HOME-LAND, SINGS TO HER CHILD IN SWAHILI AND ENGLISH.
AS SHE SINGS TO HER NOW, SO WILL SHE SING TO HER FOR MANY TIMES TO COME.

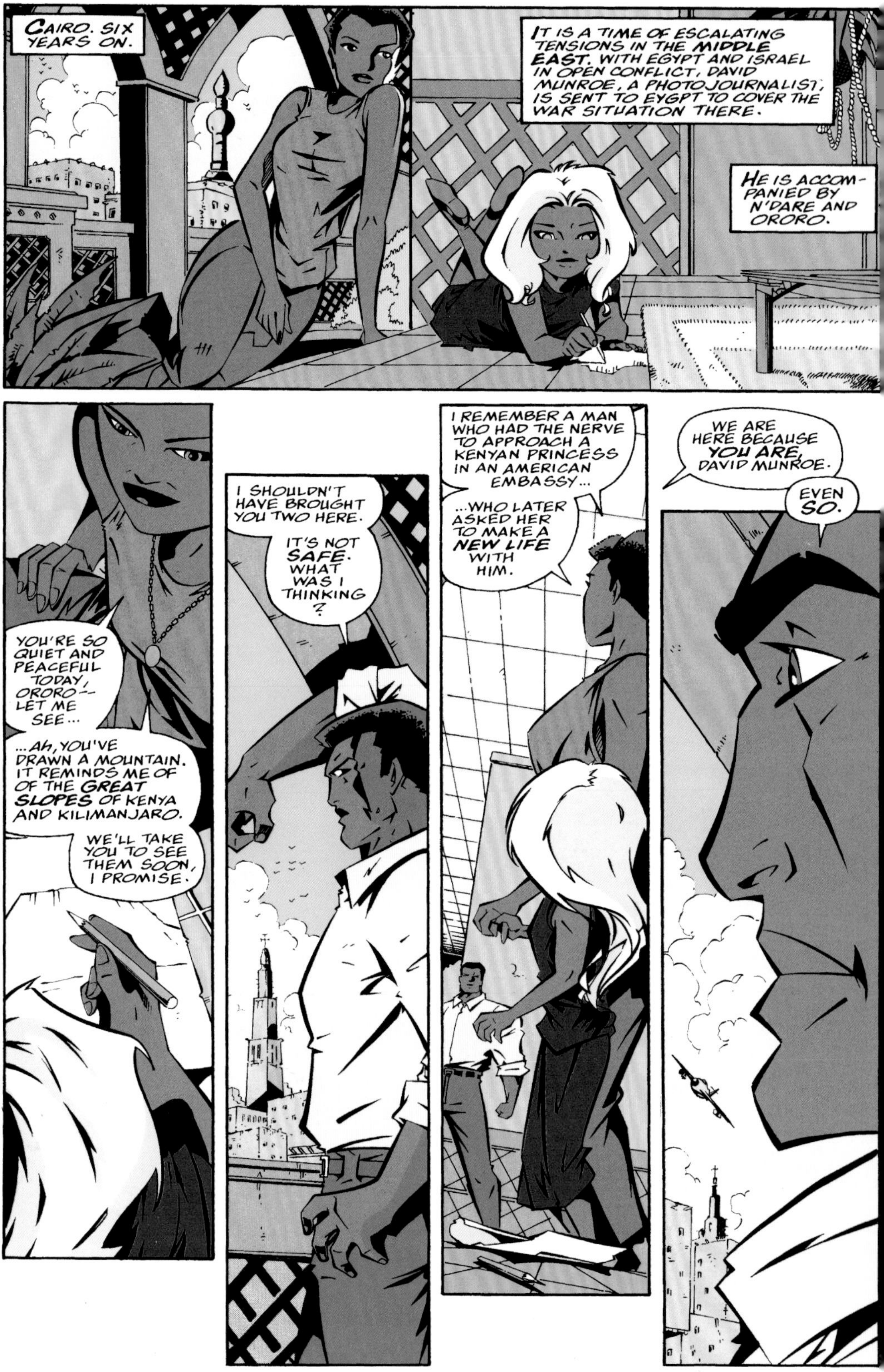
CAIRO. SIX YEARS ON.
IT IS A TIME OF ESCALATING TENSIONS IN THE MIDDLE EAST. WITH EGYPT AND ISRAEL IN OPEN CONFLICT, DAVID MUNROE, A PHOTOJOURNALIST, IS SENT TO EYGPT TO COVER THE WAR SITUATION THERE.
HE IS ACCOMPANIED BY N'DARE AND ORORO.
YOU'RE SO QUIET AND PEACEFUL TODAY, ORORO-- LET ME SEE...
...AH, YOU'VE DRAWN A MOUNTAIN. IT REMINDS ME OF THE GREAT SLOPES OF KENYA AND KILIMANJARO.
WE'LL TAKE YOU TO SEE THEM SOON, I PROMISE.
I SHOULDN'T HAVE BROUGHT YOU TWO HERE.
IT'S NOT SAFE. WHAT WAS I THINKING?
I REMEMBER A MAN WHO HAD THE NERVE TO APPROACH A KENYAN PRINCESS IN AN AMERICAN EMBASSY...
...WHO LATER ASKED HER TO MAKE A NEW LIFE WITH HIM.
WE ARE HERE BECAUSE YOU ARE, DAVID MUNROE.
EVEN SO.

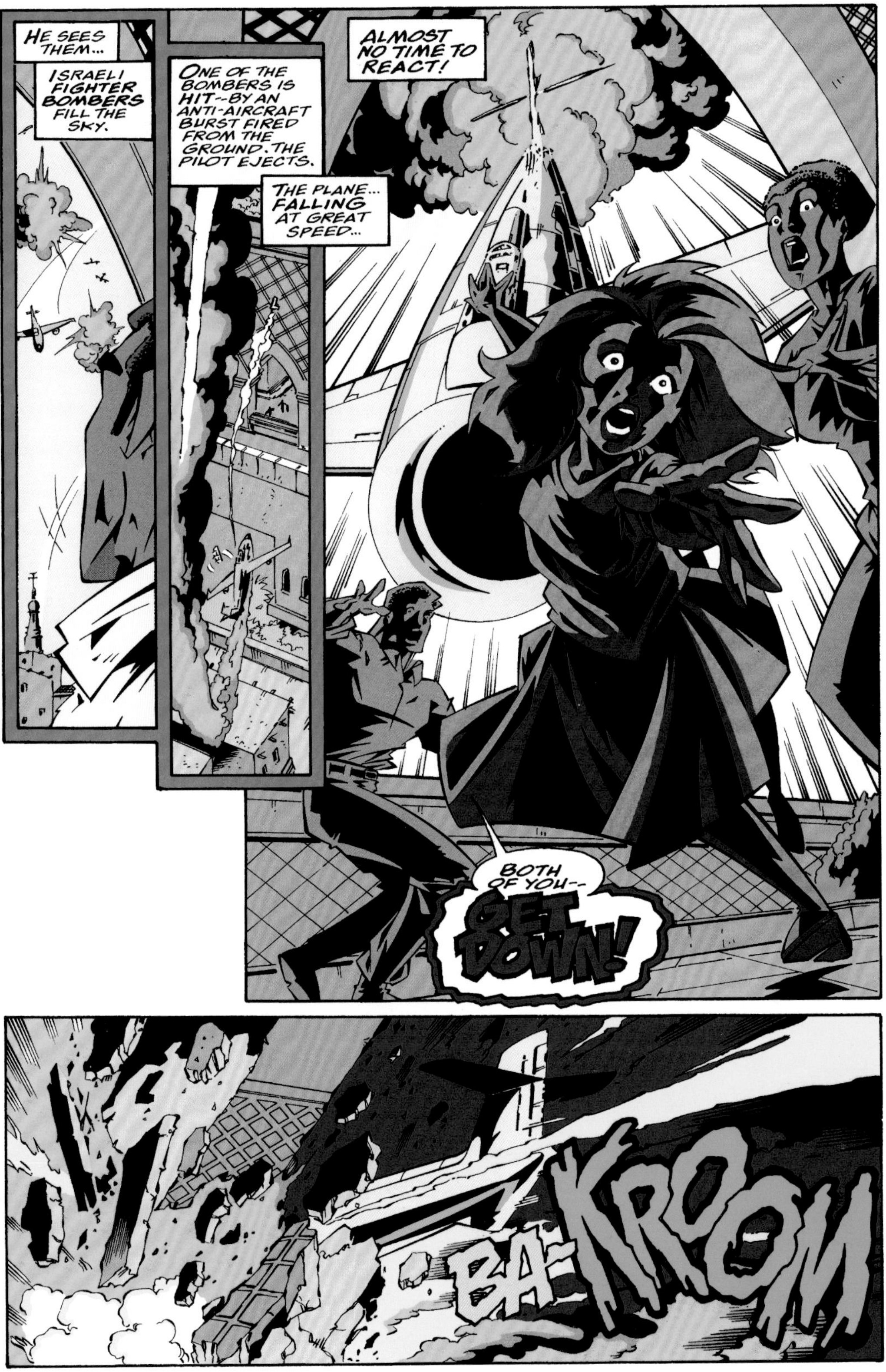
HE SEES THEM...
ISRAELI FIGHTER BOMBERS FILL THE SKY.
ONE OF THE BOMBERS IS HIT--BY AN ANTI-AIRCRAFT BURST FIRED FROM THE GROUND. THE PILOT EJECTS.
THE PLANE... FALLING AT GREAT SPEED...
ALMOST NO TIME TO REACT!
BOTH OF YOU-- GET DOWN!
BA-KROOM

ORORO WAKES IN THE DARKNESS.

SHE REMEMBERS.

HER FATHER SHOUTING A WARNING.

THEN, THE CRASH... THE NOISE OF WRENCHING STEEL AND SNAPPING TIMBER RUSHING IN ON HER SENSES LIKE A WILD AND OPPRESSIVE GALE.

SHE REMEMBERS ...THE ROOM GIVING WAY BENEATH HER...

HER FALLING INTO A PIT HOLLOWED OUT BY THE CRASH.

IT'S THEN THAT SHE REALIZES...

SHE'S STILL IN THE PIT!

PAIN BEGINS TO JAB AT HER THROUGH HER GROGGINESS. SHE'S TOO PETRIFIED TO MOVE.

ALL ALONE IN THE RUBBLE AND THE DARKNESS AND THE HORROR.

mother...?

HER MOTHER'S SONG COMES TO ORORO. BARELY A DAY WOULD GO BY WITHOUT HER MOTHER SINGING TO HER.

THE SOFT LULL OF HER MOTHER'S VOICE IS A SOOTHING RIPPLE IN A DARK, TERRIFYING SEA. IT CALMS THE YOUNG ORORO.

SHE LISTENS TO THE WORDS...

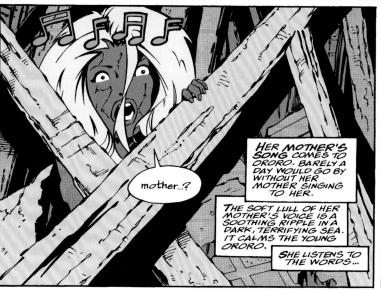

...WHICH SAY TO HER, "Be brave little bird, and climb to the SUN."

SO, USING THE SONG AS HER GUIDE, SHE CLIMBS. JUST A FEW MOMENTS MORE, SHE THINKS, AND SHE'LL BE OUT OF THE DARK ...

...SHE'LL BE SAFE WITH HER PARENTS.

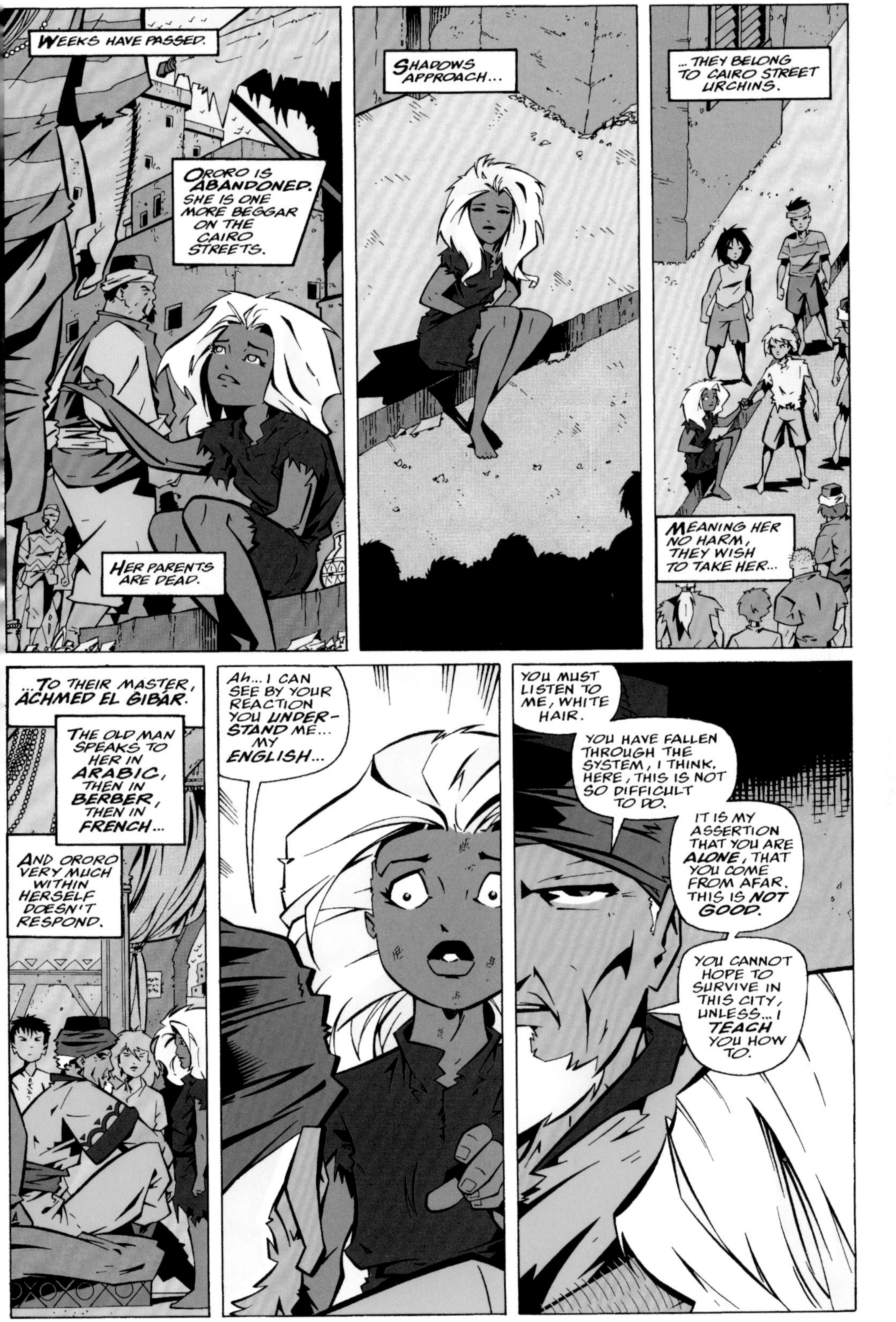
WEEKS HAVE PASSED.
ORORO IS ABANDONED. SHE IS ONE MORE BEGGAR ON THE CAIRO STREETS.
HER PARENTS ARE DEAD.
SHADOWS APPROACH...
...THEY BELONG TO CAIRO STREET URCHINS.
MEANING HER NO HARM, THEY WISH TO TAKE HER...
...TO THEIR MASTER, ACHMED EL GIBAR.
THE OLD MAN SPEAKS TO HER IN ARABIC, THEN IN BERBER, THEN IN FRENCH...
AND ORORO VERY MUCH WITHIN HERSELF DOESN'T RESPOND.
Ah... I CAN SEE BY YOUR REACTION YOU UNDERSTAND ME... MY ENGLISH...
YOU MUST LISTEN TO ME, WHITE HAIR.
YOU HAVE FALLEN THROUGH THE SYSTEM, I THINK. HERE, THIS IS NOT SO DIFFICULT TO DO.
IT IS MY ASSERTION THAT YOU ARE ALONE, THAT YOU COME FROM AFAR. THIS IS NOT GOOD.
YOU CANNOT HOPE TO SURVIVE IN THIS CITY, UNLESS... I TEACH YOU HOW TO.

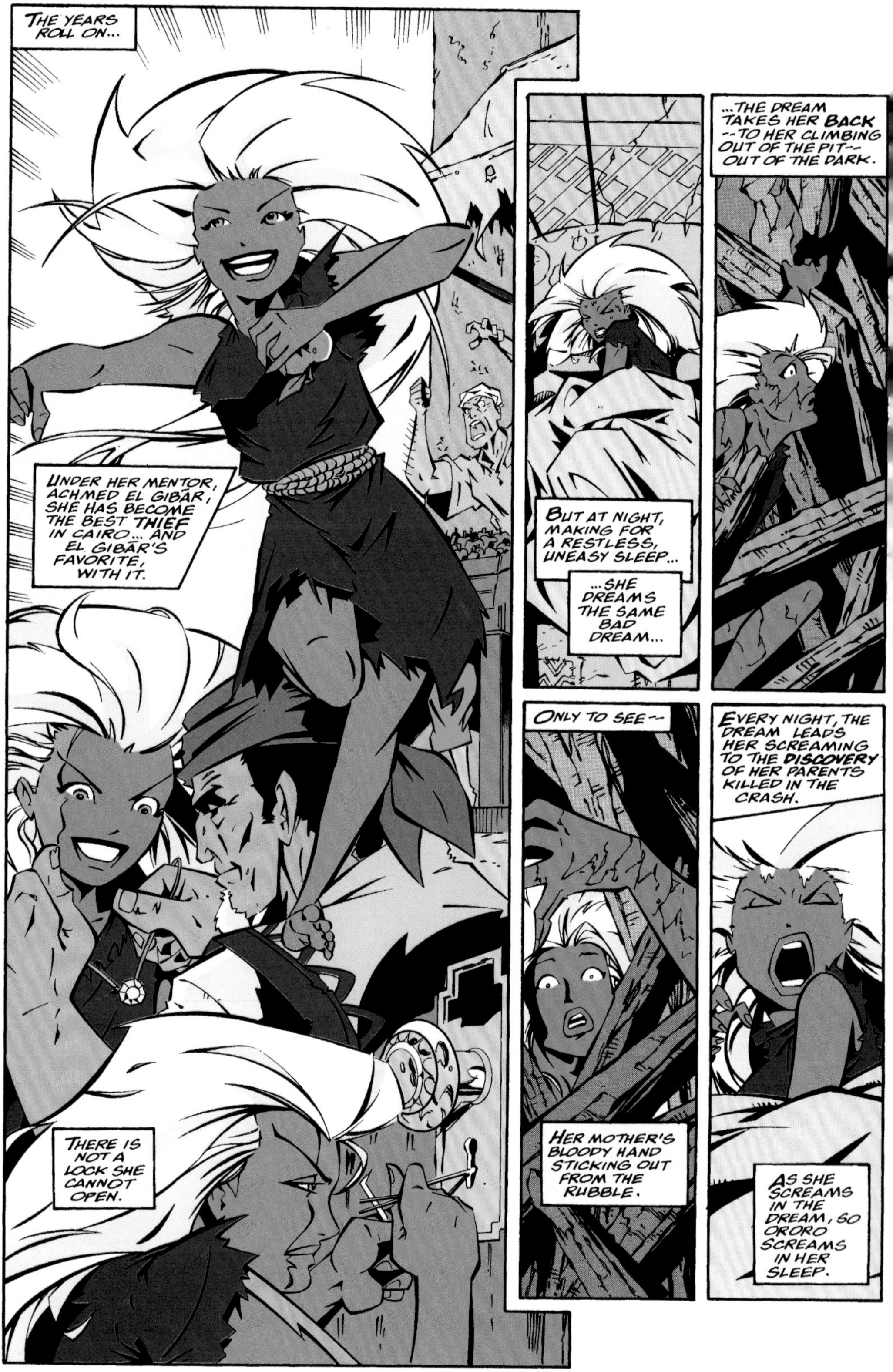
THE YEARS ROLL ON...
UNDER HER MENTOR, ACHMED EL GIBĀR, SHE HAS BECOME THE BEST THIEF IN CAIRO... AND EL GIBĀR'S FAVORITE, WITH IT.
THERE IS NOT A LOCK SHE CANNOT OPEN.
BUT AT NIGHT, MAKING FOR A RESTLESS, UNEASY SLEEP...
...SHE DREAMS THE SAME BAD DREAM...
...THE DREAM TAKES HER BACK --TO HER CLIMBING OUT OF THE PIT-- OUT OF THE DARK.
ONLY TO SEE--
HER MOTHER'S BLOODY HAND STICKING OUT FROM THE RUBBLE.
EVERY NIGHT, THE DREAM LEADS HER SCREAMING TO THE DISCOVERY OF HER PARENTS KILLED IN THE CRASH.
AS SHE SCREAMS IN THE DREAM, SO ORORO SCREAMS IN HER SLEEP.

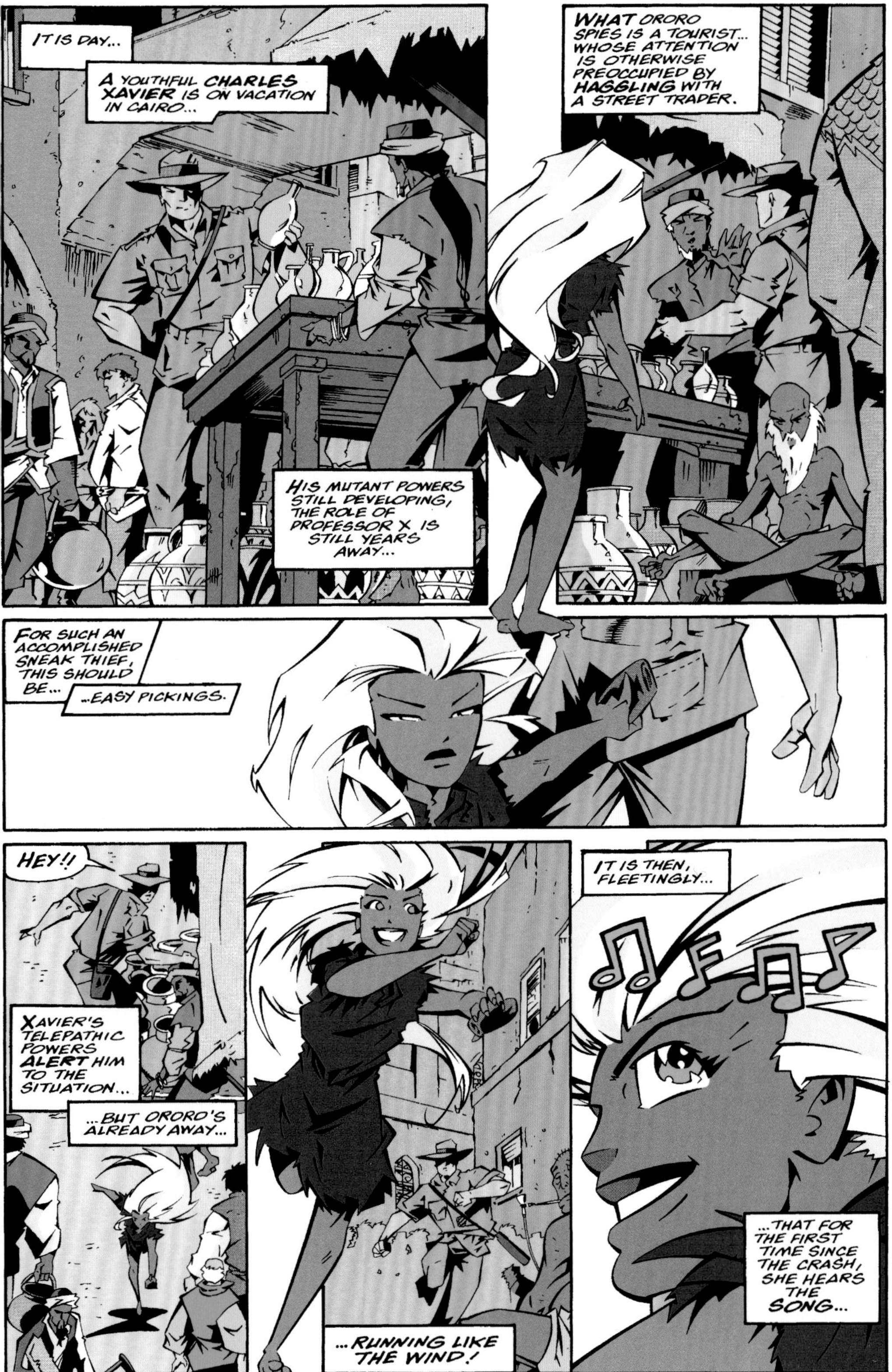
IT IS DAY...
A YOUTHFUL CHARLES XAVIER IS ON VACATION IN CAIRO...
HIS MUTANT POWERS STILL DEVELOPING, THE ROLE OF PROFESSOR X IS STILL YEARS AWAY...
WHAT ORORO SPIES IS A TOURIST... WHOSE ATTENTION IS OTHERWISE PREOCCUPIED BY HAGGLING WITH A STREET TRADER.
FOR SUCH AN ACCOMPLISHED SNEAK THIEF, THIS SHOULD BE...
...EASY PICKINGS.
HEY!!
XAVIER'S TELEPATHIC POWERS ALERT HIM TO THE SITUATION...
...BUT ORORO'S ALREADY AWAY...
...RUNNING LIKE THE WIND!
IT IS THEN, FLEETINGLY...
...THAT FOR THE FIRST TIME SINCE THE CRASH, SHE HEARS THE SONG...

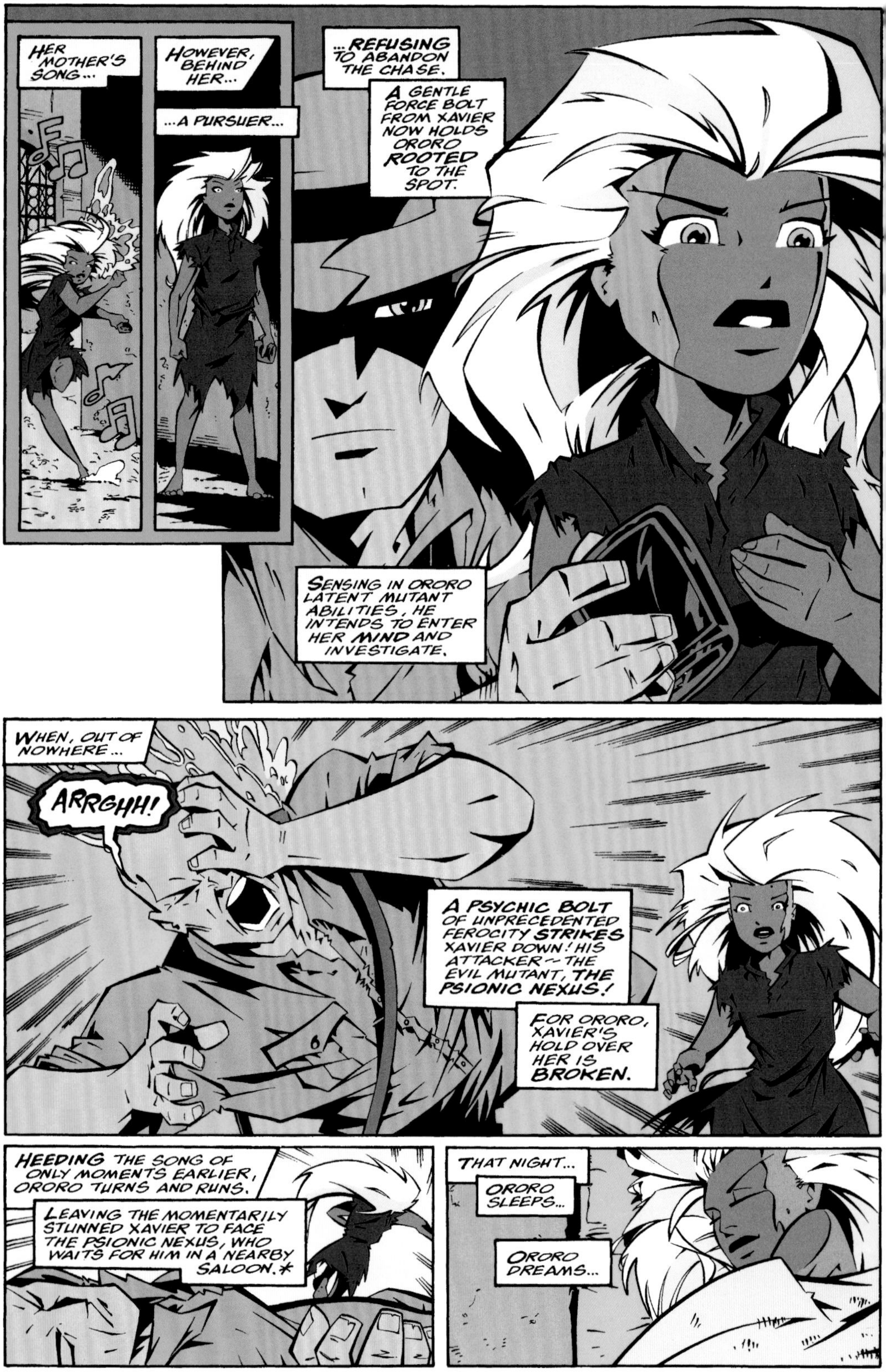

HER MOTHER'S SONG...
HOWEVER, BEHIND HER...
...A PURSUER...
...REFUSING TO ABANDON THE CHASE.
A GENTLE FORCE BOLT FROM XAVIER NOW HOLDS ORORO ROOTED TO THE SPOT.
SENSING IN ORORO LATENT MUTANT ABILITIES, HE INTENDS TO ENTER HER MIND AND INVESTIGATE.
WHEN, OUT OF NOWHERE...
ARRGHH!
A PSYCHIC BOLT OF UNPRECEDENTED FEROCITY STRIKES XAVIER DOWN! HIS ATTACKER -- THE EVIL MUTANT, THE PSIONIC NEXUS!
FOR ORORO, XAVIER'S HOLD OVER HER IS BROKEN.
HEEDING THE SONG OF ONLY MOMENTS EARLIER, ORORO TURNS AND RUNS.
LEAVING THE MOMENTARILY STUNNED XAVIER TO FACE THE PSIONIC NEXUS, WHO WAITS FOR HIM IN A NEARBY SALOON.*
THAT NIGHT...
ORORO SLEEPS...
ORORO DREAMS...

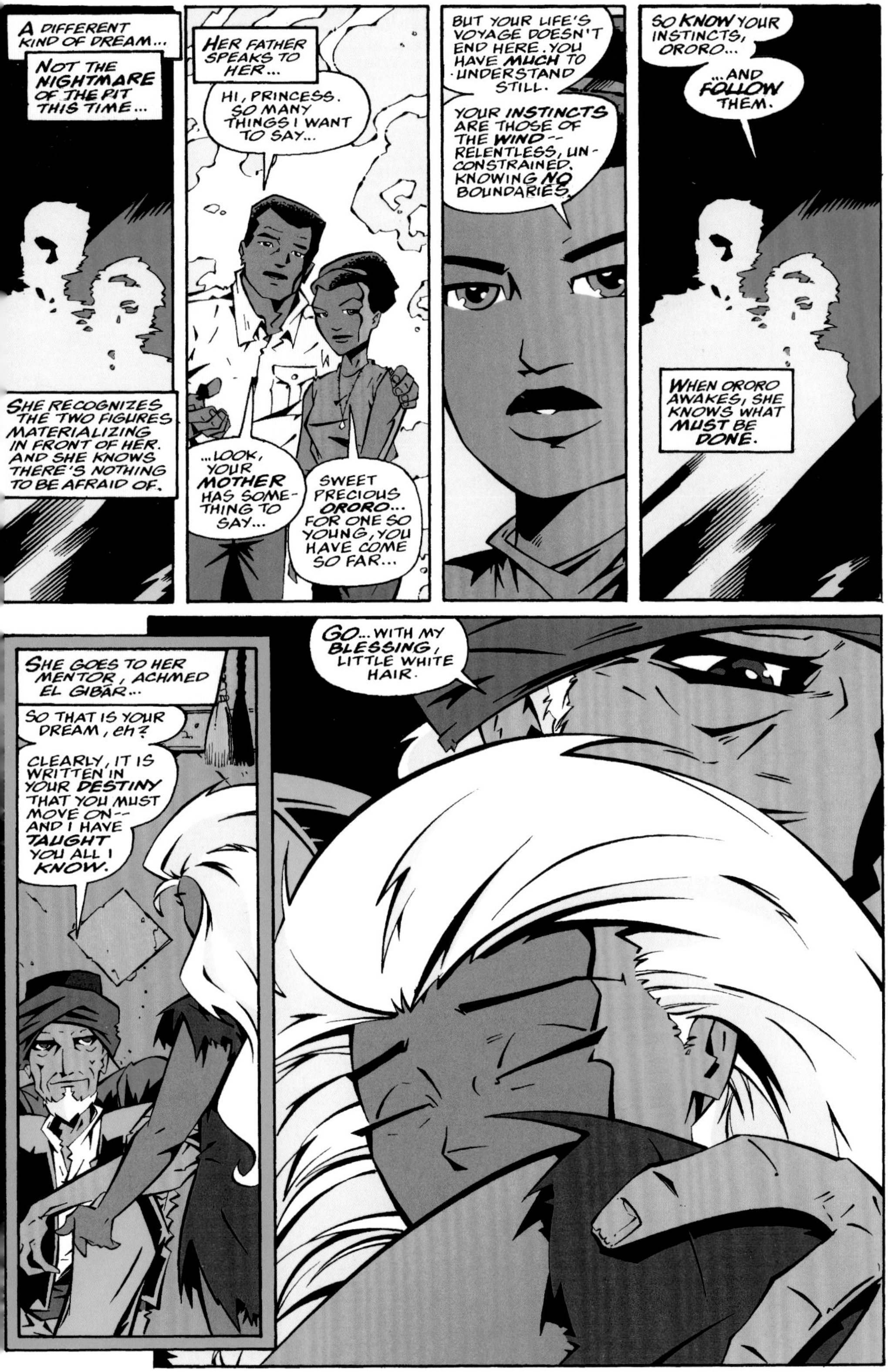
A DIFFERENT KIND OF DREAM...
NOT THE NIGHTMARE OF THE PIT THIS TIME...
SHE RECOGNIZES THE TWO FIGURES MATERIALIZING IN FRONT OF HER. AND SHE KNOWS THERE'S NOTHING TO BE AFRAID OF.
HER FATHER SPEAKS TO HER...
HI, PRINCESS. SO MANY THINGS I WANT TO SAY...
...LOOK, YOUR MOTHER HAS SOMETHING TO SAY...
SWEET PRECIOUS ORORO... FOR ONE SO YOUNG, YOU HAVE COME SO FAR...
BUT YOUR LIFE'S VOYAGE DOESN'T END HERE. YOU HAVE MUCH TO UNDERSTAND STILL.
YOUR INSTINCTS ARE THOSE OF THE WIND-- RELENTLESS, UNCONSTRAINED, KNOWING NO BOUNDARIES.
SO KNOW YOUR INSTINCTS, ORORO...
...AND FOLLOW THEM.
WHEN ORORO AWAKES, SHE KNOWS WHAT MUST BE DONE.
SHE GOES TO HER MENTOR, ACHMED EL GIBÁR...
SO THAT IS YOUR DREAM, eh?
CLEARLY, IT IS WRITTEN IN YOUR DESTINY THAT YOU MUST MOVE ON-- AND I HAVE TAUGHT YOU ALL I KNOW.
GO... WITH MY BLESSING, LITTLE WHITE HAIR.

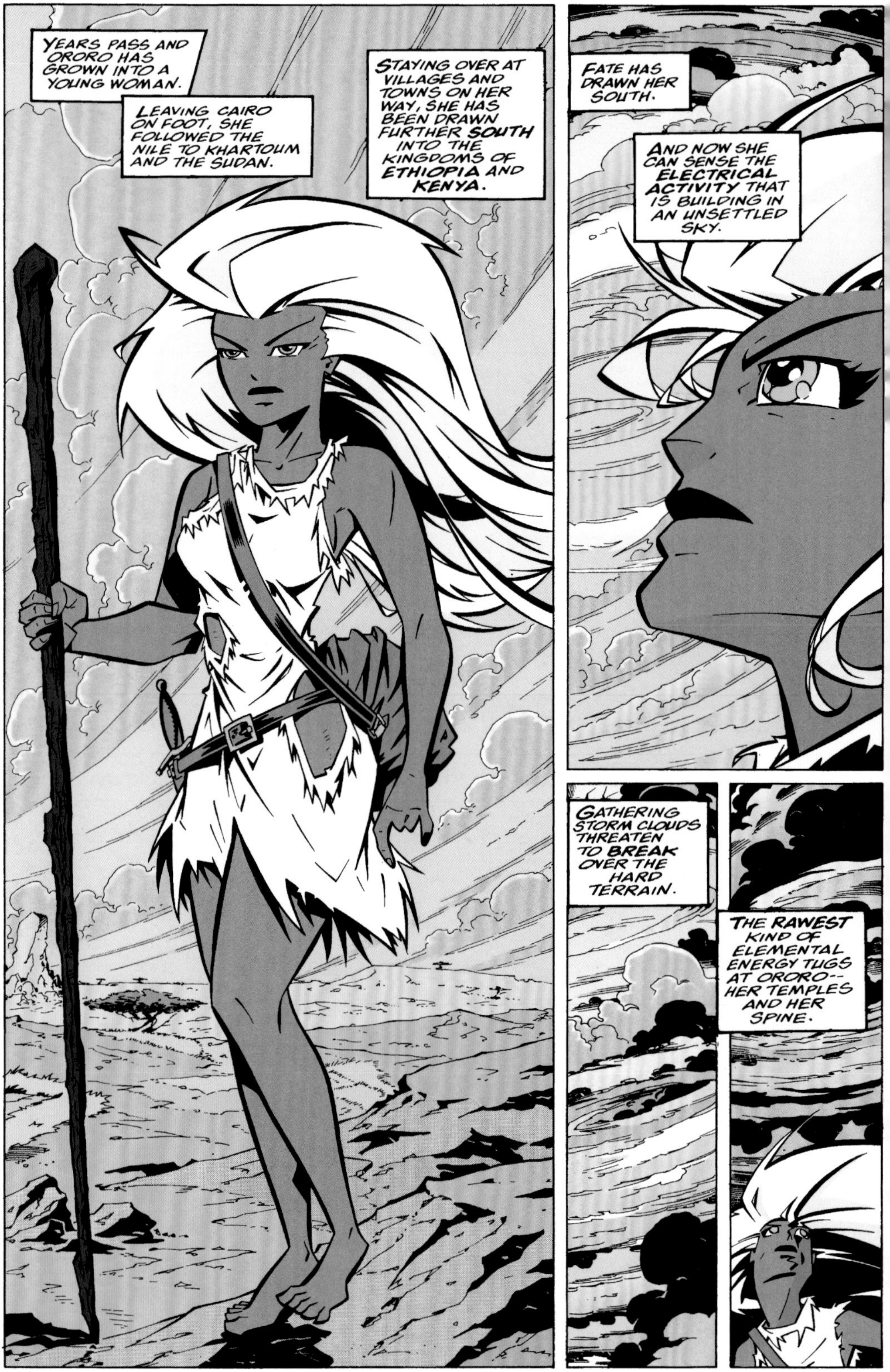
YEARS PASS AND ORORO HAS GROWN INTO A YOUNG WOMAN.
LEAVING CAIRO ON FOOT, SHE FOLLOWED THE NILE TO KHARTOUM AND THE SUDAN.
STAYING OVER AT VILLAGES AND TOWNS ON HER WAY, SHE HAS BEEN DRAWN FURTHER SOUTH INTO THE KINGDOMS OF ETHIOPIA AND KENYA.
FATE HAS DRAWN HER SOUTH.
AND NOW SHE CAN SENSE THE ELECTRICAL ACTIVITY THAT IS BUILDING IN AN UNSETTLED SKY.
GATHERING STORM CLOUDS THREATEN TO BREAK OVER THE HARD TERRAIN.
THE RAWEST KIND OF ELEMENTAL ENERGY TUGS AT ORORO-- HER TEMPLES AND HER SPINE.

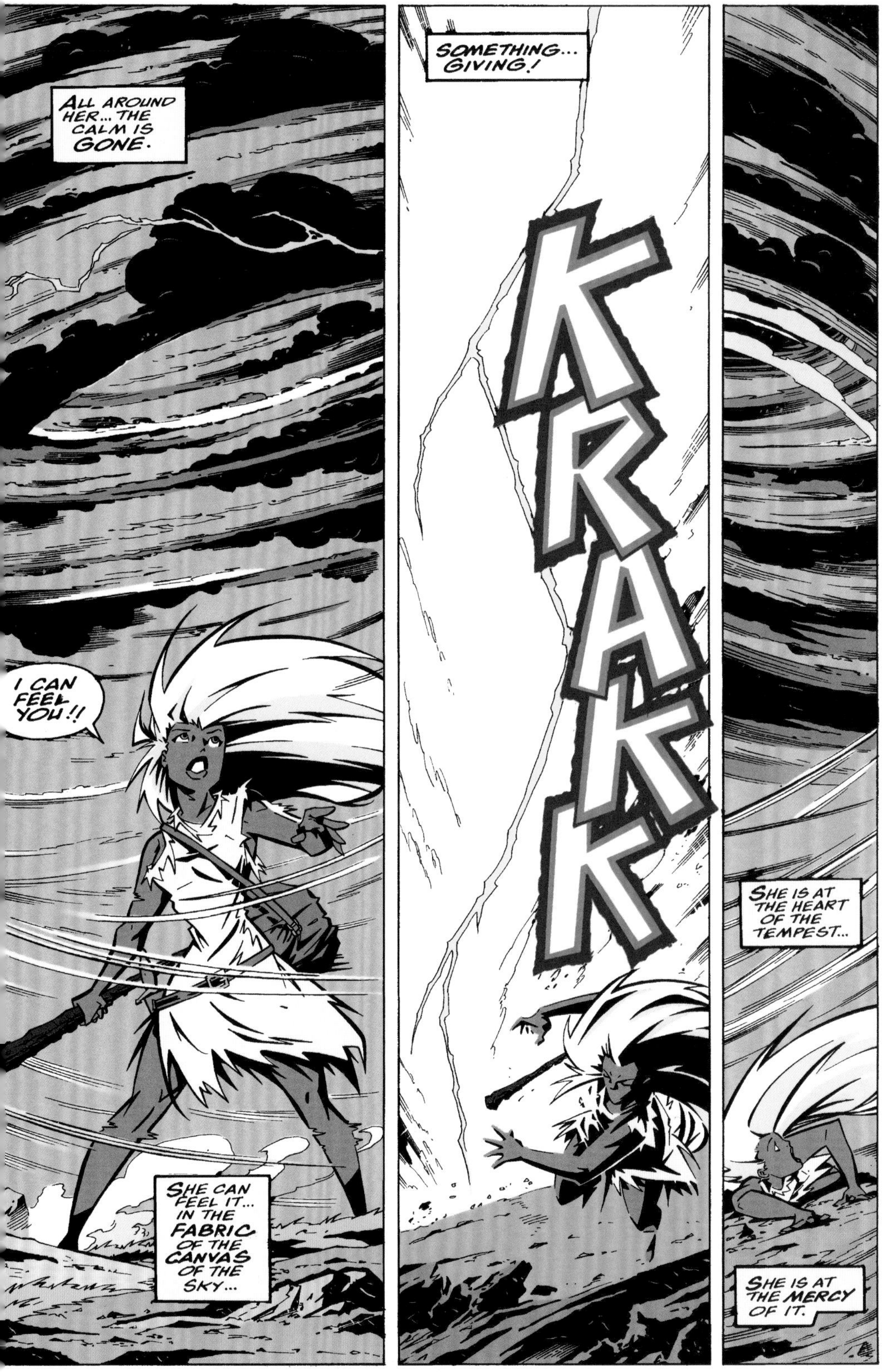
ALL AROUND HER... THE CALM IS GONE.
I CAN FEEL YOU!!
SHE CAN FEEL IT... IN THE FABRIC OF THE CANVAS OF THE SKY...
SOMETHING... GIVING!
KRAKK
SHE IS AT THE HEART OF THE TEMPEST...
SHE IS AT THE MERCY OF IT.

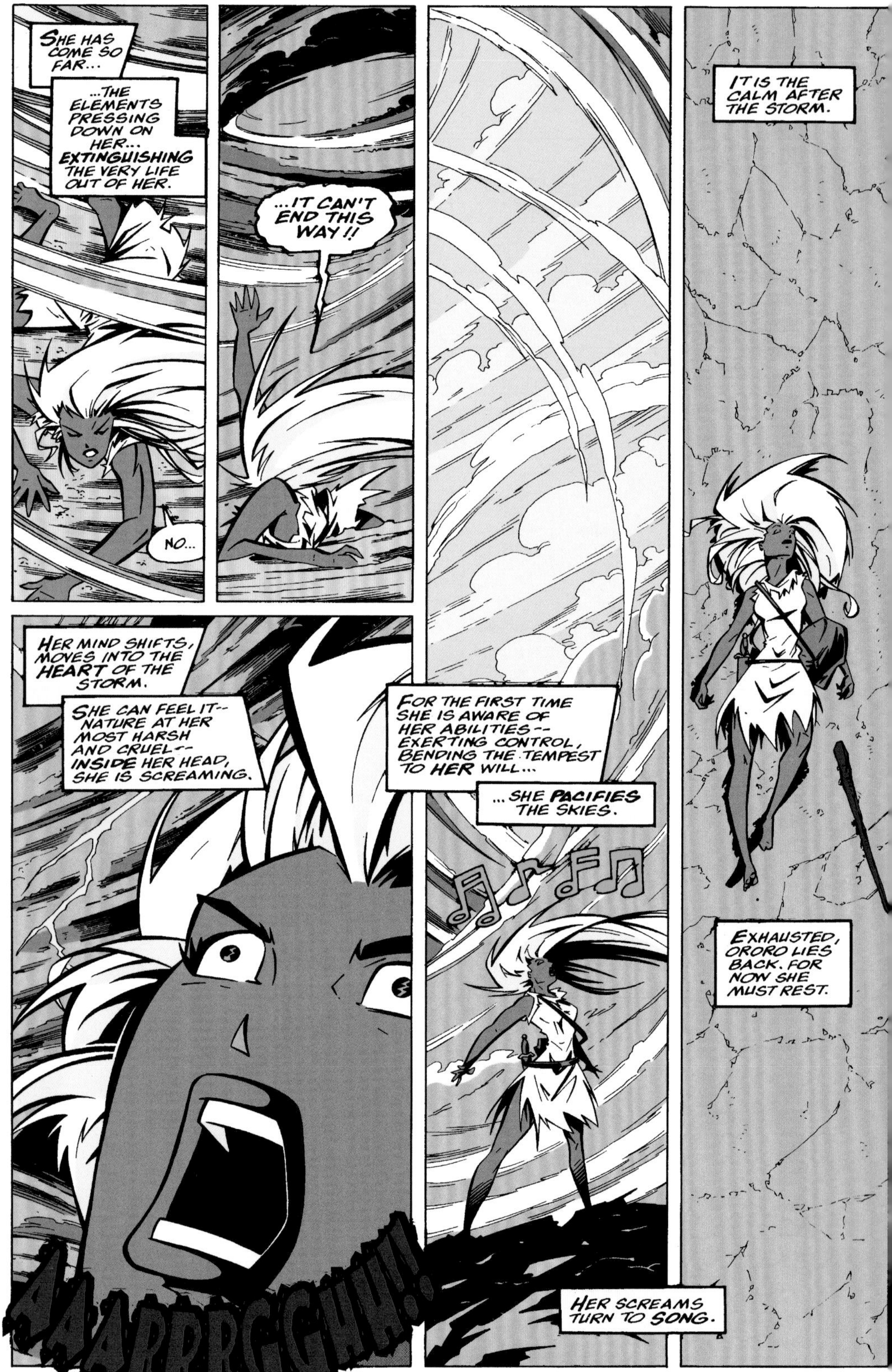
SHE HAS COME SO FAR...
...THE ELEMENTS PRESSING DOWN ON HER... EXTINGUISHING THE VERY LIFE OUT OF HER.
NO...
...IT CAN'T END THIS WAY!!
HER MIND SHIFTS, MOVES INTO THE HEART OF THE STORM.
SHE CAN FEEL IT-- NATURE AT HER MOST HARSH AND CRUEL-- INSIDE HER HEAD, SHE IS SCREAMING.
AAAARRRGGHH!!
FOR THE FIRST TIME SHE IS AWARE OF HER ABILITIES-- EXERTING CONTROL, BENDING THE TEMPEST TO HER WILL...
...SHE PACIFIES THE SKIES.
HER SCREAMS TURN TO SONG.
IT IS THE CALM AFTER THE STORM.
EXHAUSTED, ORORO LIES BACK. FOR NOW SHE MUST REST.

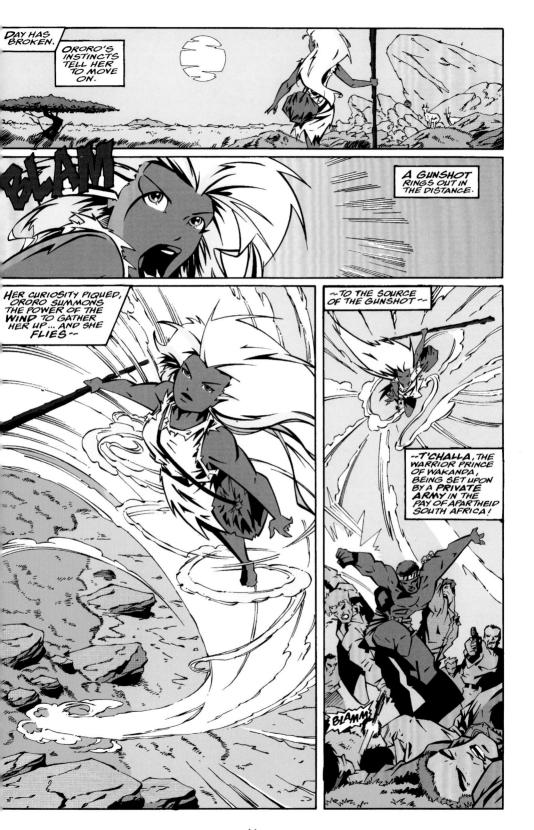

DAY HAS BROKEN.

ORORO'S INSTINCTS TELL HER TO MOVE ON.

BLAM

A GUNSHOT RINGS OUT IN THE DISTANCE.

HER CURIOSITY PIQUED, ORORO SUMMONS THE POWER OF THE WIND TO GATHER HER UP... AND SHE FLIES--

--TO THE SOURCE OF THE GUNSHOT--

--T'CHALLA, THE WARRIOR PRINCE OF WAKANDA, BEING SET UPON BY A PRIVATE ARMY IN THE PAY OF APARTHEID SOUTH AFRICA!

BLAMM!

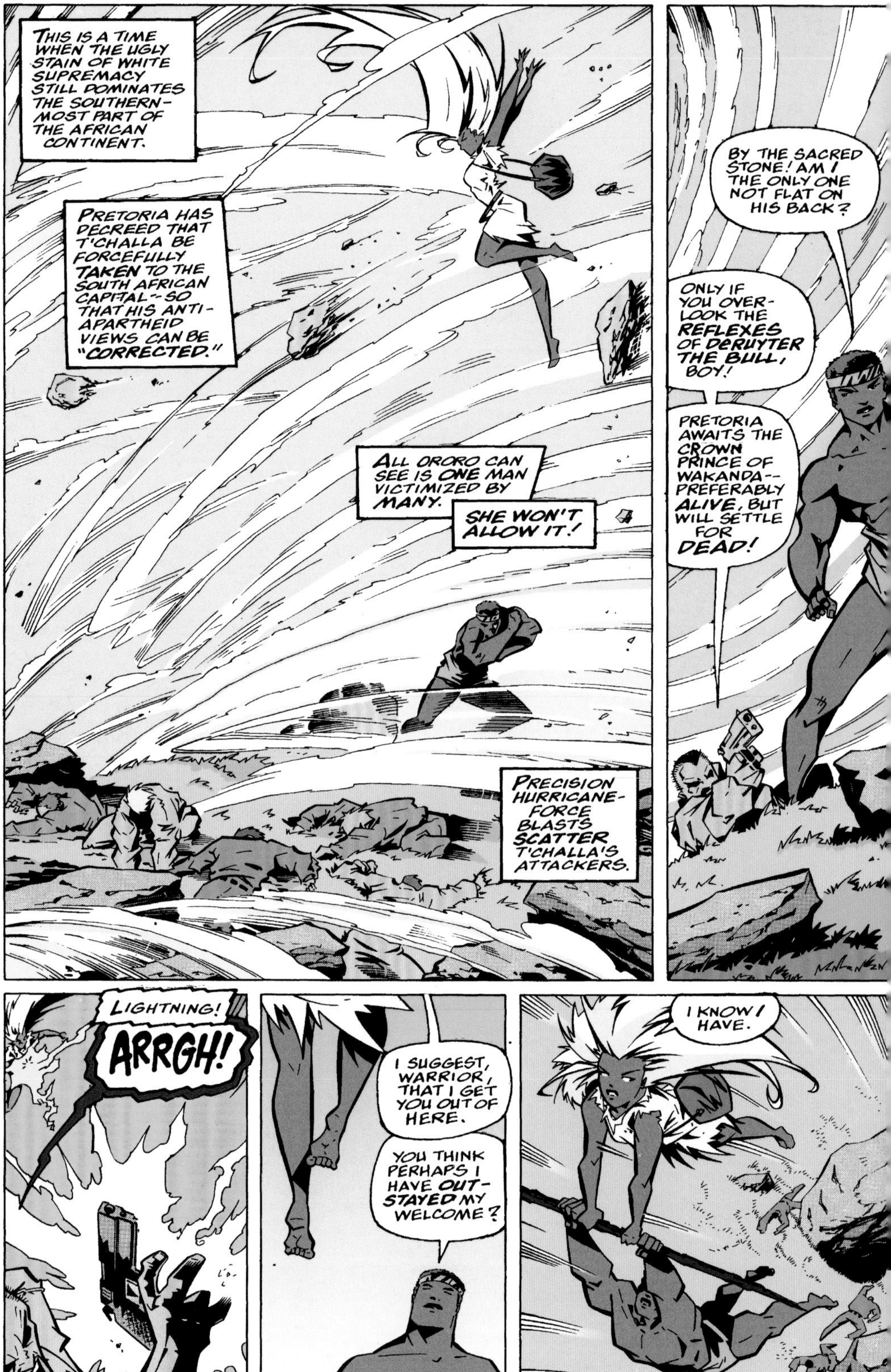

THIS IS A TIME WHEN THE UGLY STAIN OF WHITE SUPREMACY STILL DOMINATES THE SOUTHERN-MOST PART OF THE AFRICAN CONTINENT.
PRETORIA HAS DECREED THAT T'CHALLA BE FORCEFULLY TAKEN TO THE SOUTH AFRICAN CAPITAL--SO THAT HIS ANTI-APARTHEID VIEWS CAN BE "CORRECTED."
ALL ORORO CAN SEE IS ONE MAN VICTIMIZED BY MANY.
SHE WON'T ALLOW IT!
PRECISION HURRICANE-FORCE BLASTS SCATTER T'CHALLA'S ATTACKERS.
BY THE SACRED STONE! AM I THE ONLY ONE NOT FLAT ON HIS BACK?
ONLY IF YOU OVER-LOOK THE REFLEXES OF DERUYTER THE BULL, BOY!
PRETORIA AWAITS THE CROWN PRINCE OF WAKANDA--PREFERABLY ALIVE, BUT WILL SETTLE FOR DEAD!
LIGHTNING!
ARRGH!
I SUGGEST, WARRIOR, THAT I GET YOU OUT OF HERE.
YOU THINK PERHAPS I HAVE OUT-STAYED MY WELCOME?
I KNOW I HAVE.

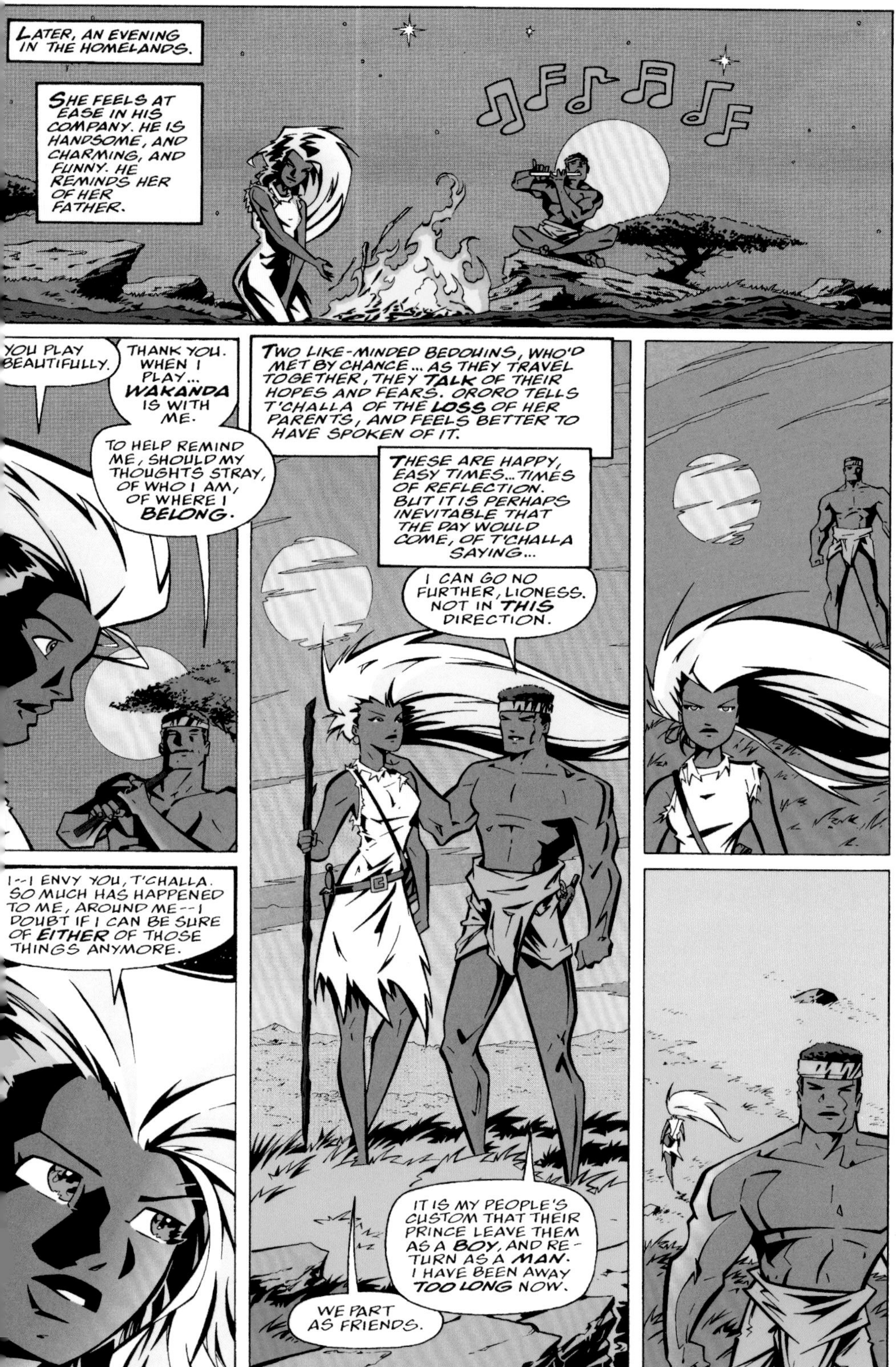
LATER, AN EVENING IN THE HOMELANDS.
SHE FEELS AT EASE IN HIS COMPANY. HE IS HANDSOME, AND CHARMING, AND FUNNY. HE REMINDS HER OF HER FATHER.
YOU PLAY BEAUTIFULLY.
THANK YOU. WHEN I PLAY... WAKANDA IS WITH ME.
TO HELP REMIND ME, SHOULD MY THOUGHTS STRAY, OF WHO I AM, OF WHERE I BELONG.
I--I ENVY YOU, T'CHALLA. SO MUCH HAS HAPPENED TO ME, AROUND ME--I DOUBT IF I CAN BE SURE OF EITHER OF THOSE THINGS ANYMORE.
TWO LIKE-MINDED BEDOUINS, WHO'D MET BY CHANCE... AS THEY TRAVEL TOGETHER, THEY TALK OF THEIR HOPES AND FEARS. ORORO TELLS T'CHALLA OF THE LOSS OF HER PARENTS, AND FEELS BETTER TO HAVE SPOKEN OF IT.
THESE ARE HAPPY, EASY TIMES... TIMES OF REFLECTION. BUT IT IS PERHAPS INEVITABLE THAT THE DAY WOULD COME, OF T'CHALLA SAYING...
I CAN GO NO FURTHER, LIONESS. NOT IN THIS DIRECTION.
IT IS MY PEOPLE'S CUSTOM THAT THEIR PRINCE LEAVE THEM AS A BOY, AND RE-TURN AS A MAN. I HAVE BEEN AWAY TOO LONG NOW.
WE PART AS FRIENDS.

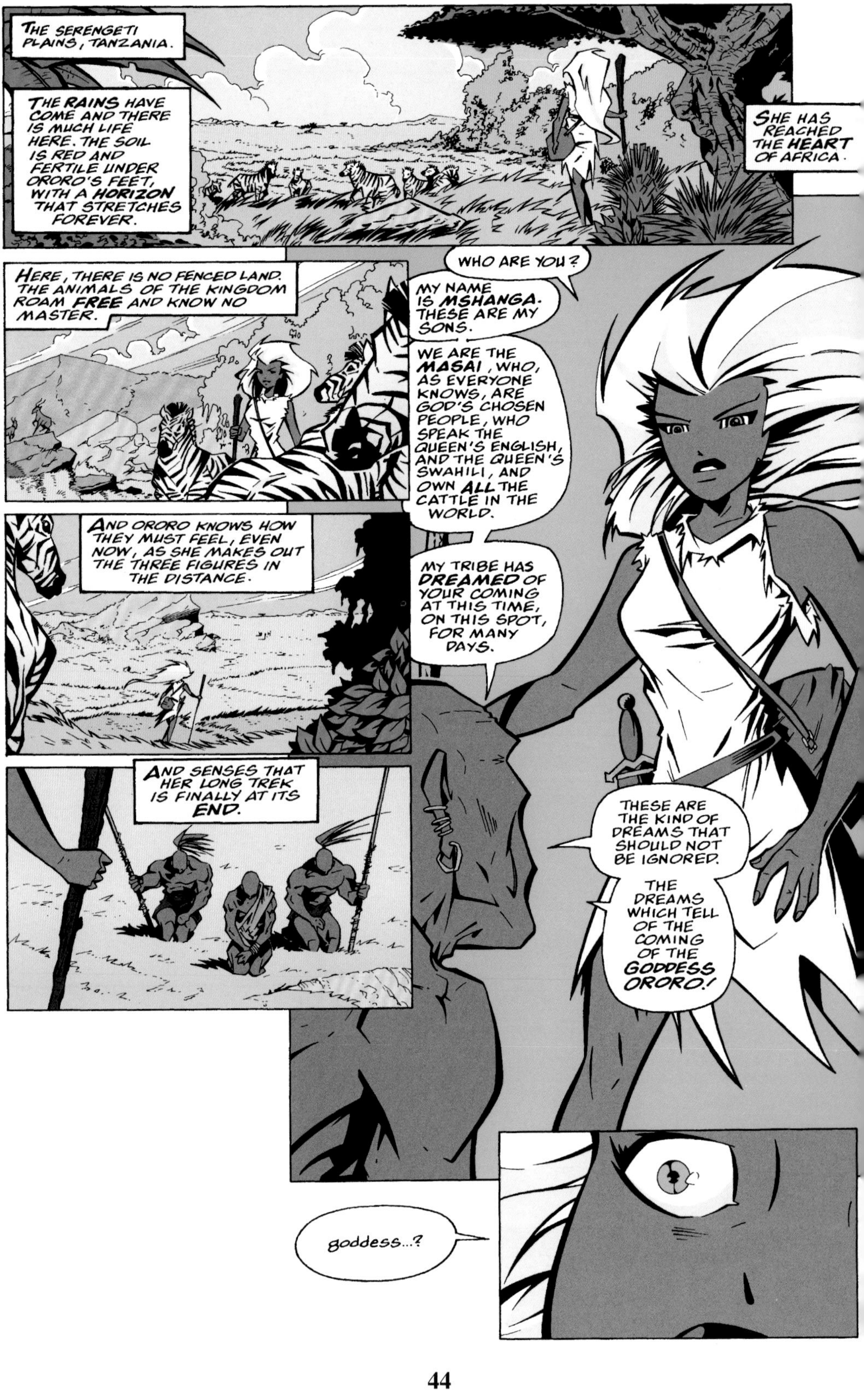
THE SERENGETI PLAINS, TANZANIA.
THE RAINS HAVE COME AND THERE IS MUCH LIFE HERE. THE SOIL IS RED AND FERTILE UNDER ORORO'S FEET, WITH A HORIZON THAT STRETCHES FOREVER.
SHE HAS REACHED THE HEART OF AFRICA.
HERE, THERE IS NO FENCED LAND. THE ANIMALS OF THE KINGDOM ROAM FREE AND KNOW NO MASTER.
AND ORORO KNOWS HOW THEY MUST FEEL, EVEN NOW, AS SHE MAKES OUT THE THREE FIGURES IN THE DISTANCE.
AND SENSES THAT HER LONG TREK IS FINALLY AT ITS END.
WHO ARE YOU?
MY NAME IS MSHANGA. THESE ARE MY SONS.
WE ARE THE MASAI, WHO, AS EVERYONE KNOWS, ARE GOD'S CHOSEN PEOPLE, WHO SPEAK THE QUEEN'S ENGLISH, AND THE QUEEN'S SWAHILI, AND OWN ALL THE CATTLE IN THE WORLD.
MY TRIBE HAS DREAMED OF YOUR COMING AT THIS TIME, ON THIS SPOT, FOR MANY DAYS.
THESE ARE THE KIND OF DREAMS THAT SHOULD NOT BE IGNORED.
THE DREAMS WHICH TELL OF THE COMING OF THE GODDESS ORORO!
goddess...?

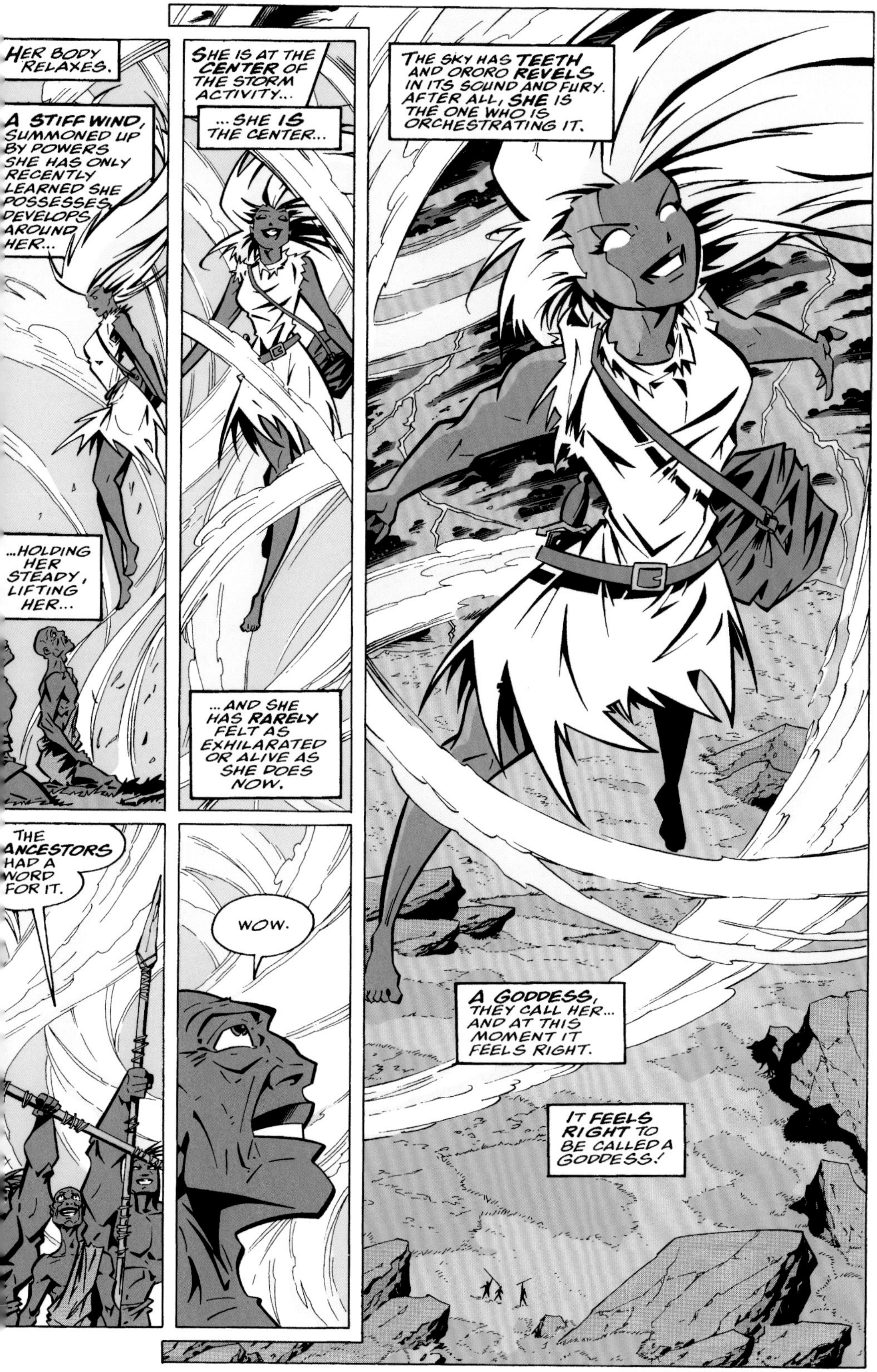
HER BODY RELAXES.
A STIFF WIND, SUMMONED UP BY POWERS SHE HAS ONLY RECENTLY LEARNED SHE POSSESSES, DEVELOPS AROUND HER...
...HOLDING HER STEADY, LIFTING HER...
SHE IS AT THE CENTER OF THE STORM ACTIVITY...
...SHE IS THE CENTER...
...AND SHE HAS RARELY FELT AS EXHILARATED OR ALIVE AS SHE DOES NOW.
THE SKY HAS TEETH AND ORORO REVELS IN ITS SOUND AND FURY. AFTER ALL, SHE IS THE ONE WHO IS ORCHESTRATING IT.
THE ANCESTORS HAD A WORD FOR IT.
WOW.
A GODDESS, THEY CALL HER... AND AT THIS MOMENT IT FEELS RIGHT.
IT FEELS RIGHT TO BE CALLED A GODDESS!

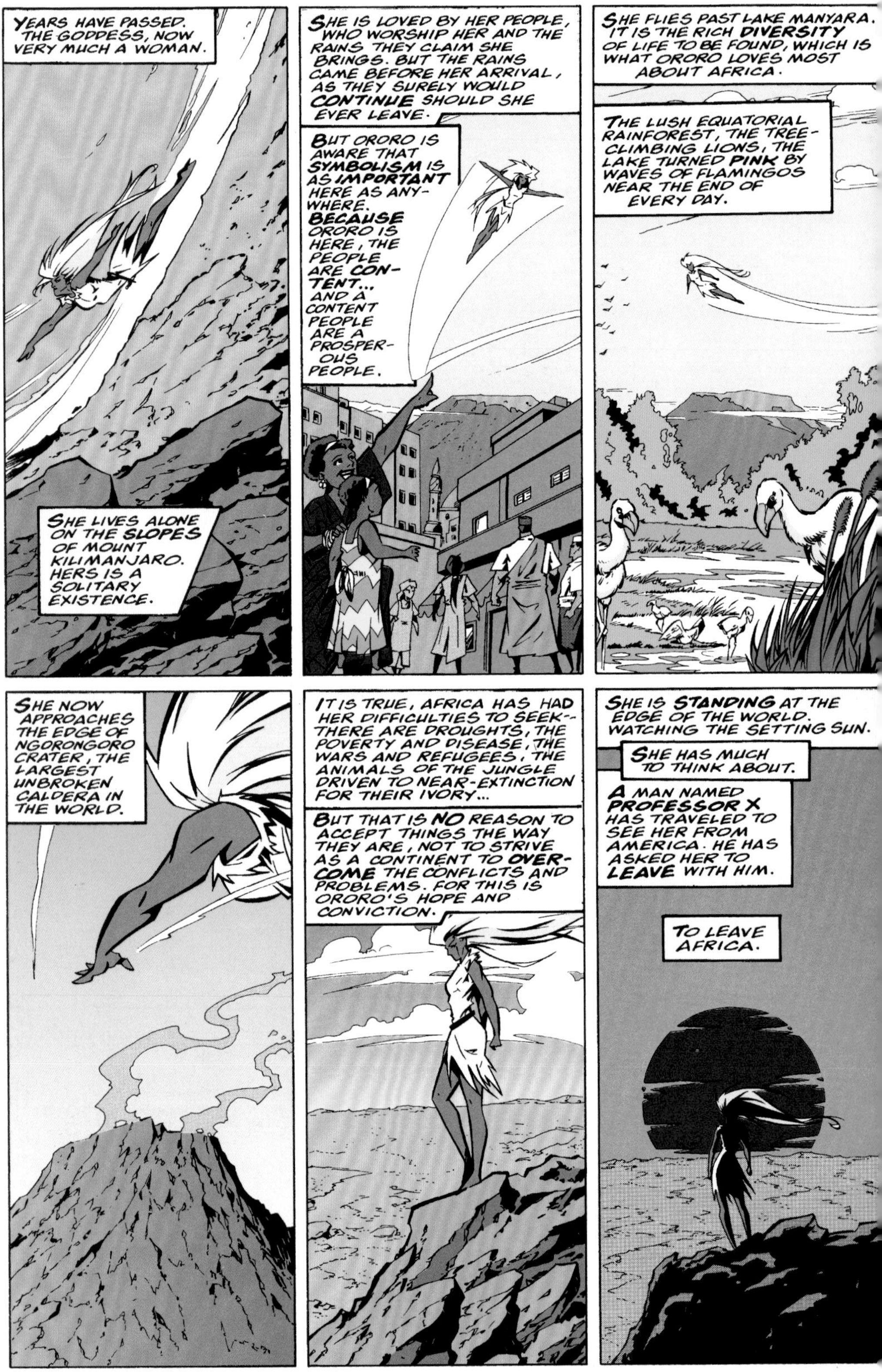
YEARS HAVE PASSED. THE GODDESS, NOW VERY MUCH A WOMAN.
SHE LIVES ALONE ON THE SLOPES OF MOUNT KILIMANJARO. HERS IS A SOLITARY EXISTENCE.
SHE IS LOVED BY HER PEOPLE, WHO WORSHIP HER AND THE RAINS THEY CLAIM SHE BRINGS. BUT THE RAINS CAME BEFORE HER ARRIVAL, AS THEY SURELY WOULD CONTINUE SHOULD SHE EVER LEAVE.
BUT ORORO IS AWARE THAT SYMBOLISM IS AS IMPORTANT HERE AS ANYWHERE. BECAUSE ORORO IS HERE, THE PEOPLE ARE CONTENT... AND A CONTENT PEOPLE ARE A PROSPEROUS PEOPLE.
SHE FLIES PAST LAKE MANYARA. IT IS THE RICH DIVERSITY OF LIFE TO BE FOUND, WHICH IS WHAT ORORO LOVES MOST ABOUT AFRICA.
THE LUSH EQUATORIAL RAINFOREST, THE TREE-CLIMBING LIONS, THE LAKE TURNED PINK BY WAVES OF FLAMINGOS NEAR THE END OF EVERY DAY.
SHE NOW APPROACHES THE EDGE OF NGORONGORO CRATER, THE LARGEST UNBROKEN CALDERA IN THE WORLD.
IT IS TRUE, AFRICA HAS HAD HER DIFFICULTIES TO SEEK--THERE ARE DROUGHTS, THE POVERTY AND DISEASE, THE WARS AND REFUGEES, THE ANIMALS OF THE JUNGLE DRIVEN TO NEAR-EXTINCTION FOR THEIR IVORY...
BUT THAT IS NO REASON TO ACCEPT THINGS THE WAY THEY ARE, NOT TO STRIVE AS A CONTINENT TO OVERCOME THE CONFLICTS AND PROBLEMS. FOR THIS IS ORORO'S HOPE AND CONVICTION.
SHE IS STANDING AT THE EDGE OF THE WORLD. WATCHING THE SETTING SUN.
SHE HAS MUCH TO THINK ABOUT.
A MAN NAMED PROFESSOR X HAS TRAVELED TO SEE HER FROM AMERICA. HE HAS ASKED HER TO LEAVE WITH HIM.
TO LEAVE AFRICA.

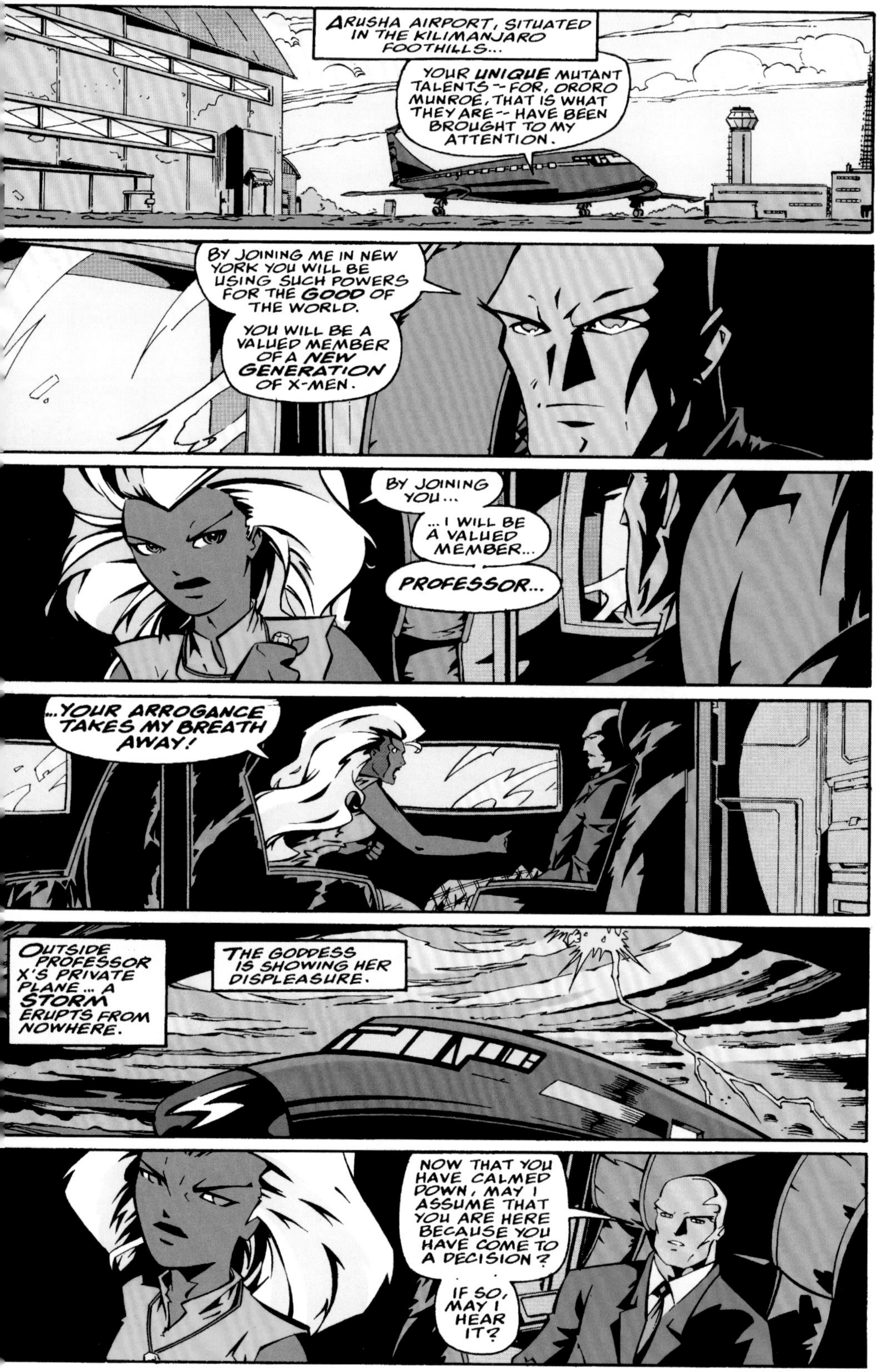
ARUSHA AIRPORT, SITUATED IN THE KILIMANJARO FOOTHILLS...
YOUR UNIQUE MUTANT TALENTS -- FOR, ORORO MUNROE, THAT IS WHAT THEY ARE -- HAVE BEEN BROUGHT TO MY ATTENTION.
BY JOINING ME IN NEW YORK YOU WILL BE USING SUCH POWERS FOR THE GOOD OF THE WORLD.
YOU WILL BE A VALUED MEMBER OF A NEW GENERATION OF X-MEN.
BY JOINING YOU...
...I WILL BE A VALUED MEMBER...
PROFESSOR...
...YOUR ARROGANCE TAKES MY BREATH AWAY!
OUTSIDE PROFESSOR X'S PRIVATE PLANE... A STORM ERUPTS FROM NOWHERE.
THE GODDESS IS SHOWING HER DISPLEASURE.
NOW THAT YOU HAVE CALMED DOWN, MAY I ASSUME THAT YOU ARE HERE BECAUSE YOU HAVE COME TO A DECISION?
IF SO, MAY I HEAR IT?

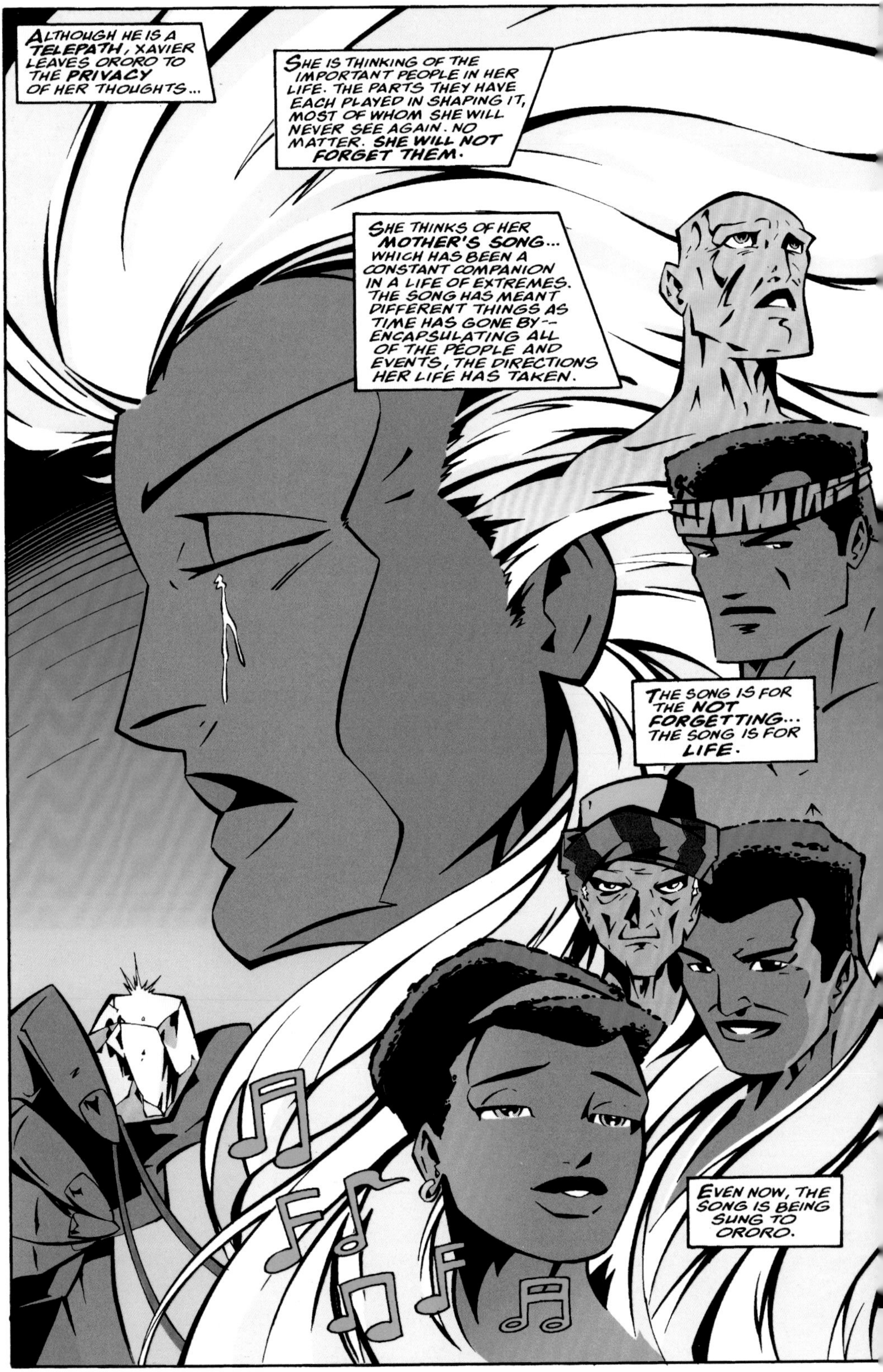

ALTHOUGH HE IS A TELEPATH, XAVIER LEAVES ORORO TO THE PRIVACY OF HER THOUGHTS...
SHE IS THINKING OF THE IMPORTANT PEOPLE IN HER LIFE. THE PARTS THEY HAVE EACH PLAYED IN SHAPING IT, MOST OF WHOM SHE WILL NEVER SEE AGAIN. NO MATTER. SHE WILL NOT FORGET THEM.
SHE THINKS OF HER MOTHER'S SONG... WHICH HAS BEEN A CONSTANT COMPANION IN A LIFE OF EXTREMES. THE SONG HAS MEANT DIFFERENT THINGS AS TIME HAS GONE BY-- ENCAPSULATING ALL OF THE PEOPLE AND EVENTS, THE DIRECTIONS HER LIFE HAS TAKEN.
THE SONG IS FOR THE NOT FORGETTING... THE SONG IS FOR LIFE.
EVEN NOW, THE SONG IS BEING SUNG TO ORORO.

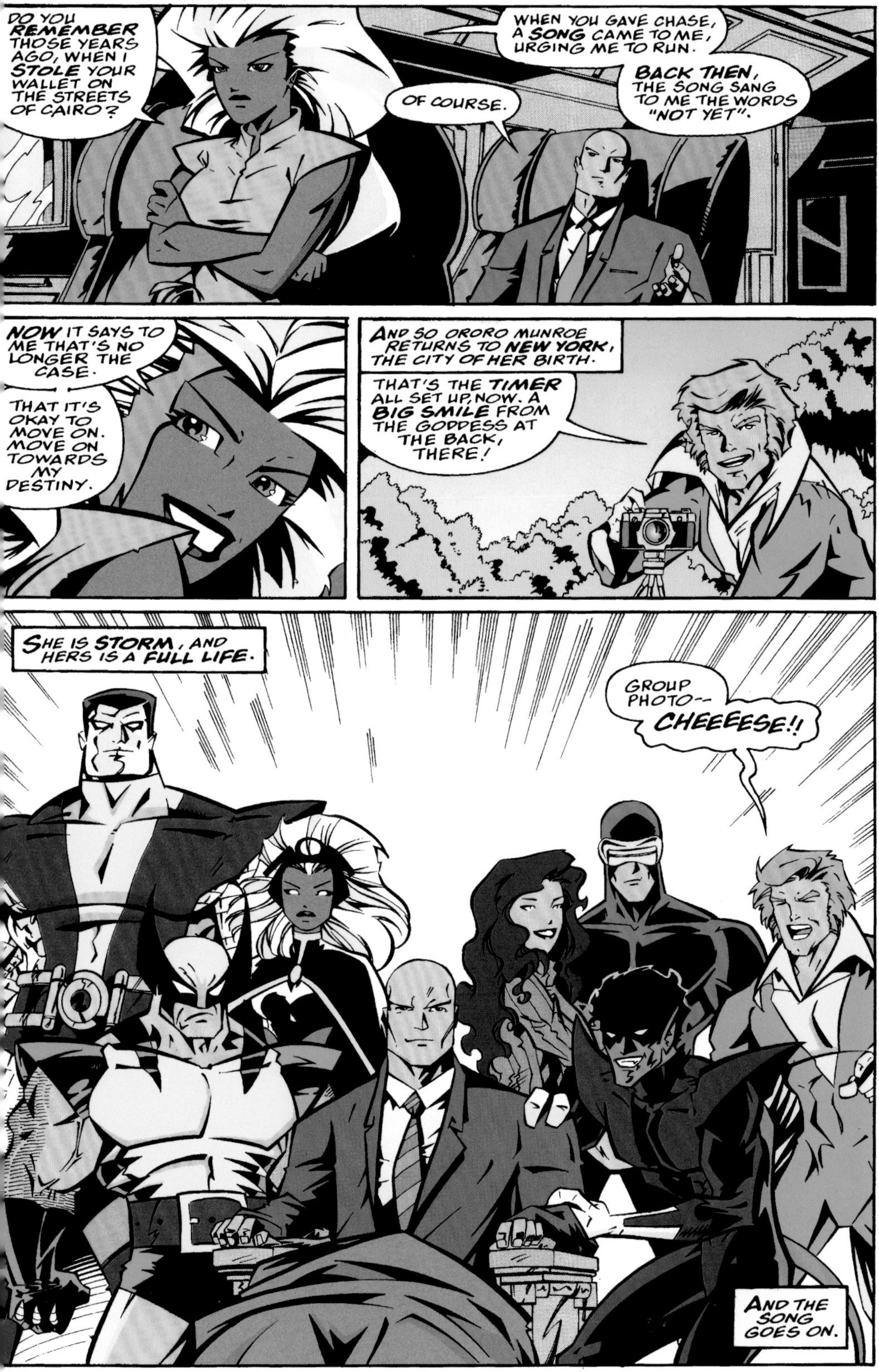
DO YOU REMEMBER THOSE YEARS AGO, WHEN I STOLE YOUR WALLET ON THE STREETS OF CAIRO?
OF COURSE.
WHEN YOU GAVE CHASE, A SONG CAME TO ME, URGING ME TO RUN.
BACK THEN, THE SONG SANG TO ME THE WORDS "NOT YET".
NOW IT SAYS TO ME THAT'S NO LONGER THE CASE.
THAT IT'S OKAY TO MOVE ON. MOVE ON TOWARDS MY DESTINY.
AND SO ORORO MUNROE RETURNS TO NEW YORK, THE CITY OF HER BIRTH.
THAT'S THE TIMER ALL SET UP, NOW. A BIG SMILE FROM THE GODDESS AT THE BACK, THERE!
SHE IS STORM, AND HERS IS A FULL LIFE.
GROUP PHOTO-- CHEEEESE!!
AND THE SONG GOES ON.

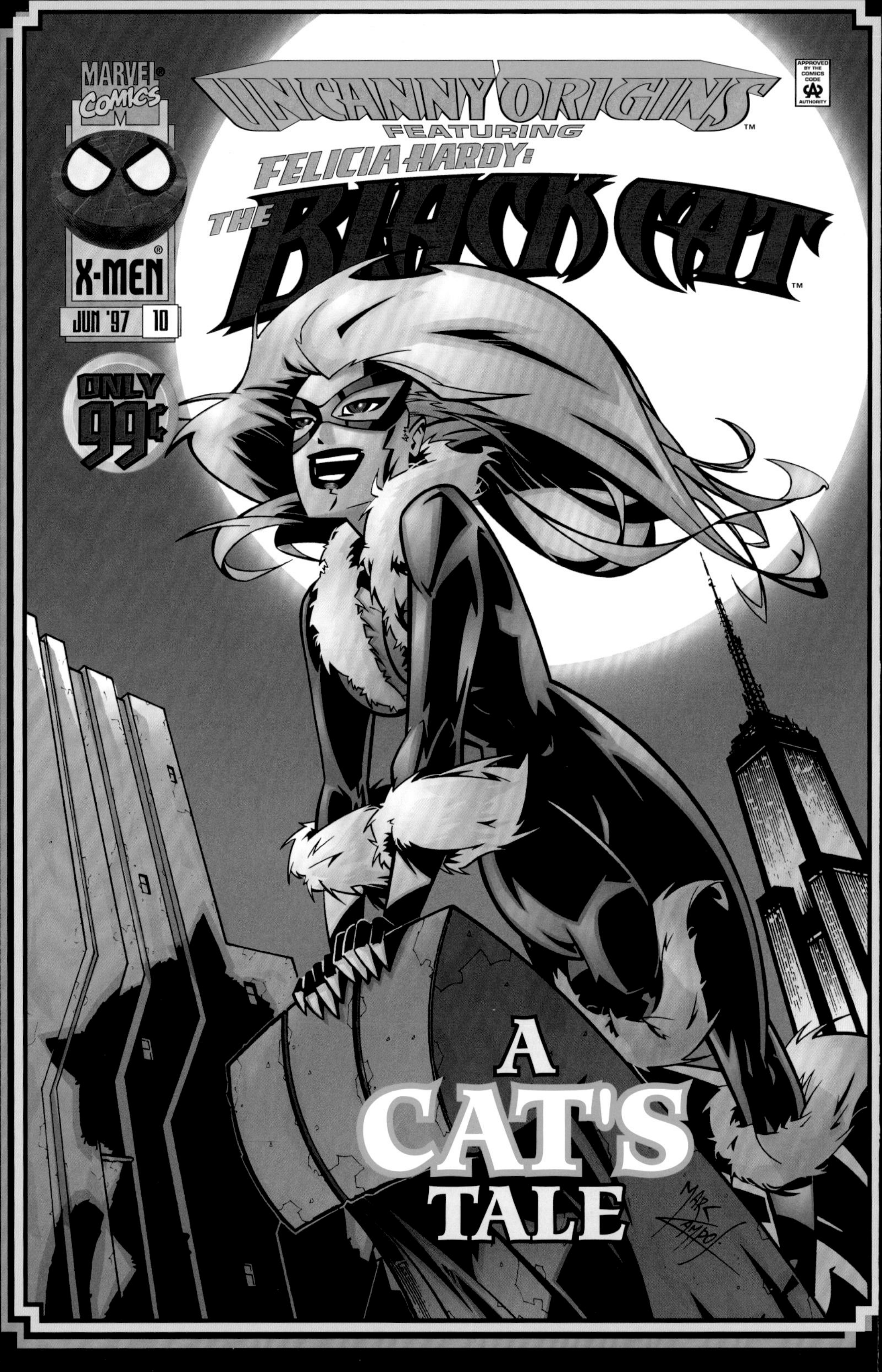
MARVEL® COMICS
X-MEN®
JUN '97 10
ONLY 99¢
UNCANNY ORIGINS™
FEATURING
FELICIA HARDY:
THE BLACK CAT™
APPROVED BY THE COMICS CODE AUTHORITY
A CAT'S TALE

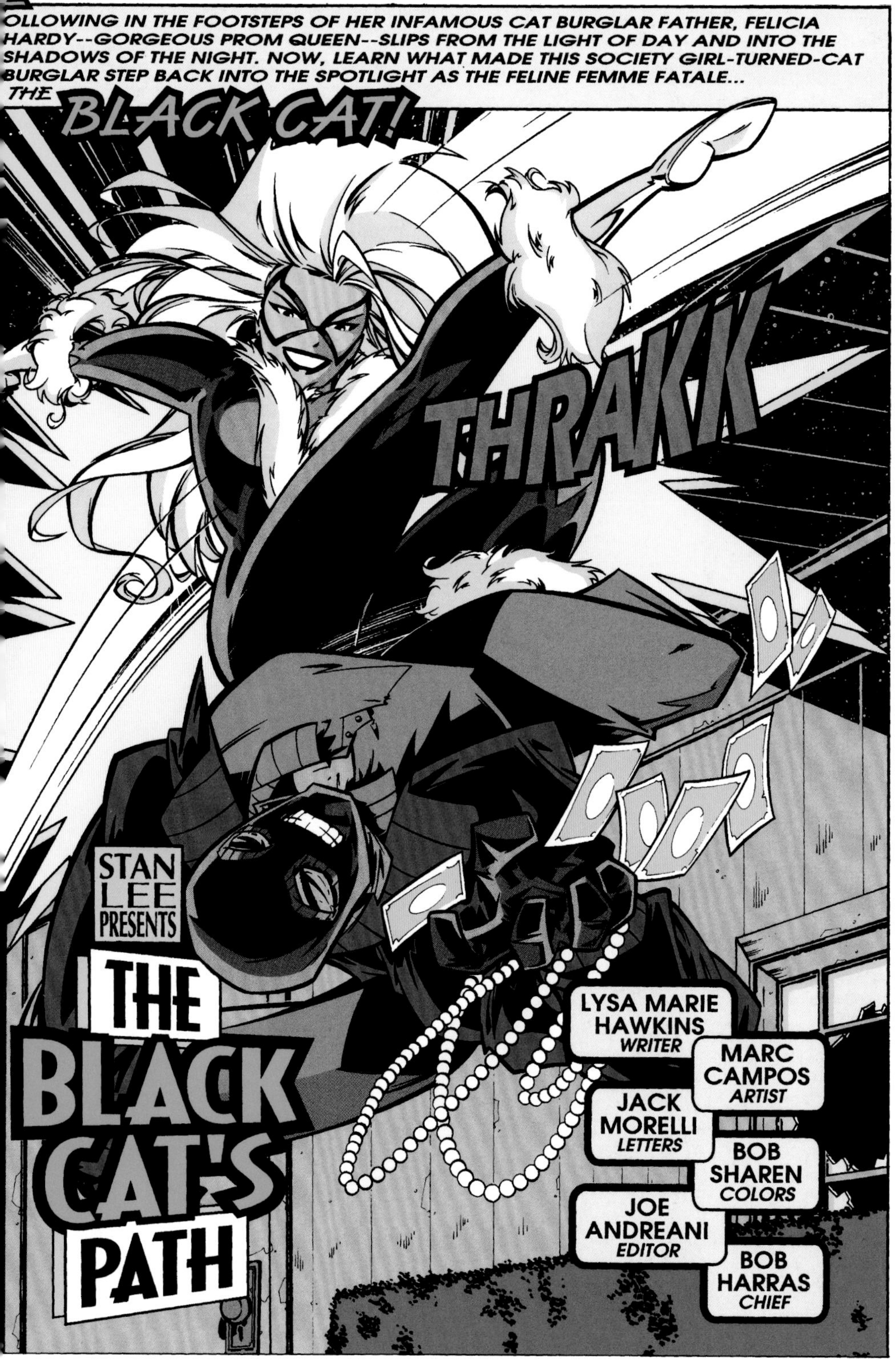

FOLLOWING IN THE FOOTSTEPS OF HER INFAMOUS CAT BURGLAR FATHER, FELICIA HARDY--GORGEOUS PROM QUEEN--SLIPS FROM THE LIGHT OF DAY AND INTO THE SHADOWS OF THE NIGHT. NOW, LEARN WHAT MADE THIS SOCIETY GIRL-TURNED-CAT BURGLAR STEP BACK INTO THE SPOTLIGHT AS THE FELINE FEMME FATALE... THE BLACK CAT!
THRAKK
STAN LEE PRESENTS
THE BLACK CAT'S PATH
LYSA MARIE HAWKINS WRITER
MARC CAMPOS ARTIST
JACK MORELLI LETTERS
BOB SHAREN COLORS
JOE ANDREANI EDITOR
BOB HARRAS CHIEF

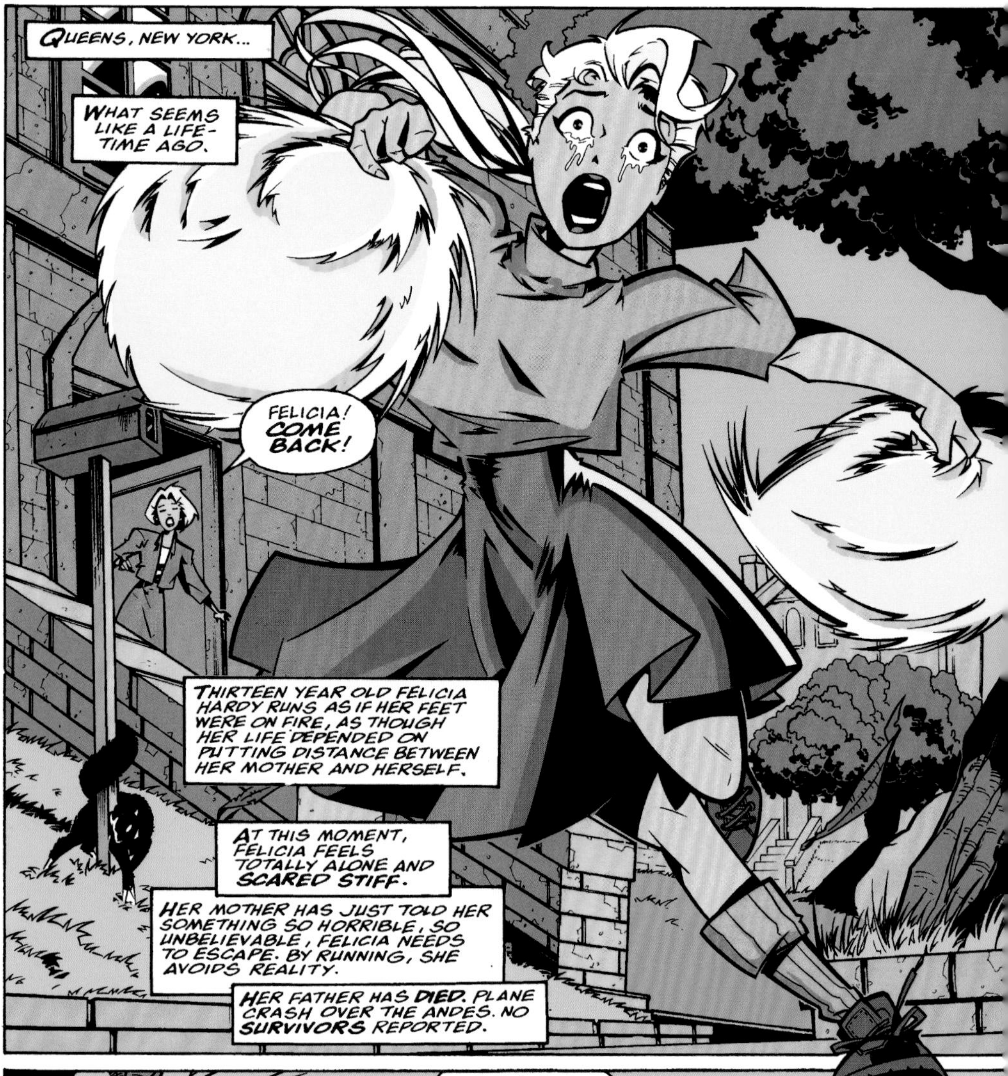
QUEENS, NEW YORK...
WHAT SEEMS LIKE A LIFE-TIME AGO.
FELICIA! COME BACK!
THIRTEEN YEAR OLD FELICIA HARDY RUNS AS IF HER FEET WERE ON FIRE, AS THOUGH HER LIFE DEPENDED ON PUTTING DISTANCE BETWEEN HER MOTHER AND HERSELF.
AT THIS MOMENT, FELICIA FEELS TOTALLY ALONE AND SCARED STIFF.
HER MOTHER HAS JUST TOLD HER SOMETHING SO HORRIBLE, SO UNBELIEVABLE, FELICIA NEEDS TO ESCAPE. BY RUNNING, SHE AVOIDS REALITY.
HER FATHER HAS DIED. PLANE CRASH OVER THE ANDES. NO SURVIVORS REPORTED.

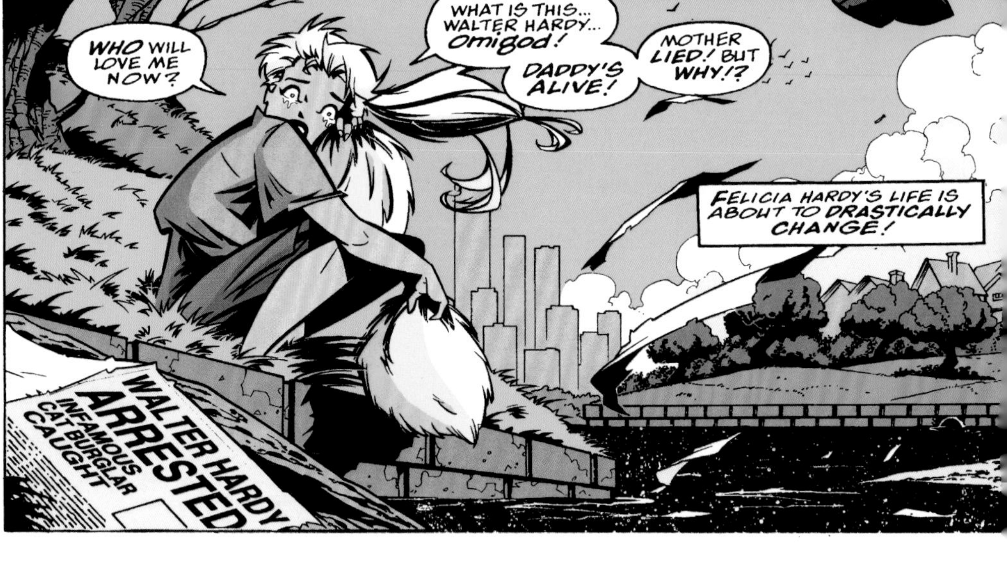
WHO WILL LOVE ME NOW?
WHAT IS THIS... WALTER HARDY... OMIGOD!
DADDY'S ALIVE!
MOTHER LIED! BUT WHY!?
FELICIA HARDY'S LIFE IS ABOUT TO DRASTICALLY CHANGE!
WALTER HARDY ARRESTED
INFAMOUS CAT BURGLAR CAUGHT

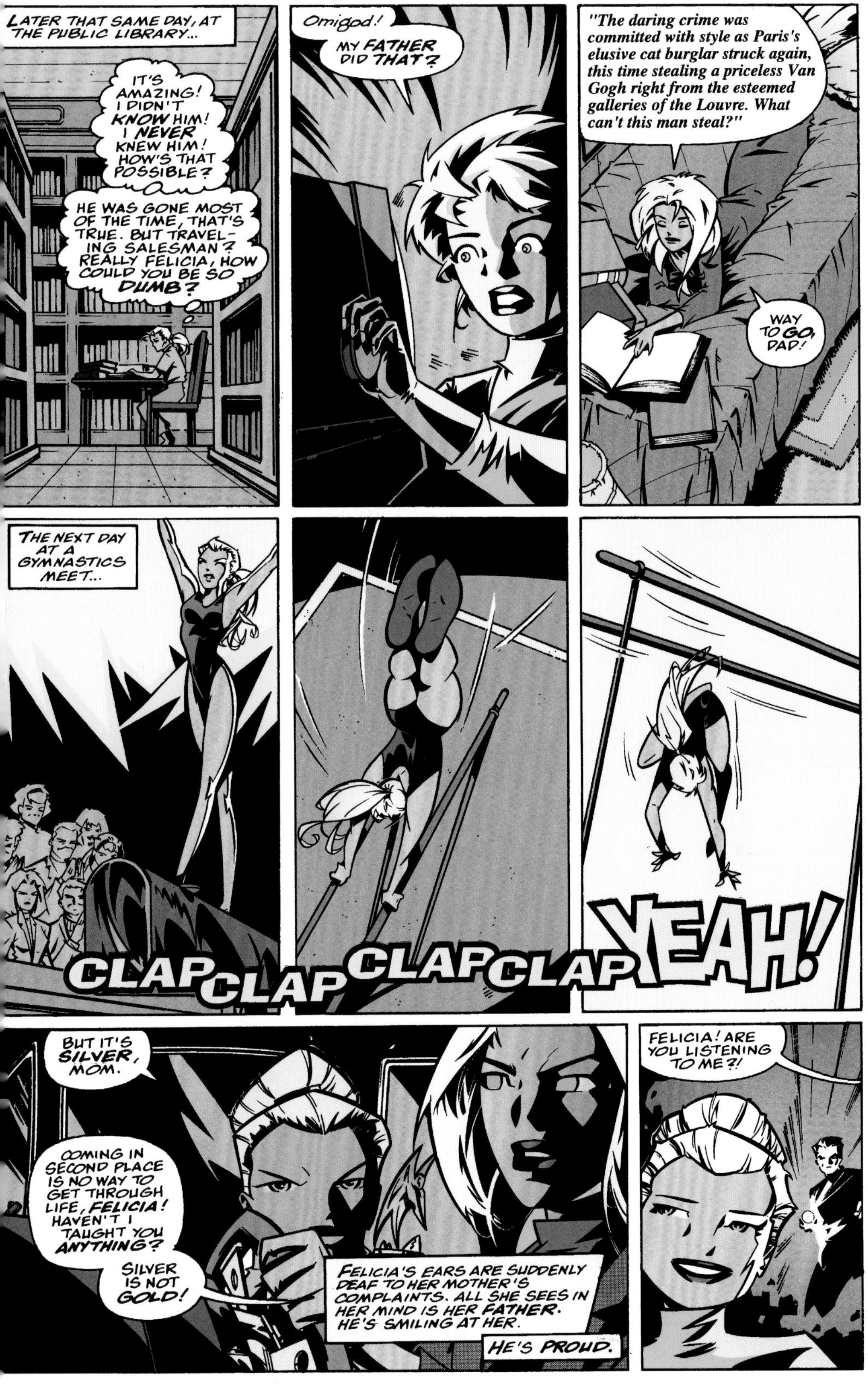

LATER THAT SAME DAY, AT THE PUBLIC LIBRARY...
IT'S AMAZING! I DIDN'T KNOW HIM! I NEVER KNEW HIM! HOW'S THAT POSSIBLE?
HE WAS GONE MOST OF THE TIME, THAT'S TRUE. BUT TRAVELING SALESMAN? REALLY FELICIA, HOW COULD YOU BE SO DUMB?
Omigod!
MY FATHER DID THAT?
"The daring crime was committed with style as Paris's elusive cat burglar struck again, this time stealing a priceless Van Gogh right from the esteemed galleries of the Louvre. What can't this man steal?"
WAY TO GO, DAD!
THE NEXT DAY AT A GYMNASTICS MEET...
CLAP CLAP CLAP CLAP YEAH!
BUT IT'S SILVER, MOM.
COMING IN SECOND PLACE IS NO WAY TO GET THROUGH LIFE, FELICIA! HAVEN'T I TAUGHT YOU ANYTHING?
SILVER IS NOT GOLD!
FELICIA'S EARS ARE SUDDENLY DEAF TO HER MOTHER'S COMPLAINTS. ALL SHE SEES IN HER MIND IS HER FATHER. HE'S SMILING AT HER.
HE'S PROUD.
FELICIA! ARE YOU LISTENING TO ME?!

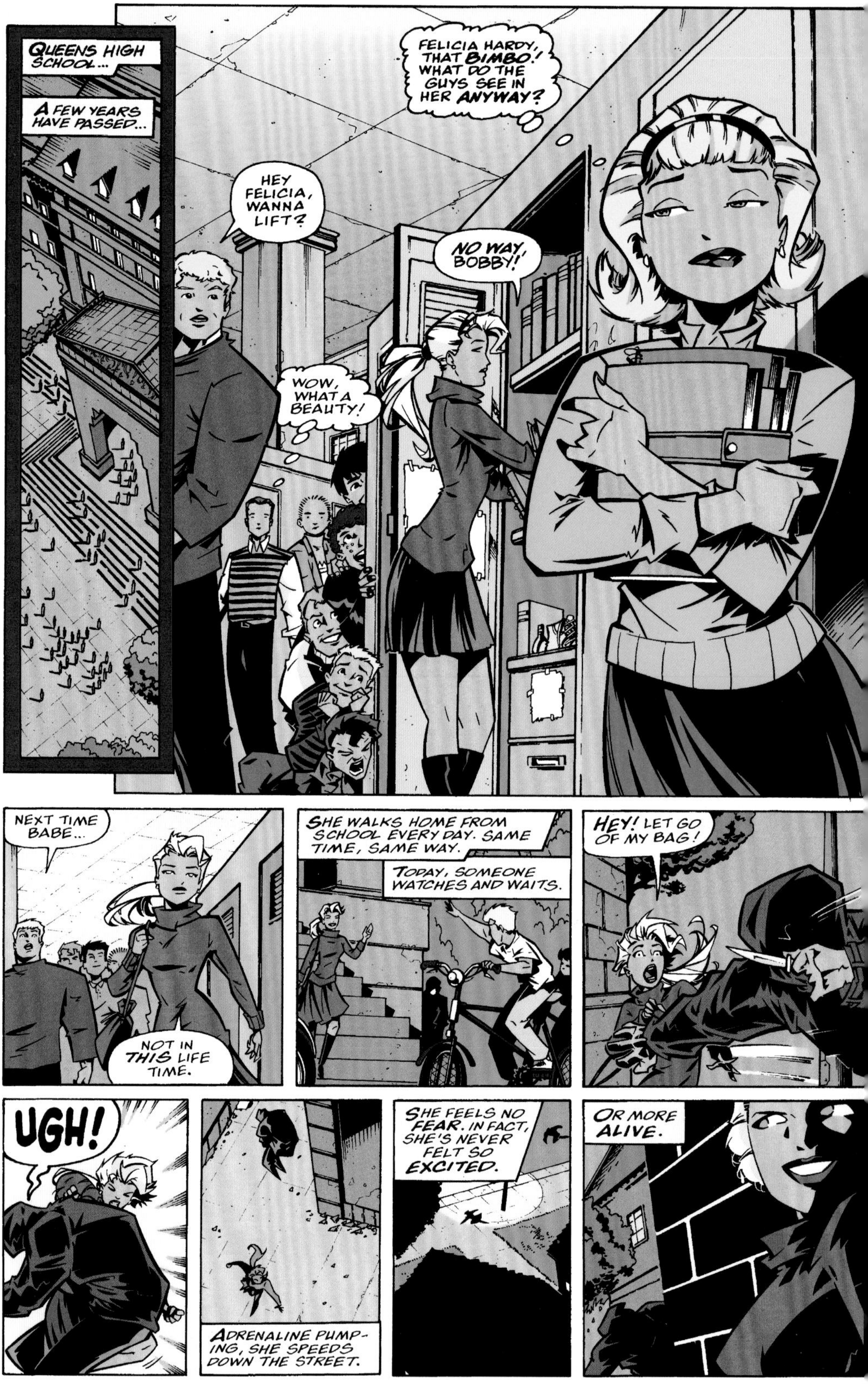
QUEENS HIGH SCHOOL...
A FEW YEARS HAVE PASSED...
FELICIA HARDY, THAT BIMBO! WHAT DO THE GUYS SEE IN HER ANYWAY?
HEY FELICIA, WANNA LIFT?
NO WAY, BOBBY!
WOW, WHAT A BEAUTY!
NEXT TIME BABE...
NOT IN THIS LIFE TIME.
SHE WALKS HOME FROM SCHOOL EVERY DAY. SAME TIME, SAME WAY.
TODAY, SOMEONE WATCHES AND WAITS.
HEY! LET GO OF MY BAG!
UGH!
ADRENALINE PUMPING, SHE SPEEDS DOWN THE STREET.
SHE FEELS NO FEAR. IN FACT, SHE'S NEVER FELT SO EXCITED.
OR MORE ALIVE.

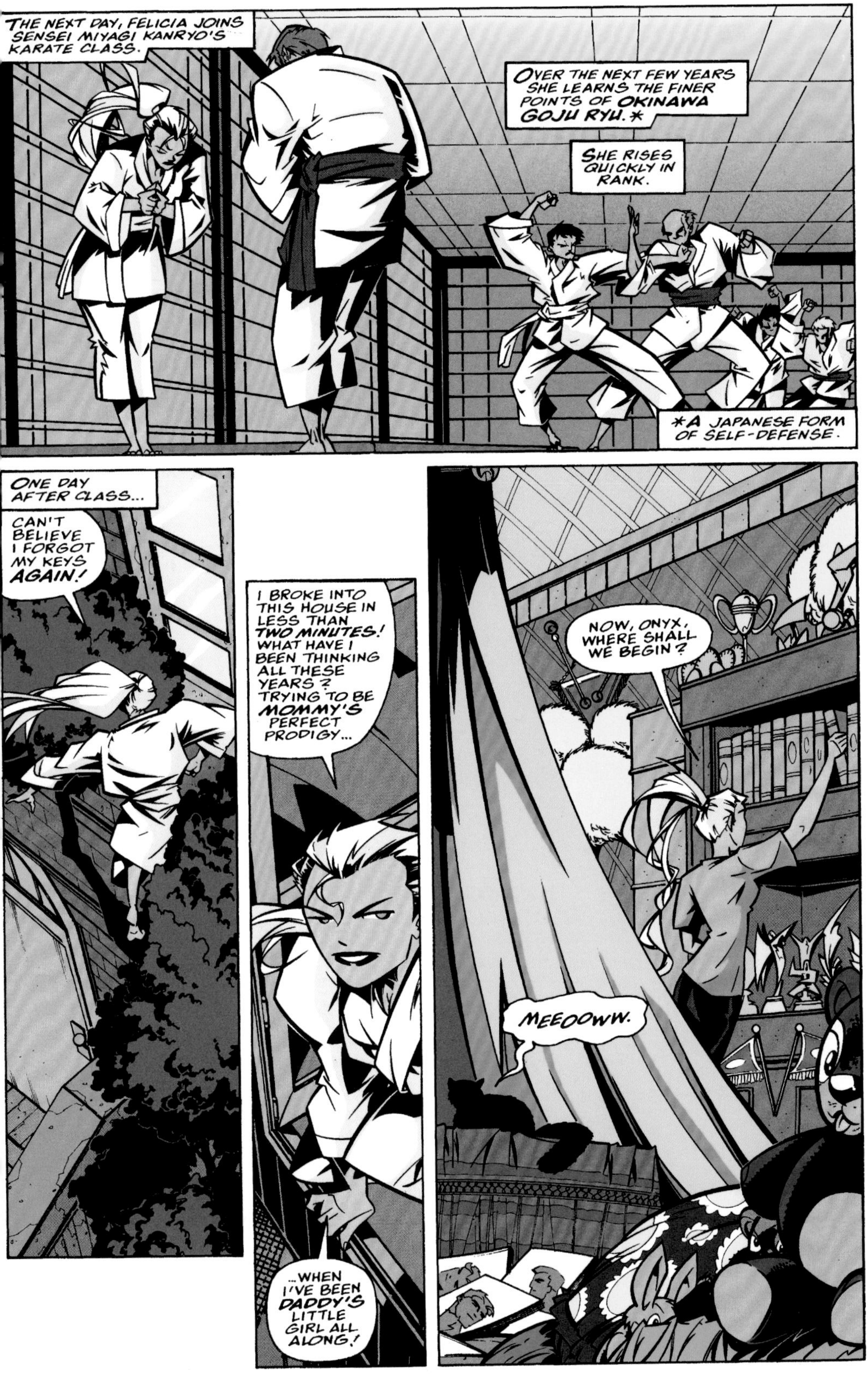
THE NEXT DAY, FELICIA JOINS SENSEI MIYAGI KANRYO'S KARATE CLASS.
OVER THE NEXT FEW YEARS SHE LEARNS THE FINER POINTS OF OKINAWA GOJU RYU.*
SHE RISES QUICKLY IN RANK.
*A JAPANESE FORM OF SELF-DEFENSE.
ONE DAY AFTER CLASS...
CAN'T BELIEVE I FORGOT MY KEYS AGAIN!
I BROKE INTO THIS HOUSE IN LESS THAN TWO MINUTES! WHAT HAVE I BEEN THINKING ALL THESE YEARS? TRYING TO BE MOMMY'S PERFECT PRODIGY...
...WHEN I'VE BEEN DADDY'S LITTLE GIRL ALL ALONG!
NOW, ONYX, WHERE SHALL WE BEGIN?
MEEOOWW.

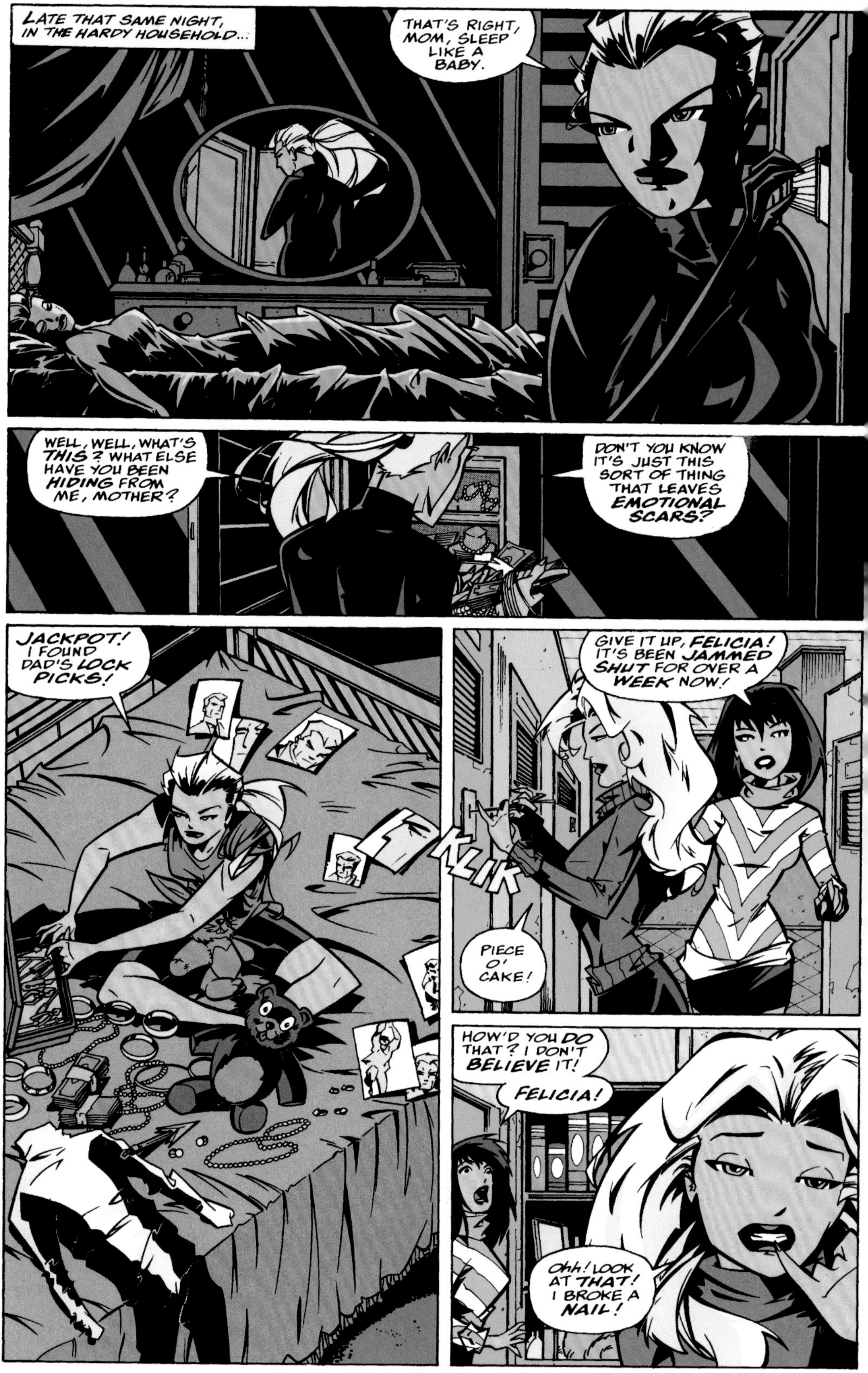
LATE THAT SAME NIGHT, IN THE HARDY HOUSEHOLD...
THAT'S RIGHT, MOM, SLEEP LIKE A BABY.
WELL, WELL, WHAT'S THIS? WHAT ELSE HAVE YOU BEEN HIDING FROM ME, MOTHER?
DON'T YOU KNOW IT'S JUST THIS SORT OF THING THAT LEAVES EMOTIONAL SCARS?
JACKPOT! I FOUND DAD'S LOCK PICKS!
GIVE IT UP, FELICIA! IT'S BEEN JAMMED SHUT FOR OVER A WEEK NOW!
KLIK
PIECE O' CAKE!
HOW'D YOU DO THAT? I DON'T BELIEVE IT!
FELICIA!
Ohh! LOOK AT THAT! I BROKE A NAIL!

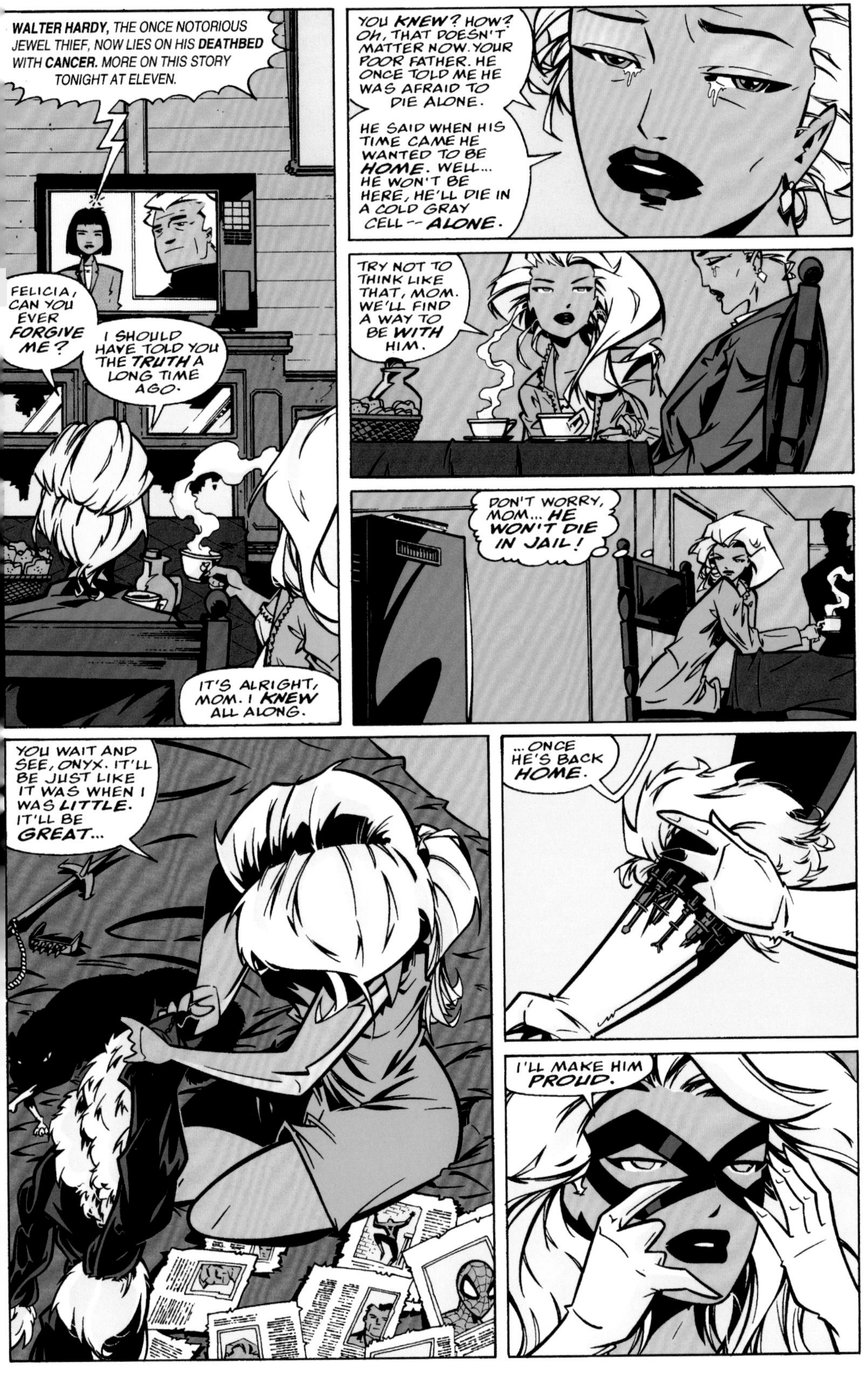
WALTER HARDY, THE ONCE NOTORIOUS JEWEL THIEF, NOW LIES ON HIS DEATHBED WITH CANCER. MORE ON THIS STORY TONIGHT AT ELEVEN.
FELICIA, CAN YOU EVER FORGIVE ME?
I SHOULD HAVE TOLD YOU THE TRUTH A LONG TIME AGO.
IT'S ALRIGHT, MOM. I KNEW ALL ALONG.
YOU KNEW? HOW? OH, THAT DOESN'T MATTER NOW. YOUR POOR FATHER. HE ONCE TOLD ME HE WAS AFRAID TO DIE ALONE.
HE SAID WHEN HIS TIME CAME HE WANTED TO BE HOME. WELL... HE WON'T BE HERE, HE'LL DIE IN A COLD GRAY CELL -- ALONE.
TRY NOT TO THINK LIKE THAT, MOM. WE'LL FIND A WAY TO BE WITH HIM.
DON'T WORRY, MOM... HE WON'T DIE IN JAIL!
YOU WAIT AND SEE, ONYX. IT'LL BE JUST LIKE IT WAS WHEN I WAS LITTLE. IT'LL BE GREAT...
...ONCE HE'S BACK HOME.
I'LL MAKE HIM PROUD.

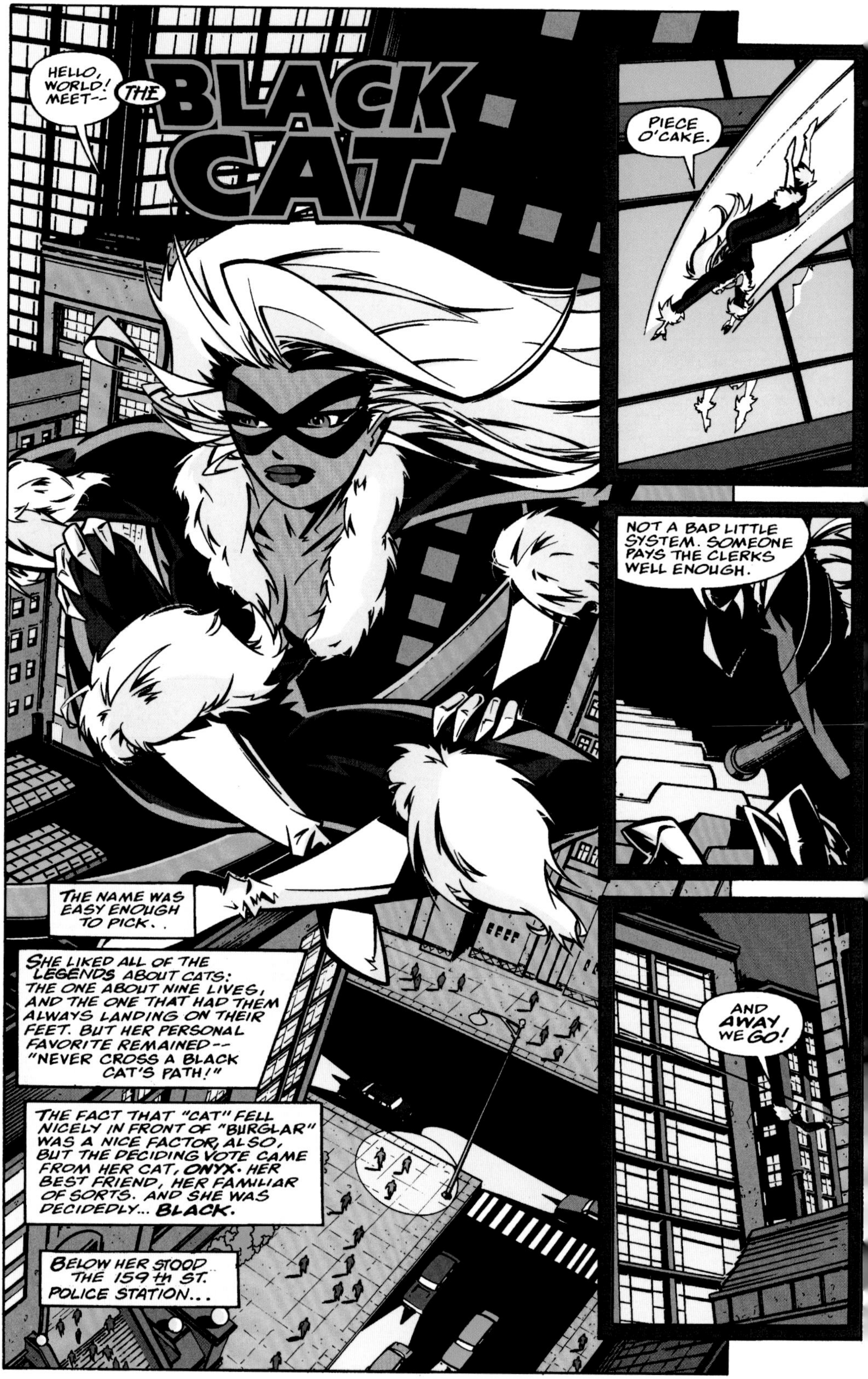
HELLO, WORLD! MEET--
THE BLACK CAT
PIECE O'CAKE.
NOT A BAD LITTLE SYSTEM. SOMEONE PAYS THE CLERKS WELL ENOUGH.
THE NAME WAS EASY ENOUGH TO PICK..
SHE LIKED ALL OF THE LEGENDS ABOUT CATS: THE ONE ABOUT NINE LIVES, AND THE ONE THAT HAD THEM ALWAYS LANDING ON THEIR FEET. BUT HER PERSONAL FAVORITE REMAINED-- "NEVER CROSS A BLACK CAT'S PATH!"
THE FACT THAT "CAT" FELL NICELY IN FRONT OF "BURGLAR" WAS A NICE FACTOR, ALSO, BUT THE DECIDING VOTE CAME FROM HER CAT, ONYX. HER BEST FRIEND, HER FAMILIAR OF SORTS. AND SHE WAS DECIDEDLY... BLACK.
BELOW HER STOOD THE 159th ST. POLICE STATION...
AND AWAY WE GO!

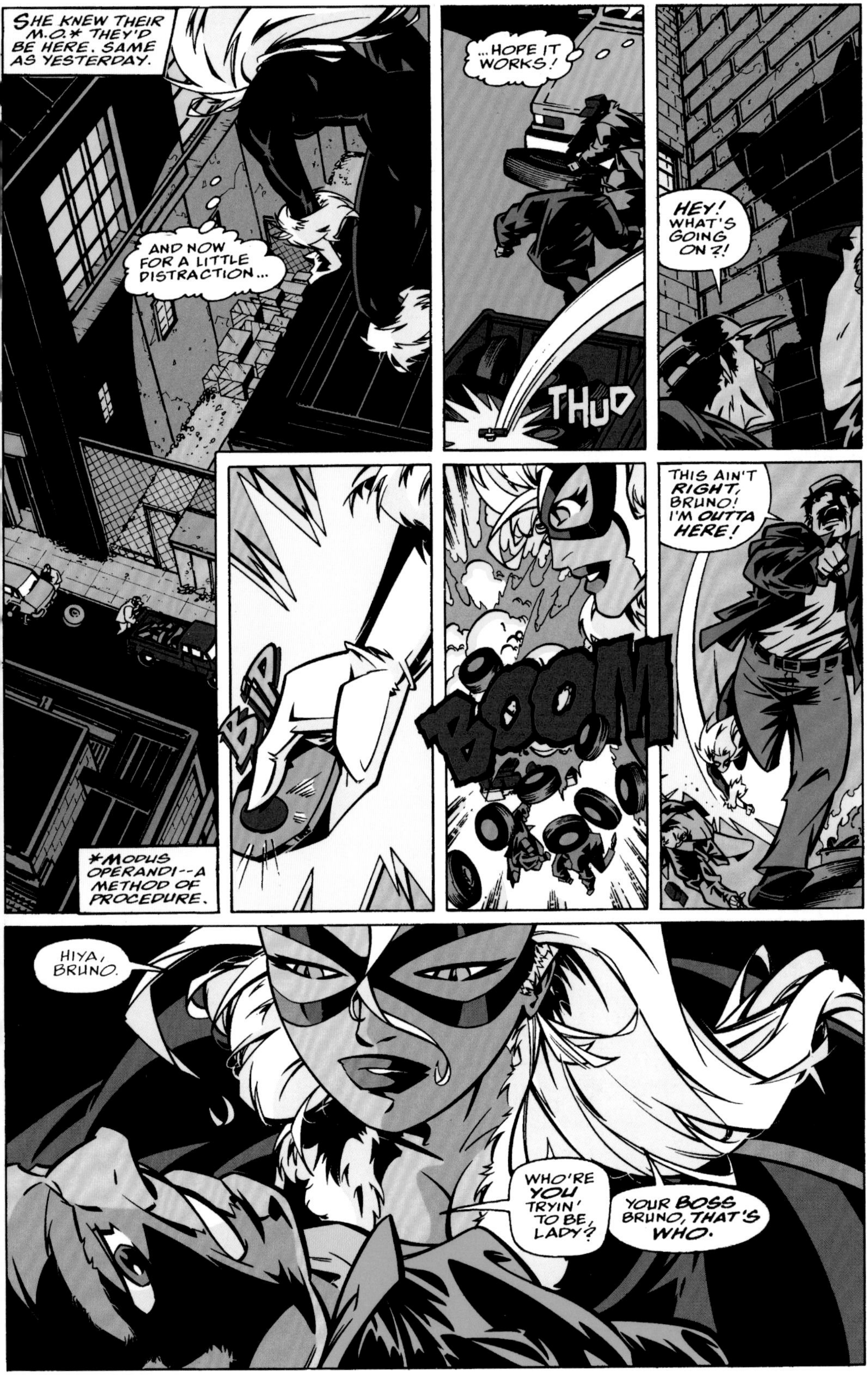
SHE KNEW THEIR M.O.* THEY'D BE HERE. SAME AS YESTERDAY.
AND NOW FOR A LITTLE DISTRACTION...
...HOPE IT WORKS!
THUD
HEY! WHAT'S GOING ON?!
*MODUS OPERANDI--A METHOD OF PROCEDURE.
BIP
BOOM
THIS AIN'T RIGHT, BRUNO! I'M OUTTA HERE!
HIYA, BRUNO.
WHO'RE YOU TRYIN' TO BE, LADY?
YOUR BOSS BRUNO, THAT'S WHO.

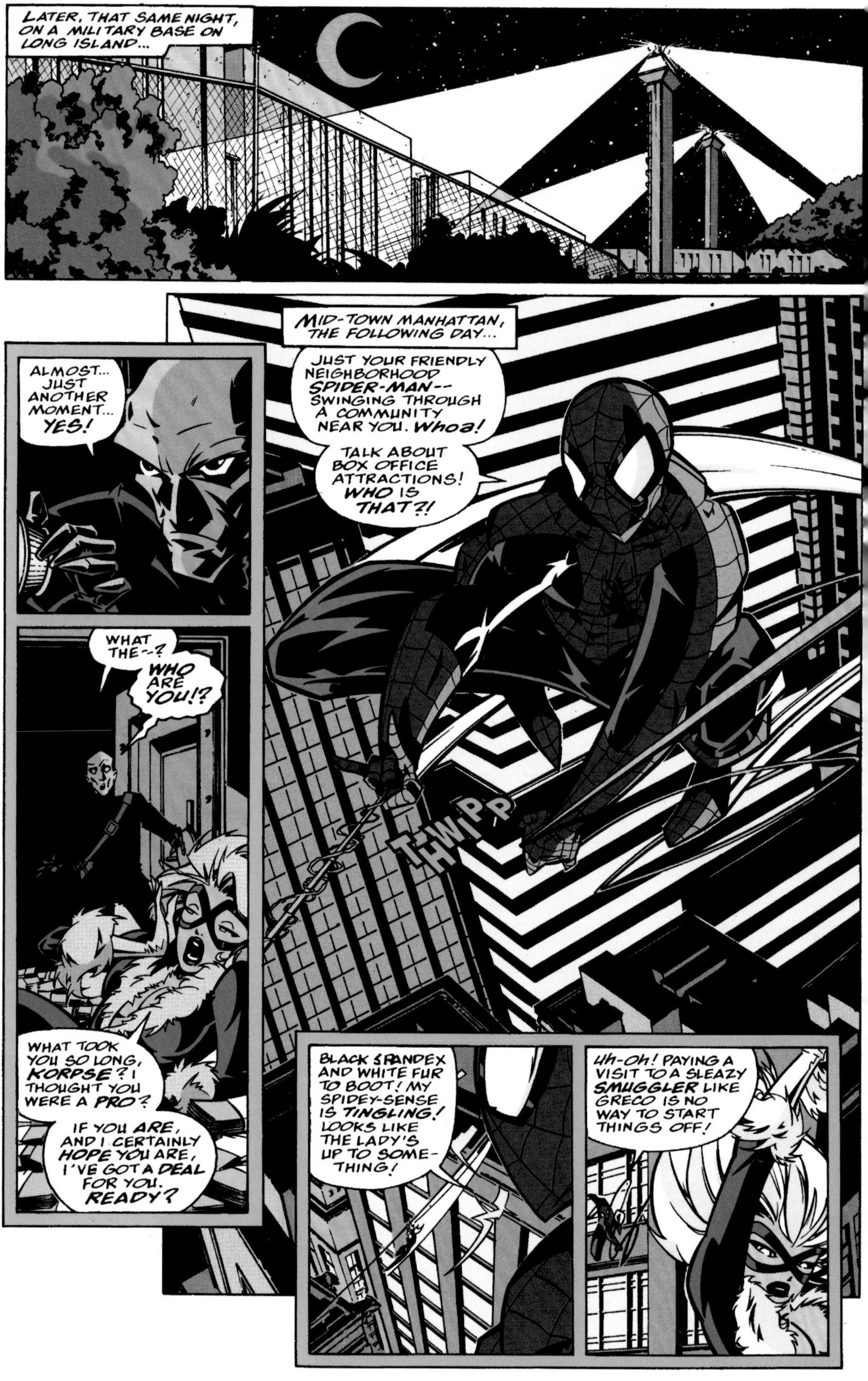
LATER, THAT SAME NIGHT, ON A MILITARY BASE ON LONG ISLAND...
MID-TOWN MANHATTAN, THE FOLLOWING DAY...
ALMOST... JUST ANOTHER MOMENT... YES!
WHAT THE--? WHO ARE YOU!?
WHAT TOOK YOU SO LONG, KORPSE? I THOUGHT YOU WERE A PRO?
IF YOU ARE, AND I CERTAINLY HOPE YOU ARE, I'VE GOT A DEAL FOR YOU. READY?
JUST YOUR FRIENDLY NEIGHBORHOOD SPIDER-MAN-- SWINGING THROUGH A COMMUNITY NEAR YOU. Whoa!
TALK ABOUT BOX OFFICE ATTRACTIONS! WHO IS THAT?!
THWIPP
BLACK SPANDEX AND WHITE FUR TO BOOT! MY SPIDEY-SENSE IS TINGLING! LOOKS LIKE THE LADY'S UP TO SOME-THING!
Uh-Oh! PAYING A VISIT TO A SLEAZY SMUGGLER LIKE GRECO IS NO WAY TO START THINGS OFF!

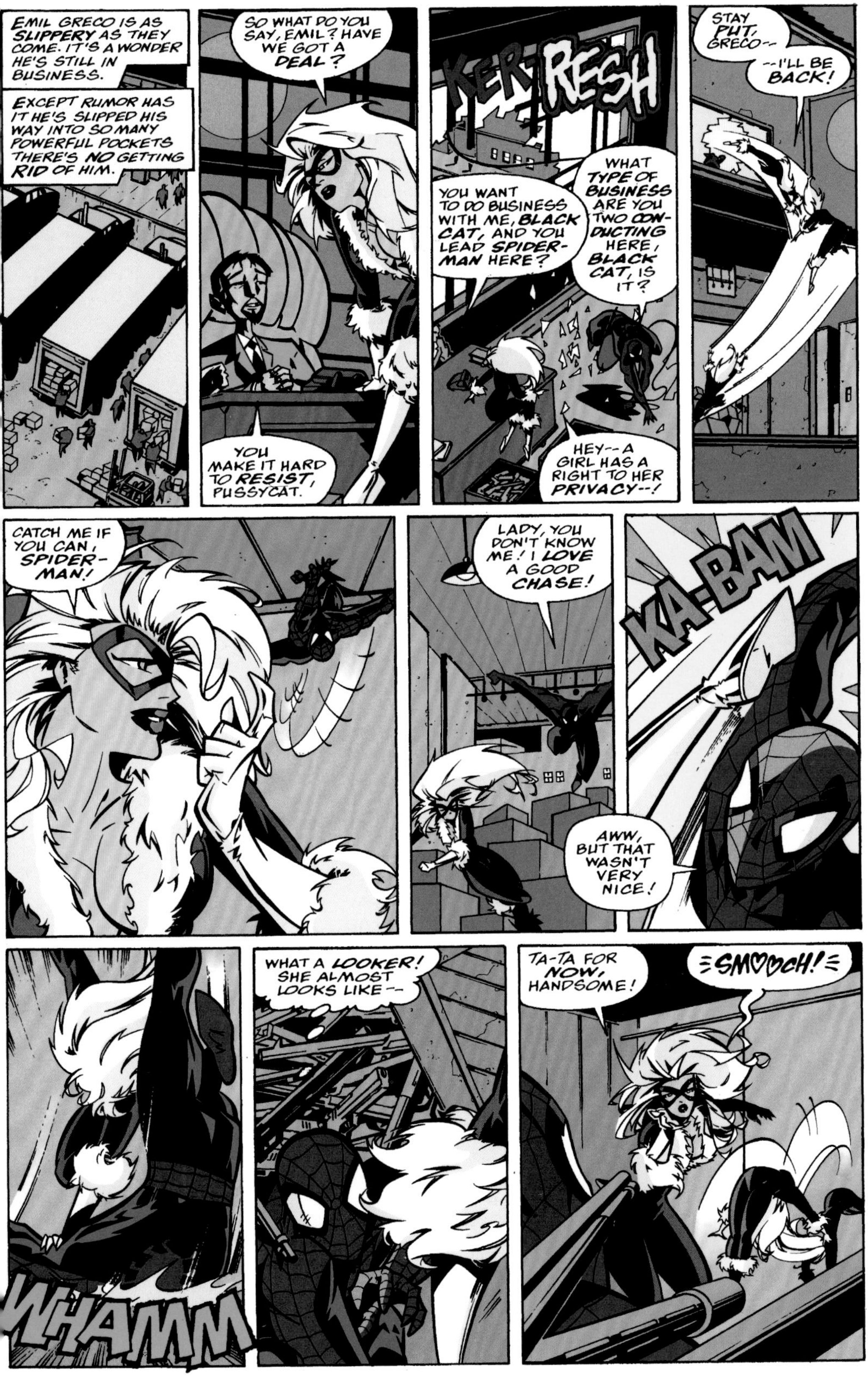
EMIL GRECO IS AS SLIPPERY AS THEY COME. IT'S A WONDER HE'S STILL IN BUSINESS.
EXCEPT RUMOR HAS IT HE'S SLIPPED HIS WAY INTO SO MANY POWERFUL POCKETS THERE'S NO GETTING RID OF HIM.
SO WHAT DO YOU SAY, EMIL? HAVE WE GOT A DEAL?
YOU MAKE IT HARD TO RESIST, PUSSYCAT.
KER-RESH
YOU WANT TO DO BUSINESS WITH ME, BLACK CAT, AND YOU LEAD SPIDER-MAN HERE?
WHAT TYPE OF BUSINESS ARE YOU TWO CONDUCTING HERE, BLACK CAT, IS IT?
HEY-- A GIRL HAS A RIGHT TO HER PRIVACY--!
STAY PUT, GRECO--
--I'LL BE BACK!
CATCH ME IF YOU CAN, SPIDER-MAN!
LADY, YOU DON'T KNOW ME! I LOVE A GOOD CHASE!
KA-BAM
AWW, BUT THAT WASN'T VERY NICE!
WHAMM
WHAT A LOOKER! SHE ALMOST LOOKS LIKE--
TA-TA FOR NOW, HANDSOME!
SMOOCH!

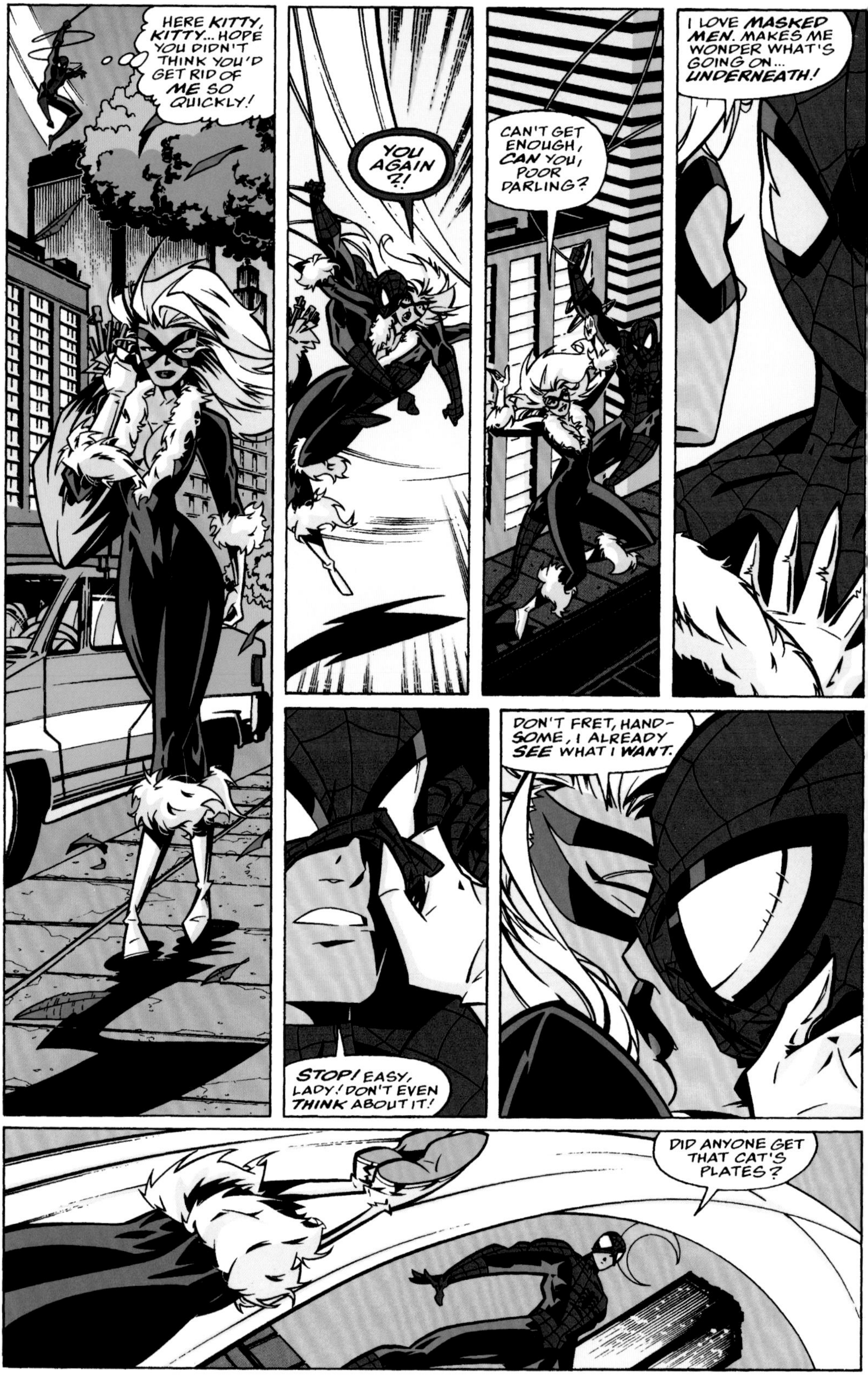
HERE KITTY, KITTY... HOPE YOU DIDN'T THINK YOU'D GET RID OF ME SO QUICKLY!
YOU AGAIN ?!
CAN'T GET ENOUGH, CAN YOU, POOR DARLING?
I LOVE MASKED MEN. MAKES ME WONDER WHAT'S GOING ON... UNDERNEATH!
STOP! EASY, LADY! DON'T EVEN THINK ABOUT IT!
DON'T FRET, HANDSOME, I ALREADY SEE WHAT I WANT.
DID ANYONE GET THAT CAT'S PLATES?

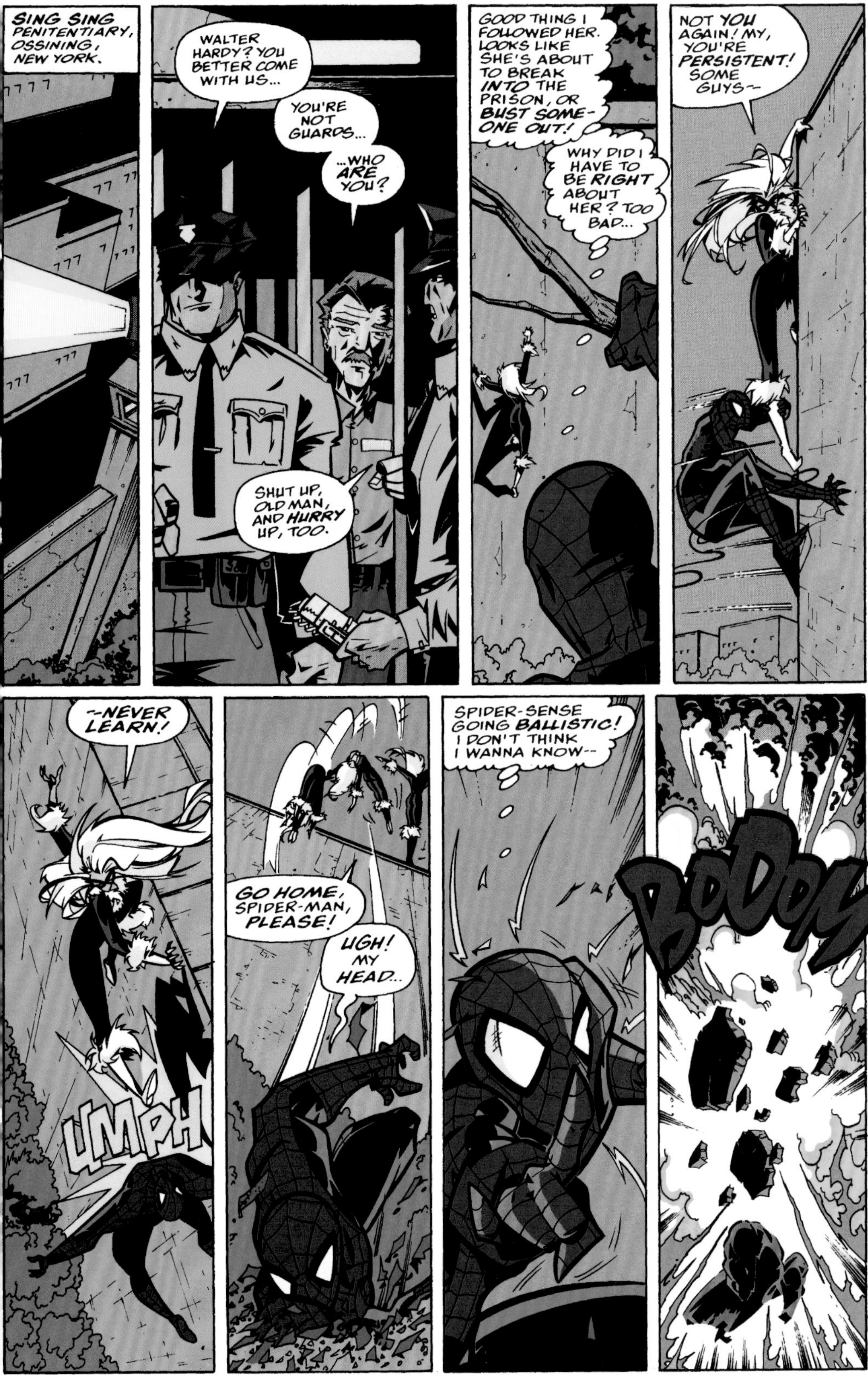
SING SING PENITENTIARY, OSSINING, NEW YORK.
WALTER HARDY? YOU BETTER COME WITH US...
YOU'RE NOT GUARDS...
...WHO ARE YOU?
SHUT UP, OLD MAN, AND HURRY UP, TOO.
GOOD THING I FOLLOWED HER. LOOKS LIKE SHE'S ABOUT TO BREAK INTO THE PRISON, OR BUST SOME-ONE OUT!
WHY DID I HAVE TO BE RIGHT ABOUT HER? TOO BAD...
NOT YOU AGAIN! MY, YOU'RE PERSISTENT! SOME GUYS--
--NEVER LEARN!
UMPH
GO HOME, SPIDER-MAN, PLEASE!
UGH! MY HEAD...
SPIDER-SENSE GOING BALLISTIC! I DON'T THINK I WANNA KNOW--
BOOOM

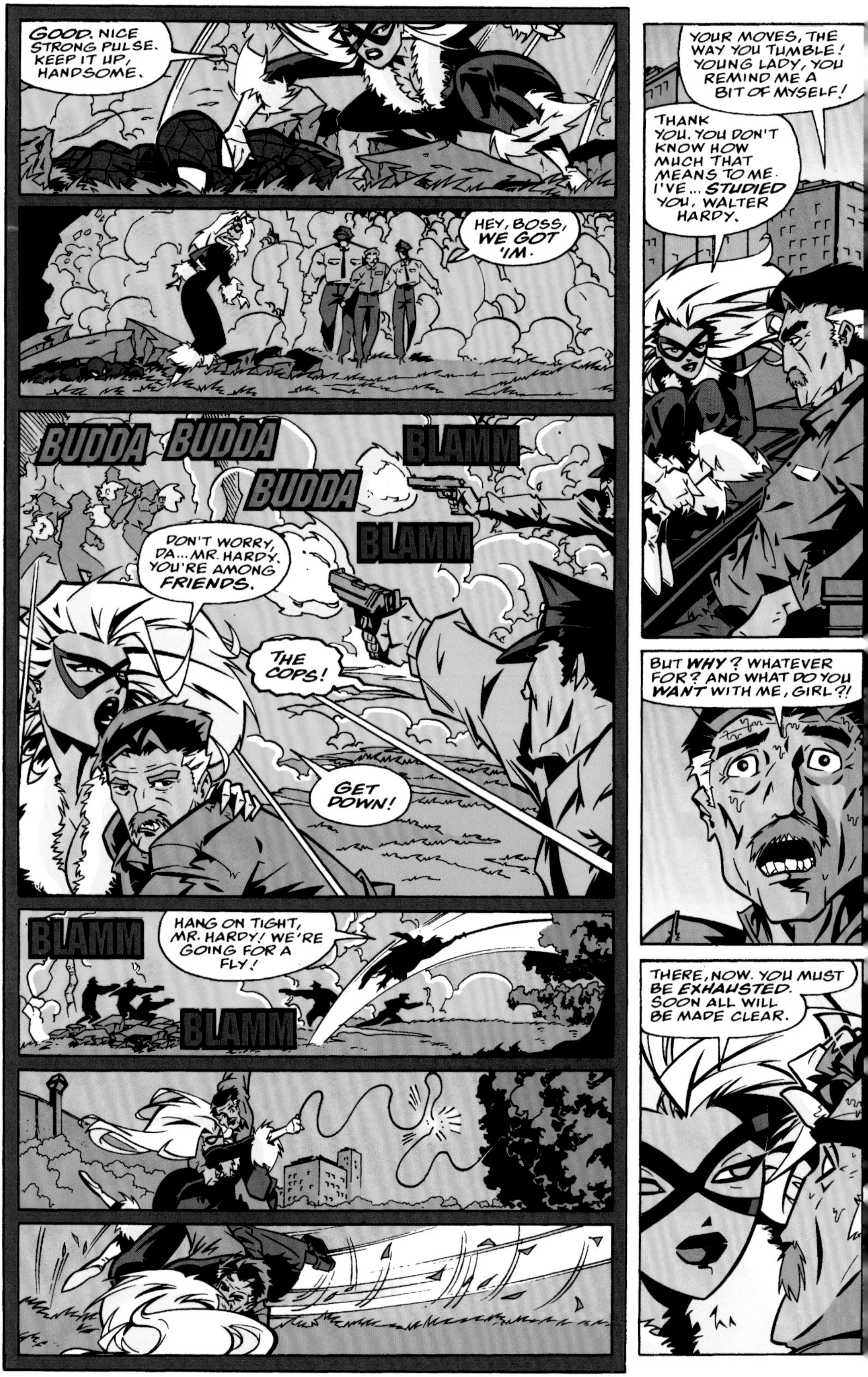
GOOD. NICE STRONG PULSE. KEEP IT UP, HANDSOME.
HEY, BOSS, WE GOT 'IM.
BUDDA BUDDA BUDDA
BLAMM
BLAMM
DON'T WORRY, DA... MR. HARDY. YOU'RE AMONG FRIENDS.
THE COPS!
GET DOWN!
BLAMM
HANG ON TIGHT, MR. HARDY! WE'RE GOING FOR A FLY!
BLAMM
YOUR MOVES, THE WAY YOU TUMBLE! YOUNG LADY, YOU REMIND ME A BIT OF MYSELF!
THANK YOU. YOU DON'T KNOW HOW MUCH THAT MEANS TO ME. I'VE... STUDIED YOU, WALTER HARDY.
BUT WHY? WHATEVER FOR? AND WHAT DO YOU WANT WITH ME, GIRL?!
THERE, NOW. YOU MUST BE EXHAUSTED. SOON ALL WILL BE MADE CLEAR.

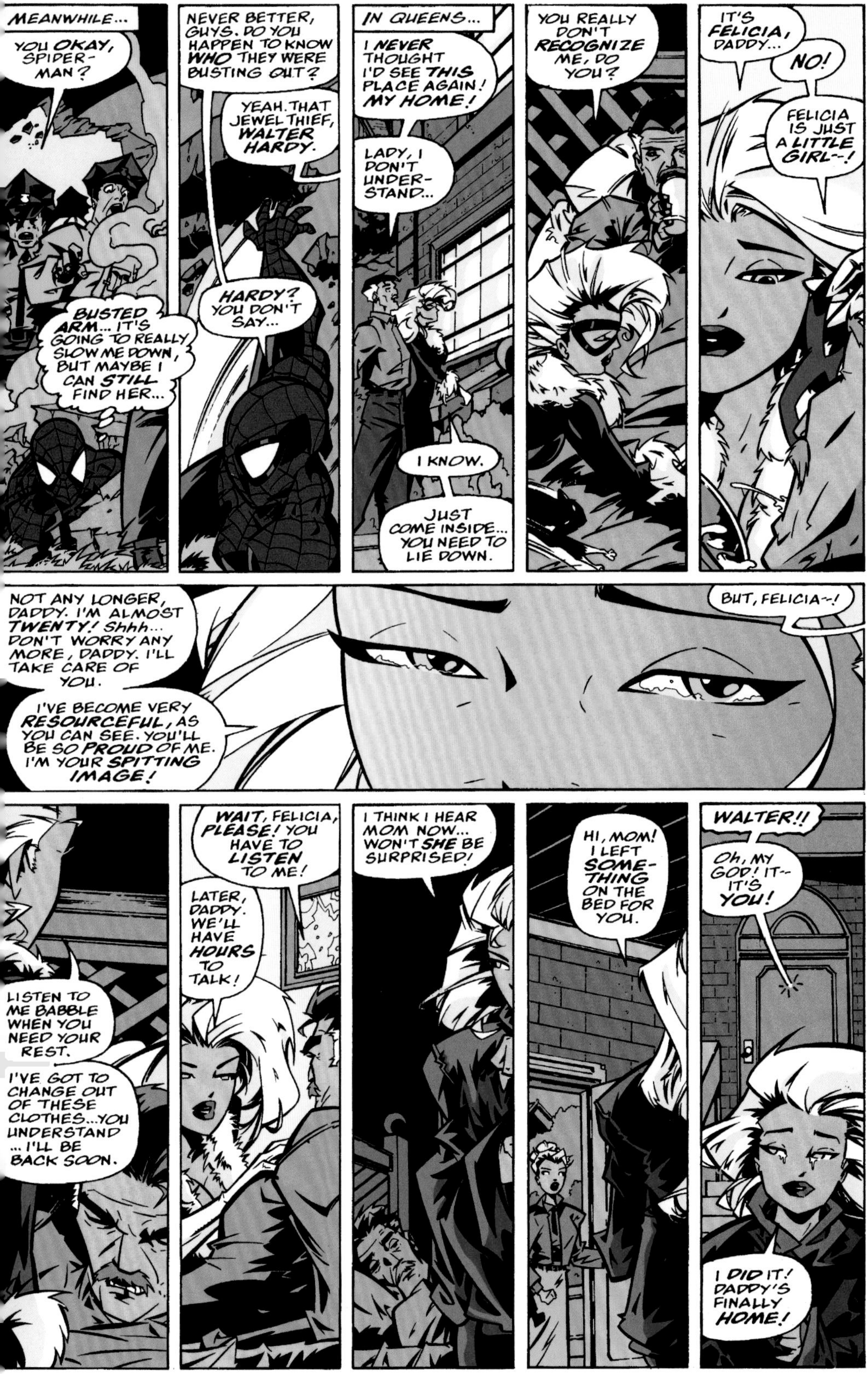
MEANWHILE...
YOU OKAY, SPIDER-MAN?
BUSTED ARM... IT'S GOING TO REALLY SLOW ME DOWN, BUT MAYBE I CAN STILL FIND HER...
NEVER BETTER, GUYS. DO YOU HAPPEN TO KNOW WHO THEY WERE BUSTING OUT?
YEAH. THAT JEWEL THIEF, WALTER HARDY.
HARDY? YOU DON'T SAY...
IN QUEENS...
I NEVER THOUGHT I'D SEE THIS PLACE AGAIN! MY HOME!
LADY, I DON'T UNDER-STAND...
I KNOW.
JUST COME INSIDE... YOU NEED TO LIE DOWN.
YOU REALLY DON'T RECOGNIZE ME, DO YOU?
IT'S FELICIA, DADDY...
NO!
FELICIA IS JUST A LITTLE GIRL--!
NOT ANY LONGER, DADDY. I'M ALMOST TWENTY! Shhh... DON'T WORRY ANY MORE, DADDY. I'LL TAKE CARE OF YOU.
I'VE BECOME VERY RESOURCEFUL, AS YOU CAN SEE. YOU'LL BE SO PROUD OF ME. I'M YOUR SPITTING IMAGE!
BUT, FELICIA--!
LISTEN TO ME BABBLE WHEN YOU NEED YOUR REST.
I'VE GOT TO CHANGE OUT OF THESE CLOTHES... YOU UNDERSTAND ...I'LL BE BACK SOON.
WAIT, FELICIA, PLEASE! YOU HAVE TO LISTEN TO ME!
LATER, DADDY. WE'LL HAVE HOURS TO TALK!
I THINK I HEAR MOM NOW... WON'T SHE BE SURPRISED!
HI, MOM! I LEFT SOME-THING ON THE BED FOR YOU.
WALTER!!
Oh, MY GOD! IT-- IT'S YOU!
I DID IT! DADDY'S FINALLY HOME!

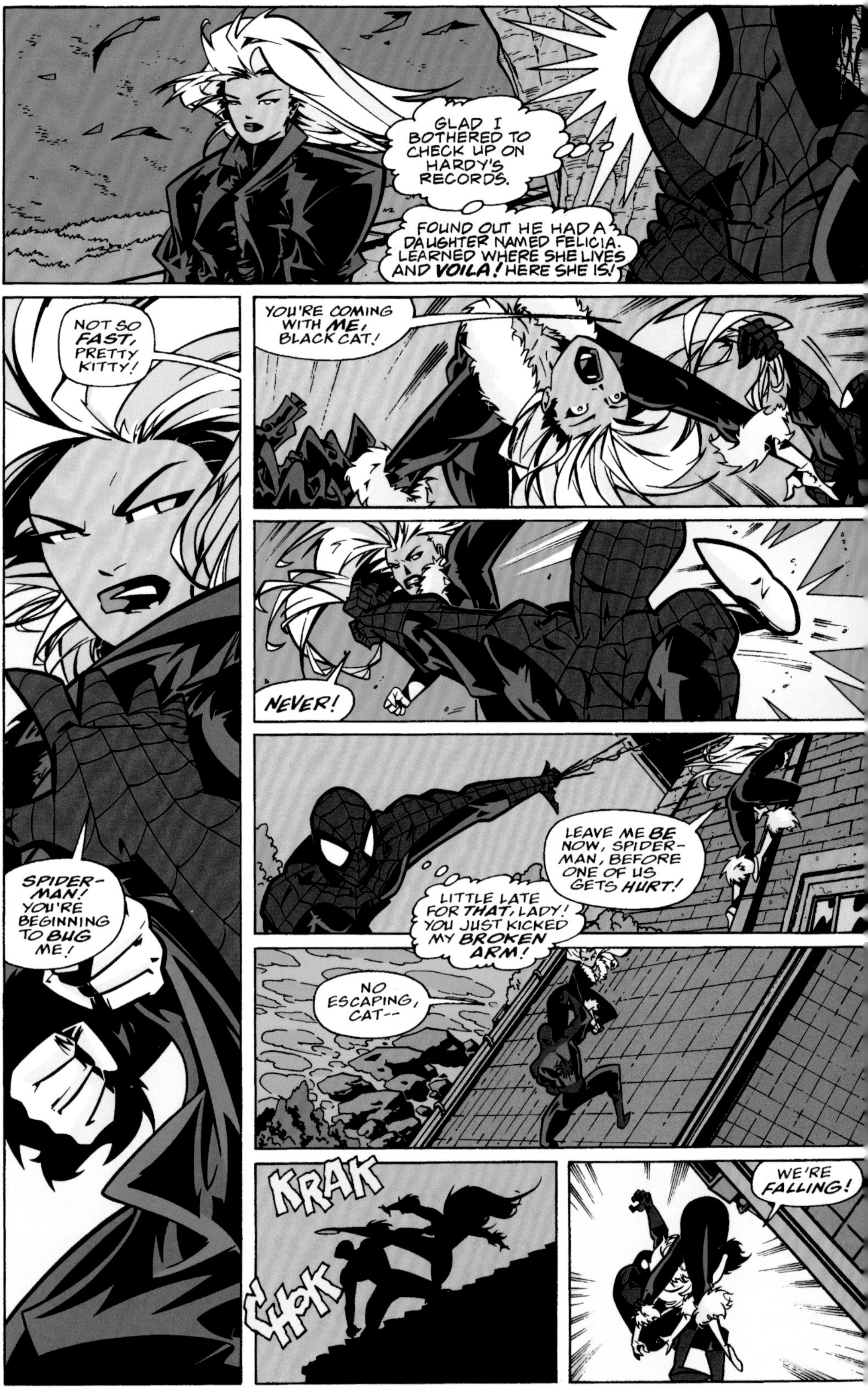
GLAD I BOTHERED TO CHECK UP ON HARDY'S RECORDS.
FOUND OUT HE HAD A DAUGHTER NAMED FELICIA. LEARNED WHERE SHE LIVES AND VOILA! HERE SHE IS!
NOT SO FAST, PRETTY KITTY!
SPIDER-MAN! YOU'RE BEGINNING TO BUG ME!
YOU'RE COMING WITH ME, BLACK CAT!
NEVER!
LEAVE ME BE NOW, SPIDER-MAN, BEFORE ONE OF US GETS HURT!
LITTLE LATE FOR THAT, LADY! YOU JUST KICKED MY BROKEN ARM!
NO ESCAPING, CAT--
KRAK
CHOK
WE'RE FALLING!

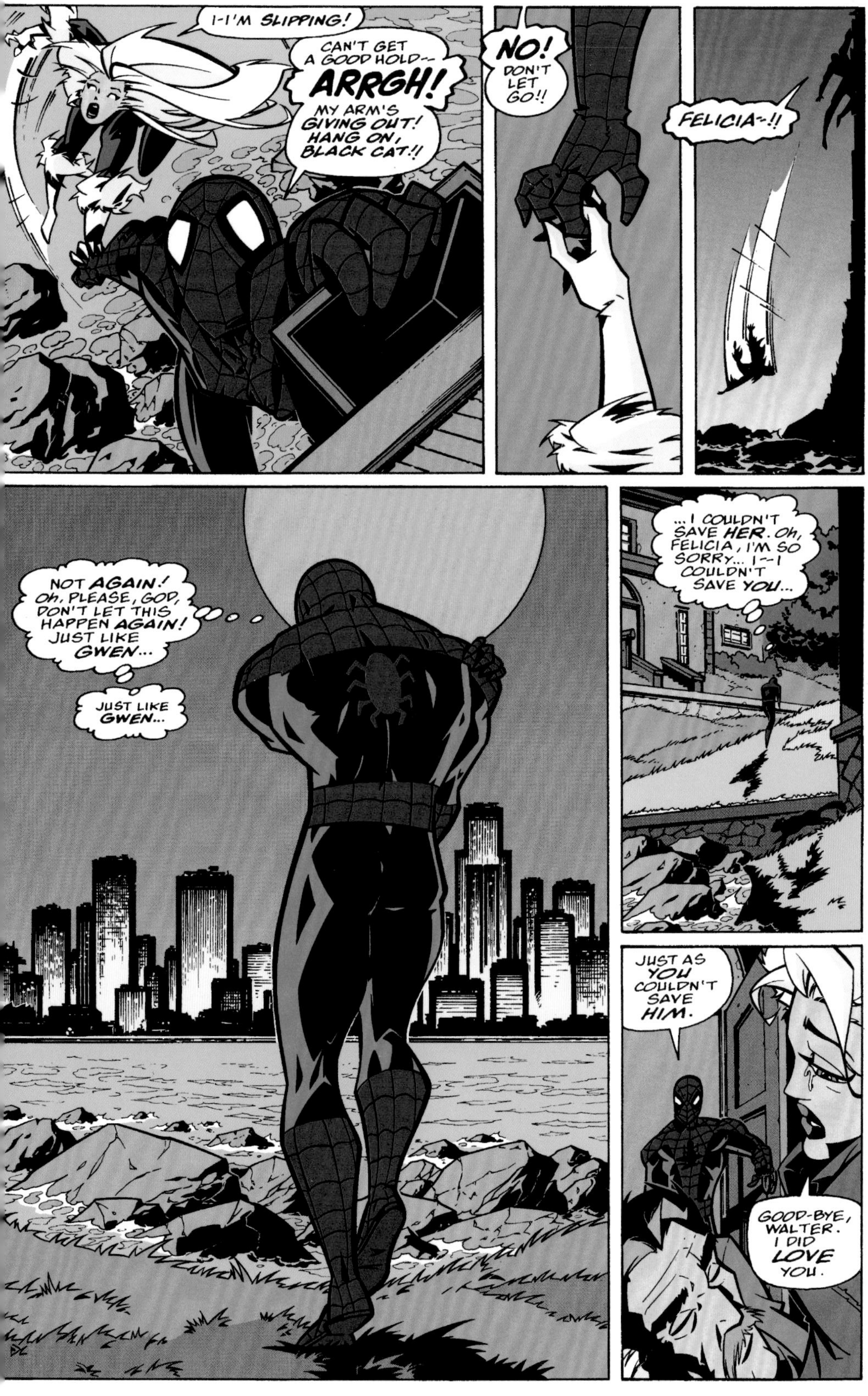
I-I'M SLIPPING!
CAN'T GET A GOOD HOLD-- ARRGH! MY ARM'S GIVING OUT! HANG ON, BLACK CAT!!
NO! DON'T LET GO!!
FELICIA--!!
NOT AGAIN! Oh, PLEASE, GOD, DON'T LET THIS HAPPEN AGAIN! JUST LIKE GWEN...
JUST LIKE GWEN...
...I COULDN'T SAVE HER. Oh, FELICIA, I'M SO SORRY... I--I COULDN'T SAVE YOU...
JUST AS YOU COULDN'T SAVE HIM.
GOOD-BYE, WALTER. I DID LOVE YOU.

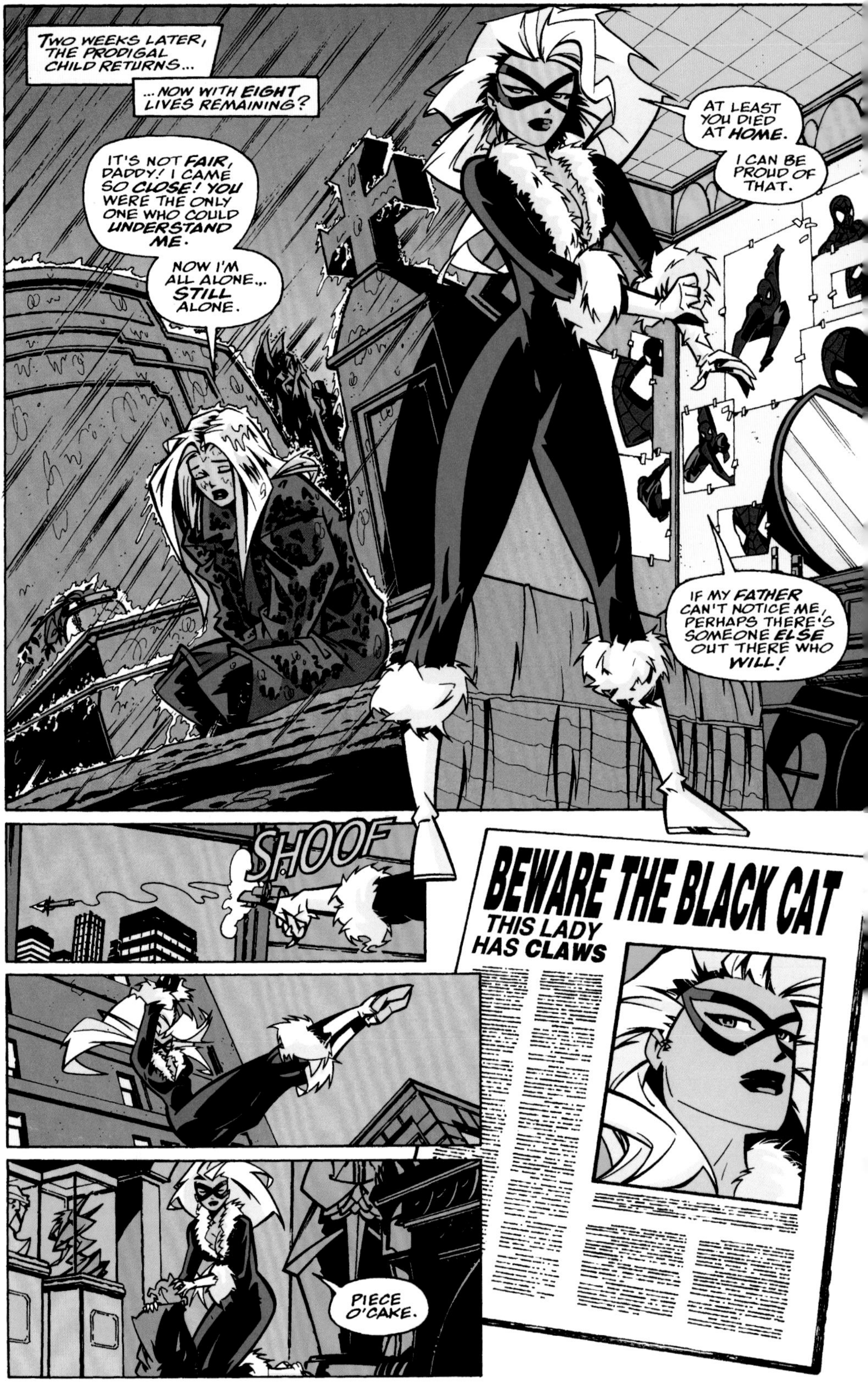

TWO WEEKS LATER, THE PRODIGAL CHILD RETURNS...
...NOW WITH EIGHT LIVES REMAINING?
IT'S NOT FAIR, DADDY! I CAME SO CLOSE! YOU WERE THE ONLY ONE WHO COULD UNDERSTAND ME.
NOW I'M ALL ALONE... STILL ALONE.
AT LEAST YOU DIED AT HOME.
I CAN BE PROUD OF THAT.
IF MY FATHER CAN'T NOTICE ME, PERHAPS THERE'S SOMEONE ELSE OUT THERE WHO WILL!
SHOOF
BEWARE THE BLACK CAT
THIS LADY HAS CLAWS
PIECE O'CAKE.

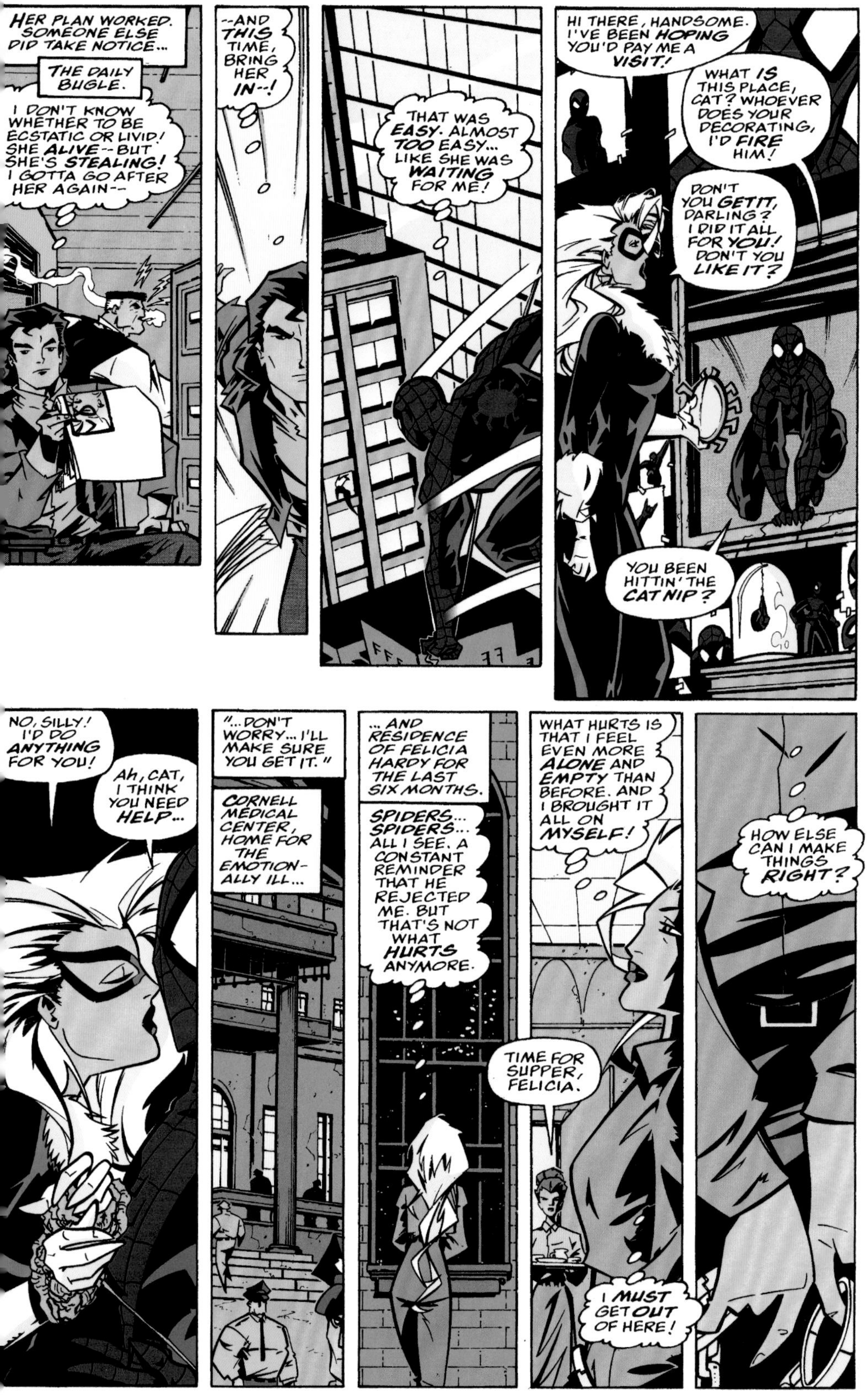
HER PLAN WORKED. SOMEONE ELSE DID TAKE NOTICE...
THE DAILY BUGLE.
I DON'T KNOW WHETHER TO BE ECSTATIC OR LIVID! SHE ALIVE--BUT SHE'S STEALING! I GOTTA GO AFTER HER AGAIN--
--AND THIS TIME, BRING HER IN--!
THAT WAS EASY. ALMOST TOO EASY... LIKE SHE WAS WAITING FOR ME!
HI THERE, HANDSOME. I'VE BEEN HOPING YOU'D PAY ME A VISIT!
WHAT IS THIS PLACE, CAT? WHOEVER DOES YOUR DECORATING, I'D FIRE HIM!
DON'T YOU GET IT, DARLING? I DID IT ALL FOR YOU! DON'T YOU LIKE IT?
YOU BEEN HITTIN' THE CATNIP?
NO, SILLY! I'D DO ANYTHING FOR YOU!
Ah, CAT, I THINK YOU NEED HELP...
"...DON'T WORRY... I'LL MAKE SURE YOU GET IT."
CORNELL MEDICAL CENTER, HOME FOR THE EMOTIONALLY ILL...
...AND RESIDENCE OF FELICIA HARDY FOR THE LAST SIX MONTHS.
SPIDERS... SPIDERS... ALL I SEE. A CONSTANT REMINDER THAT HE REJECTED ME. BUT THAT'S NOT WHAT HURTS ANYMORE.
WHAT HURTS IS THAT I FEEL EVEN MORE ALONE AND EMPTY THAN BEFORE. AND I BROUGHT IT ALL ON MYSELF!
TIME FOR SUPPER, FELICIA.
I MUST GET OUT OF HERE!
HOW ELSE CAN I MAKE THINGS RIGHT?

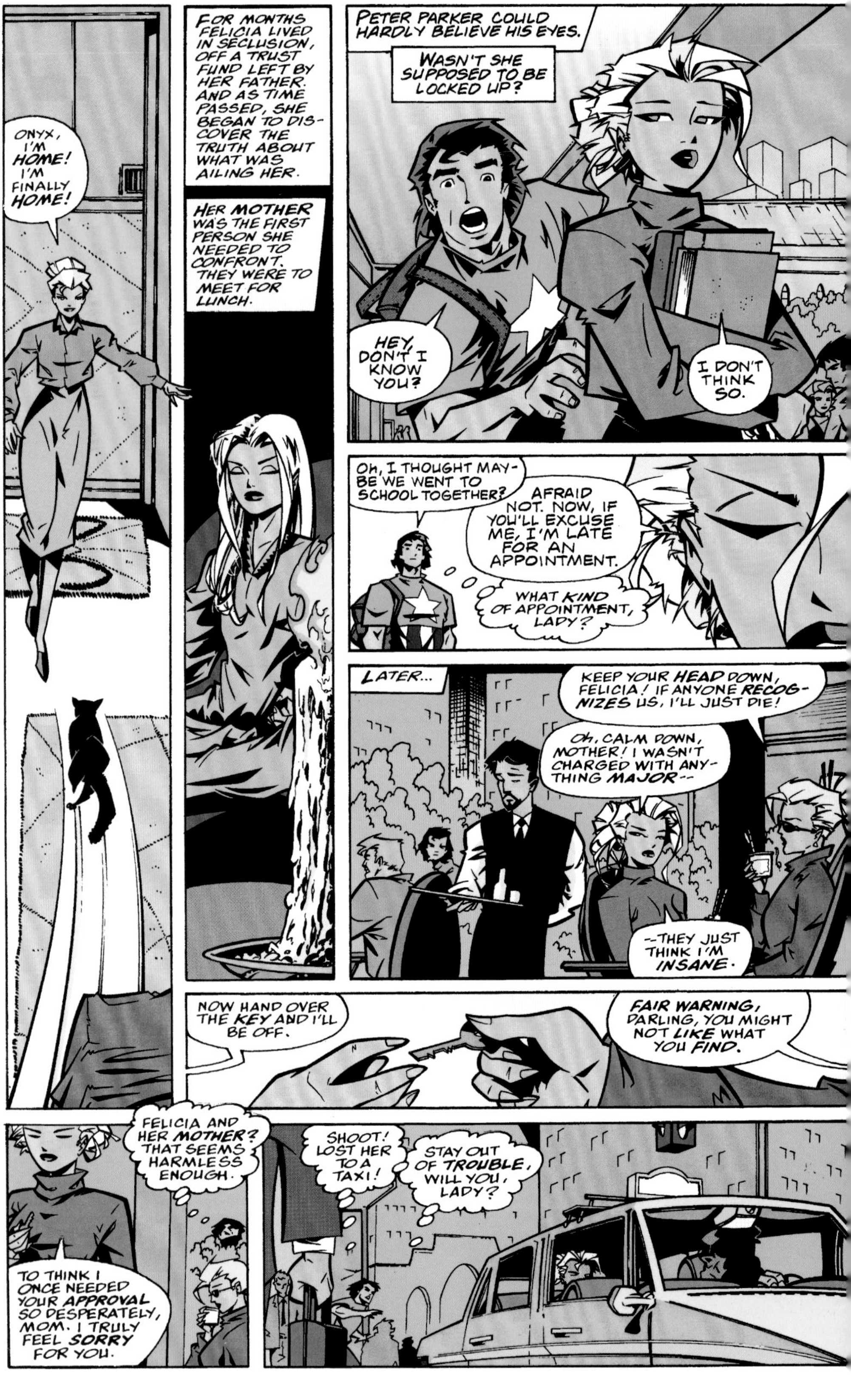
ONYX, I'M HOME! I'M FINALLY HOME!
FOR MONTHS FELICIA LIVED IN SECLUSION, OFF A TRUST FUND LEFT BY HER FATHER. AND AS TIME PASSED, SHE BEGAN TO DISCOVER THE TRUTH ABOUT WHAT WAS AILING HER.
HER MOTHER WAS THE FIRST PERSON SHE NEEDED TO CONFRONT. THEY WERE TO MEET FOR LUNCH.
PETER PARKER COULD HARDLY BELIEVE HIS EYES.
WASN'T SHE SUPPOSED TO BE LOCKED UP?
HEY, DON'T I KNOW YOU?
I DON'T THINK SO.
OH, I THOUGHT MAYBE WE WENT TO SCHOOL TOGETHER?
AFRAID NOT. NOW, IF YOU'LL EXCUSE ME, I'M LATE FOR AN APPOINTMENT.
WHAT KIND OF APPOINTMENT, LADY?
LATER...
KEEP YOUR HEAD DOWN, FELICIA! IF ANYONE RECOGNIZES US, I'LL JUST DIE!
OH, CALM DOWN, MOTHER! I WASN'T CHARGED WITH ANYTHING MAJOR--
--THEY JUST THINK I'M INSANE.
NOW HAND OVER THE KEY AND I'LL BE OFF.
FAIR WARNING, DARLING, YOU MIGHT NOT LIKE WHAT YOU FIND.
TO THINK I ONCE NEEDED YOUR APPROVAL SO DESPERATELY, MOM. I TRULY FEEL SORRY FOR YOU.
FELICIA AND HER MOTHER? THAT SEEMS HARMLESS ENOUGH.
SHOOT! LOST HER TO A TAXI!
STAY OUT OF TROUBLE, WILL YOU, LADY?

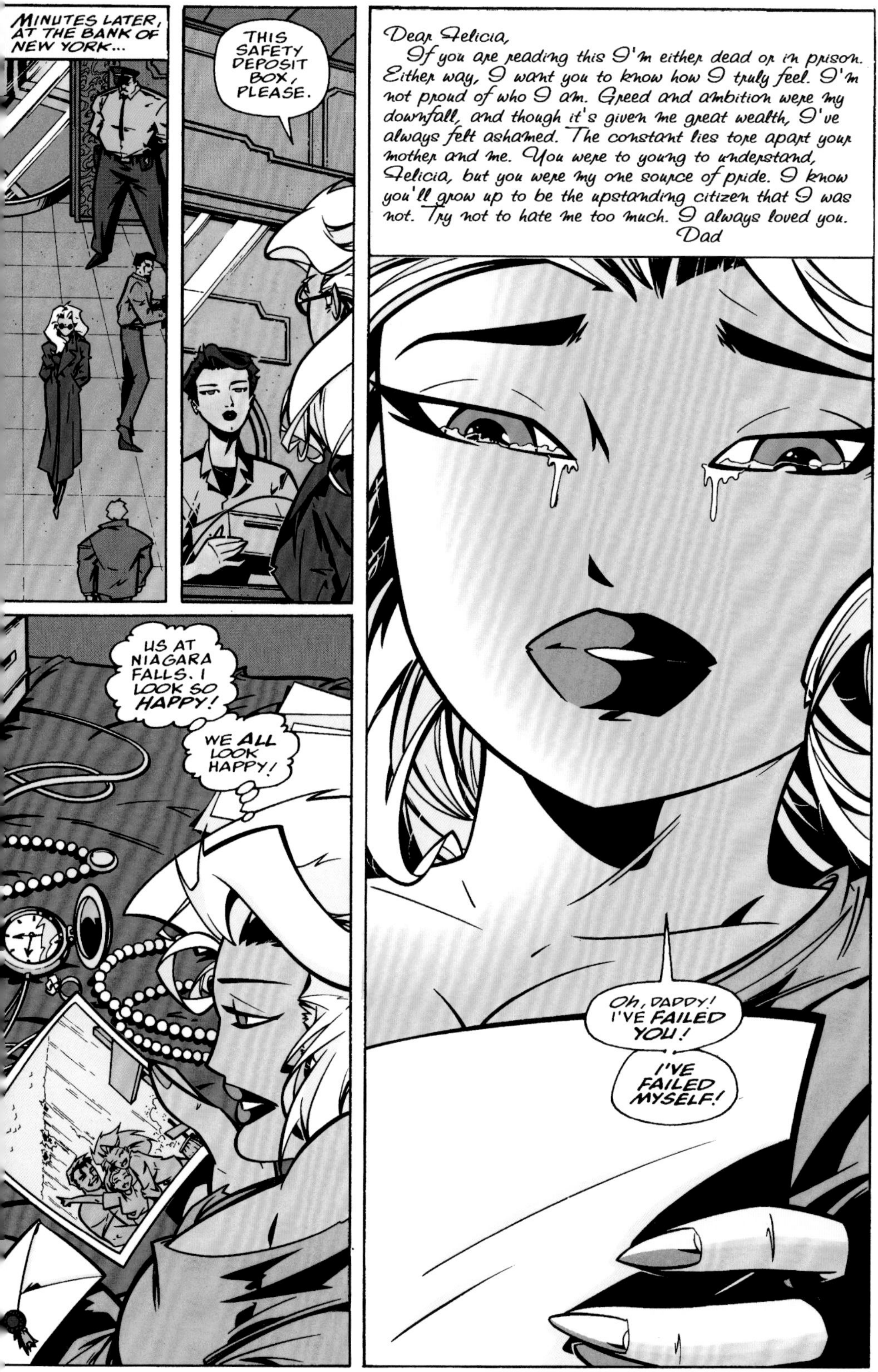
MINUTES LATER, AT THE BANK OF NEW YORK...
THIS SAFETY DEPOSIT BOX, PLEASE.
Dear Felicia,
If you are reading this I'm either dead or in prison. Either way, I want you to know how I truly feel. I'm not proud of who I am. Greed and ambition were my downfall, and though it's given me great wealth, I've always felt ashamed. The constant lies tore apart your mother and me. You were to young to understand, Felicia, but you were my one source of pride. I know you'll grow up to be the upstanding citizen that I was not. Try not to hate me too much. I always loved you.
Dad
US AT NIAGARA FALLS. I LOOK SO HAPPY!
WE ALL LOOK HAPPY!
Oh, DADDY! I'VE FAILED YOU!
I'VE FAILED MYSELF!

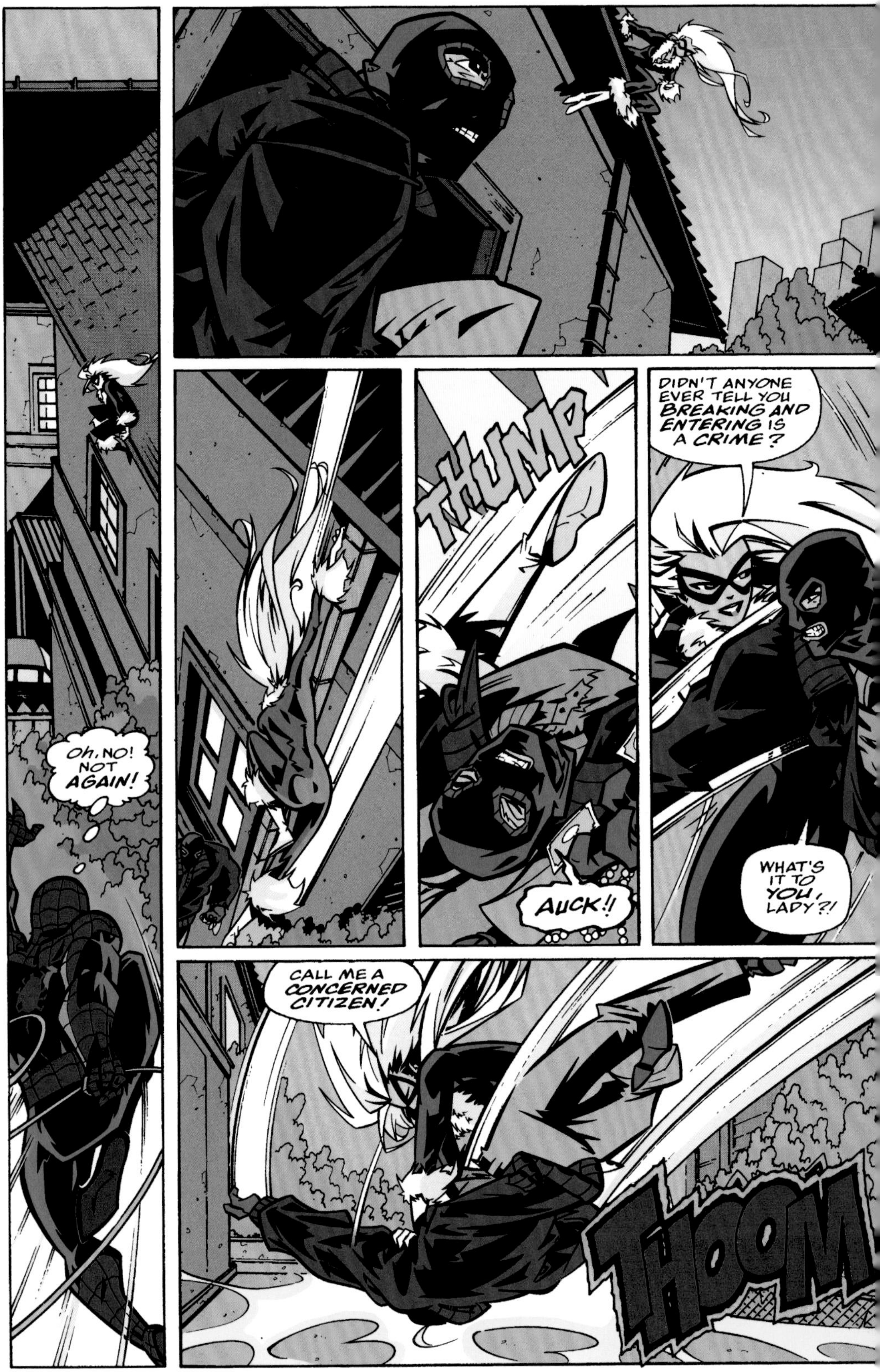

Oh, NO! NOT AGAIN!
THUMP
AUCK!!
DIDN'T ANYONE EVER TELL YOU BREAKING AND ENTERING IS A CRIME?
WHAT'S IT TO YOU, LADY?!
CALL ME A CONCERNED CITIZEN!
THOOM

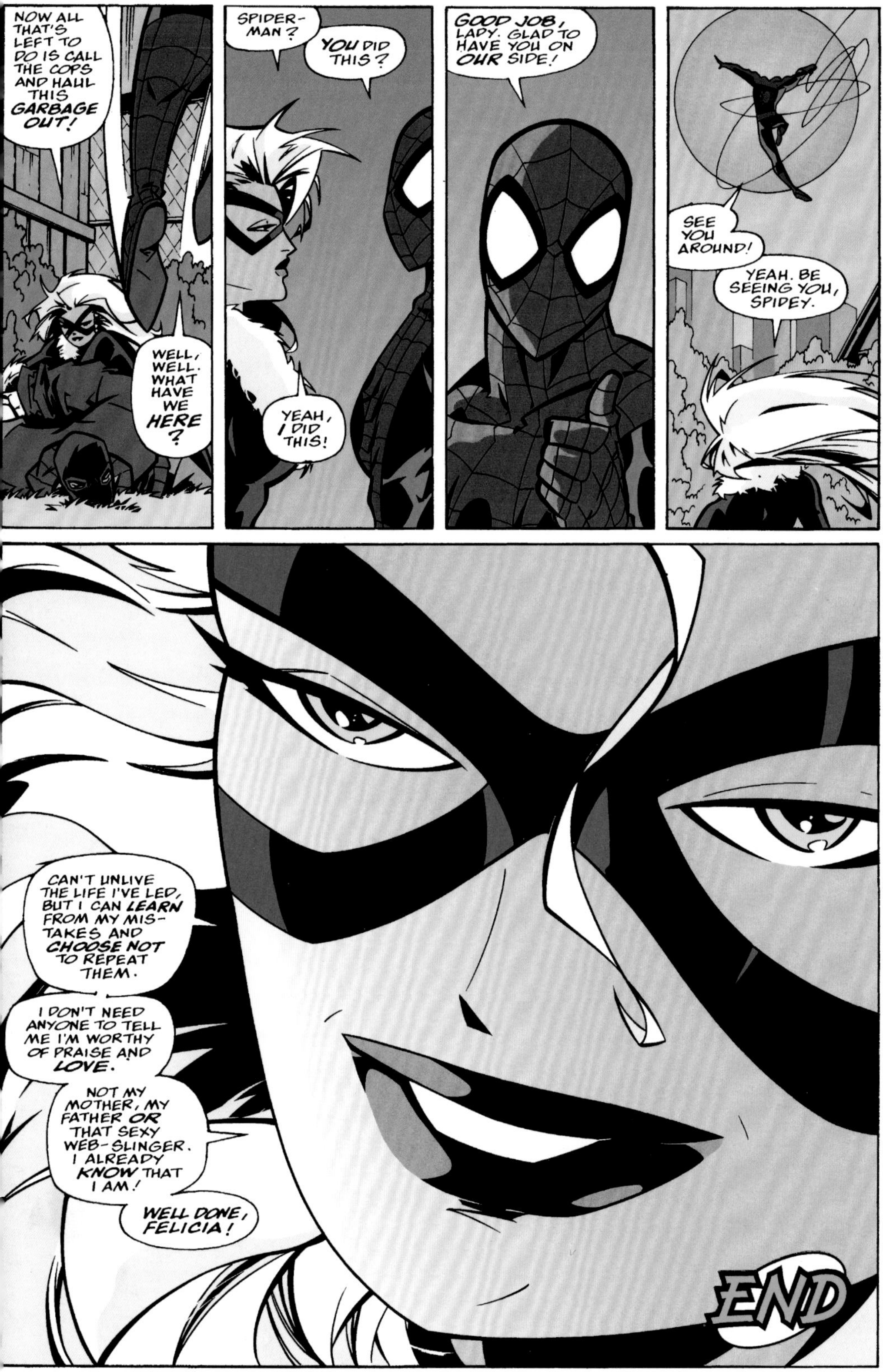
NOW ALL THAT'S LEFT TO DO IS CALL THE COPS AND HAUL THIS GARBAGE OUT!
WELL, WELL. WHAT HAVE WE HERE?
SPIDER-MAN?
YOU DID THIS?
YEAH, I DID THIS!
GOOD JOB, LADY. GLAD TO HAVE YOU ON OUR SIDE!
SEE YOU AROUND!
YEAH. BE SEEING YOU, SPIDEY.
CAN'T UNLIVE THE LIFE I'VE LED, BUT I CAN LEARN FROM MY MIS-TAKES AND CHOOSE NOT TO REPEAT THEM.
I DON'T NEED ANYONE TO TELL ME I'M WORTHY OF PRAISE AND LOVE.
NOT MY MOTHER, MY FATHER OR THAT SEXY WEB-SLINGER. I ALREADY KNOW THAT I AM!
WELL DONE, FELICIA!
END

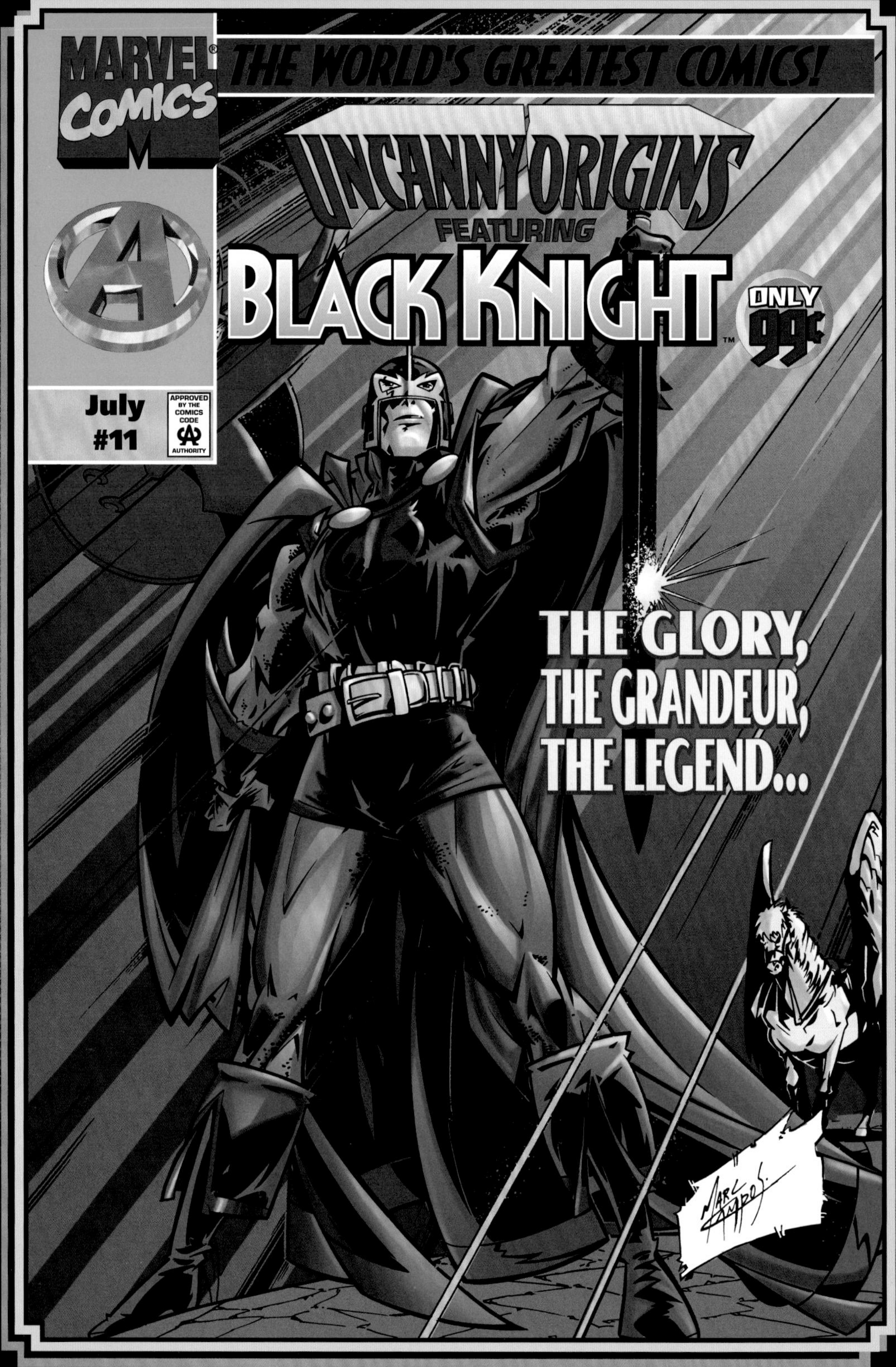
MARVEL COMICS
THE WORLD'S GREATEST COMICS!
UNCANNY ORIGINS
FEATURING
BLACK KNIGHT™
ONLY 99¢
July
#11
APPROVED BY THE COMICS CODE AUTHORITY
THE GLORY,
THE GRANDEUR,
THE LEGEND...

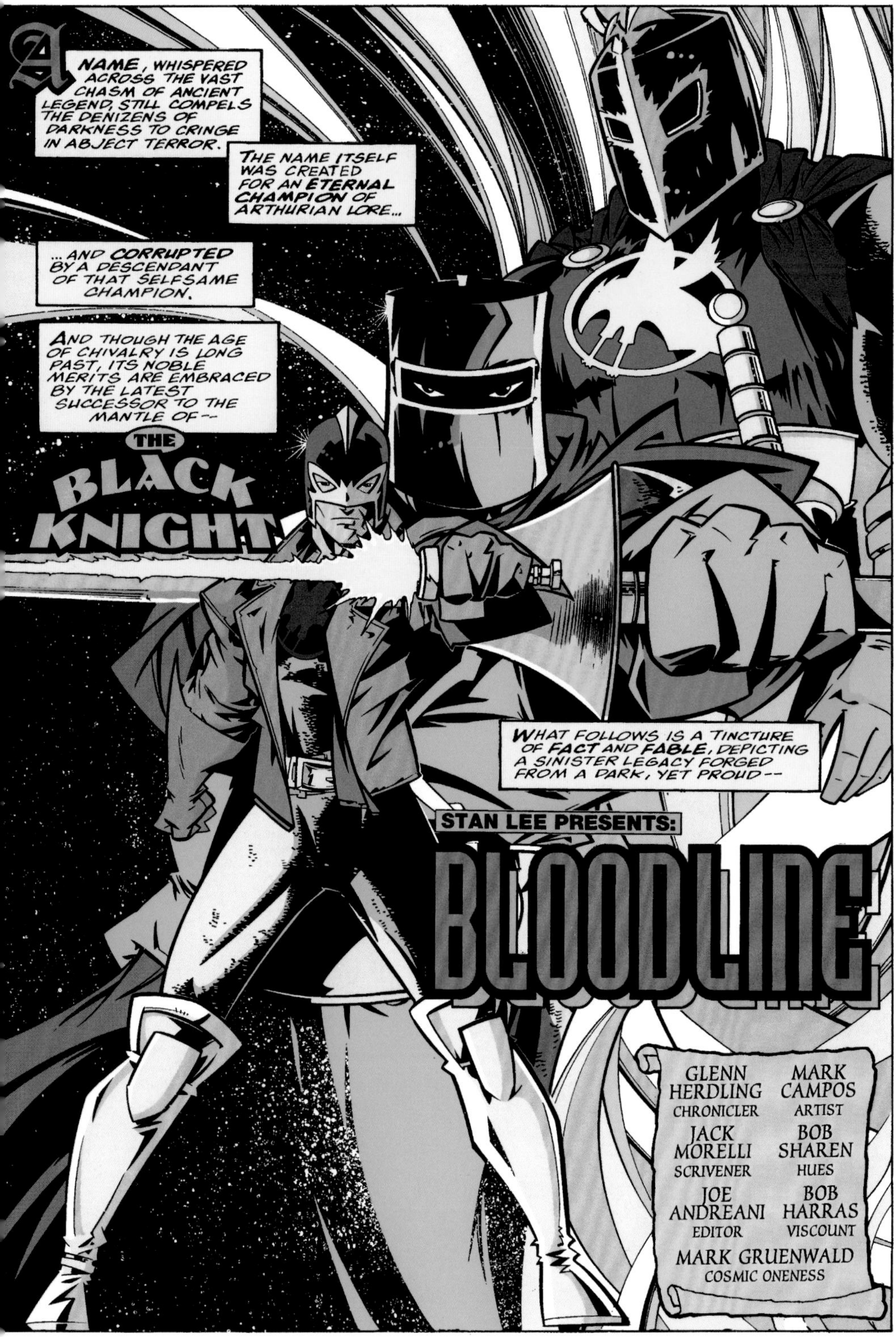
A NAME, WHISPERED ACROSS THE VAST CHASM OF ANCIENT LEGEND, STILL COMPELS THE DENIZENS OF DARKNESS TO CRINGE IN ABJECT TERROR.
THE NAME ITSELF WAS CREATED FOR AN ETERNAL CHAMPION OF ARTHURIAN LORE...
...AND CORRUPTED BY A DESCENDANT OF THAT SELFSAME CHAMPION.
AND THOUGH THE AGE OF CHIVALRY IS LONG PAST, ITS NOBLE MERITS ARE EMBRACED BY THE LATEST SUCCESSOR TO THE MANTLE OF--
THE BLACK KNIGHT
WHAT FOLLOWS IS A TINCTURE OF FACT AND FABLE, DEPICTING A SINISTER LEGACY FORGED FROM A DARK, YET PROUD--
STAN LEE PRESENTS:
BLOODLINE
GLENN HERDLING CHRONICLER
MARK CAMPOS ARTIST
JACK MORELLI SCRIVENER
BOB SHAREN HUES
JOE ANDREANI EDITOR
BOB HARRAS VISCOUNT
MARK GRUENWALD COSMIC ONENESS

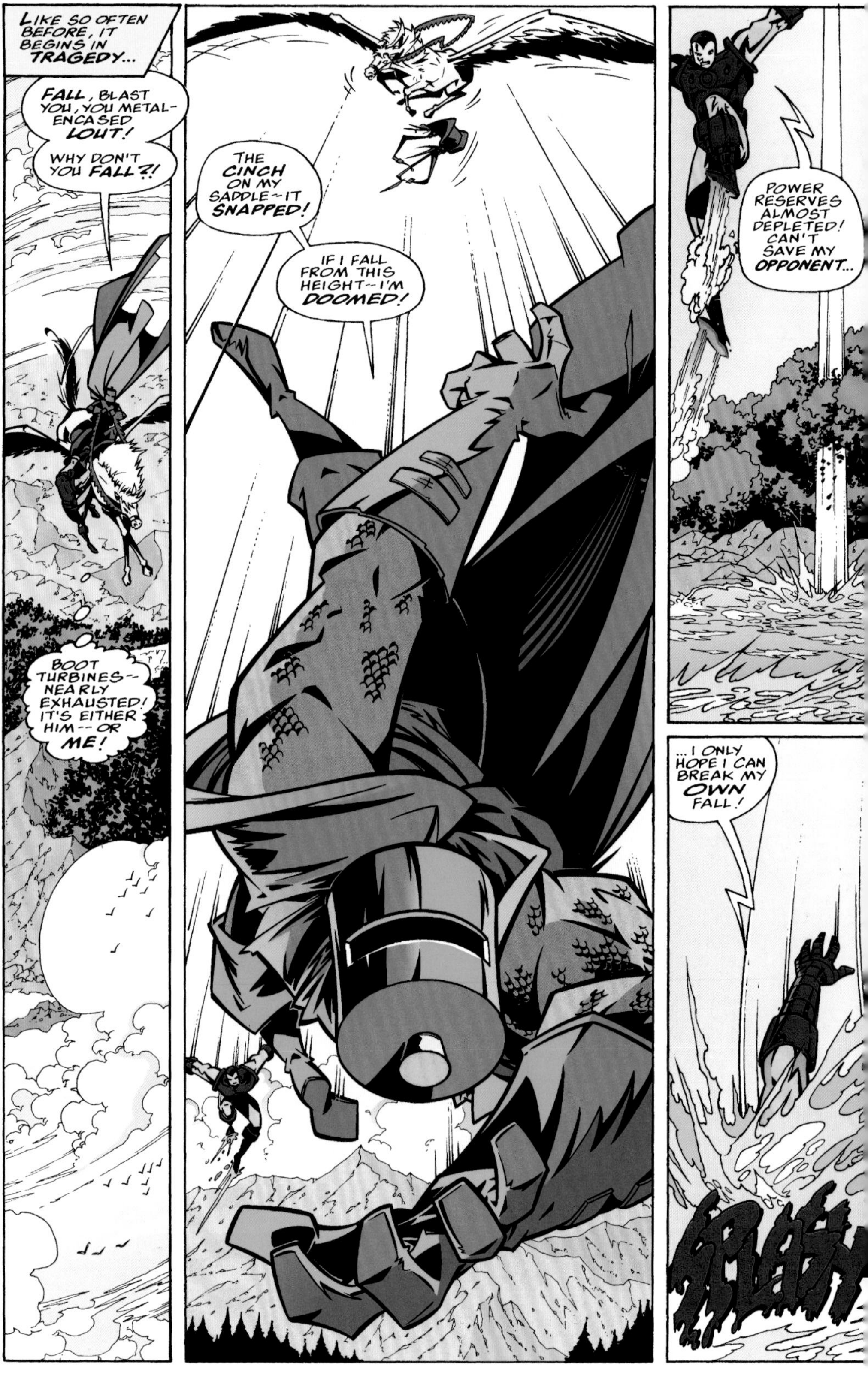
LIKE SO OFTEN BEFORE, IT BEGINS IN TRAGEDY...
FALL, BLAST YOU, YOU METAL-ENCASED LOUT!
WHY DON'T YOU FALL?!
BOOT TURBINES-- NEARLY EXHAUSTED! IT'S EITHER HIM -- OR ME!
THE CINCH ON MY SADDLE-- IT SNAPPED!
IF I FALL FROM THIS HEIGHT-- I'M DOOMED!
POWER RESERVES ALMOST DEPLETED! CAN'T SAVE MY OPPONENT...
...I ONLY HOPE I CAN BREAK MY OWN FALL!
SPLASH

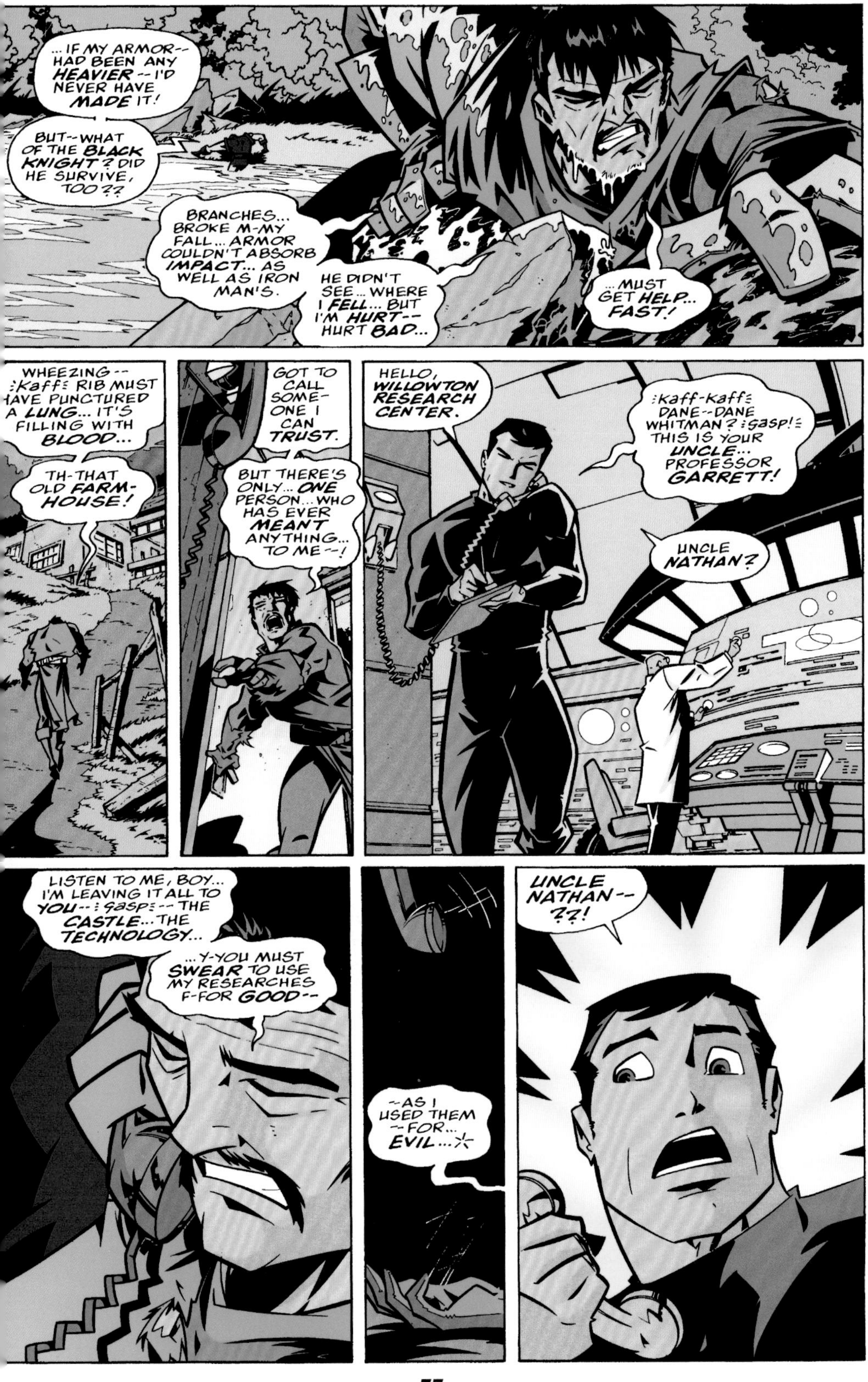
...IF MY ARMOR-- HAD BEEN ANY HEAVIER--I'D NEVER HAVE MADE IT!
BUT--WHAT OF THE BLACK KNIGHT? DID HE SURVIVE, TOO??
BRANCHES... BROKE M-MY FALL... ARMOR COULDN'T ABSORB IMPACT... AS WELL AS IRON MAN'S.
HE DIDN'T SEE... WHERE I FELL... BUT I'M HURT--HURT BAD...
...MUST GET HELP... FAST!
WHEEZING-- :Kaff: RIB MUST HAVE PUNCTURED A LUNG... IT'S FILLING WITH BLOOD...
TH-THAT OLD FARM-HOUSE!
GOT TO CALL SOME-ONE I CAN TRUST.
BUT THERE'S ONLY... ONE PERSON... WHO HAS EVER MEANT ANYTHING... TO ME--!
HELLO, WILLOWTON RESEARCH CENTER.
:Kaff-Kaff: DANE--DANE WHITMAN? :gasp!: THIS IS YOUR UNCLE... PROFESSOR GARRETT!
UNCLE NATHAN?
LISTEN TO ME, BOY... I'M LEAVING IT ALL TO YOU--:gasp:--THE CASTLE... THE TECHNOLOGY...
...Y-YOU MUST SWEAR TO USE MY RESEARCHES F-FOR GOOD--
--AS I USED THEM --FOR... EVIL...
UNCLE NATHAN--??!

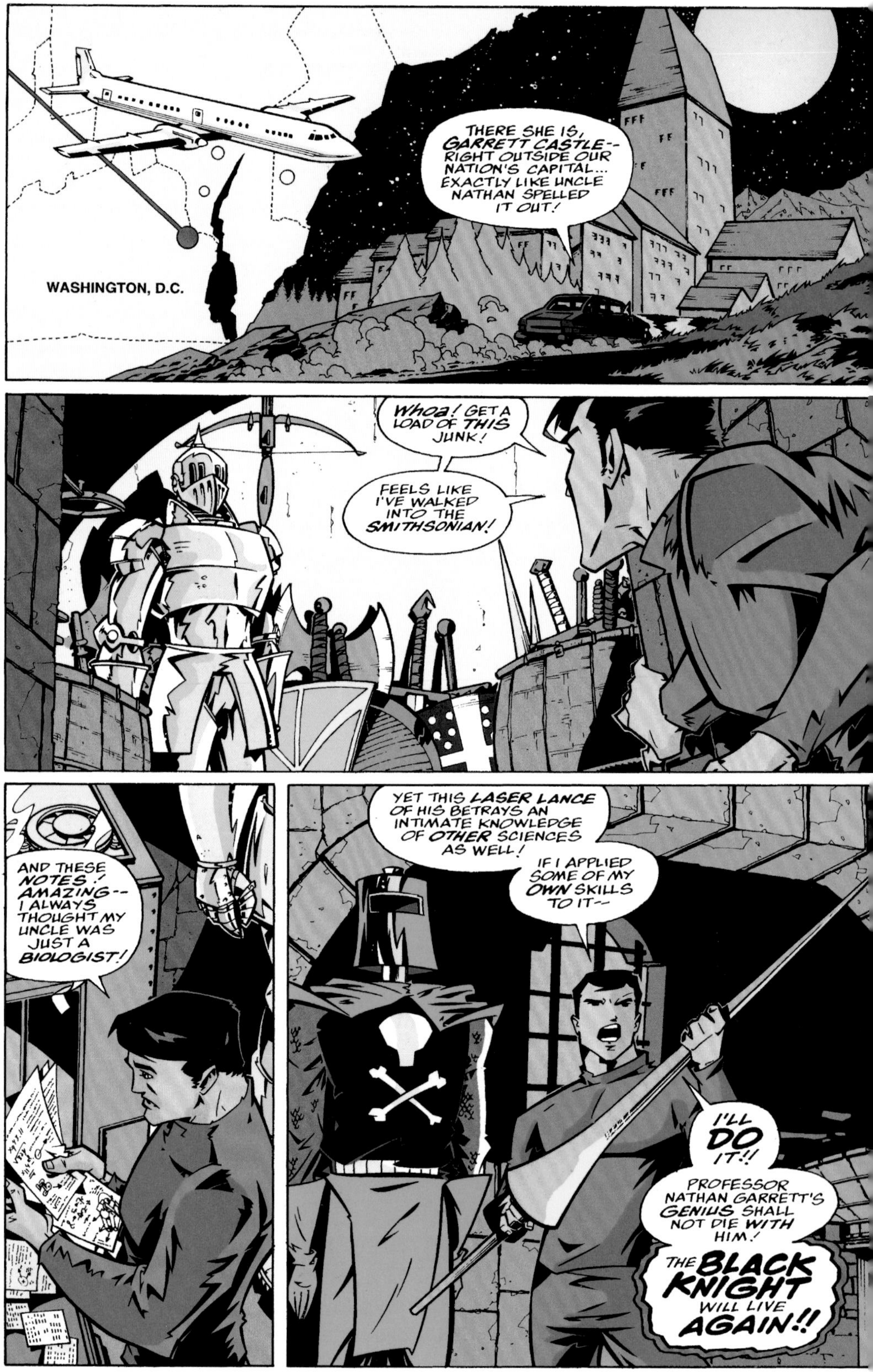
WASHINGTON, D.C.
THERE SHE IS, GARRETT CASTLE-- RIGHT OUTSIDE OUR NATION'S CAPITAL... EXACTLY LIKE UNCLE NATHAN SPELLED IT OUT!
Whoa! GET A LOAD OF THIS JUNK!
FEELS LIKE I'VE WALKED INTO THE SMITHSONIAN!
AND THESE NOTES! AMAZING-- I ALWAYS THOUGHT MY UNCLE WAS JUST A BIOLOGIST!
YET THIS LASER LANCE OF HIS BETRAYS AN INTIMATE KNOWLEDGE OF OTHER SCIENCES AS WELL!
IF I APPLIED SOME OF MY OWN SKILLS TO IT--
I'LL DO IT!!
PROFESSOR NATHAN GARRETT'S GENIUS SHALL NOT DIE WITH HIM!
THE BLACK KNIGHT WILL LIVE AGAIN!!

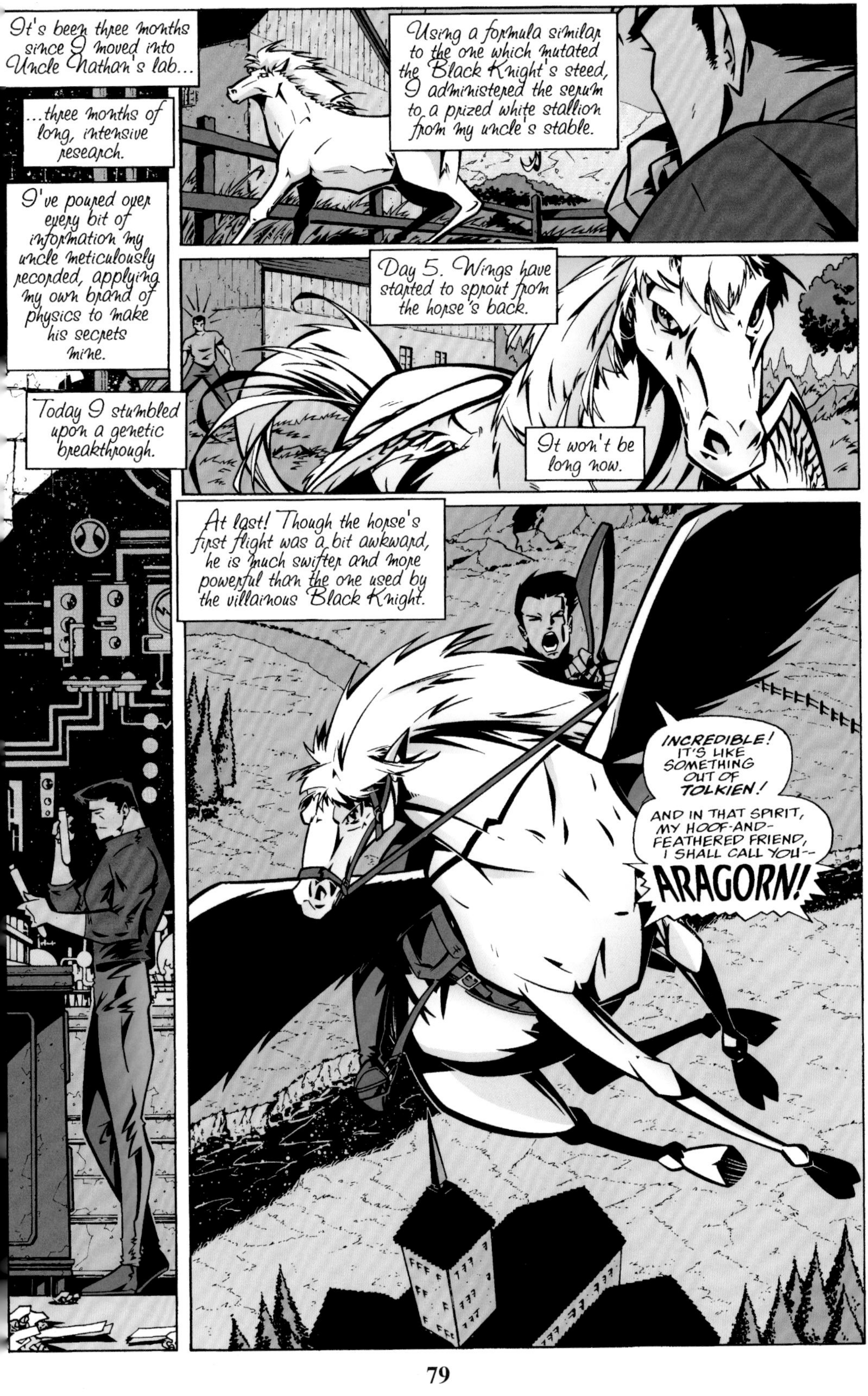

It's been three months since I moved into Uncle Nathan's lab...
...three months of long, intensive research.
I've poured over every bit of information my uncle meticulously recorded, applying my own brand of physics to make his secrets mine.
Today I stumbled upon a genetic breakthrough.
Using a formula similar to the one which mutated the Black Knight's steed, I administered the serum to a prized white stallion from my uncle's stable.
Day 5. Wings have started to sprout from the horse's back.
It won't be long now.
At last! Though the horse's first flight was a bit awkward, he is much swifter and more powerful than the one used by the villainous Black Knight.
INCREDIBLE! IT'S LIKE SOMETHING OUT OF TOLKIEN!
AND IN THAT SPIRIT, MY HOOF-AND-FEATHERED FRIEND, I SHALL CALL YOU--
ARAGORN!

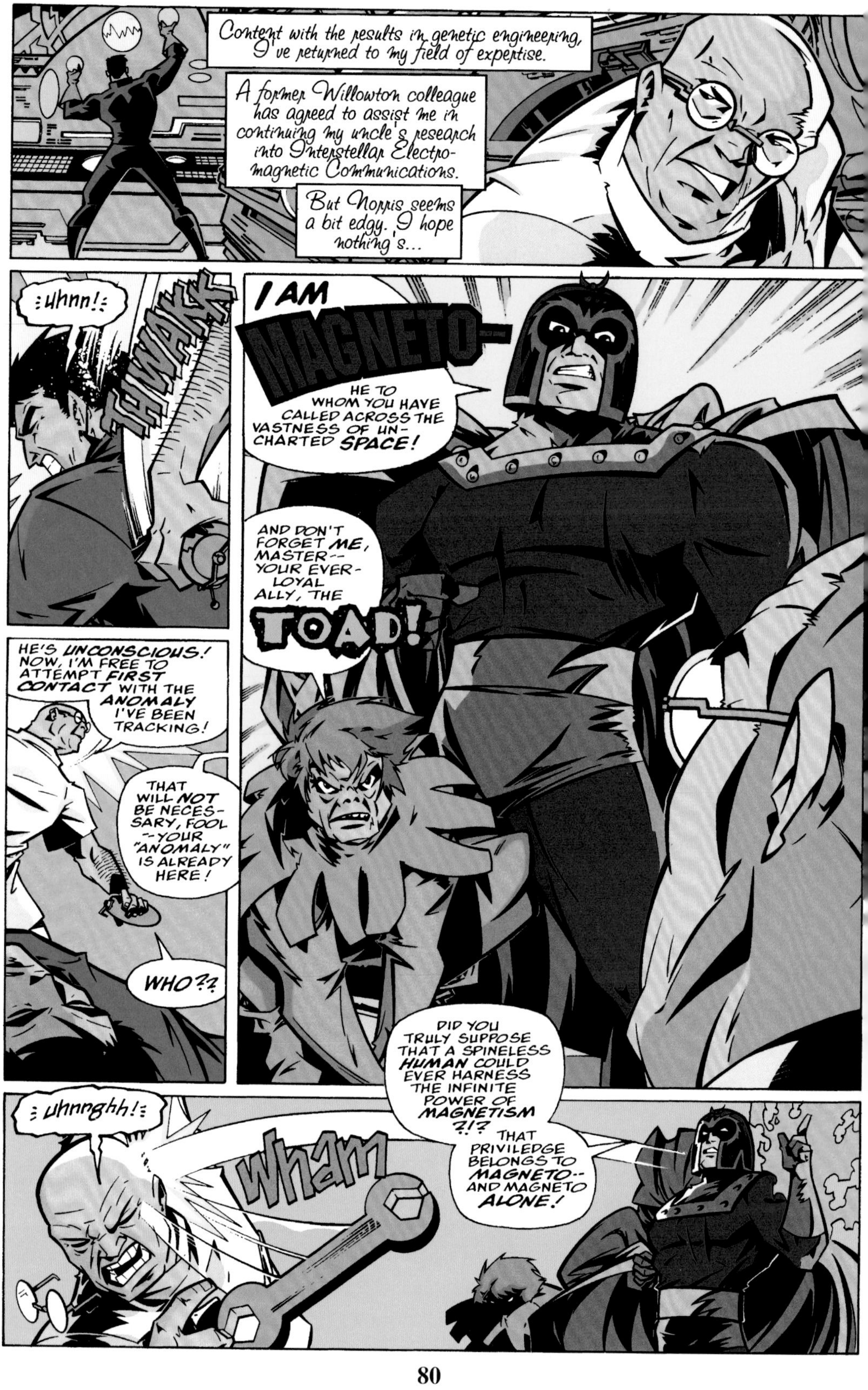
Content with the results in genetic engineering, I've returned to my field of expertise.
A former Willowton colleague has agreed to assist me in continuing my uncle's research into Interstellar Electromagnetic Communications.
But Norris seems a bit edgy. I hope nothing's...
:uhnn!:
THWAK
I AM MAGNETO--
HE TO WHOM YOU HAVE CALLED ACROSS THE VASTNESS OF UNCHARTED SPACE!
AND DON'T FORGET ME, MASTER-- YOUR EVER-LOYAL ALLY, THE TOAD!
HE'S UNCONSCIOUS! NOW, I'M FREE TO ATTEMPT FIRST CONTACT WITH THE ANOMALY I'VE BEEN TRACKING!
THAT WILL NOT BE NECESSARY, FOOL --YOUR "ANOMALY" IS ALREADY HERE!
WHO?!?
DID YOU TRULY SUPPOSE THAT A SPINELESS HUMAN COULD EVER HARNESS THE INFINITE POWER OF MAGNETISM ?!?
THAT PRIVILEDGE BELONGS TO MAGNETO-- AND MAGNETO ALONE!
:uhnnghh!:
Wham

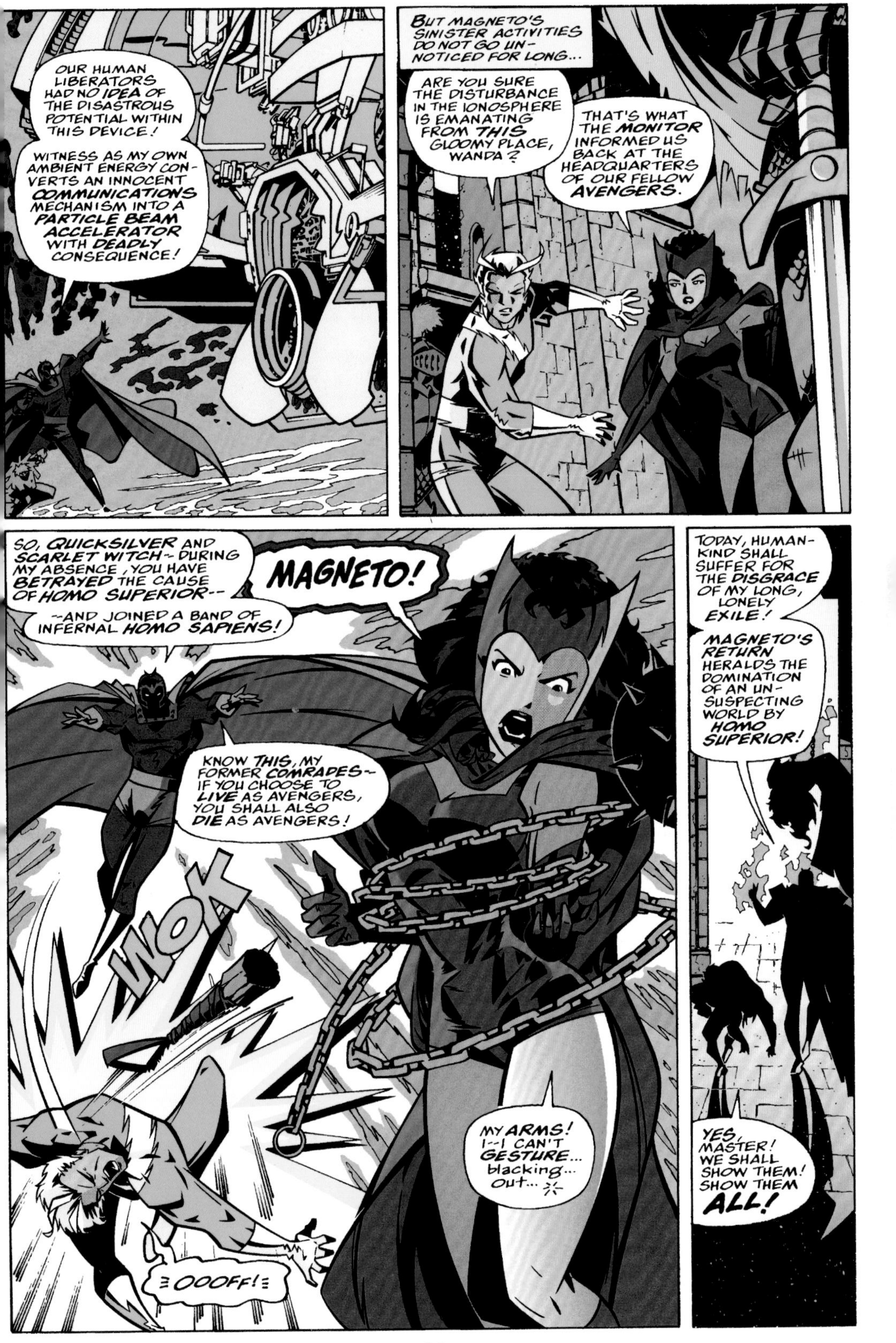
OUR HUMAN LIBERATORS HAD NO IDEA OF THE DISASTROUS POTENTIAL WITHIN THIS DEVICE!
WITNESS AS MY OWN AMBIENT ENERGY CONVERTS AN INNOCENT COMMUNICATIONS MECHANISM INTO A PARTICLE BEAM ACCELERATOR WITH DEADLY CONSEQUENCE!
BUT MAGNETO'S SINISTER ACTIVITIES DO NOT GO UNNOTICED FOR LONG...
ARE YOU SURE THE DISTURBANCE IN THE IONOSPHERE IS EMANATING FROM THIS GLOOMY PLACE, WANDA?
THAT'S WHAT THE MONITOR INFORMED US BACK AT THE HEADQUARTERS OF OUR FELLOW AVENGERS.
SO, QUICKSILVER AND SCARLET WITCH-- DURING MY ABSENCE, YOU HAVE BETRAYED THE CAUSE OF HOMO SUPERIOR--
--AND JOINED A BAND OF INFERNAL HOMO SAPIENS!
MAGNETO!
KNOW THIS, MY FORMER COMRADES-- IF YOU CHOOSE TO LIVE AS AVENGERS, YOU SHALL ALSO DIE AS AVENGERS!
WOK
MY ARMS! I--I CAN'T GESTURE... blacking... out...
OOOFF!
TODAY, HUMANKIND SHALL SUFFER FOR THE DISGRACE OF MY LONG, LONELY EXILE!
MAGNETO'S RETURN HERALDS THE DOMINATION OF AN UNSUSPECTING WORLD BY HOMO SUPERIOR!
YES, MASTER! WE SHALL SHOW THEM! SHOW THEM ALL!

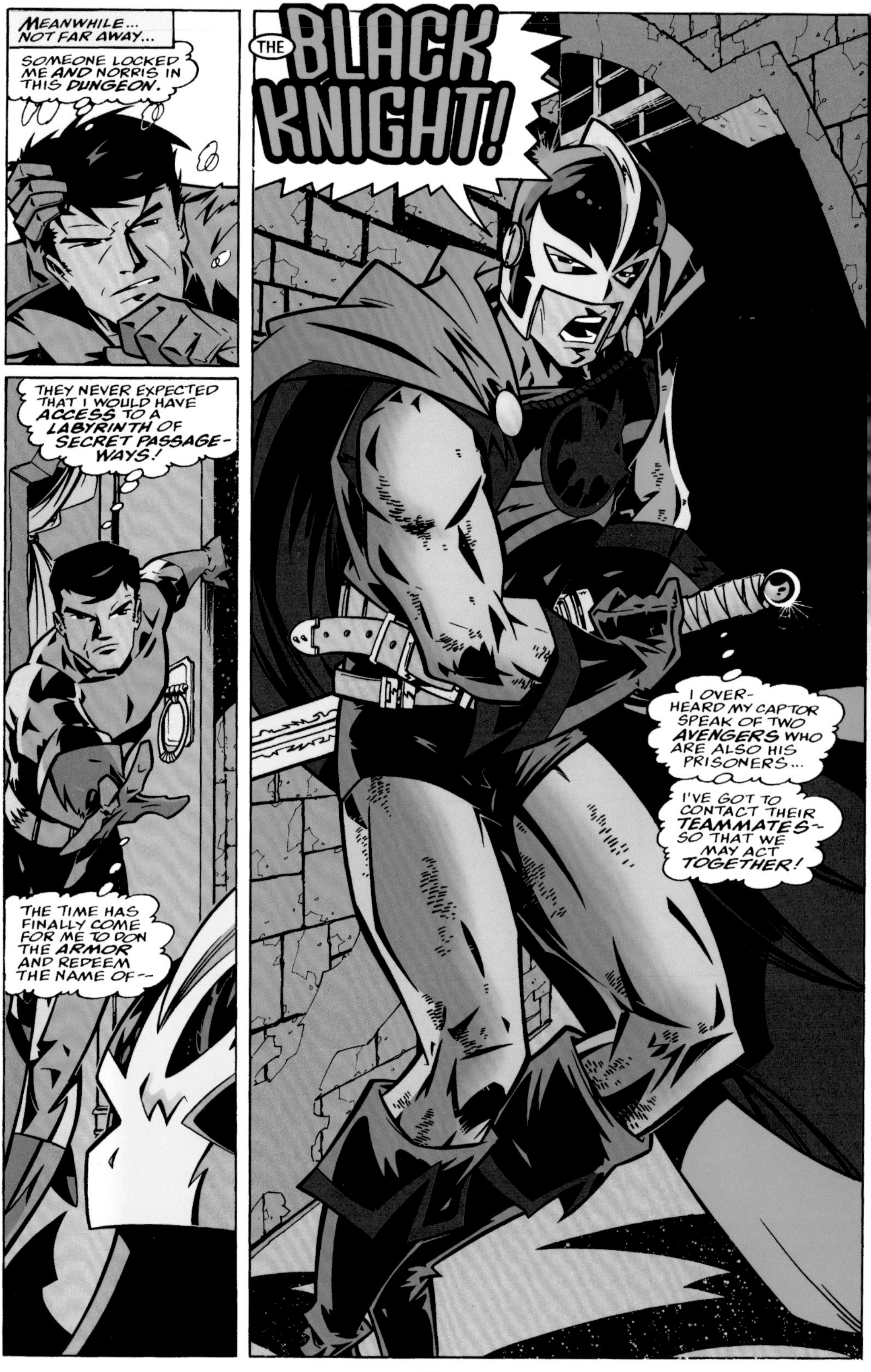
MEANWHILE... NOT FAR AWAY...
SOMEONE LOCKED ME AND NORRIS IN THIS DUNGEON.
THEY NEVER EXPECTED THAT I WOULD HAVE ACCESS TO A LABYRINTH OF SECRET PASSAGE-WAYS!
THE TIME HAS FINALLY COME FOR ME TO DON THE ARMOR AND REDEEM THE NAME OF--
THE BLACK KNIGHT!
I OVER-HEARD MY CAPTOR SPEAK OF TWO AVENGERS WHO ARE ALSO HIS PRISONERS...
I'VE GOT TO CONTACT THEIR TEAMMATES-- SO THAT WE MAY ACT TOGETHER!

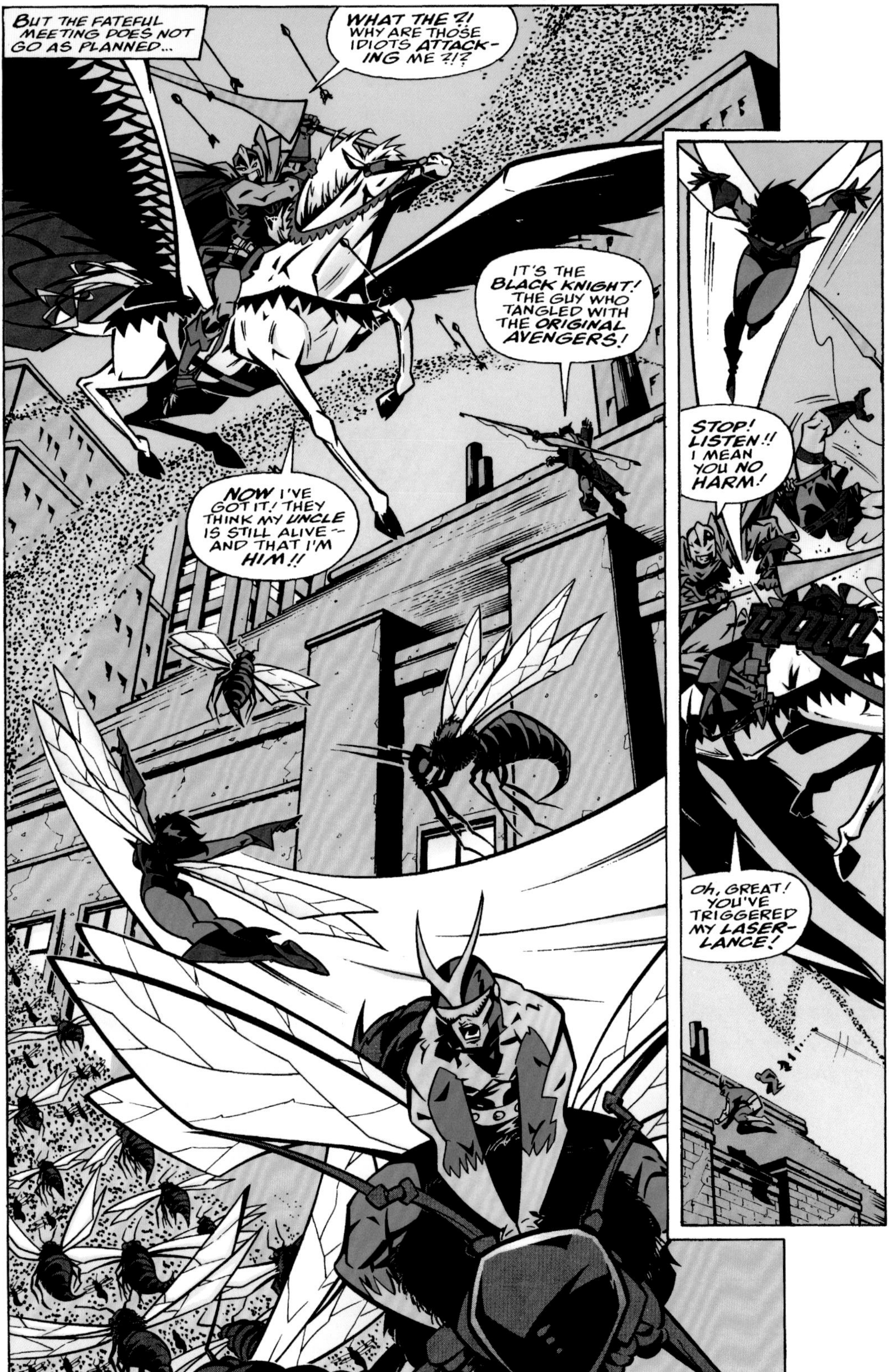
BUT THE FATEFUL MEETING DOES NOT GO AS PLANNED...
WHAT THE ?! WHY ARE THOSE IDIOTS ATTACKING ME ?!?
IT'S THE BLACK KNIGHT! THE GUY WHO TANGLED WITH THE ORIGINAL AVENGERS!
NOW I'VE GOT IT! THEY THINK MY UNCLE IS STILL ALIVE-- AND THAT I'M HIM!!
STOP! LISTEN!! I MEAN YOU NO HARM!
OH, GREAT! YOU'VE TRIGGERED MY LASER-LANCE!

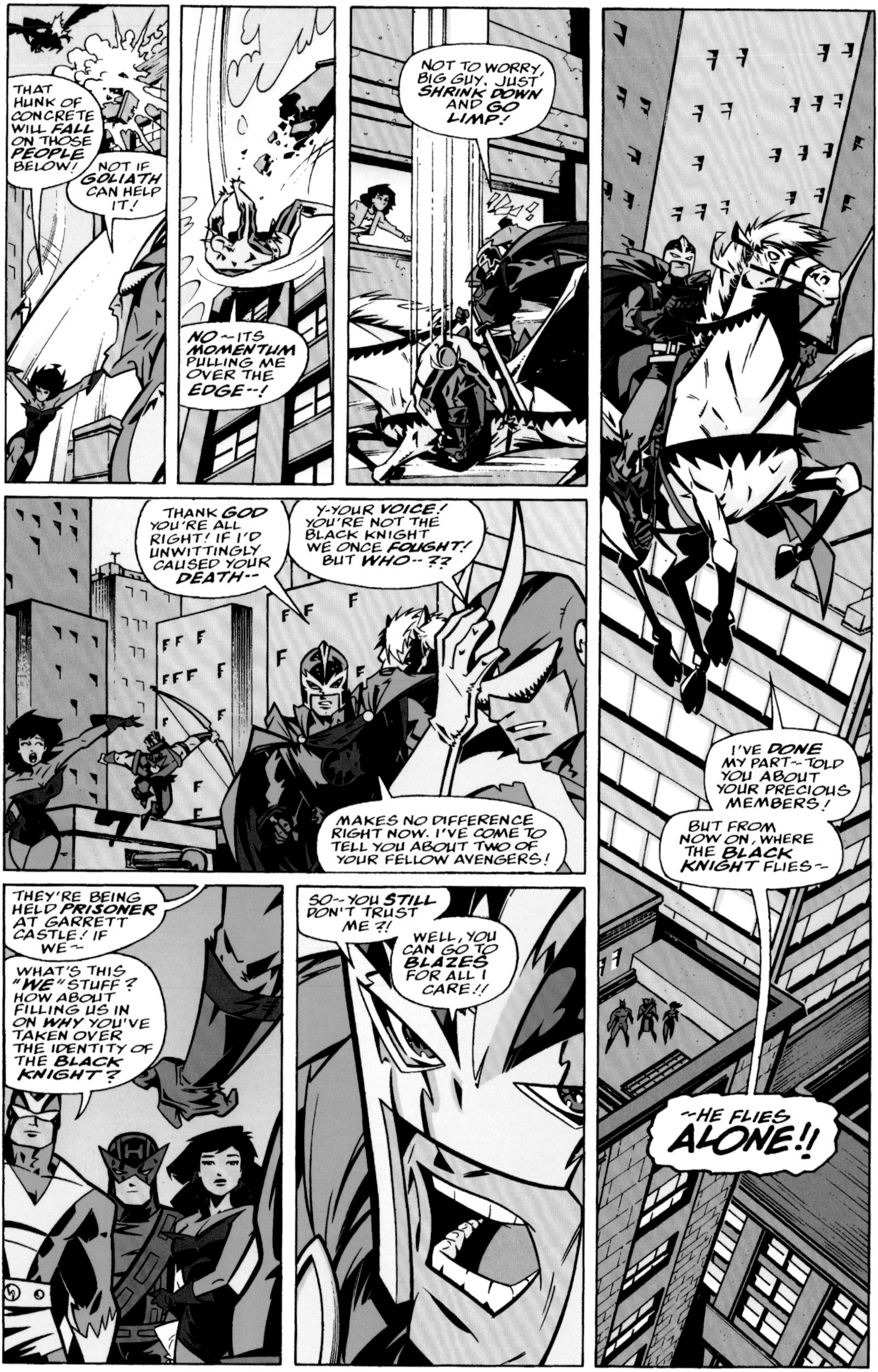
THAT HUNK OF CONCRETE WILL FALL ON THOSE PEOPLE BELOW!
NOT IF GOLIATH CAN HELP IT!
NO--ITS MOMENTUM PULLING ME OVER THE EDGE--!
NOT TO WORRY, BIG GUY. JUST SHRINK DOWN AND GO LIMP!
THANK GOD YOU'RE ALL RIGHT! IF I'D UNWITTINGLY CAUSED YOUR DEATH--
Y-YOUR VOICE! YOU'RE NOT THE BLACK KNIGHT WE ONCE FOUGHT! BUT WHO--??
MAKES NO DIFFERENCE RIGHT NOW. I'VE COME TO TELL YOU ABOUT TWO OF YOUR FELLOW AVENGERS!
THEY'RE BEING HELD PRISONER AT GARRETT CASTLE! IF WE--
WHAT'S THIS "WE" STUFF? HOW ABOUT FILLING US IN ON WHY YOU'VE TAKEN OVER THE IDENTITY OF THE BLACK KNIGHT?
SO--YOU STILL DON'T TRUST ME?!
WELL, YOU CAN GO TO BLAZES FOR ALL I CARE!!
I'VE DONE MY PART--TOLD YOU ABOUT YOUR PRECIOUS MEMBERS!
BUT FROM NOW ON, WHERE THE BLACK KNIGHT FLIES--
--HE FLIES ALONE!!

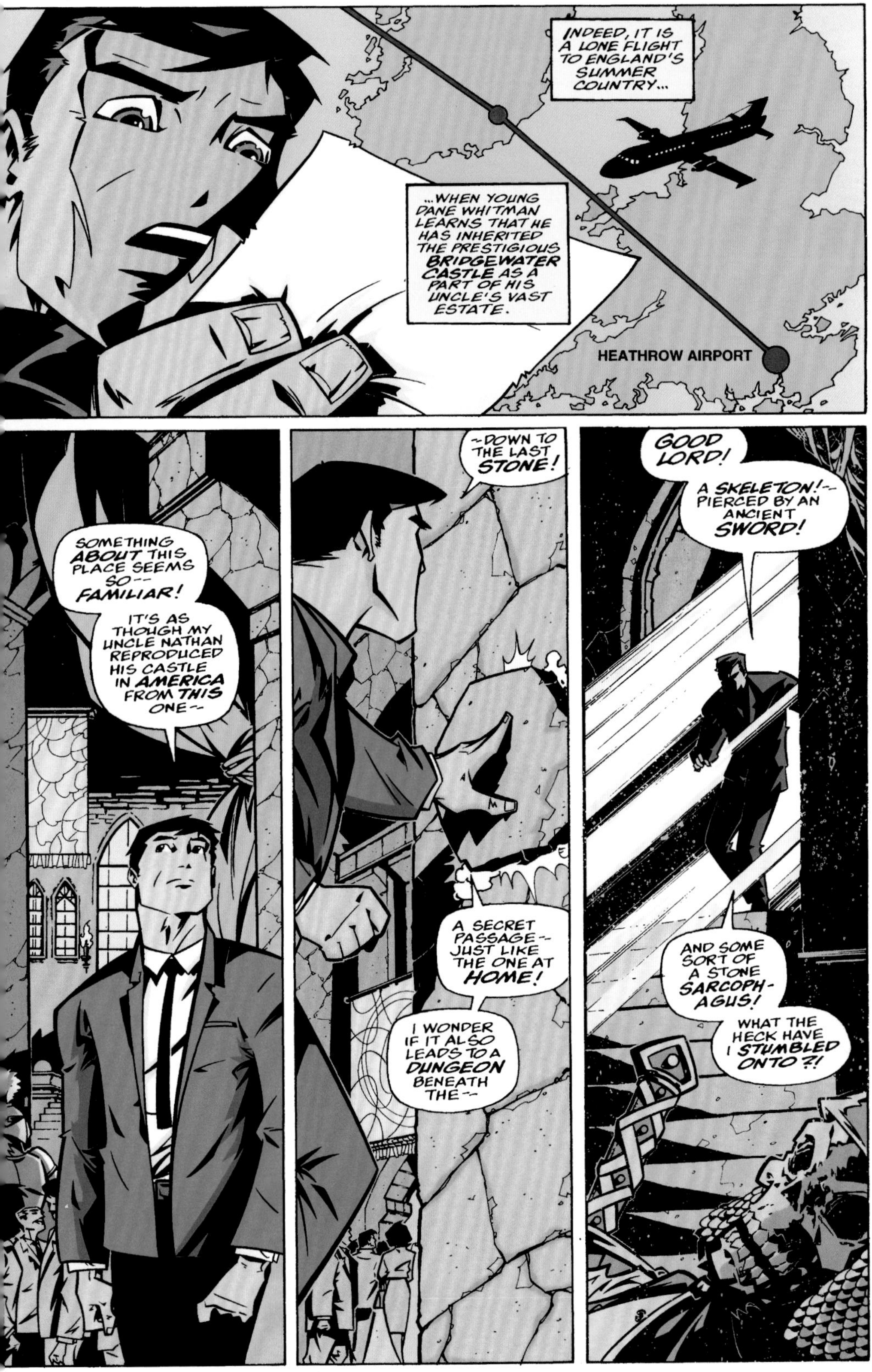
INDEED, IT IS A LONE FLIGHT TO ENGLAND'S SUMMER COUNTRY...
...WHEN YOUNG DANE WHITMAN LEARNS THAT HE HAS INHERITED THE PRESTIGIOUS BRIDGEWATER CASTLE AS A PART OF HIS UNCLE'S VAST ESTATE.
HEATHROW AIRPORT
SOMETHING ABOUT THIS PLACE SEEMS SO-- FAMILIAR!
IT'S AS THOUGH MY UNCLE NATHAN REPRODUCED HIS CASTLE IN AMERICA FROM THIS ONE--
--DOWN TO THE LAST STONE!
A SECRET PASSAGE-- JUST LIKE THE ONE AT HOME!
I WONDER IF IT ALSO LEADS TO A DUNGEON BENEATH THE--
GOOD LORD!
A SKELETON!-- PIERCED BY AN ANCIENT SWORD!
AND SOME SORT OF A STONE SARCOPH-AGUS!
WHAT THE HECK HAVE I STUMBLED ONTO?!

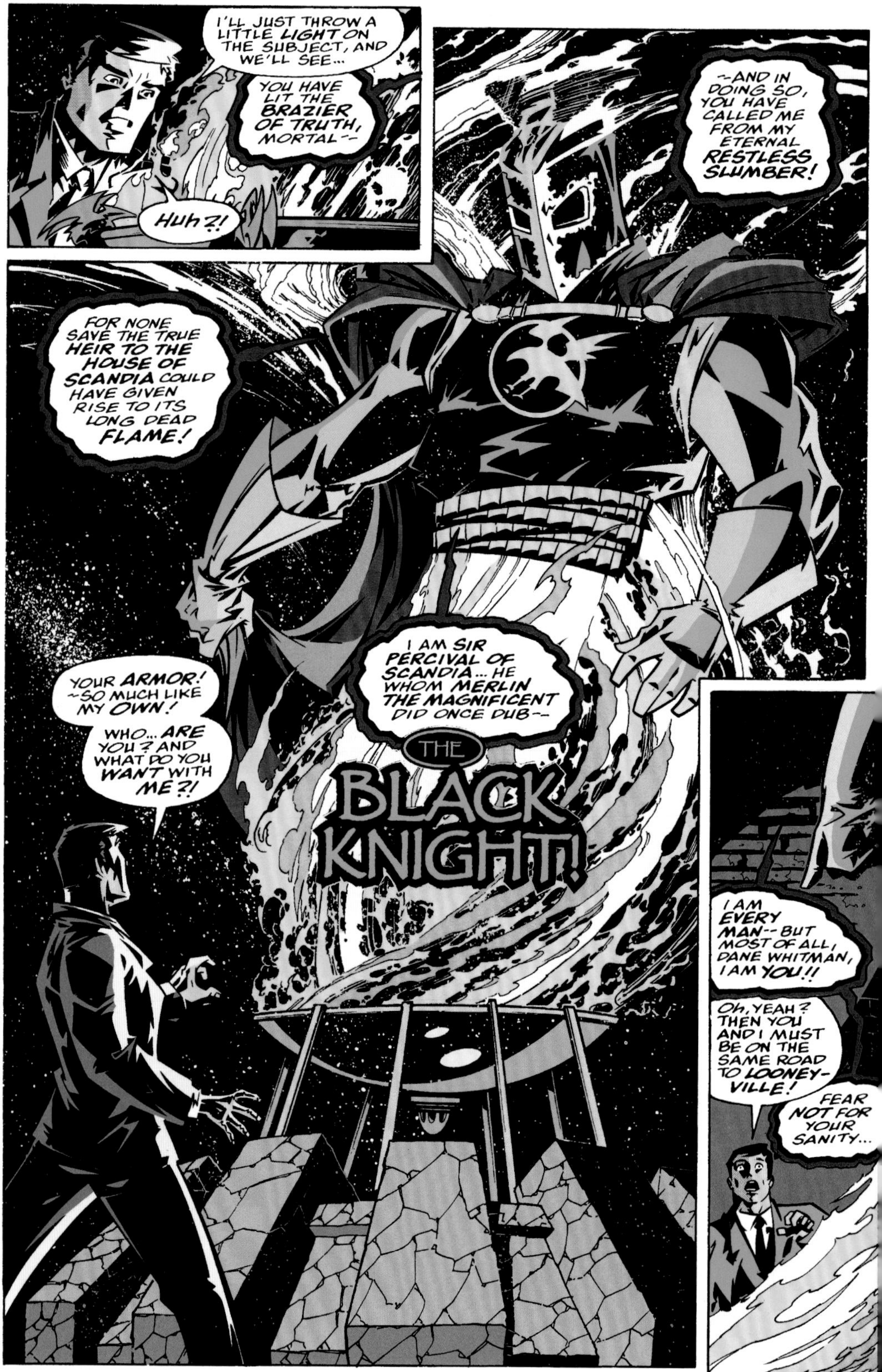
I'LL JUST THROW A LITTLE LIGHT ON THE SUBJECT, AND WE'LL SEE...
YOU HAVE LIT THE BRAZIER OF TRUTH, MORTAL--
HUH?!
--AND IN DOING SO, YOU HAVE CALLED ME FROM MY ETERNAL RESTLESS SLUMBER!
FOR NONE SAVE THE TRUE HEIR TO THE HOUSE OF SCANDIA COULD HAVE GIVEN RISE TO ITS LONG DEAD FLAME!
YOUR ARMOR! --SO MUCH LIKE MY OWN!
WHO... ARE YOU? AND WHAT DO YOU WANT WITH ME?!
I AM SIR PERCIVAL OF SCANDIA... HE WHOM MERLIN THE MAGNIFICENT DID ONCE DUB--
THE BLACK KNIGHT!
I AM EVERY MAN-- BUT MOST OF ALL, DANE WHITMAN, I AM YOU!!
OH, YEAH? THEN YOU AND I MUST BE ON THE SAME ROAD TO LOONEY-VILLE!
FEAR NOT FOR YOUR SANITY...

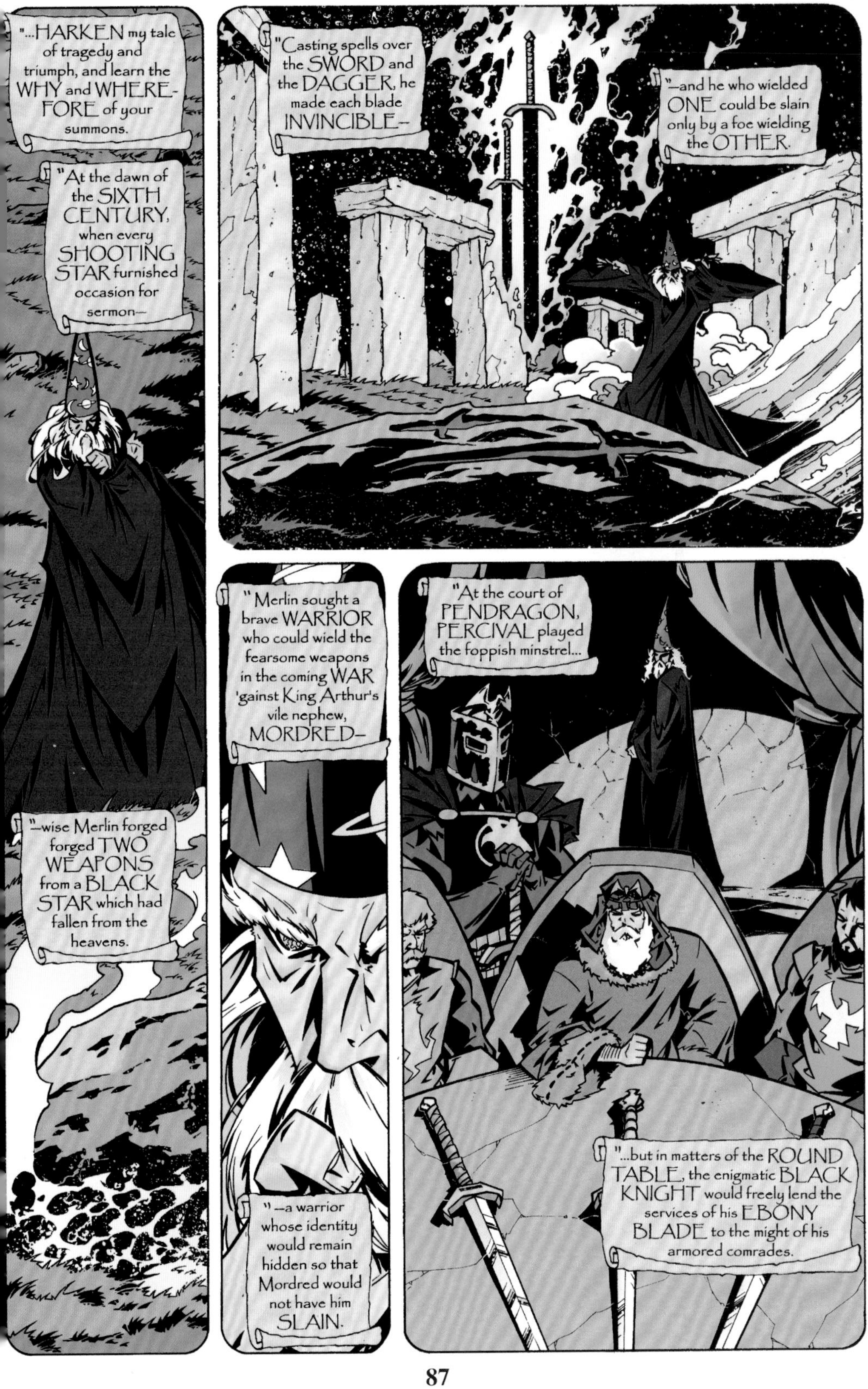
"...HARKEN my tale of tragedy and triumph, and learn the WHY and WHERE-FORE of your summons.
"At the dawn of the SIXTH CENTURY, when every SHOOTING STAR furnished occasion for sermon—
"—wise Merlin forged forged TWO WEAPONS from a BLACK STAR which had fallen from the heavens.
"Casting spells over the SWORD and the DAGGER, he made each blade INVINCIBLE—
"—and he who wielded ONE could be slain only by a foe wielding the OTHER.
"Merlin sought a brave WARRIOR who could wield the fearsome weapons in the coming WAR 'gainst King Arthur's vile nephew, MORDRED—
"—a warrior whose identity would remain hidden so that Mordred would not have him SLAIN.
"At the court of PENDRAGON, PERCIVAL played the foppish minstrel...
"...but in matters of the ROUND TABLE, the enigmatic BLACK KNIGHT would freely lend the services of his EBONY BLADE to the might of his armored comrades.

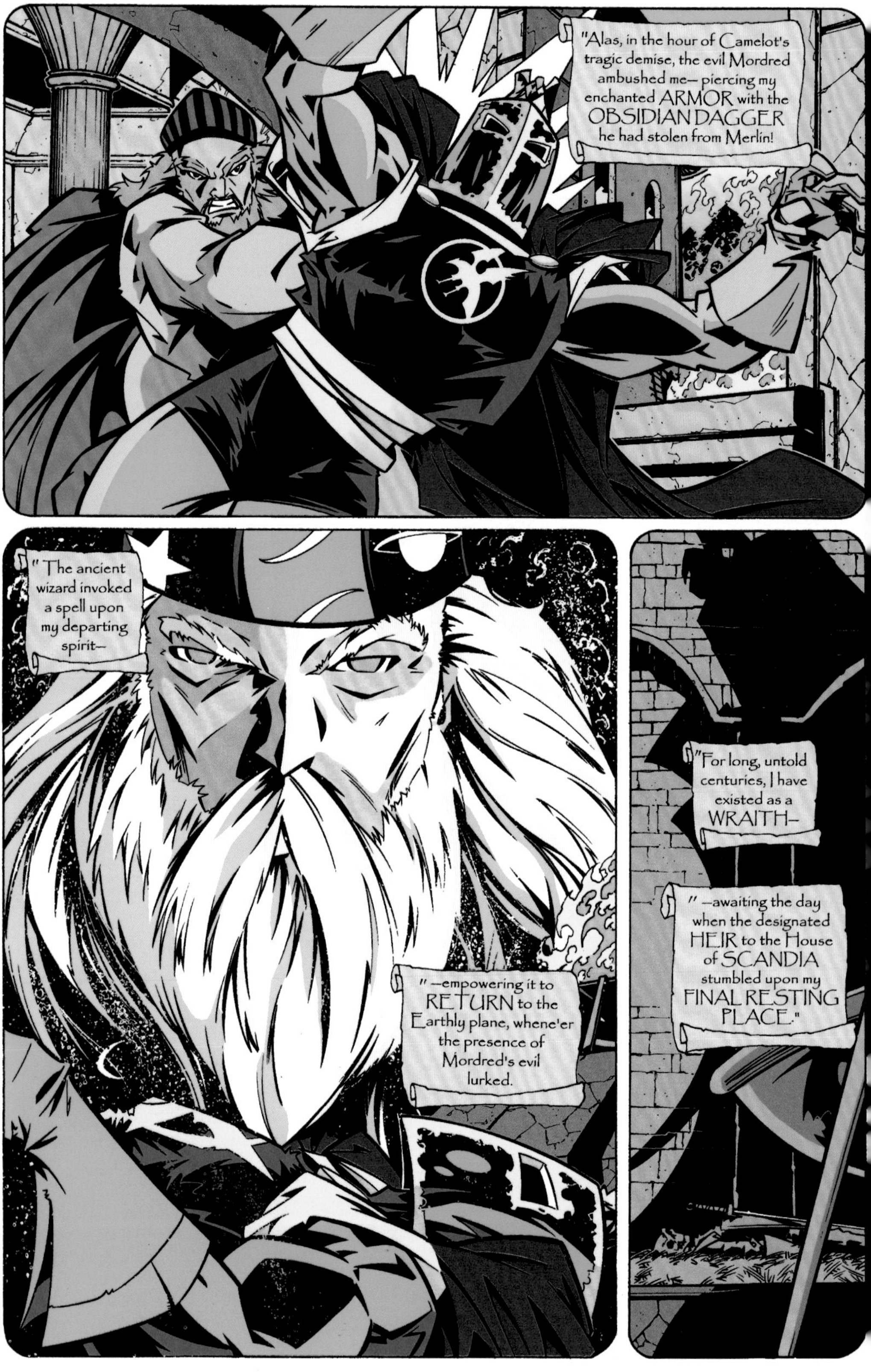
"Alas, in the hour of Camelot's tragic demise, the evil Mordred ambushed me— piercing my enchanted ARMOR with the OBSIDIAN DAGGER he had stolen from Merlin!
"The ancient wizard invoked a spell upon my departing spirit—
"—empowering it to RETURN to the Earthly plane, whene'er the presence of Mordred's evil lurked.
"For long, untold centuries, I have existed as a WRAITH—
"—awaiting the day when the designated HEIR to the House of SCANDIA stumbled upon my FINAL RESTING PLACE."

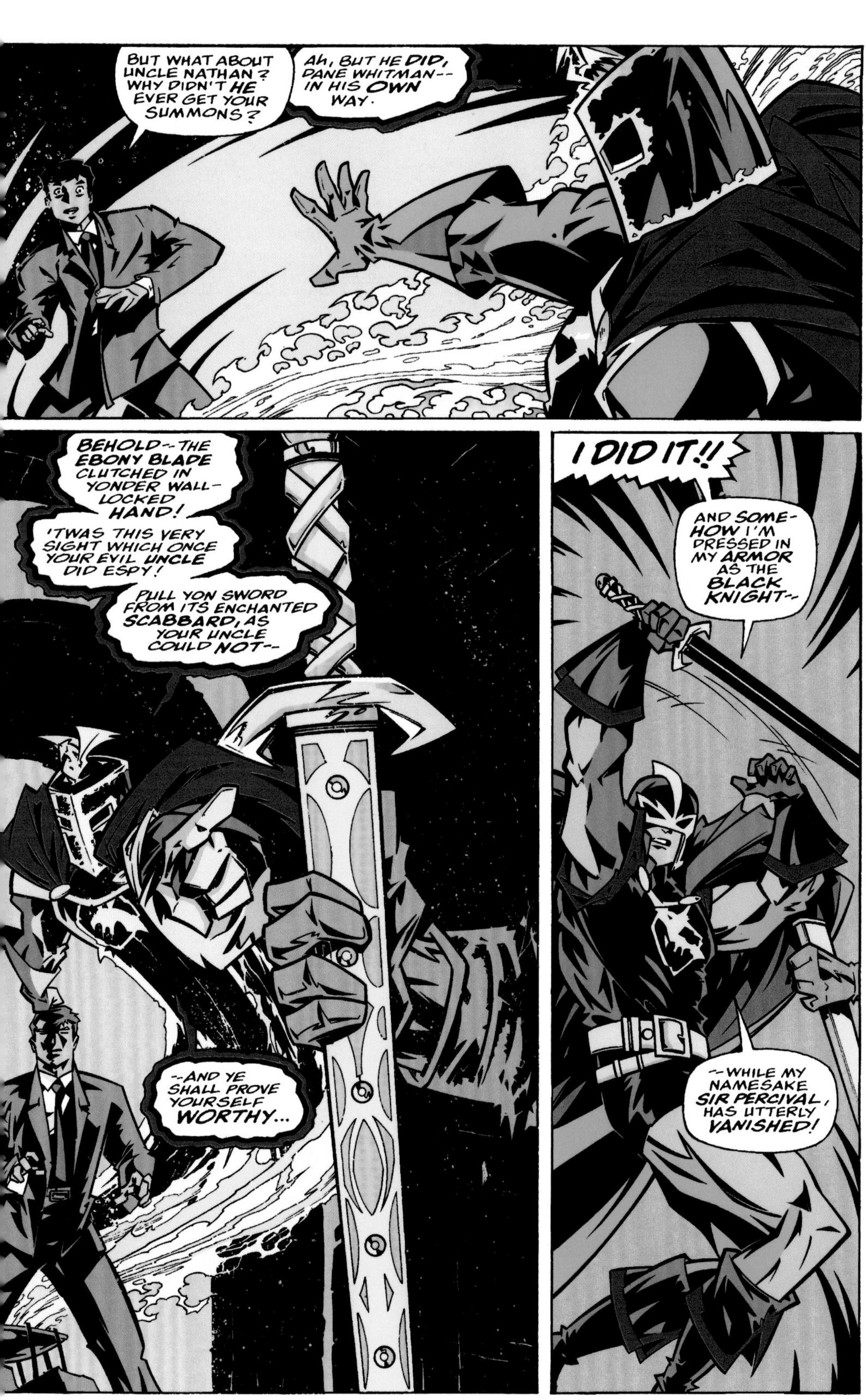

BUT WHAT ABOUT UNCLE NATHAN? WHY DIDN'T HE EVER GET YOUR SUMMONS?
AH, BUT HE DID, DANE WHITMAN-- IN HIS OWN WAY.
BEHOLD-- THE EBONY BLADE CLUTCHED IN YONDER WALL-LOCKED HAND!
'TWAS THIS VERY SIGHT WHICH ONCE YOUR EVIL UNCLE DID ESPY!
PULL YON SWORD FROM ITS ENCHANTED SCABBARD, AS YOUR UNCLE COULD NOT--
--AND YE SHALL PROVE YOURSELF WORTHY...
I DID IT!!
AND SOMEHOW I'M DRESSED IN MY ARMOR AS THE BLACK KNIGHT--
--WHILE MY NAMESAKE SIR PERCIVAL, HAS UTTERLY VANISHED!

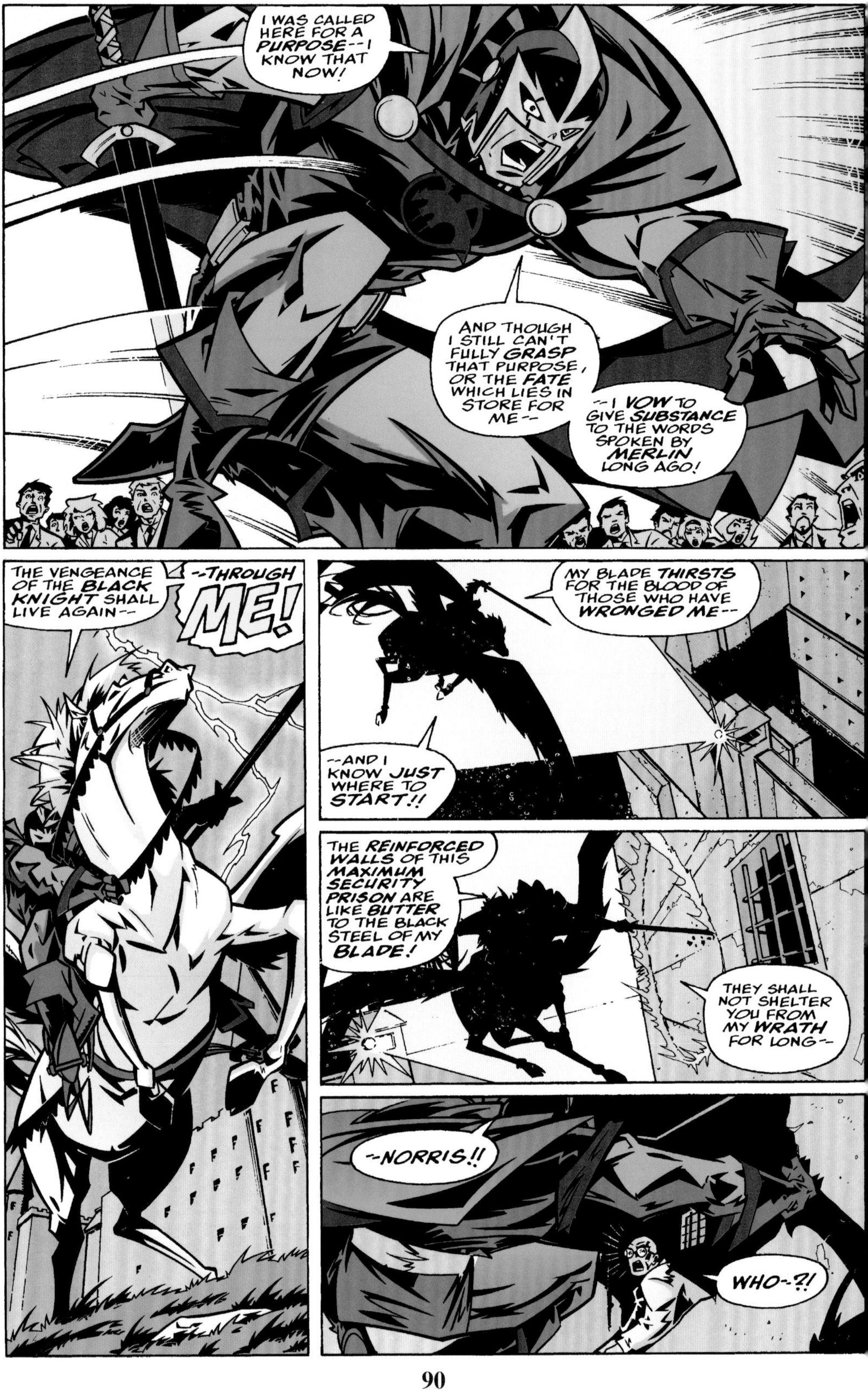
I WAS CALLED HERE FOR A PURPOSE--I KNOW THAT NOW!
AND THOUGH I STILL CAN'T FULLY GRASP THAT PURPOSE, OR THE FATE WHICH LIES IN STORE FOR ME--
--I VOW TO GIVE SUBSTANCE TO THE WORDS SPOKEN BY MERLIN LONG AGO!
THE VENGEANCE OF THE BLACK KNIGHT SHALL LIVE AGAIN--
--THROUGH ME!
MY BLADE THIRSTS FOR THE BLOOD OF THOSE WHO HAVE WRONGED ME--
--AND I KNOW JUST WHERE TO START!!
THE REINFORCED WALLS OF THIS MAXIMUM SECURITY PRISON ARE LIKE BUTTER TO THE BLACK STEEL OF MY BLADE!
THEY SHALL NOT SHELTER YOU FROM MY WRATH FOR LONG--
--NORRIS!!
WHO--?!

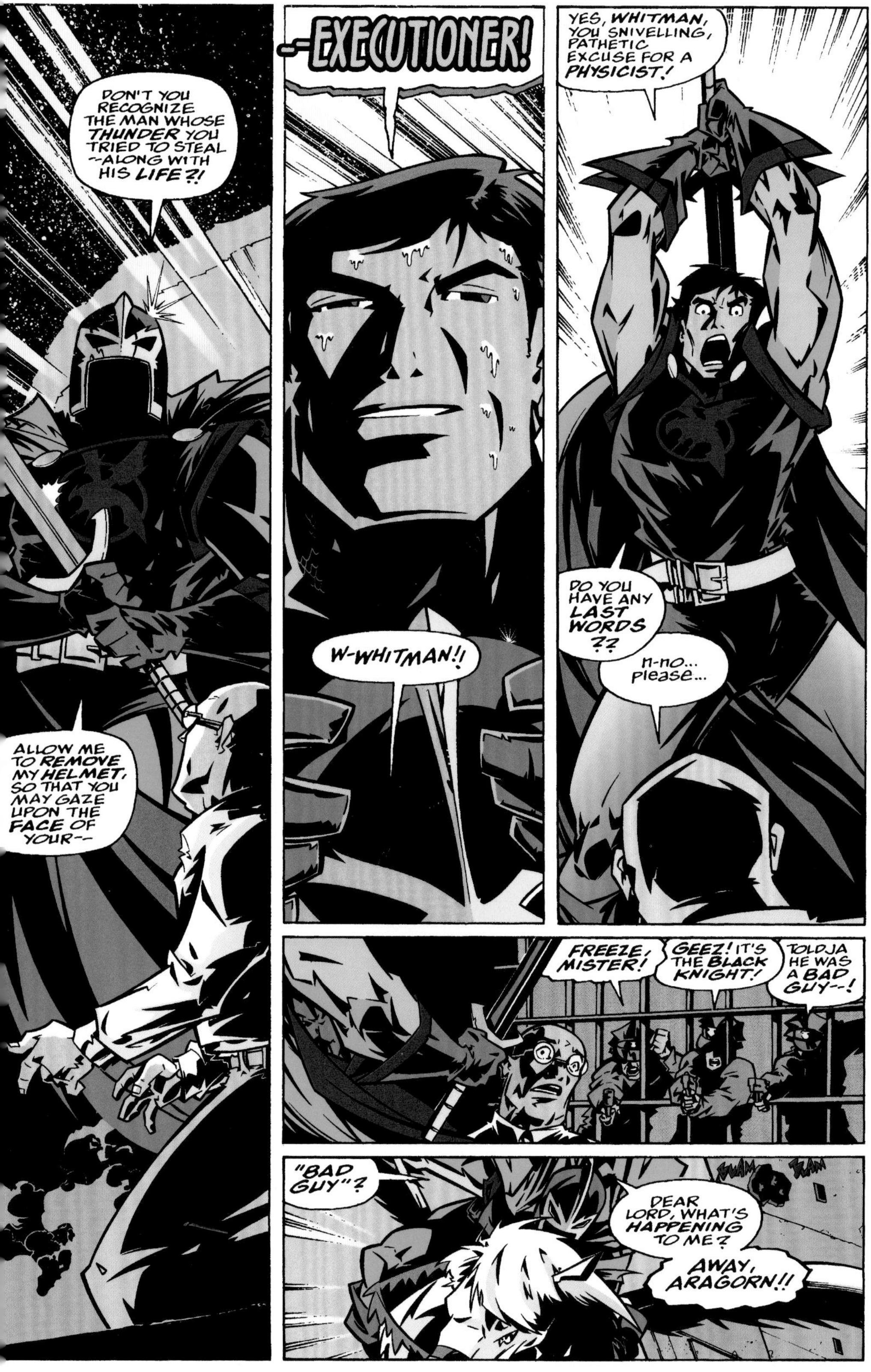
DON'T YOU RECOGNIZE THE MAN WHOSE THUNDER YOU TRIED TO STEAL --ALONG WITH HIS LIFE?!
ALLOW ME TO REMOVE MY HELMET, SO THAT YOU MAY GAZE UPON THE FACE OF YOUR--
--EXECUTIONER!
W-WHITMAN!!
YES, WHITMAN, YOU SNIVELLING, PATHETIC EXCUSE FOR A PHYSICIST!
DO YOU HAVE ANY LAST WORDS??
N-NO... PLEASE...
FREEZE, MISTER!
GEEZ! IT'S THE BLACK KNIGHT!
TOLDJA HE WAS A BAD GUY--!
"BAD GUY"?
BLAM
BLAM
DEAR LORD, WHAT'S HAPPENING TO ME?
AWAY, ARAGORN!!

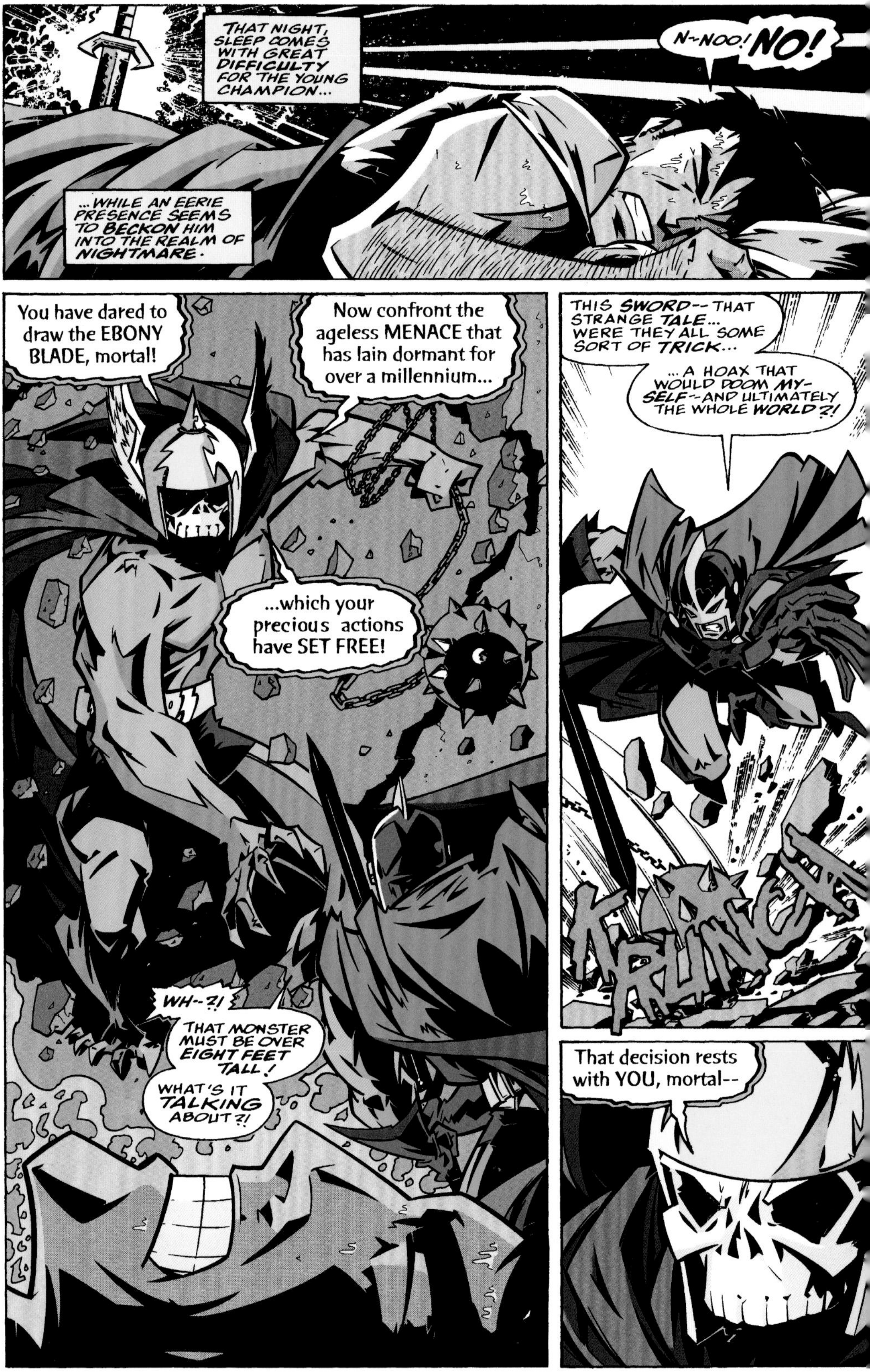
THAT NIGHT, SLEEP COMES WITH GREAT DIFFICULTY FOR THE YOUNG CHAMPION...
N--NOO! NO!
...WHILE AN EERIE PRESENCE SEEMS TO BECKON HIM INTO THE REALM OF NIGHTMARE.
You have dared to draw the EBONY BLADE, mortal!
Now confront the ageless MENACE that has lain dormant for over a millennium...
...which your precious actions have SET FREE!
WH--?!
THAT MONSTER MUST BE OVER EIGHT FEET TALL!
WHAT'S IT TALKING ABOUT?!
THIS SWORD-- THAT STRANGE TALE... WERE THEY ALL SOME SORT OF TRICK...
... A HOAX THAT WOULD DOOM MY-SELF--AND ULTIMATELY THE WHOLE WORLD?!
KRUNCH
That decision rests with YOU, mortal--

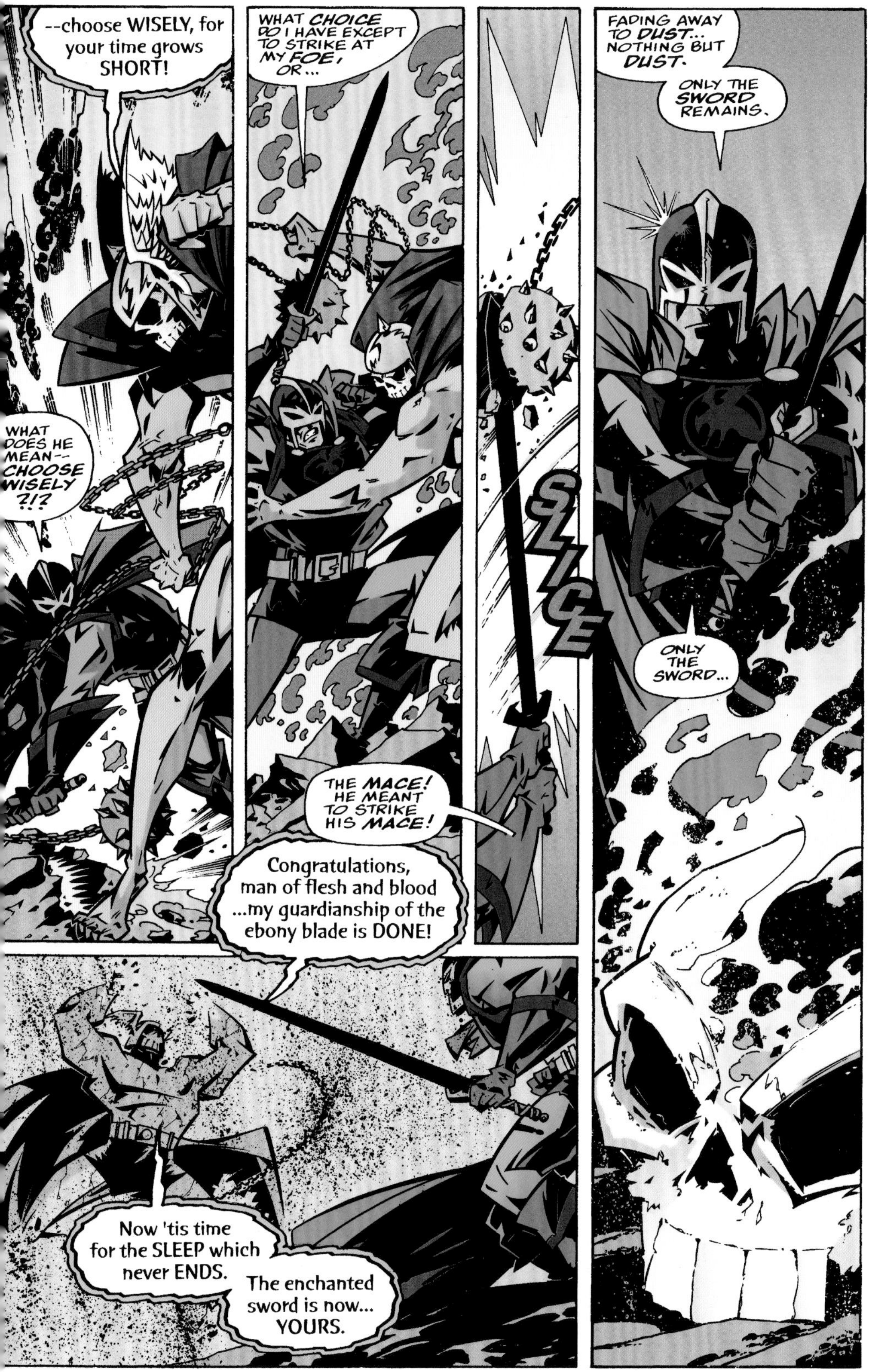

--choose WISELY, for your time grows SHORT!
WHAT DOES HE MEAN-- CHOOSE WISELY ?!?
WHAT CHOICE DO I HAVE EXCEPT TO STRIKE AT MY FOE, OR...
SLICE
THE MACE! HE MEANT TO STRIKE HIS MACE!
FADING AWAY TO DUST... NOTHING BUT DUST.
ONLY THE SWORD REMAINS.
ONLY THE SWORD...
Congratulations, man of flesh and blood ...my guardianship of the ebony blade is DONE!
Now 'tis time for the SLEEP which never ENDS.
The enchanted sword is now... YOURS.

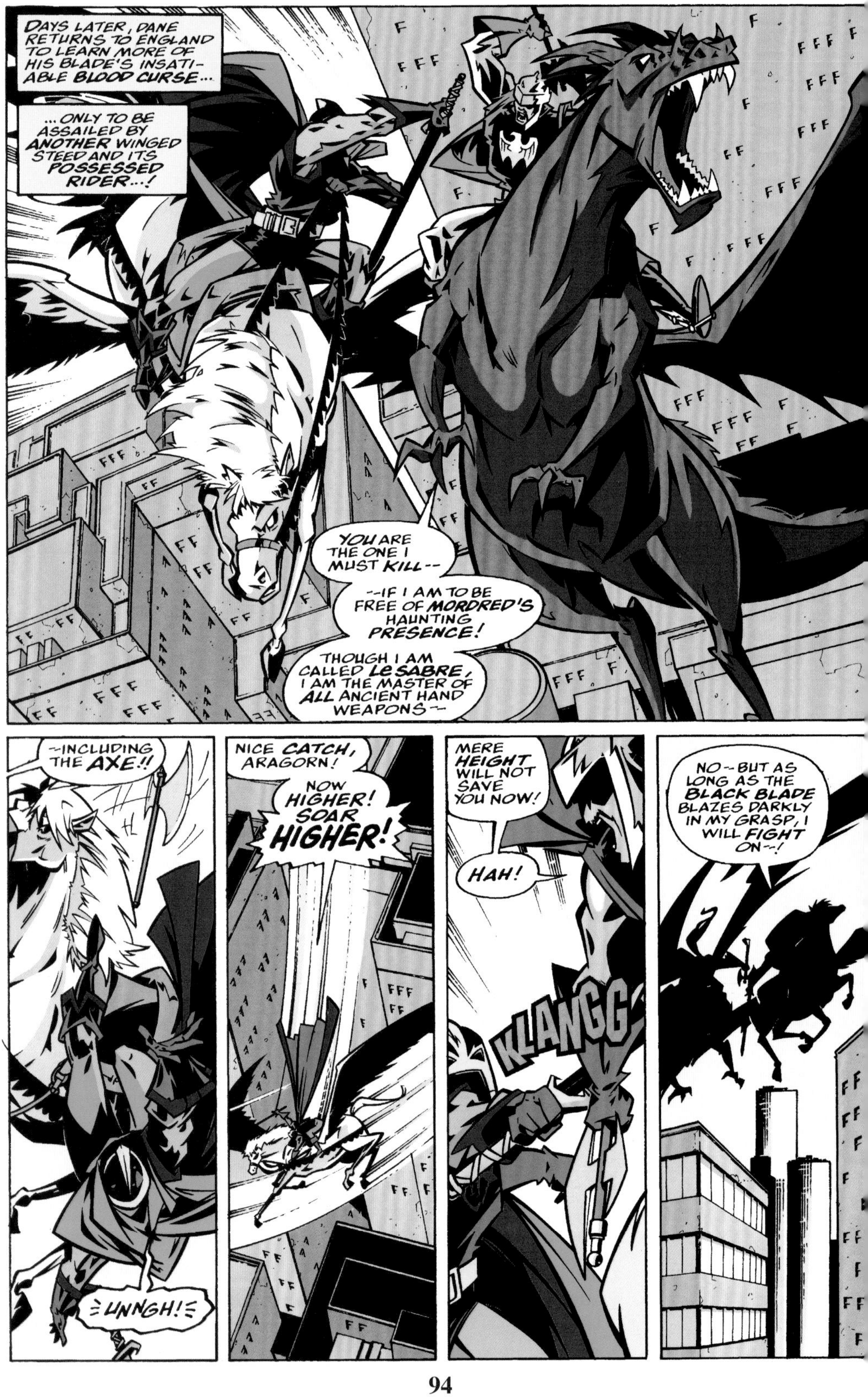
DAYS LATER, DANE RETURNS TO ENGLAND TO LEARN MORE OF HIS BLADE'S INSATIABLE BLOOD CURSE...
...ONLY TO BE ASSAILED BY ANOTHER WINGED STEED AND ITS POSSESSED RIDER...!
YOU ARE THE ONE I MUST KILL--
--IF I AM TO BE FREE OF MORDRED'S HAUNTING PRESENCE!
THOUGH I AM CALLED LE SABRE, I AM THE MASTER OF ALL ANCIENT HAND WEAPONS--
--INCLUDING THE AXE!!
UNNGH!
NICE CATCH, ARAGORN!
NOW HIGHER! SOAR HIGHER!
MERE HEIGHT WILL NOT SAVE YOU NOW!
HAH!
KLANGG
NO--BUT AS LONG AS THE BLACK BLADE BLAZES DARKLY IN MY GRASP, I WILL FIGHT ON--!

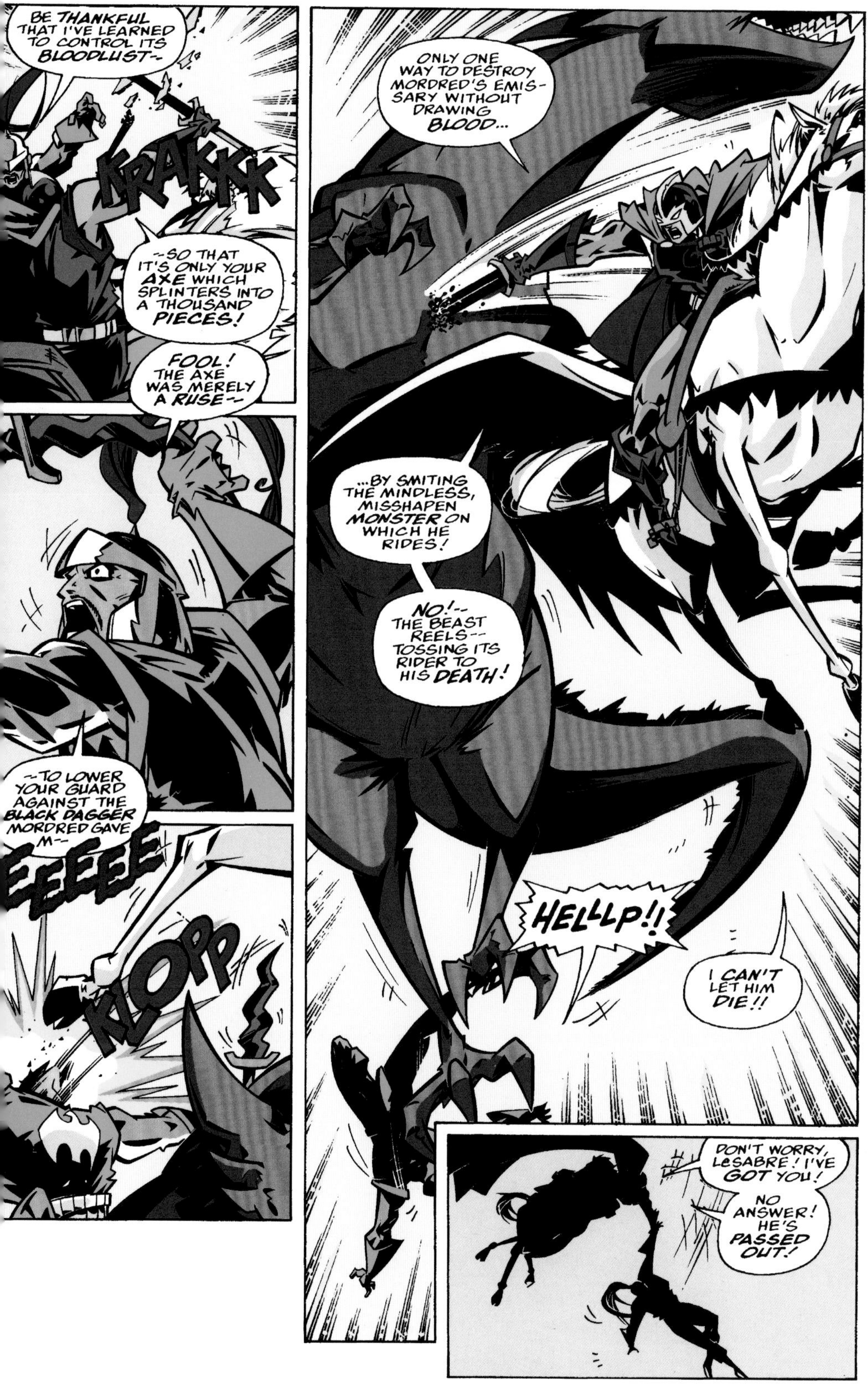
BE THANKFUL THAT I'VE LEARNED TO CONTROL ITS BLOODLUST--
KRAKKK
--SO THAT IT'S ONLY YOUR AXE WHICH SPLINTERS INTO A THOUSAND PIECES!
FOOL! THE AXE WAS MERELY A RUSE--
--TO LOWER YOUR GUARD AGAINST THE BLACK DAGGER MORDRED GAVE M--
EEEEE
KLOPP
ONLY ONE WAY TO DESTROY MORDRED'S EMISSARY WITHOUT DRAWING BLOOD...
...BY SMITING THE MINDLESS, MISSHAPEN MONSTER ON WHICH HE RIDES!
NO!-- THE BEAST REELS-- TOSSING ITS RIDER TO HIS DEATH!
HELLLP!!
I CAN'T LET HIM DIE!!
DON'T WORRY, LeSABRE! I'VE GOT YOU!
NO ANSWER! HE'S PASSED OUT!

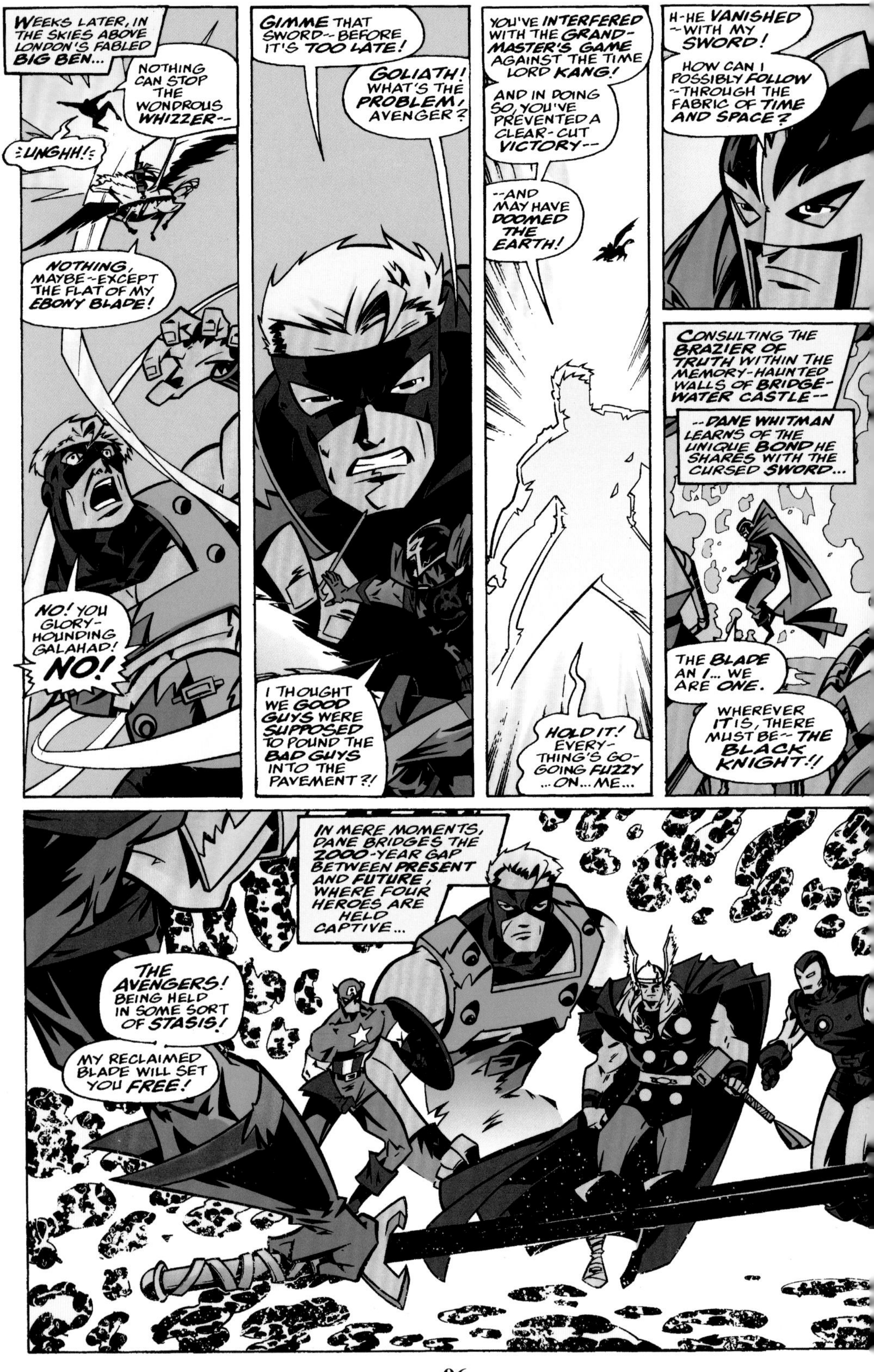
WEEKS LATER, IN THE SKIES ABOVE LONDON'S FABLED BIG BEN...
NOTHING CAN STOP THE WONDROUS WHIZZER--
UNGHH!
NOTHING, MAYBE--EXCEPT THE FLAT OF MY EBONY BLADE!
NO! YOU GLORY-HOUNDING GALAHAD! NO!
GIMME THAT SWORD--BEFORE IT'S TOO LATE!
GOLIATH! WHAT'S THE PROBLEM, AVENGER?
I THOUGHT WE GOOD GUYS WERE SUPPOSED TO POUND THE BAD GUYS INTO THE PAVEMENT?!
YOU'VE INTERFERED WITH THE GRAND-MASTER'S GAME AGAINST THE TIME LORD KANG!
AND IN DOING SO, YOU'VE PREVENTED A CLEAR-CUT VICTORY--
--AND MAY HAVE DOOMED THE EARTH!
HOLD IT! EVERY-THING'S GO-GOING FUZZY ...ON... ME...
H-HE VANISHED --WITH MY SWORD!
HOW CAN I POSSIBLY FOLLOW --THROUGH THE FABRIC OF TIME AND SPACE?
CONSULTING THE BRAZIER OF TRUTH WITHIN THE MEMORY-HAUNTED WALLS OF BRIDGE-WATER CASTLE--
--DANE WHITMAN LEARNS OF THE UNIQUE BOND HE SHARES WITH THE CURSED SWORD...
THE BLADE AN I... WE ARE ONE.
WHEREVER IT IS, THERE MUST BE--THE BLACK KNIGHT!!
IN MERE MOMENTS, DANE BRIDGES THE 2000-YEAR GAP BETWEEN PRESENT AND FUTURE, WHERE FOUR HEROES ARE HELD CAPTIVE...
THE AVENGERS! BEING HELD IN SOME SORT OF STASIS!
MY RECLAIMED BLADE WILL SET YOU FREE!

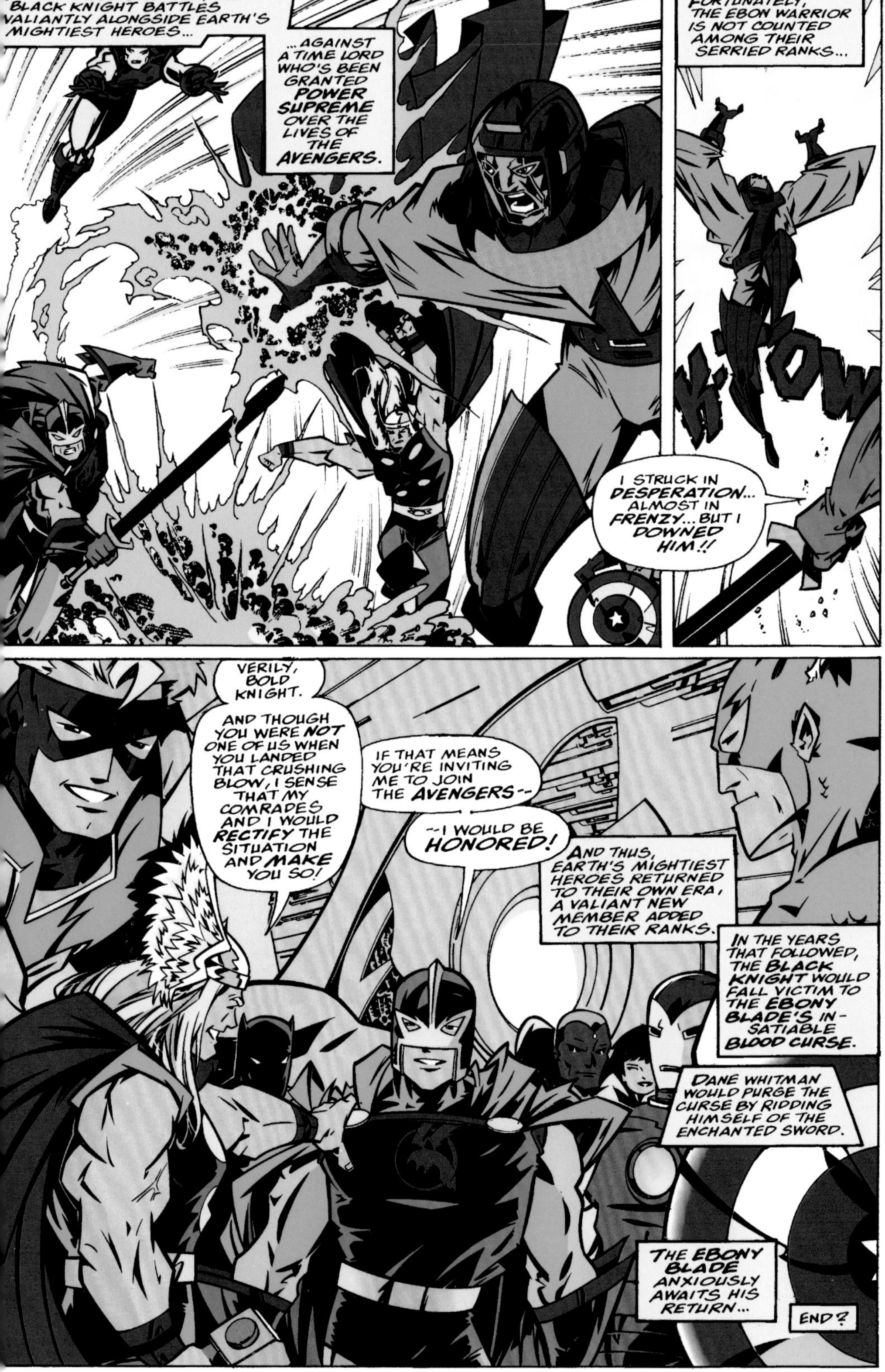

IN THE ENSUING MELEE, THE BLACK KNIGHT BATTLES VALIANTLY ALONGSIDE EARTH'S MIGHTIEST HEROES...
...AGAINST A TIME LORD WHO'S BEEN GRANTED POWER SUPREME OVER THE LIVES OF THE AVENGERS.
FORTUNATELY, THE EBON WARRIOR IS NOT COUNTED AMONG THEIR SERRIED RANKS...
K-POW
I STRUCK IN DESPERATION... ALMOST IN FRENZY... BUT I DOWNED HIM!!
VERILY, BOLD KNIGHT.
AND THOUGH YOU WERE NOT ONE OF US WHEN YOU LANDED THAT CRUSHING BLOW, I SENSE THAT MY COMRADES AND I WOULD RECTIFY THE SITUATION AND MAKE YOU SO!
IF THAT MEANS YOU'RE INVITING ME TO JOIN THE AVENGERS--
--I WOULD BE HONORED!
AND THUS, EARTH'S MIGHTIEST HEROES RETURNED TO THEIR OWN ERA, A VALIANT NEW MEMBER ADDED TO THEIR RANKS.
IN THE YEARS THAT FOLLOWED, THE BLACK KNIGHT WOULD FALL VICTIM TO THE EBONY BLADE'S IN-SATIABLE BLOOD CURSE.
DANE WHITMAN WOULD PURGE THE CURSE BY RIDDING HIMSELF OF THE ENCHANTED SWORD.
THE EBONY BLADE ANXIOUSLY AWAITS HIS RETURN...
END?

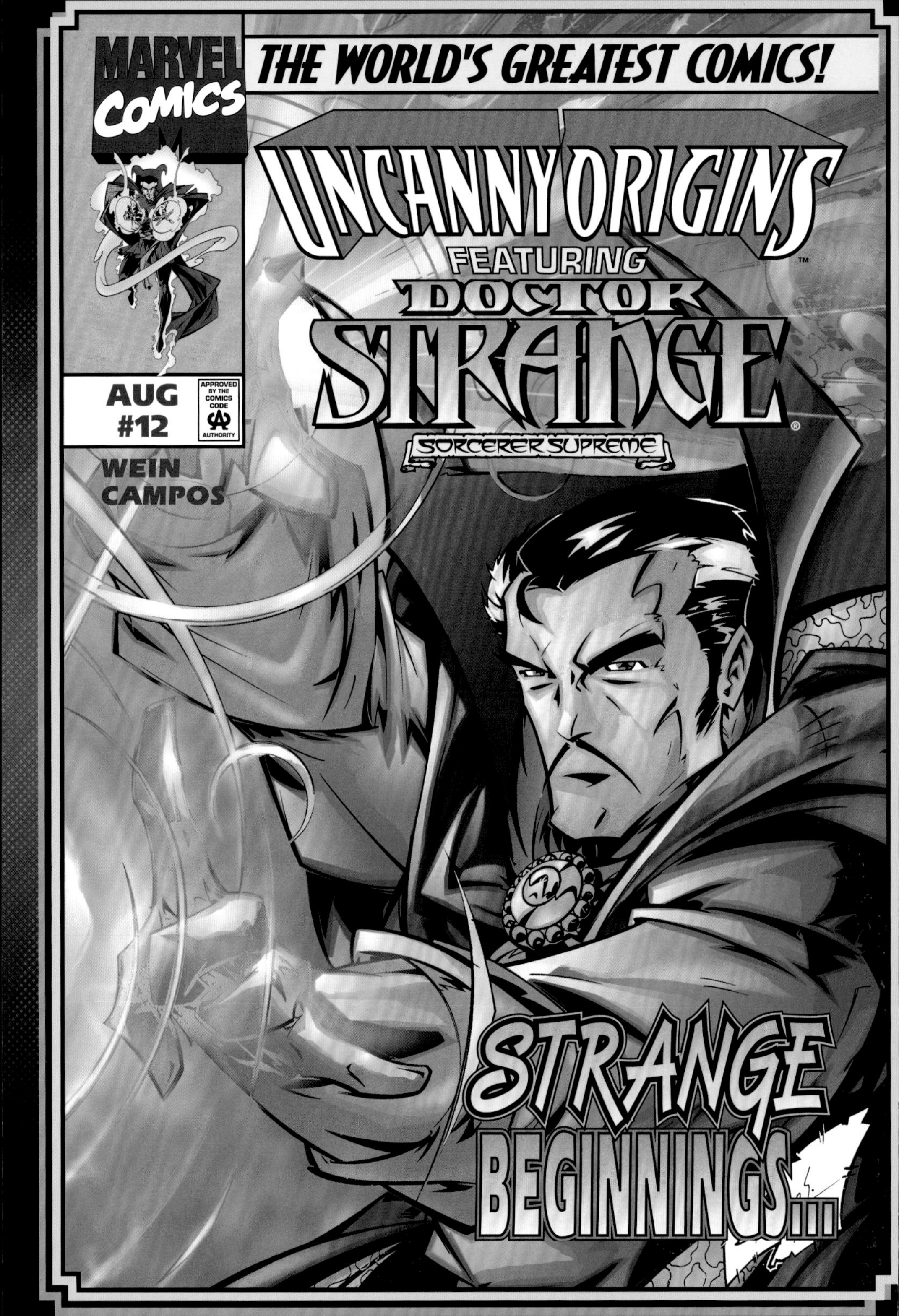
MARVEL COMICS
THE WORLD'S GREATEST COMICS!
UNCANNY ORIGINS™
FEATURING
DOCTOR STRANGE®
SORCERER SUPREME
AUG
#12
APPROVED BY THE COMICS CODE AUTHORITY
WEIN
CAMPOS
STRANGE BEGINNINGS...!

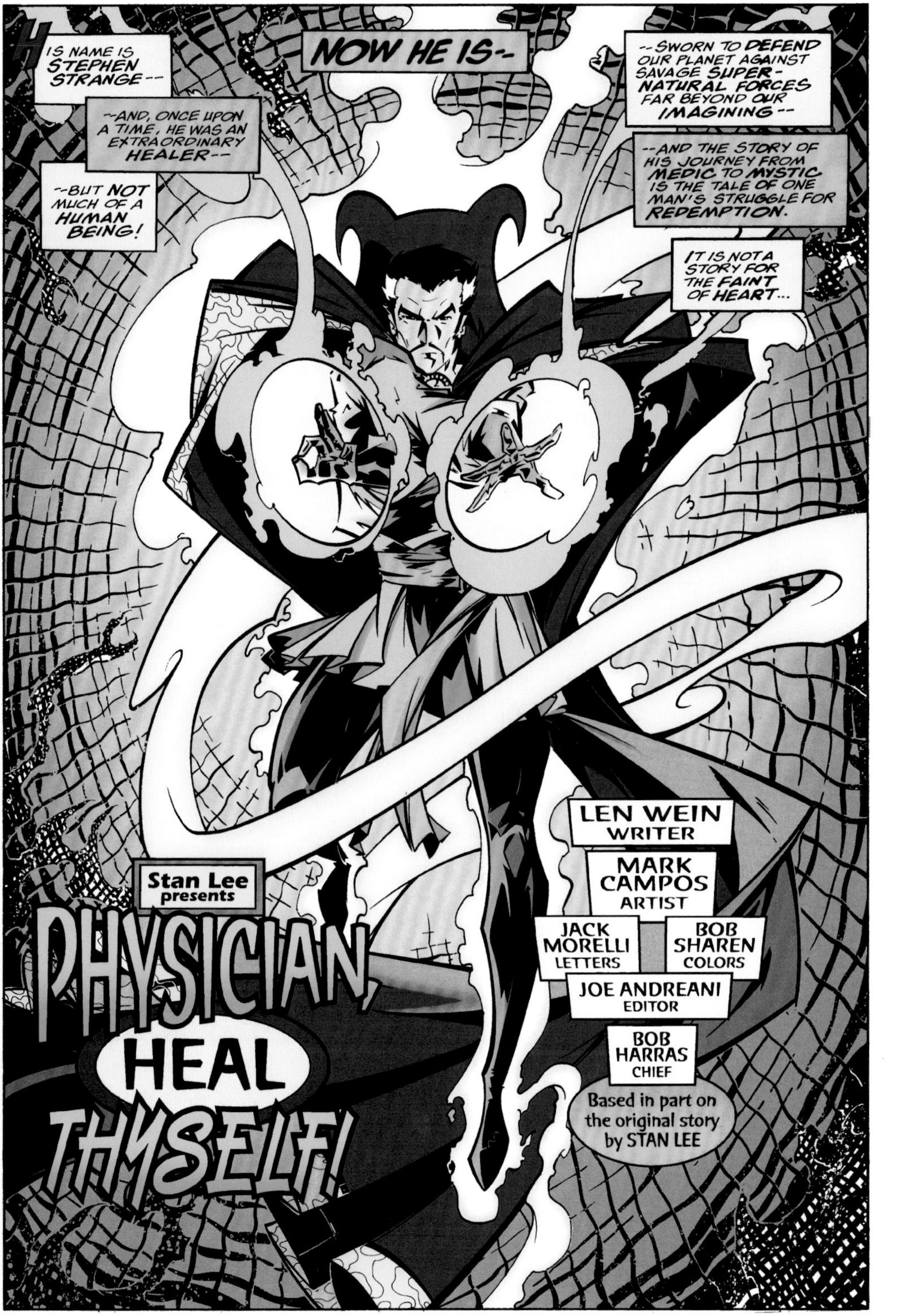
HIS NAME IS STEPHEN STRANGE--
--AND, ONCE UPON A TIME, HE WAS AN EXTRAORDINARY HEALER--
--BUT NOT MUCH OF A HUMAN BEING!
NOW HE IS--
--SWORN TO DEFEND OUR PLANET AGAINST SAVAGE SUPER-NATURAL FORCES FAR BEYOND OUR IMAGINING--
--AND THE STORY OF HIS JOURNEY FROM MEDIC TO MYSTIC IS THE TALE OF ONE MAN'S STRUGGLE FOR REDEMPTION.
IT IS NOT A STORY FOR THE FAINT OF HEART...
Stan Lee presents
PHYSICIAN, HEAL THYSELF!
LEN WEIN WRITER
MARK CAMPOS ARTIST
JACK MORELLI LETTERS
BOB SHAREN COLORS
JOE ANDREANI EDITOR
BOB HARRAS CHIEF
Based in part on the original story by STAN LEE

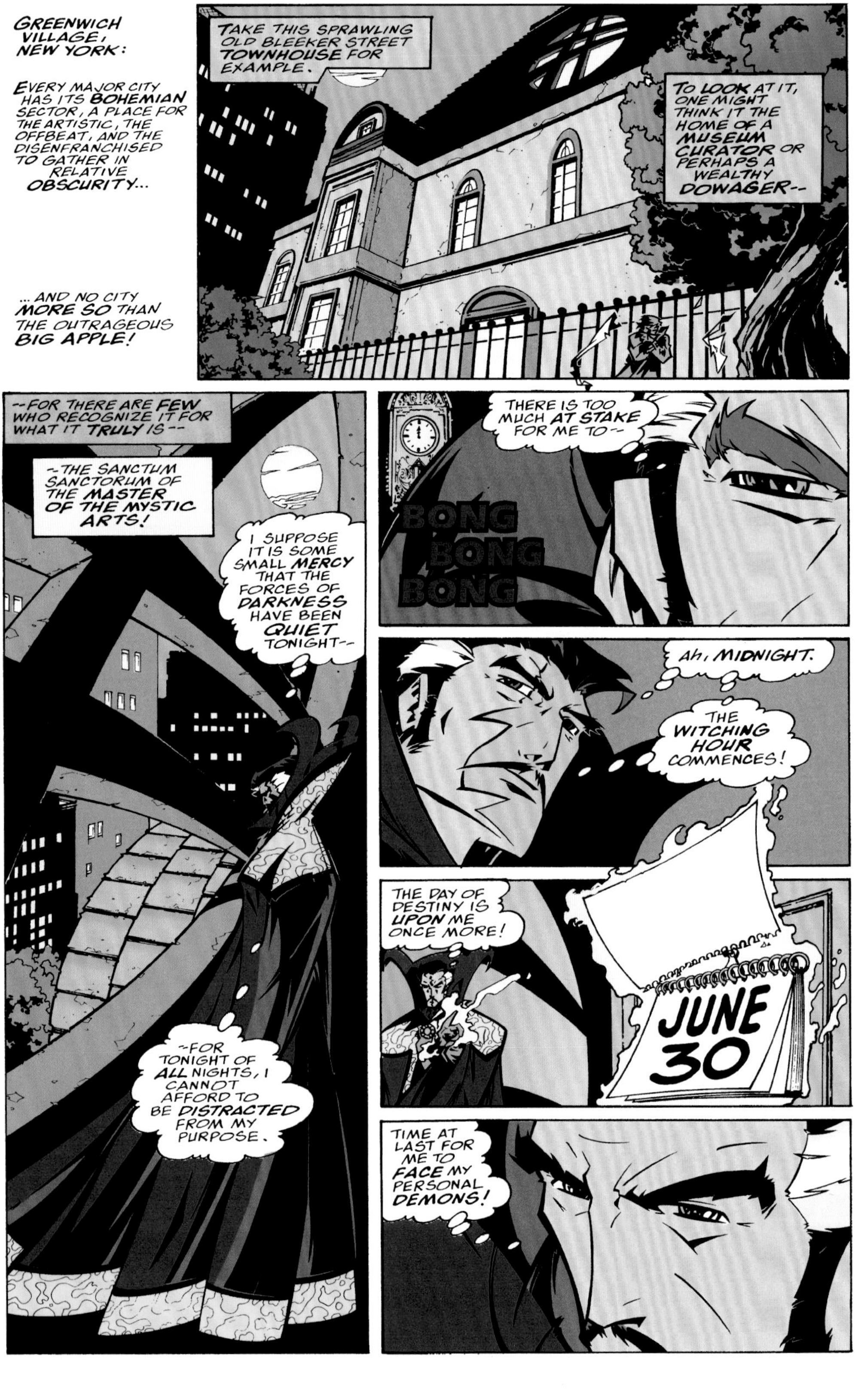

GREENWICH VILLAGE, NEW YORK:
EVERY MAJOR CITY HAS ITS BOHEMIAN SECTOR, A PLACE FOR THE ARTISTIC, THE OFFBEAT, AND THE DISENFRANCHISED TO GATHER IN RELATIVE OBSCURITY...
...AND NO CITY MORE SO THAN THE OUTRAGEOUS BIG APPLE!
TAKE THIS SPRAWLING OLD BLEEKER STREET TOWNHOUSE FOR EXAMPLE.
TO LOOK AT IT, ONE MIGHT THINK IT THE HOME OF A MUSEUM CURATOR OR PERHAPS A WEALTHY DOWAGER--
--FOR THERE ARE FEW WHO RECOGNIZE IT FOR WHAT IT TRULY IS--
--THE SANCTUM SANCTORUM OF THE MASTER OF THE MYSTIC ARTS!
I SUPPOSE IT IS SOME SMALL MERCY THAT THE FORCES OF DARKNESS HAVE BEEN QUIET TONIGHT--
--FOR TONIGHT OF ALL NIGHTS, I CANNOT AFFORD TO BE DISTRACTED FROM MY PURPOSE.
THERE IS TOO MUCH AT STAKE FOR ME TO--
BONG
BONG
BONG
Ah, MIDNIGHT.
THE WITCHING HOUR COMMENCES!
THE DAY OF DESTINY IS UPON ME ONCE MORE!
JUNE 30
TIME AT LAST FOR ME TO FACE MY PERSONAL DEMONS!

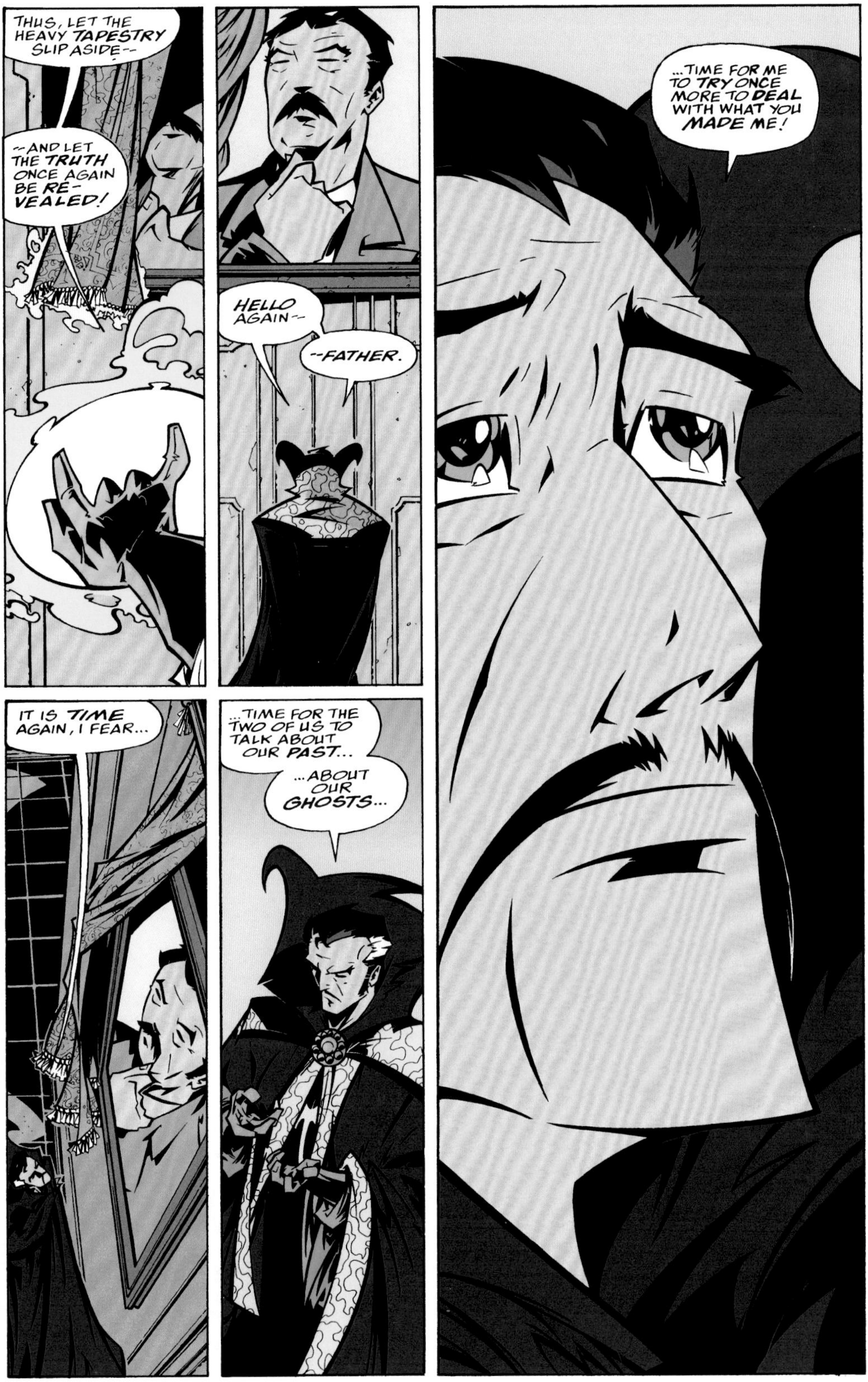
THUS, LET THE HEAVY TAPESTRY SLIP ASIDE--
--AND LET THE TRUTH ONCE AGAIN BE RE-VEALED!
HELLO AGAIN--
--FATHER.
IT IS TIME AGAIN, I FEAR...
...TIME FOR THE TWO OF US TO TALK ABOUT OUR PAST...
...ABOUT OUR GHOSTS...
...TIME FOR ME TO TRY ONCE MORE TO DEAL WITH WHAT YOU MADE ME!

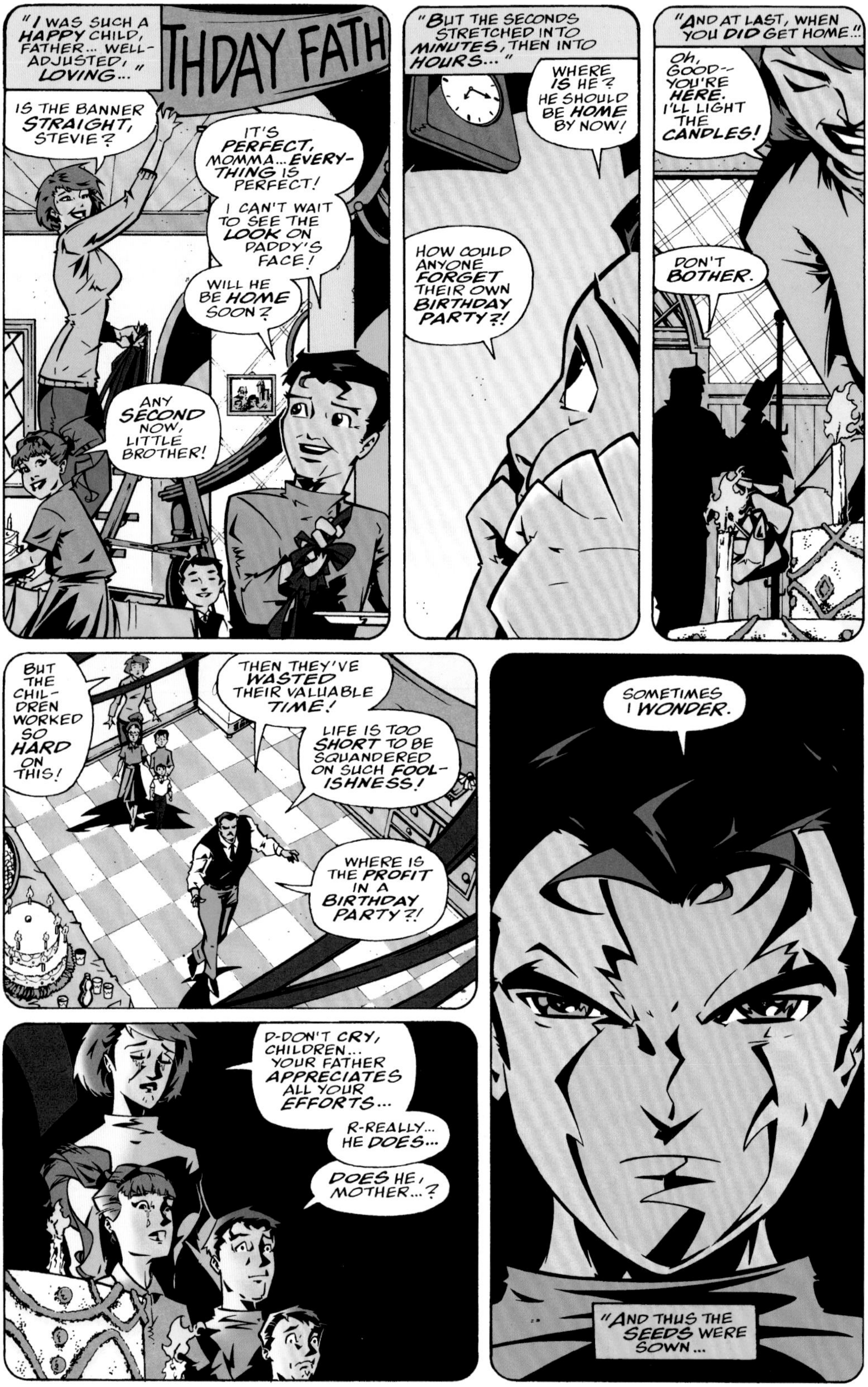

"I WAS SUCH A HAPPY CHILD, FATHER... WELL-ADJUSTED, LOVING..."
THDAY FATH
IS THE BANNER STRAIGHT, STEVIE?
IT'S PERFECT, MOMMA... EVERYTHING IS PERFECT!
I CAN'T WAIT TO SEE THE LOOK ON PADDY'S FACE!
WILL HE BE HOME SOON?
ANY SECOND NOW, LITTLE BROTHER!
"BUT THE SECONDS STRETCHED INTO MINUTES, THEN INTO HOURS..."
WHERE IS HE? HE SHOULD BE HOME BY NOW!
HOW COULD ANYONE FORGET THEIR OWN BIRTHDAY PARTY?!
"AND AT LAST, WHEN YOU DID GET HOME..."
Oh, GOOD-- YOU'RE HERE. I'LL LIGHT THE CANDLES!
DON'T BOTHER.
BUT THE CHILDREN WORKED SO HARD ON THIS!
THEN THEY'VE WASTED THEIR VALUABLE TIME!
LIFE IS TOO SHORT TO BE SQUANDERED ON SUCH FOOLISHNESS!
WHERE IS THE PROFIT IN A BIRTHDAY PARTY?!
D-DON'T CRY, CHILDREN... YOUR FATHER APPRECIATES ALL YOUR EFFORTS...
R-REALLY... HE DOES...
DOES HE, MOTHER...?
SOMETIMES I WONDER.
"AND THUS THE SEEDS WERE SOWN...

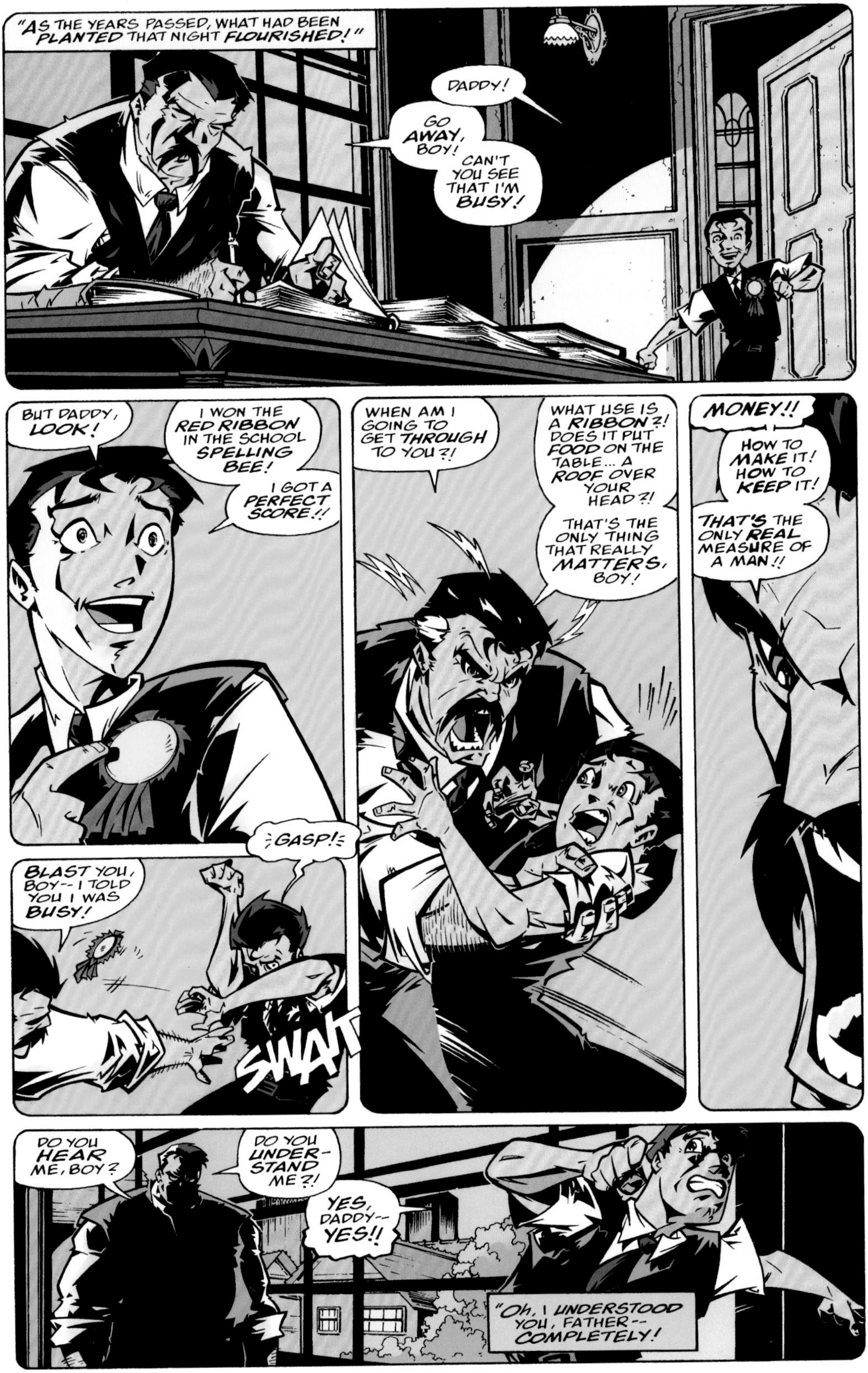
"AS THE YEARS PASSED, WHAT HAD BEEN PLANTED THAT NIGHT FLOURISHED!"
DADDY!
GO AWAY, BOY! CAN'T YOU SEE THAT I'M BUSY!
BUT DADDY, LOOK!
I WON THE RED RIBBON IN THE SCHOOL SPELLING BEE!
I GOT A PERFECT SCORE!!
BLAST YOU, BOY-- I TOLD YOU I WAS BUSY!
;GASP!;
SWAT
WHEN AM I GOING TO GET THROUGH TO YOU?!
WHAT USE IS A RIBBON?! DOES IT PUT FOOD ON THE TABLE... A ROOF OVER YOUR HEAD?!
THAT'S THE ONLY THING THAT REALLY MATTERS, BOY!
MONEY!!
HOW TO MAKE IT! HOW TO KEEP IT!
THAT'S THE ONLY REAL MEASURE OF A MAN!!
DO YOU HEAR ME, BOY?
DO YOU UNDER-STAND ME?!
YES, DADDY-- YES!!
"Oh, I UNDERSTOOD YOU, FATHER-- COMPLETELY!"

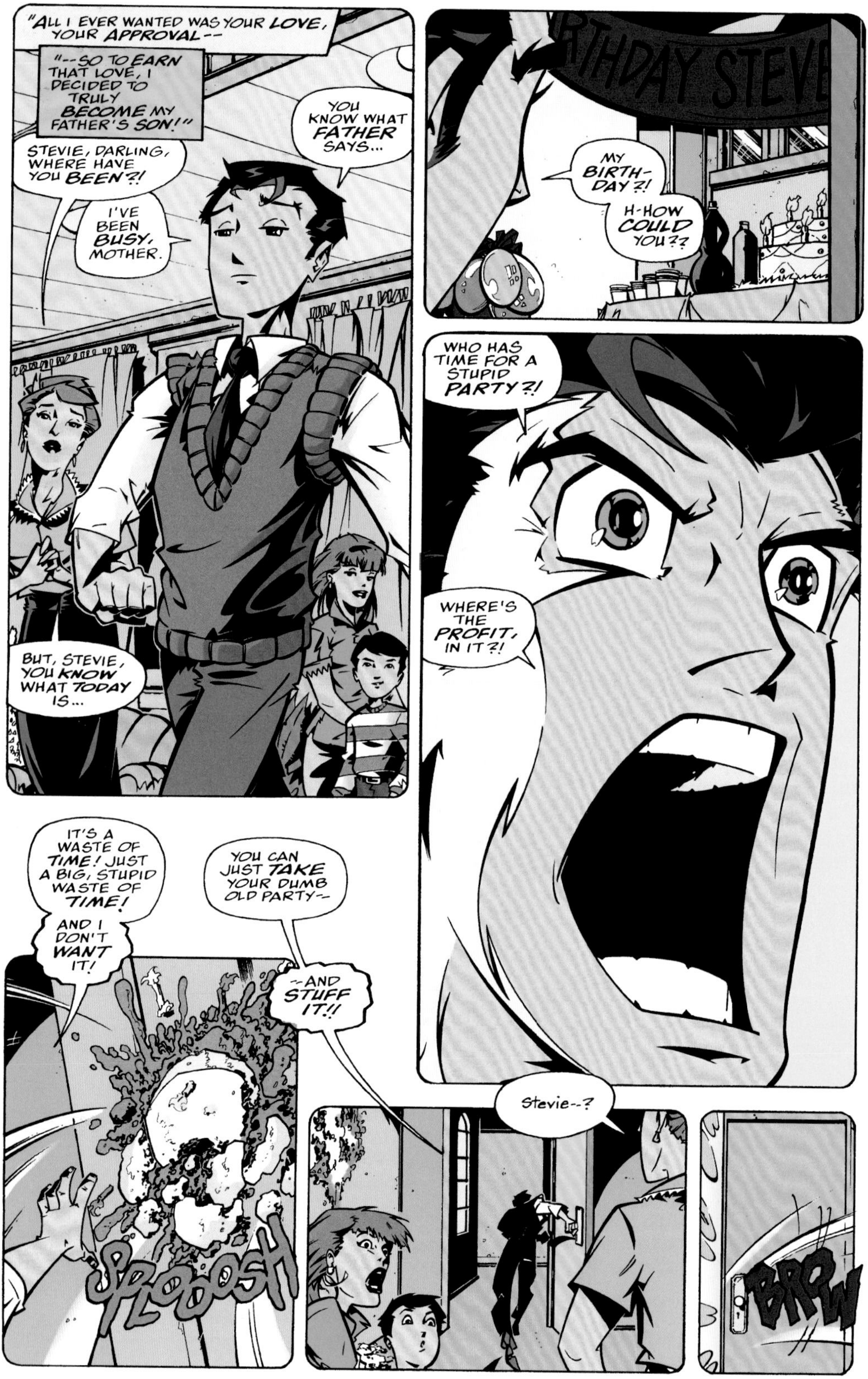
"ALL I EVER WANTED WAS YOUR LOVE, YOUR APPROVAL--
"--SO TO EARN THAT LOVE, I DECIDED TO TRULY BECOME MY FATHER'S SON!"
STEVIE, DARLING, WHERE HAVE YOU BEEN?!
I'VE BEEN BUSY, MOTHER.
YOU KNOW WHAT FATHER SAYS...
BUT, STEVIE, YOU KNOW WHAT TODAY IS...
RTHDAY STEVE
MY BIRTH-DAY?!
H-HOW COULD YOU??
WHO HAS TIME FOR A STUPID PARTY?!
WHERE'S THE PROFIT, IN IT?!
IT'S A WASTE OF TIME! JUST A BIG, STUPID WASTE OF TIME!
AND I DON'T WANT IT!
YOU CAN JUST TAKE YOUR DUMB OLD PARTY--
--AND STUFF IT!!
SPLOOSH
Stevie--?
BRAM

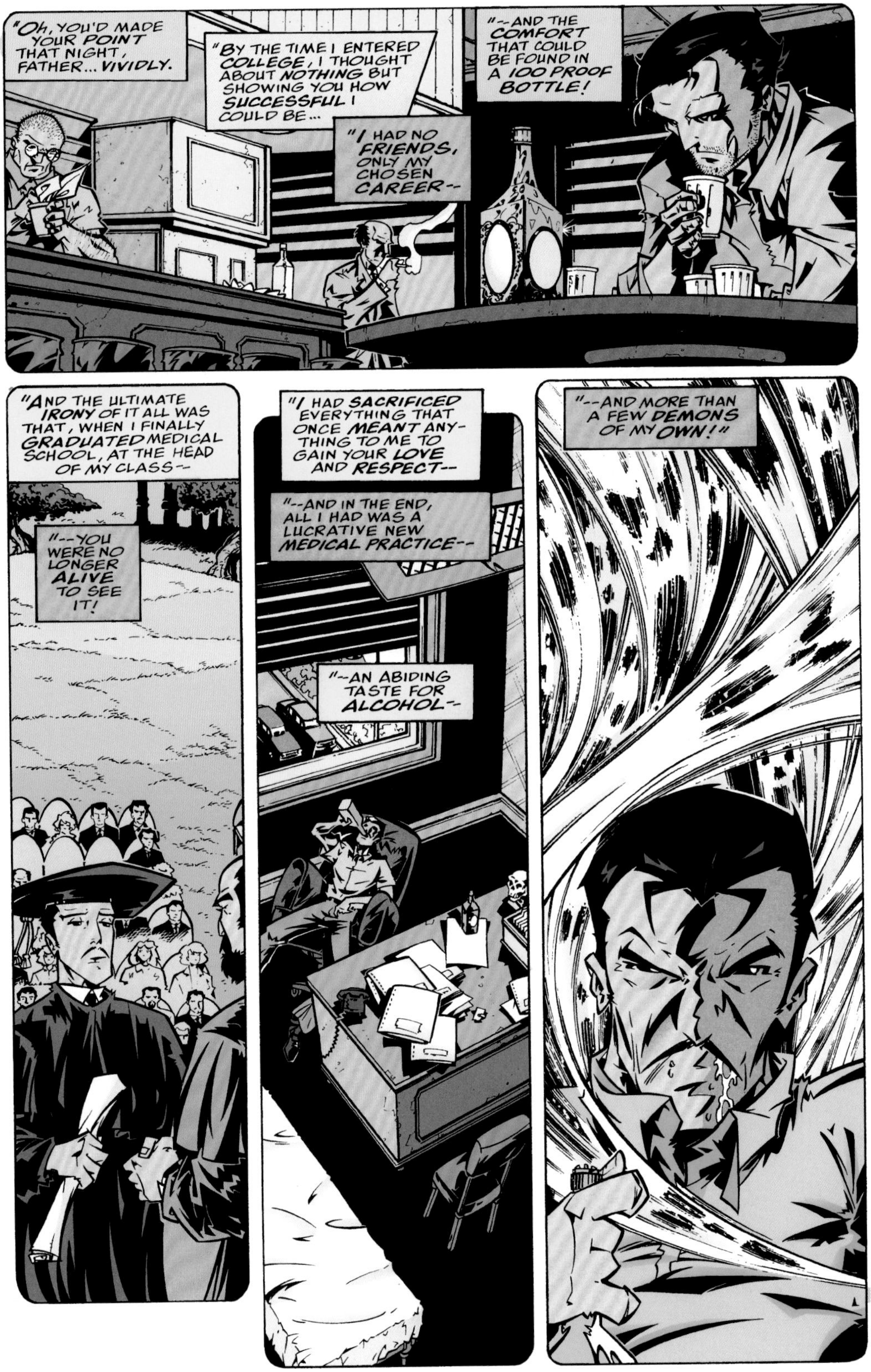
"OH, YOU'D MADE YOUR POINT THAT NIGHT, FATHER... VIVIDLY.
"BY THE TIME I ENTERED COLLEGE, I THOUGHT ABOUT NOTHING BUT SHOWING YOU HOW SUCCESSFUL I COULD BE...
"I HAD NO FRIENDS, ONLY MY CHOSEN CAREER--
"--AND THE COMFORT THAT COULD BE FOUND IN A 100 PROOF BOTTLE!
"AND THE ULTIMATE IRONY OF IT ALL WAS THAT, WHEN I FINALLY GRADUATED MEDICAL SCHOOL, AT THE HEAD OF MY CLASS--
"--YOU WERE NO LONGER ALIVE TO SEE IT!
"I HAD SACRIFICED EVERYTHING THAT ONCE MEANT ANYTHING TO ME TO GAIN YOUR LOVE AND RESPECT--
"--AND IN THE END, ALL I HAD WAS A LUCRATIVE NEW MEDICAL PRACTICE--
"--AN ABIDING TASTE FOR ALCOHOL--
"--AND MORE THAN A FEW DEMONS OF MY OWN!"

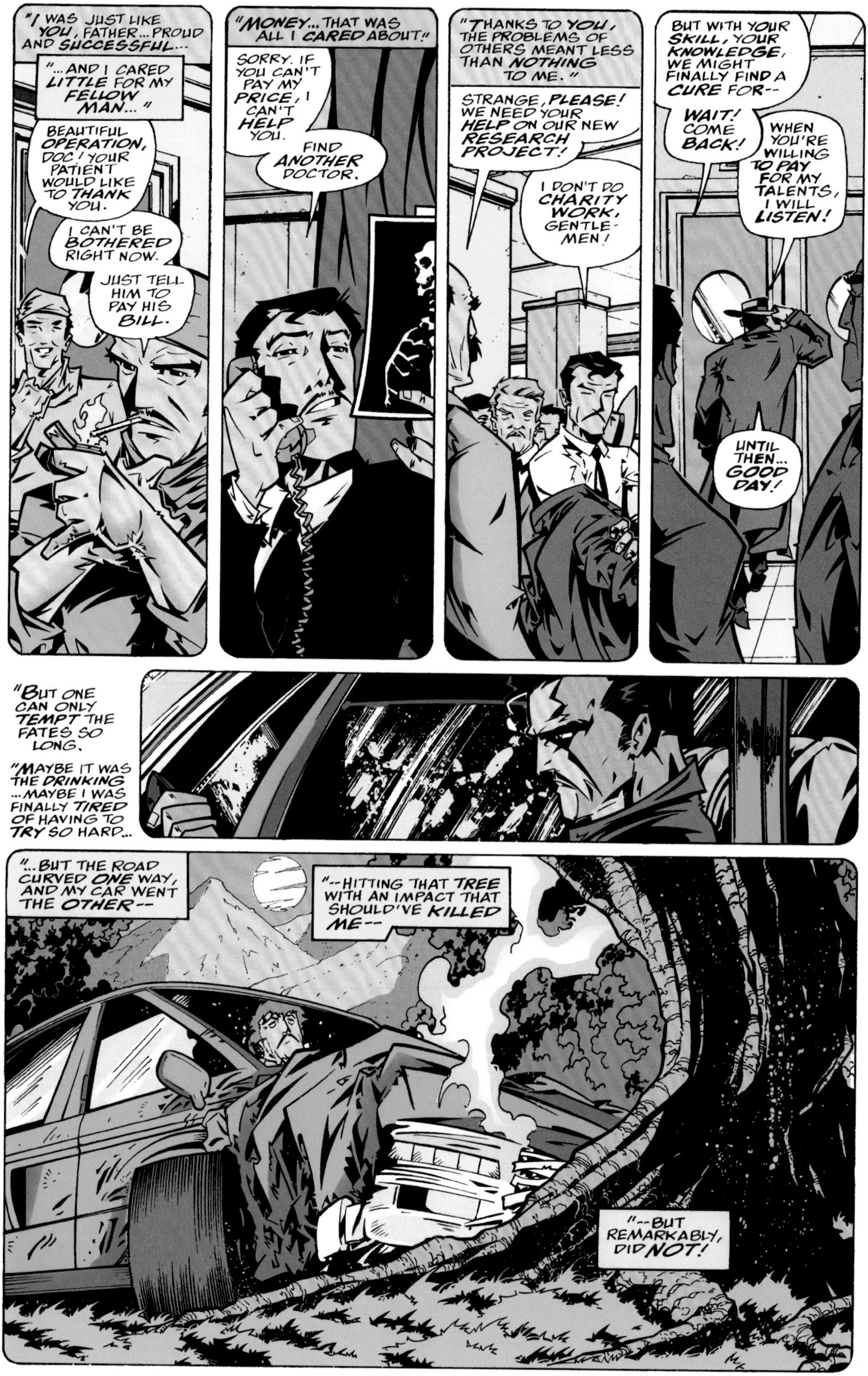
"I WAS JUST LIKE YOU, FATHER... PROUD AND SUCCESSFUL...
"...AND I CARED LITTLE FOR MY FELLOW MAN..."
BEAUTIFUL OPERATION, DOC! YOUR PATIENT WOULD LIKE TO THANK YOU.
I CAN'T BE BOTHERED RIGHT NOW.
JUST TELL HIM TO PAY HIS BILL.
"MONEY... THAT WAS ALL I CARED ABOUT!"
SORRY. IF YOU CAN'T PAY MY PRICE, I CAN'T HELP YOU.
FIND ANOTHER DOCTOR.
"THANKS TO YOU, THE PROBLEMS OF OTHERS MEANT LESS THAN NOTHING TO ME."
STRANGE, PLEASE! WE NEED YOUR HELP ON OUR NEW RESEARCH PROJECT!
I DON'T DO CHARITY WORK, GENTLEMEN!
BUT WITH YOUR SKILL, YOUR KNOWLEDGE, WE MIGHT FINALLY FIND A CURE FOR--
WAIT! COME BACK!
WHEN YOU'RE WILLING TO PAY FOR MY TALENTS, I WILL LISTEN!
UNTIL THEN... GOOD DAY!
"BUT ONE CAN ONLY TEMPT THE FATES SO LONG.
"MAYBE IT WAS THE DRINKING ...MAYBE I WAS FINALLY TIRED OF HAVING TO TRY SO HARD...
"...BUT THE ROAD CURVED ONE WAY, AND MY CAR WENT THE OTHER--
"--HITTING THAT TREE WITH AN IMPACT THAT SHOULD'VE KILLED ME--
"--BUT REMARKABLY, DID NOT!

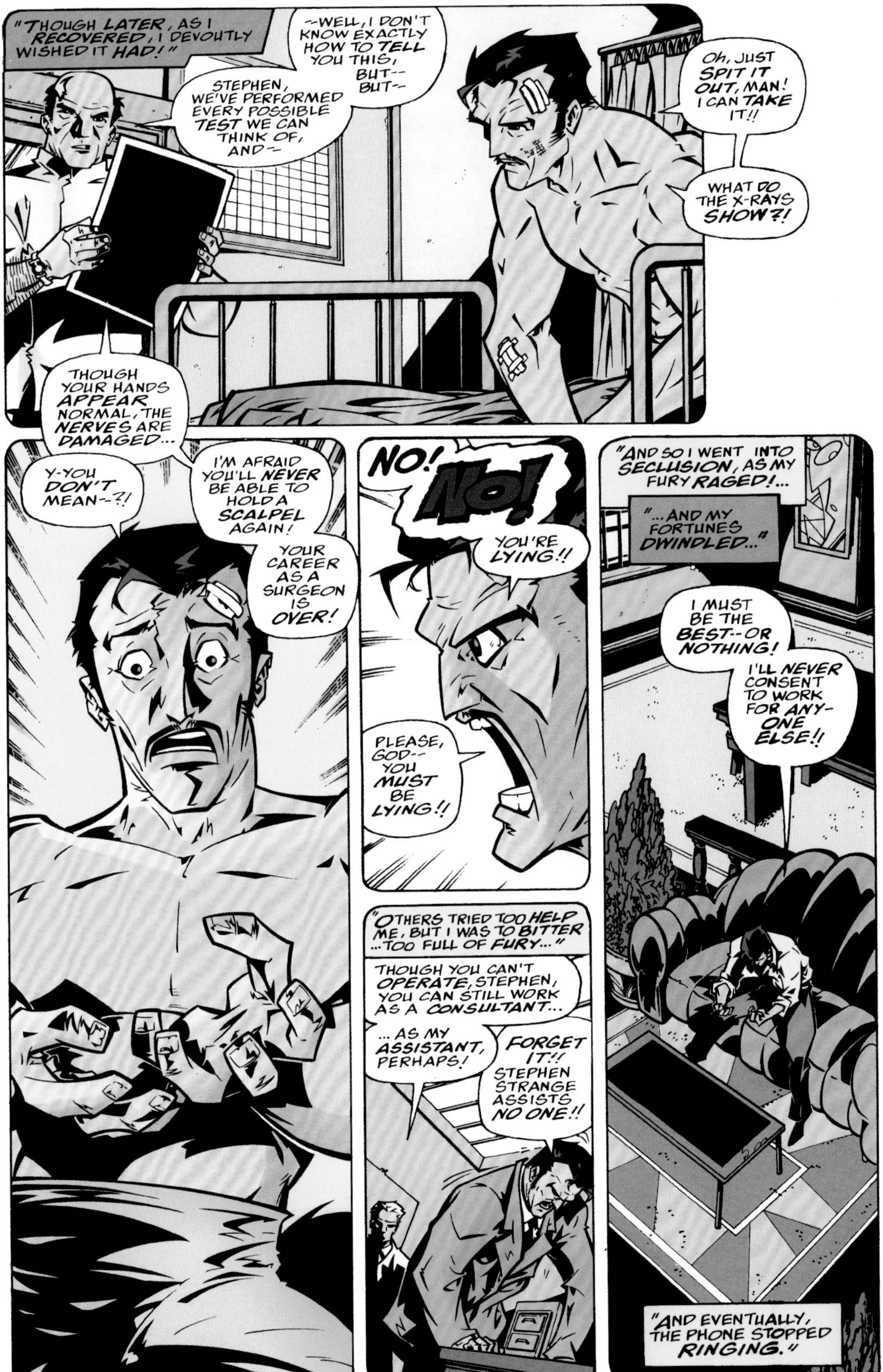
"THOUGH LATER, AS I RECOVERED, I DEVOUTLY WISHED IT HAD!"
STEPHEN, WE'VE PERFORMED EVERY POSSIBLE TEST WE CAN THINK OF, AND--
--WELL, I DON'T KNOW EXACTLY HOW TO TELL YOU THIS, BUT-- BUT--
Oh, JUST SPIT IT OUT, MAN! I CAN TAKE IT!!
WHAT DO THE X-RAYS SHOW?!
THOUGH YOUR HANDS APPEAR NORMAL, THE NERVES ARE DAMAGED...
Y-YOU DON'T MEAN--?!
I'M AFRAID YOU'LL NEVER BE ABLE TO HOLD A SCALPEL AGAIN!
YOUR CAREER AS A SURGEON IS OVER!
NO!
NO!
YOU'RE LYING!!
PLEASE, GOD-- YOU MUST BE LYING!!
"OTHERS TRIED TOO HELP ME, BUT I WAS TO BITTER ...TOO FULL OF FURY..."
THOUGH YOU CAN'T OPERATE, STEPHEN, YOU CAN STILL WORK AS A CONSULTANT...
... AS MY ASSISTANT, PERHAPS!
FORGET IT!! STEPHEN STRANGE ASSISTS NO ONE!!
"AND SO I WENT INTO SECLUSION, AS MY FURY RAGED!...
"...AND MY FORTUNES DWINDLED..."
I MUST BE THE BEST--OR NOTHING!
I'LL NEVER CONSENT TO WORK FOR ANY-ONE ELSE!!
"AND EVENTUALLY, THE PHONE STOPPED RINGING."

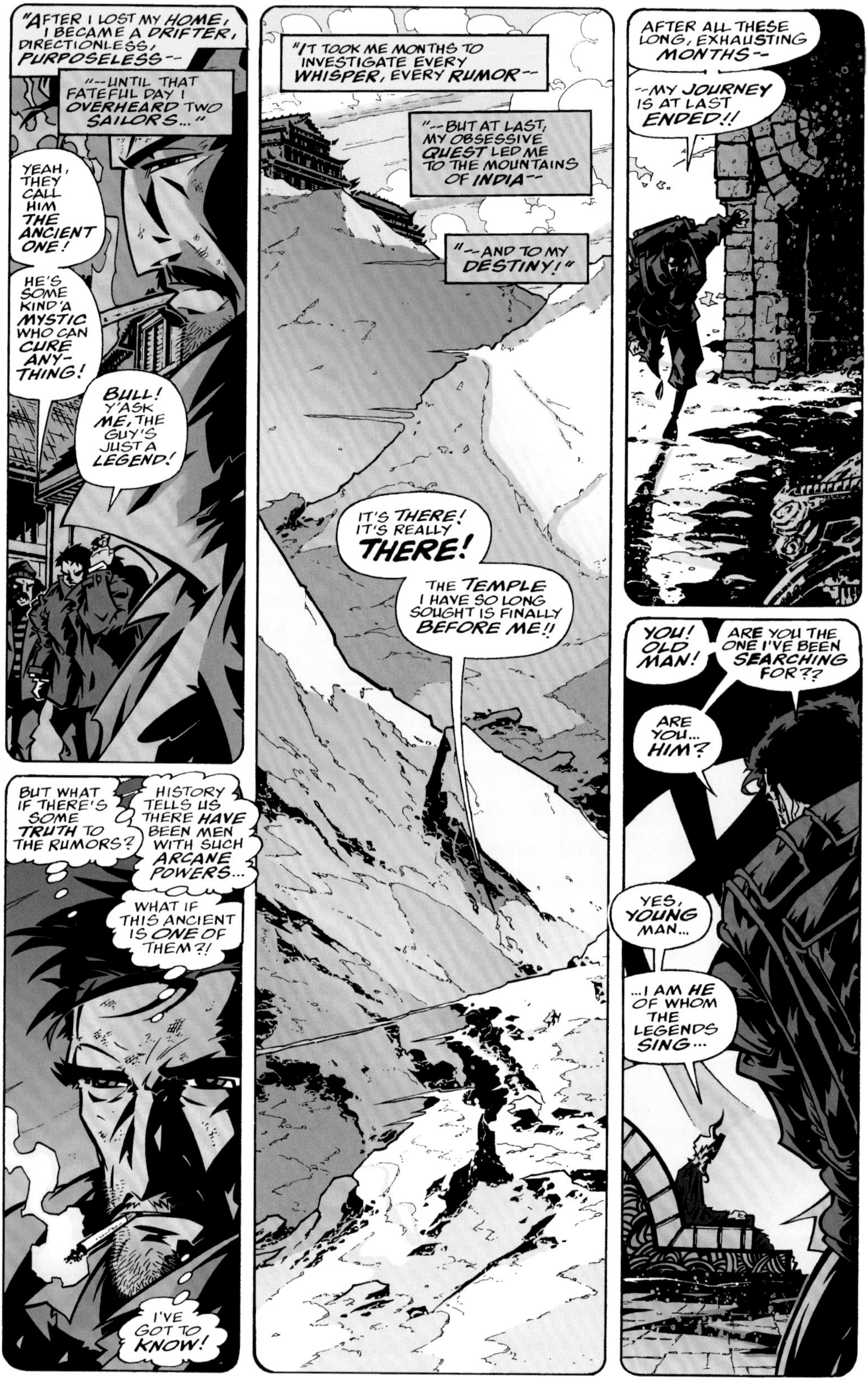
"AFTER I LOST MY HOME, I BECAME A DRIFTER, DIRECTIONLESS, PURPOSELESS--
"--UNTIL THAT FATEFUL DAY I OVERHEARD TWO SAILORS..."
YEAH, THEY CALL HIM THE ANCIENT ONE!
HE'S SOME KIND'A MYSTIC WHO CAN CURE ANY-THING!
BULL! Y'ASK ME, THE GUY'S JUST A LEGEND!
BUT WHAT IF THERE'S SOME TRUTH TO THE RUMORS?
HISTORY TELLS US THERE HAVE BEEN MEN WITH SUCH ARCANE POWERS...
WHAT IF THIS ANCIENT IS ONE OF THEM?!
I'VE GOT TO KNOW!
"IT TOOK ME MONTHS TO INVESTIGATE EVERY WHISPER, EVERY RUMOR--
"--BUT AT LAST, MY OBSESSIVE QUEST LED ME TO THE MOUNTAINS OF INDIA--
"--AND TO MY DESTINY!"
IT'S THERE! IT'S REALLY THERE!
THE TEMPLE I HAVE SO LONG SOUGHT IS FINALLY BEFORE ME!!
AFTER ALL THESE LONG, EXHAUSTING MONTHS--
--MY JOURNEY IS AT LAST ENDED!!
YOU! OLD MAN!
ARE YOU THE ONE I'VE BEEN SEARCHING FOR??
ARE YOU... HIM?
YES, YOUNG MAN...
...I AM HE OF WHOM THE LEGENDS SING...

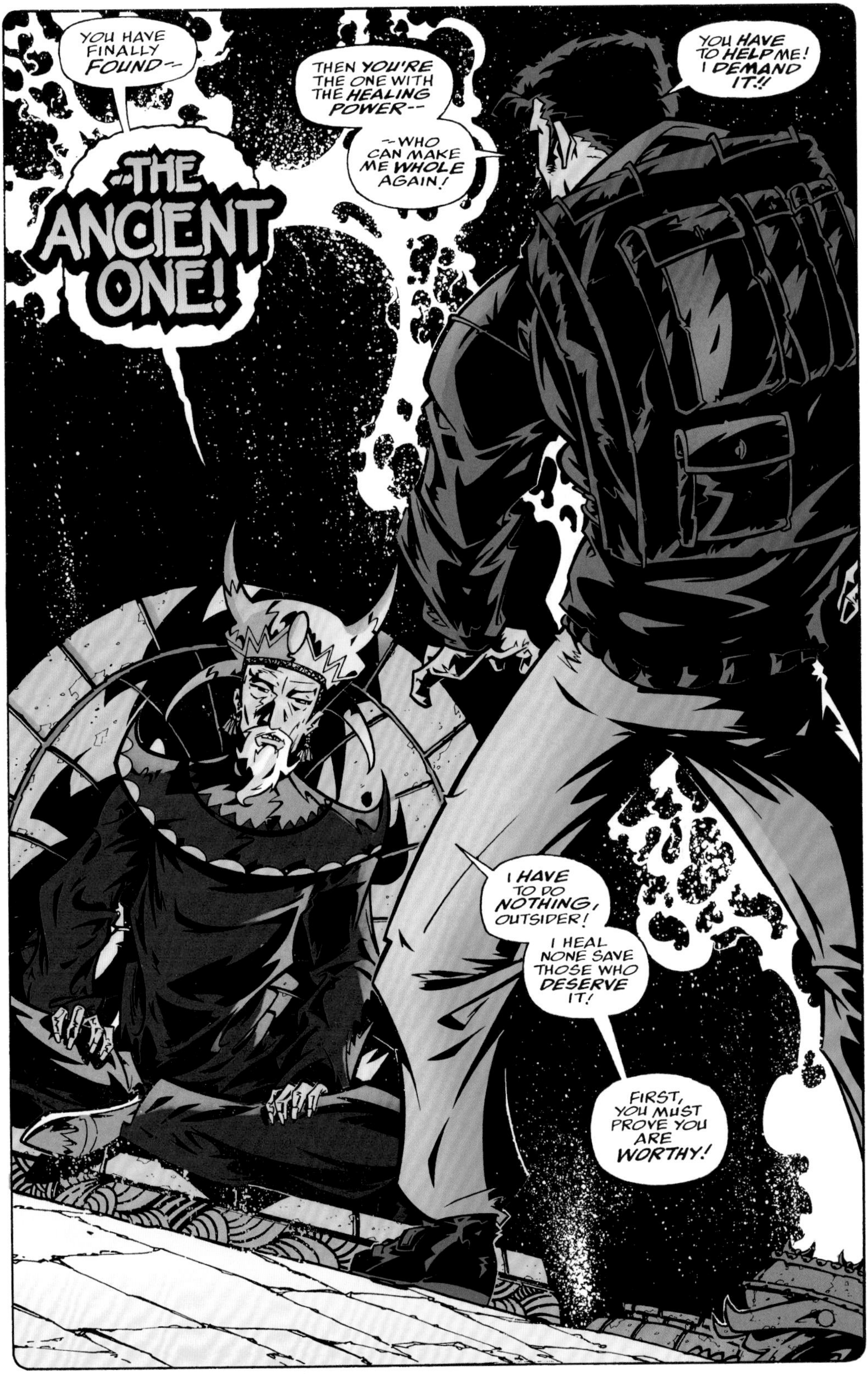
YOU HAVE FINALLY FOUND--
--THE ANCIENT ONE!
THEN YOU'RE THE ONE WITH THE HEALING POWER--
--WHO CAN MAKE ME WHOLE AGAIN!
YOU HAVE TO HELP ME! I DEMAND IT!!
I HAVE TO DO NOTHING, OUTSIDER!
I HEAL NONE SAVE THOSE WHO DESERVE IT!
FIRST, YOU MUST PROVE YOU ARE WORTHY!

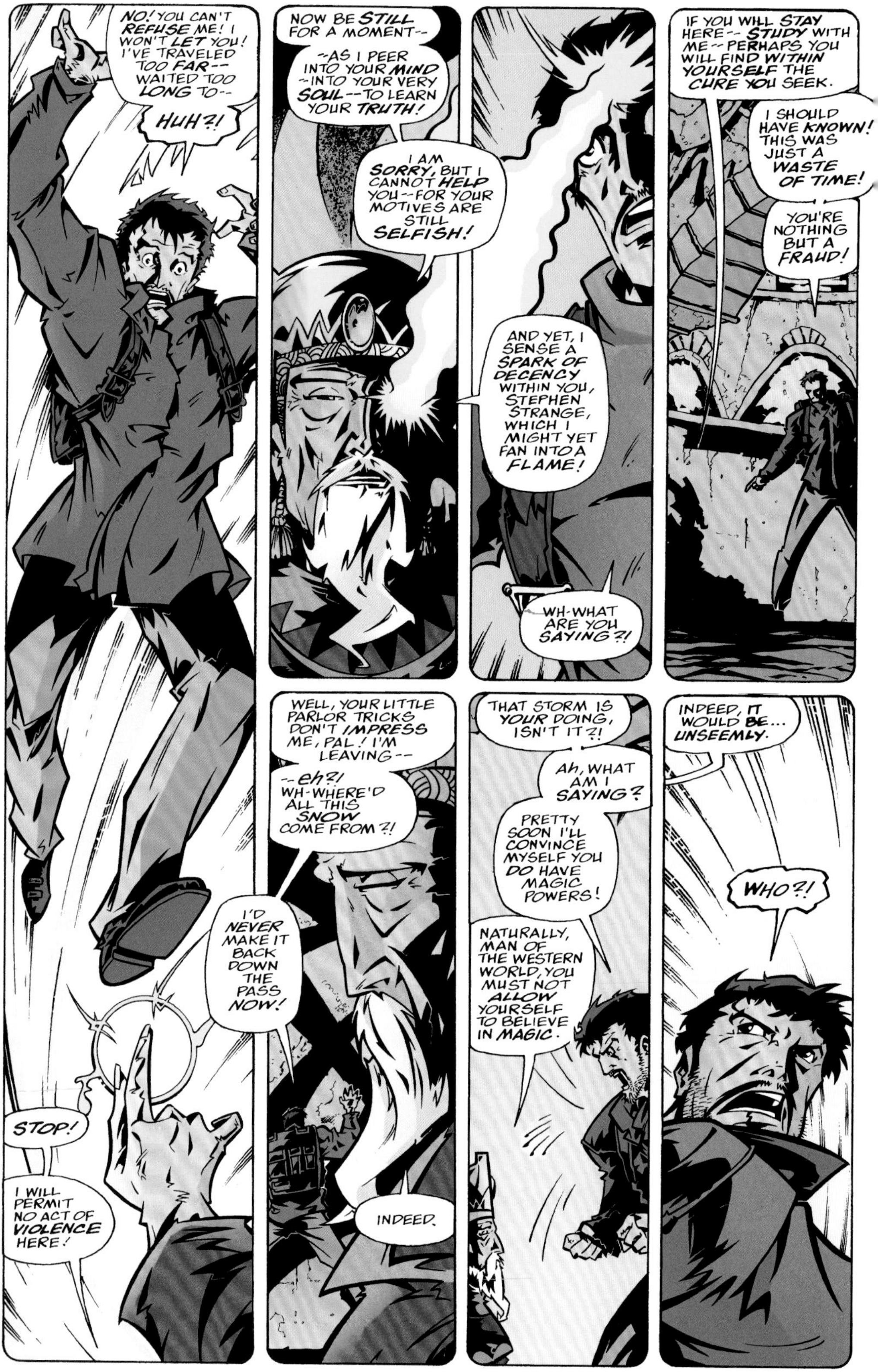
NO! YOU CAN'T REFUSE ME! I WON'T LET YOU! I'VE TRAVELED TOO FAR--WAITED TOO LONG TO--
HUH?!
STOP!
I WILL PERMIT NO ACT OF VIOLENCE HERE!
NOW BE STILL FOR A MOMENT--
--AS I PEER INTO YOUR MIND--INTO YOUR VERY SOUL--TO LEARN YOUR TRUTH!
I AM SORRY, BUT I CANNOT HELP YOU--FOR YOUR MOTIVES ARE STILL SELFISH!
AND YET, I SENSE A SPARK OF DECENCY WITHIN YOU, STEPHEN STRANGE, WHICH I MIGHT YET FAN INTO A FLAME!
WH-WHAT ARE YOU SAYING?!
IF YOU WILL STAY HERE--STUDY WITH ME--PERHAPS YOU WILL FIND WITHIN YOURSELF THE CURE YOU SEEK.
I SHOULD HAVE KNOWN! THIS WAS JUST A WASTE OF TIME!
YOU'RE NOTHING BUT A FRAUD!
WELL, YOUR LITTLE PARLOR TRICKS DON'T IMPRESS ME, PAL! I'M LEAVING--
--eh?! WH-WHERE'D ALL THIS SNOW COME FROM?!
I'D NEVER MAKE IT BACK DOWN THE PASS NOW!
INDEED.
THAT STORM IS YOUR DOING, ISN'T IT?!
Ah, WHAT AM I SAYING?
PRETTY SOON I'LL CONVINCE MYSELF YOU DO HAVE MAGIC POWERS!
NATURALLY, MAN OF THE WESTERN WORLD, YOU MUST NOT ALLOW YOURSELF TO BELIEVE IN MAGIC.
INDEED, IT WOULD BE... UNSEEMLY.
WHO?!

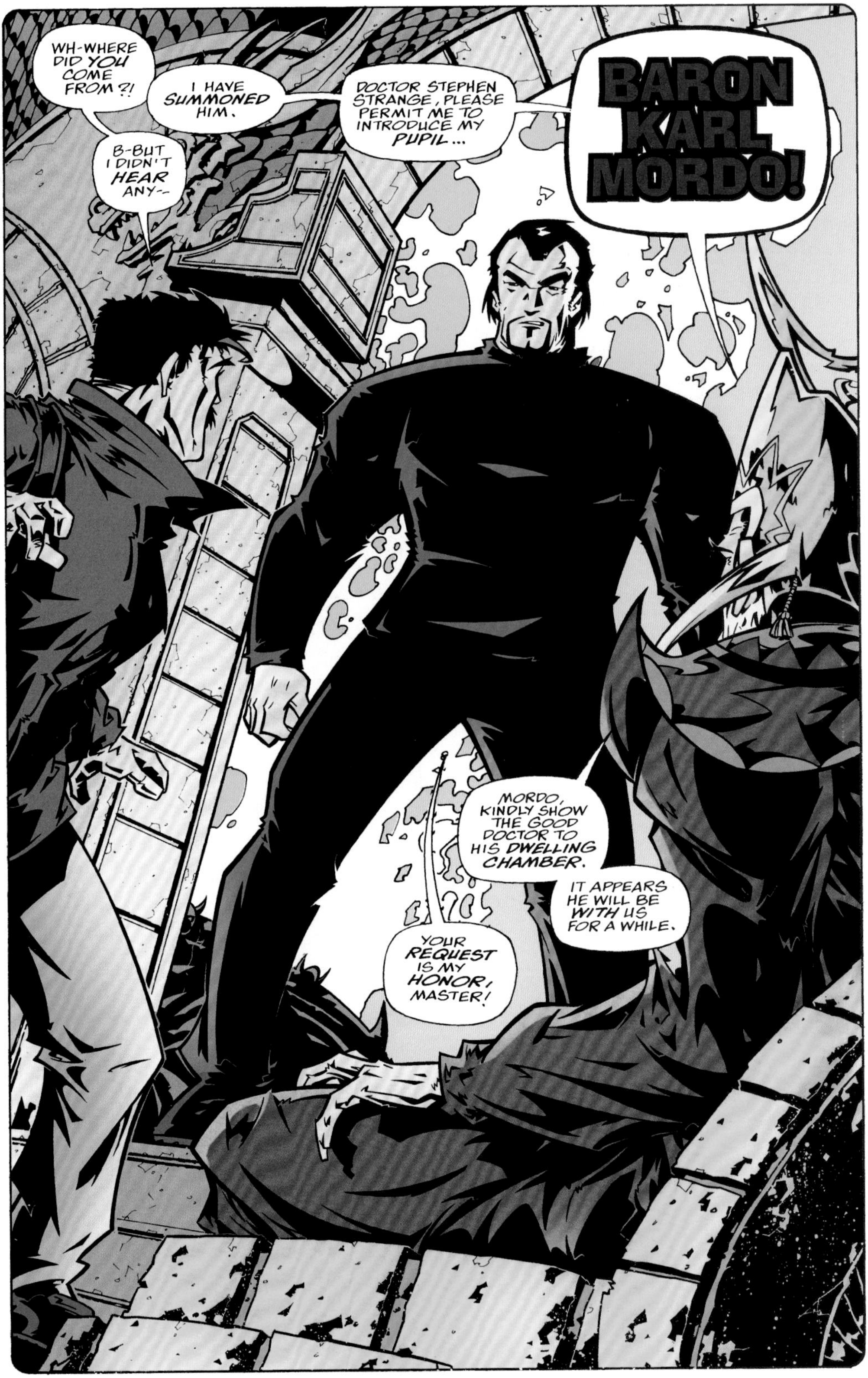
WH-WHERE DID YOU COME FROM?!
I HAVE SUMMONED HIM.
B-BUT I DIDN'T HEAR ANY--
DOCTOR STEPHEN STRANGE, PLEASE PERMIT ME TO INTRODUCE MY PUPIL...
BARON KARL MORDO!
MORDO, KINDLY SHOW THE GOOD DOCTOR TO HIS DWELLING CHAMBER.
IT APPEARS HE WILL BE WITH US FOR A WHILE.
YOUR REQUEST IS MY HONOR, MASTER!

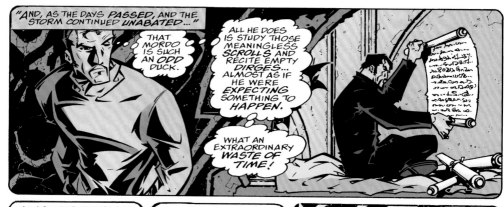

"AND, AS THE DAYS PASSED, AND THE STORM CONTINUED UNABATED..."

THAT MORDO IS SUCH AN ODD DUCK.

ALL HE DOES IS STUDY THOSE MEANINGLESS SCROLLS AND RECITE EMPTY DIRGES... ALMOST AS IF HE WERE EXPECTING SOMETHING TO HAPPEN.

WHAT AN EXTRAORDINARY WASTE OF TIME!

I'D ASK THE OLD MAN IF HE KNOWS HOW LONG IT TAKES THE SNOW TO MELT AROUND HERE --

--BUT NATURALLY, HE'S SLEEPING AGAIN--

--EH? WHAT IN BLAZES IS THAT ?!

THE VAPORS OF VALTORR.!!

I AM BEING ATTACKED BY SOME ENEMY.!!

THESE VAPORS WERE SPAWNED BY BLACK MAGIC, AND ONLY BY SUCH MAGIC CAN THEY BE DIS-SPELLED!

DARK FORCES-- BEGONE!

THUS DO I SUMMON THE POWERS OF THE VISHANTI!

BY THE SPELL OF THE DREAD DORMAMMU, IN THE NAME OF THE ALL-SEEING AGAMOTTO--

ALL THY STRENGTH I NOW DO SUMMON...

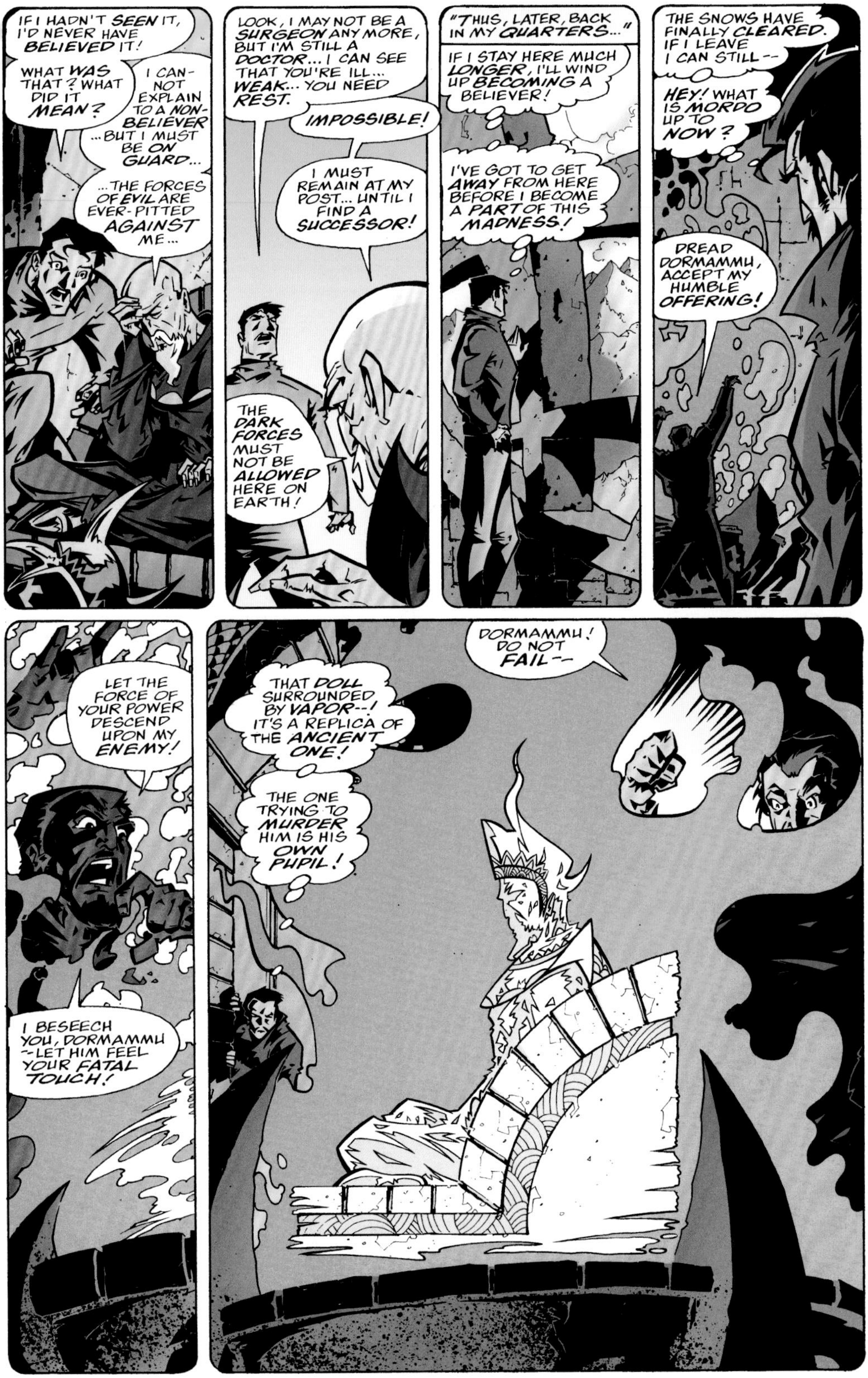
IF I HADN'T SEEN IT, I'D NEVER HAVE BELIEVED IT!
WHAT WAS THAT? WHAT DID IT MEAN?
I CANNOT EXPLAIN TO A NON-BELIEVER ...BUT I MUST BE ON GUARD...
...THE FORCES OF EVIL ARE EVER-PITTED AGAINST ME...
LOOK, I MAY NOT BE A SURGEON ANY MORE, BUT I'M STILL A DOCTOR... I CAN SEE THAT YOU'RE ILL... WEAK... YOU NEED REST.
IMPOSSIBLE!
I MUST REMAIN AT MY POST... UNTIL I FIND A SUCCESSOR!
THE DARK FORCES MUST NOT BE ALLOWED HERE ON EARTH!
"THUS, LATER, BACK IN MY QUARTERS..."
IF I STAY HERE MUCH LONGER, I'LL WIND UP BECOMING A BELIEVER!
I'VE GOT TO GET AWAY FROM HERE BEFORE I BECOME A PART OF THIS MADNESS!
THE SNOWS HAVE FINALLY CLEARED. IF I LEAVE I CAN STILL --
HEY! WHAT IS MORDO UP TO NOW?
DREAD DORMAMMU, ACCEPT MY HUMBLE OFFERING!
LET THE FORCE OF YOUR POWER DESCEND UPON MY ENEMY!
I BESEECH YOU, DORMAMMU --LET HIM FEEL YOUR FATAL TOUCH!
DORMAMMU! DO NOT FAIL--
THAT DOLL SURROUNDED BY VAPOR--! IT'S A REPLICA OF THE ANCIENT ONE!
THE ONE TRYING TO MURDER HIM IS HIS OWN PUPIL!

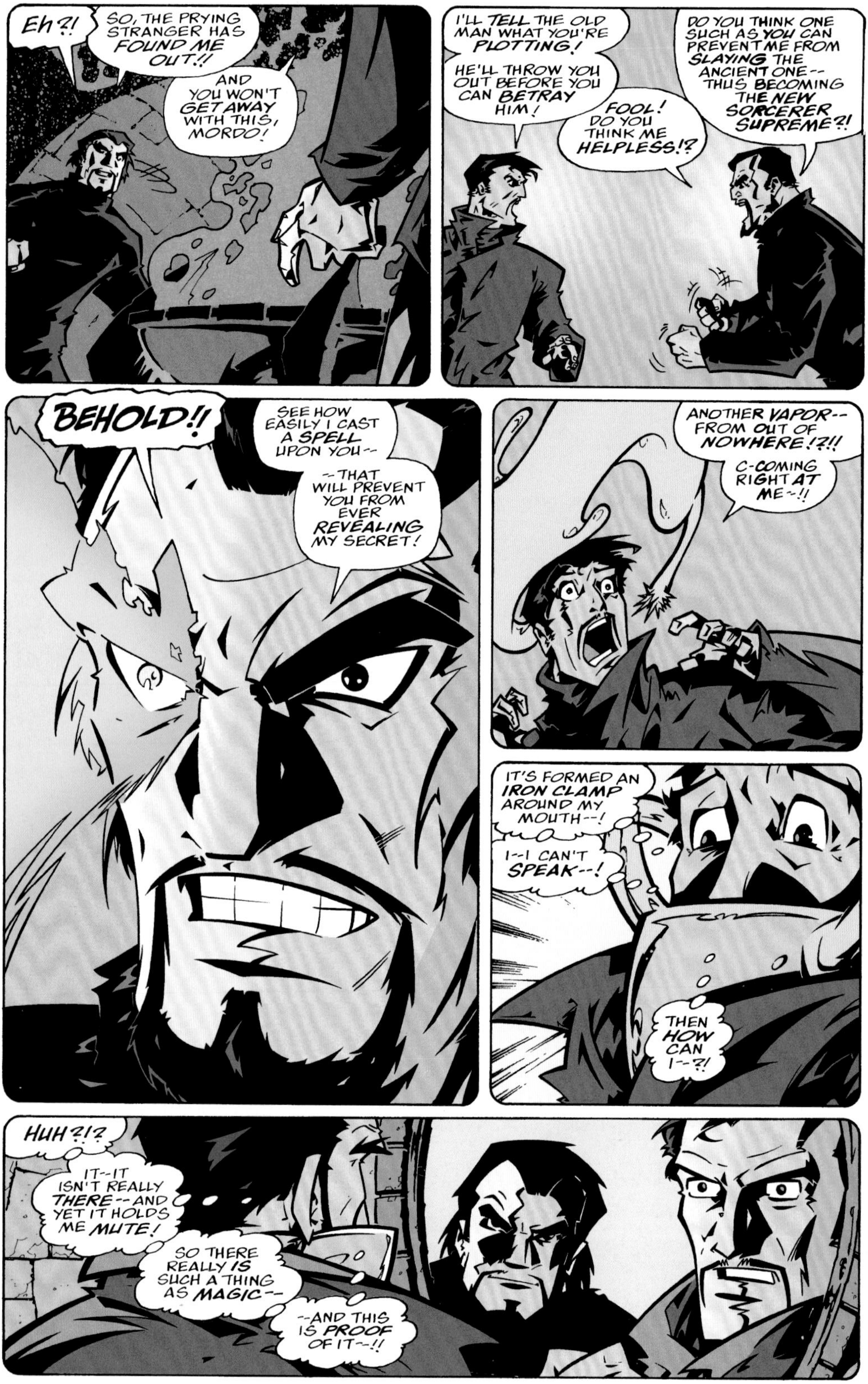

Eh?!
SO, THE PRYING STRANGER HAS FOUND ME OUT!!
AND YOU WON'T GET AWAY WITH THIS, MORDO!
I'LL TELL THE OLD MAN WHAT YOU'RE PLOTTING!
HE'LL THROW YOU OUT BEFORE YOU CAN BETRAY HIM!
FOOL! DO YOU THINK ME HELPLESS!?
DO YOU THINK ONE SUCH AS YOU CAN PREVENT ME FROM SLAYING THE ANCIENT ONE-- THUS BECOMING THE NEW SORCERER SUPREME?!
BEHOLD!!
SEE HOW EASILY I CAST A SPELL UPON YOU--
--THAT WILL PREVENT YOU FROM EVER REVEALING MY SECRET!
ANOTHER VAPOR-- FROM OUT OF NOWHERE!?!!
C-COMING RIGHT AT ME--!!
IT'S FORMED AN IRON CLAMP AROUND MY MOUTH--!
I--I CAN'T SPEAK--!
THEN HOW CAN I--?!
HUH?!?
IT--IT ISN'T REALLY THERE--AND YET IT HOLDS ME MUTE!
SO THERE REALLY IS SUCH A THING AS MAGIC--
--AND THIS IS PROOF OF IT--!!

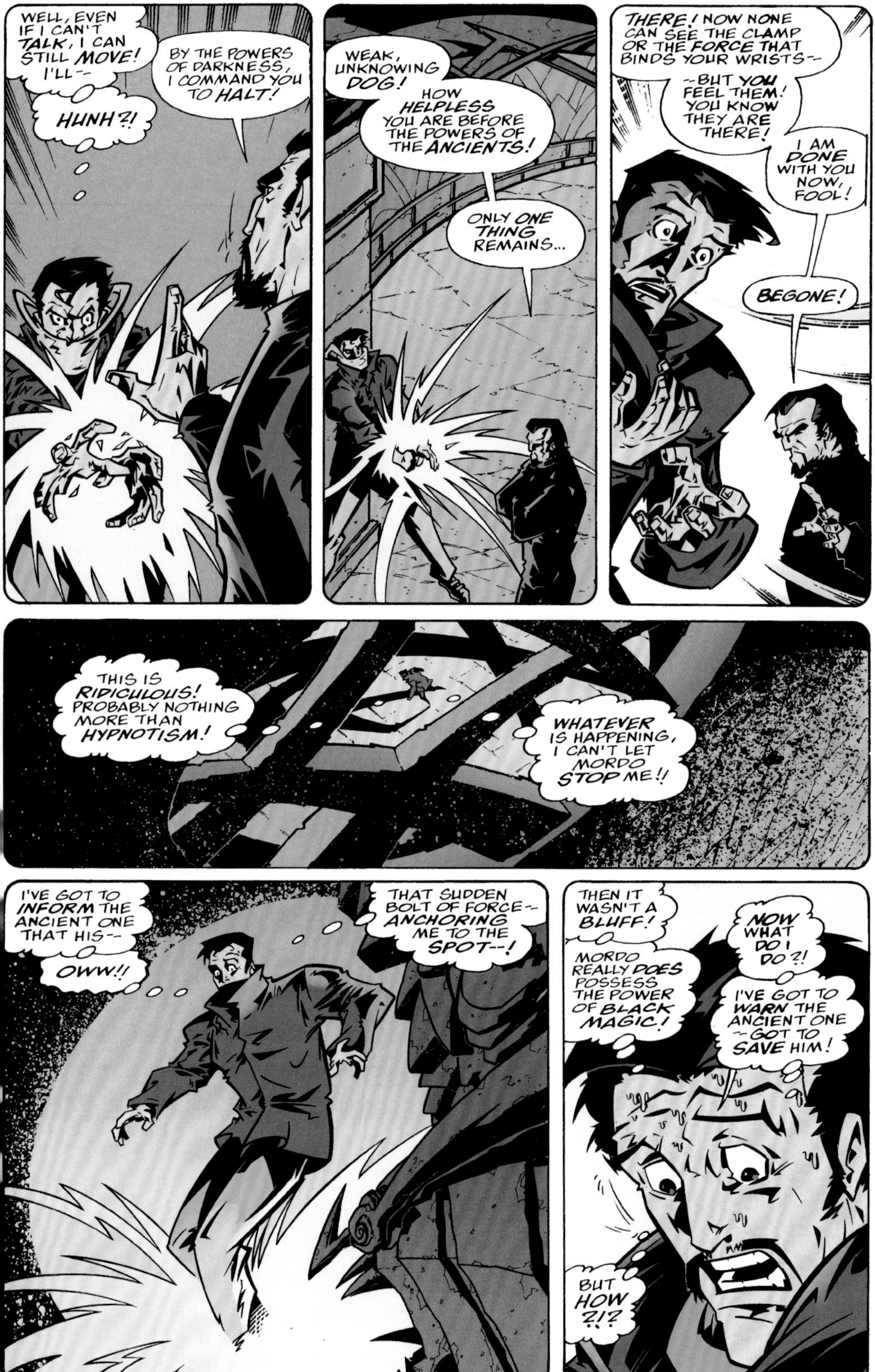
WELL, EVEN IF I CAN'T TALK, I CAN STILL MOVE! I'LL--
HUNH?!
BY THE POWERS OF DARKNESS, I COMMAND YOU TO HALT!
WEAK, UNKNOWING DOG!
HOW HELPLESS YOU ARE BEFORE THE POWERS OF THE ANCIENTS!
ONLY ONE THING REMAINS...
THERE! NOW NONE CAN SEE THE CLAMP OR THE FORCE THAT BINDS YOUR WRISTS--
--BUT YOU FEEL THEM! YOU KNOW THEY ARE THERE!
I AM DONE WITH YOU NOW, FOOL!
BEGONE!
THIS IS RIDICULOUS! PROBABLY NOTHING MORE THAN HYPNOTISM!
WHATEVER IS HAPPENING, I CAN'T LET MORDO STOP ME!!
I'VE GOT TO INFORM THE ANCIENT ONE THAT HIS--
OWW!!
THAT SUDDEN BOLT OF FORCE-- ANCHORING ME TO THE SPOT--!
THEN IT WASN'T A BLUFF!
MORDO REALLY DOES POSSESS THE POWER OF BLACK MAGIC!
NOW WHAT DO I DO?!
I'VE GOT TO WARN THE ANCIENT ONE --GOT TO SAVE HIM!
BUT HOW?!?

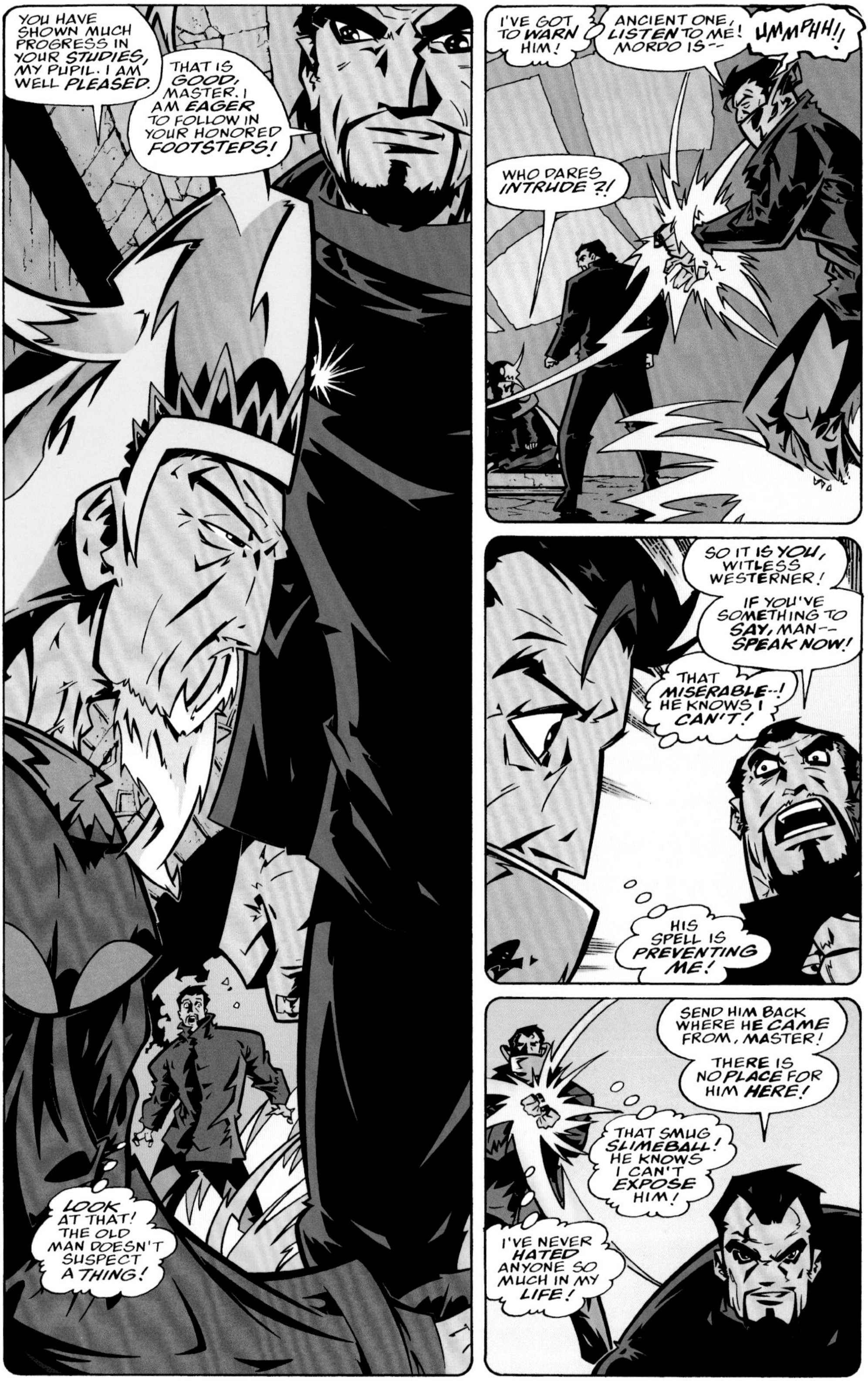
YOU HAVE SHOWN MUCH PROGRESS IN YOUR STUDIES, MY PUPIL. I AM WELL PLEASED.
THAT IS GOOD, MASTER. I AM EAGER TO FOLLOW IN YOUR HONORED FOOTSTEPS!
LOOK AT THAT! THE OLD MAN DOESN'T SUSPECT A THING!
I'VE GOT TO WARN HIM!
ANCIENT ONE, LISTEN TO ME! MORDO IS--
UMMPHH!!
WHO DARES INTRUDE ?!
SO IT IS YOU, WITLESS WESTERNER!
IF YOU'VE SOMETHING TO SAY, MAN-- SPEAK NOW!
THAT MISERABLE--! HE KNOWS I CAN'T!
HIS SPELL IS PREVENTING ME!
SEND HIM BACK WHERE HE CAME FROM, MASTER!
THERE IS NO PLACE FOR HIM HERE!
THAT SMUG SLIMEBALL! HE KNOWS I CAN'T EXPOSE HIM!
I'VE NEVER HATED ANYONE SO MUCH IN MY LIFE!

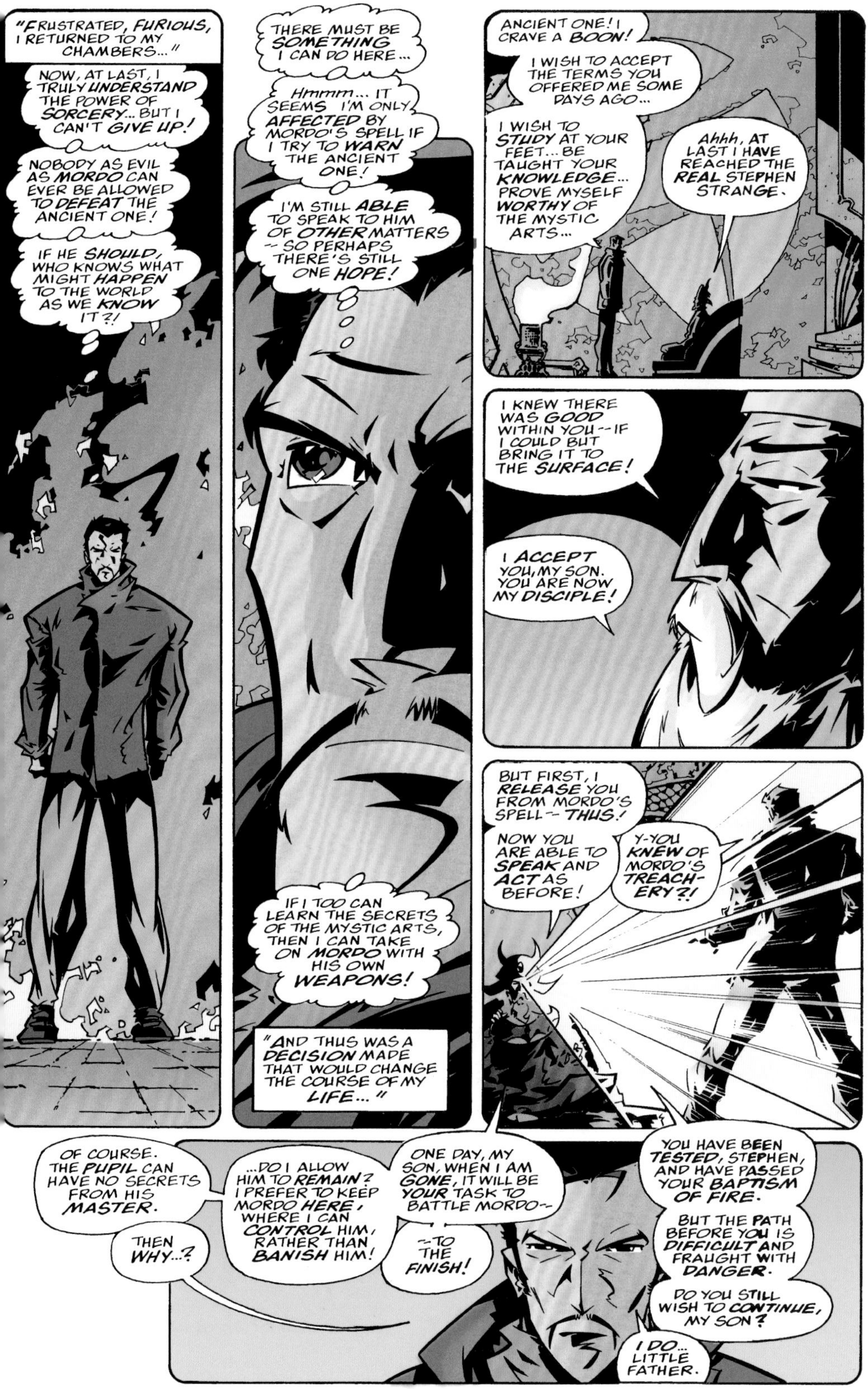
"FRUSTRATED, FURIOUS, I RETURNED TO MY CHAMBERS..."
NOW, AT LAST, I TRULY UNDERSTAND THE POWER OF SORCERY... BUT I CAN'T GIVE UP!
NOBODY AS EVIL AS MORDO CAN EVER BE ALLOWED TO DEFEAT THE ANCIENT ONE!
IF HE SHOULD, WHO KNOWS WHAT MIGHT HAPPEN TO THE WORLD AS WE KNOW IT?!
THERE MUST BE SOMETHING I CAN DO HERE...
Hmmm... IT SEEMS I'M ONLY AFFECTED BY MORDO'S SPELL IF I TRY TO WARN THE ANCIENT ONE!
I'M STILL ABLE TO SPEAK TO HIM OF OTHER MATTERS -- SO PERHAPS THERE'S STILL ONE HOPE!
IF I TOO CAN LEARN THE SECRETS OF THE MYSTIC ARTS, THEN I CAN TAKE ON MORDO WITH HIS OWN WEAPONS!
"AND THUS WAS A DECISION MADE THAT WOULD CHANGE THE COURSE OF MY LIFE..."
ANCIENT ONE! I CRAVE A BOON!
I WISH TO ACCEPT THE TERMS YOU OFFERED ME SOME DAYS AGO...
I WISH TO STUDY AT YOUR FEET... BE TAUGHT YOUR KNOWLEDGE... PROVE MYSELF WORTHY OF THE MYSTIC ARTS...
Ahhh, AT LAST I HAVE REACHED THE REAL STEPHEN STRANGE.
I KNEW THERE WAS GOOD WITHIN YOU -- IF I COULD BUT BRING IT TO THE SURFACE!
I ACCEPT YOU, MY SON. YOU ARE NOW MY DISCIPLE!
BUT FIRST, I RELEASE YOU FROM MORDO'S SPELL -- THUS!
NOW YOU ARE ABLE TO SPEAK AND ACT AS BEFORE!
Y-YOU KNEW OF MORDO'S TREACHERY?!
OF COURSE. THE PUPIL CAN HAVE NO SECRETS FROM HIS MASTER.
THEN WHY...?
...DO I ALLOW HIM TO REMAIN? I PREFER TO KEEP MORDO HERE, WHERE I CAN CONTROL HIM, RATHER THAN BANISH HIM!
ONE DAY, MY SON, WHEN I AM GONE, IT WILL BE YOUR TASK TO BATTLE MORDO--
--TO THE FINISH!
YOU HAVE BEEN TESTED, STEPHEN, AND HAVE PASSED YOUR BAPTISM OF FIRE.
BUT THE PATH BEFORE YOU IS DIFFICULT AND FRAUGHT WITH DANGER.
DO YOU STILL WISH TO CONTINUE, MY SON?
I DO... LITTLE FATHER.

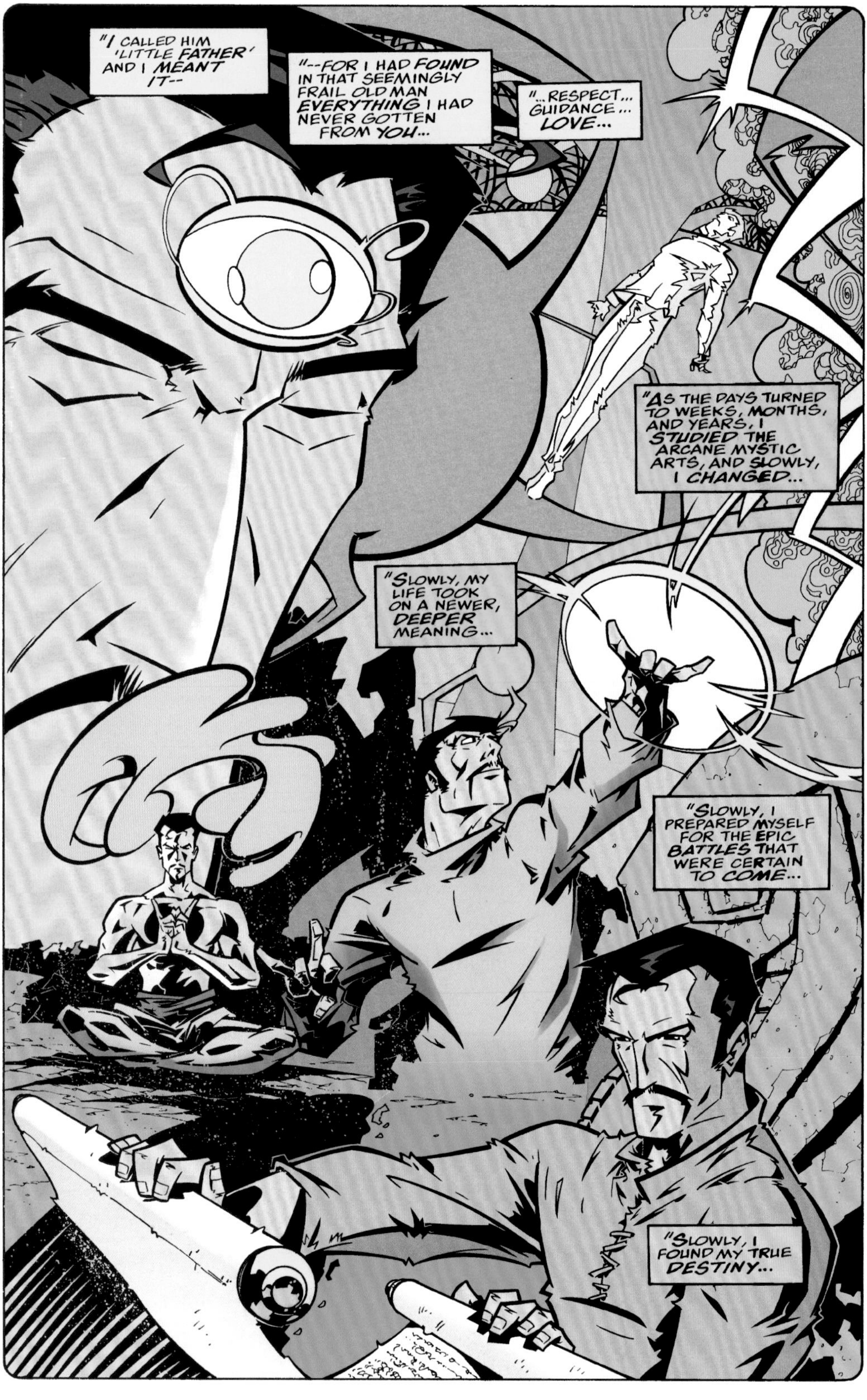
"I CALLED HIM 'LITTLE FATHER' AND I MEANT IT--
"--FOR I HAD FOUND IN THAT SEEMINGLY FRAIL OLD MAN EVERYTHING I HAD NEVER GOTTEN FROM YOU...
"...RESPECT... GUIDANCE... LOVE...
"AS THE DAYS TURNED TO WEEKS, MONTHS, AND YEARS, I STUDIED THE ARCANE MYSTIC ARTS, AND SLOWLY, I CHANGED...
"SLOWLY, MY LIFE TOOK ON A NEWER, DEEPER MEANING...
"SLOWLY, I PREPARED MYSELF FOR THE EPIC BATTLES THAT WERE CERTAIN TO COME...
"SLOWLY, I FOUND MY TRUE DESTINY...

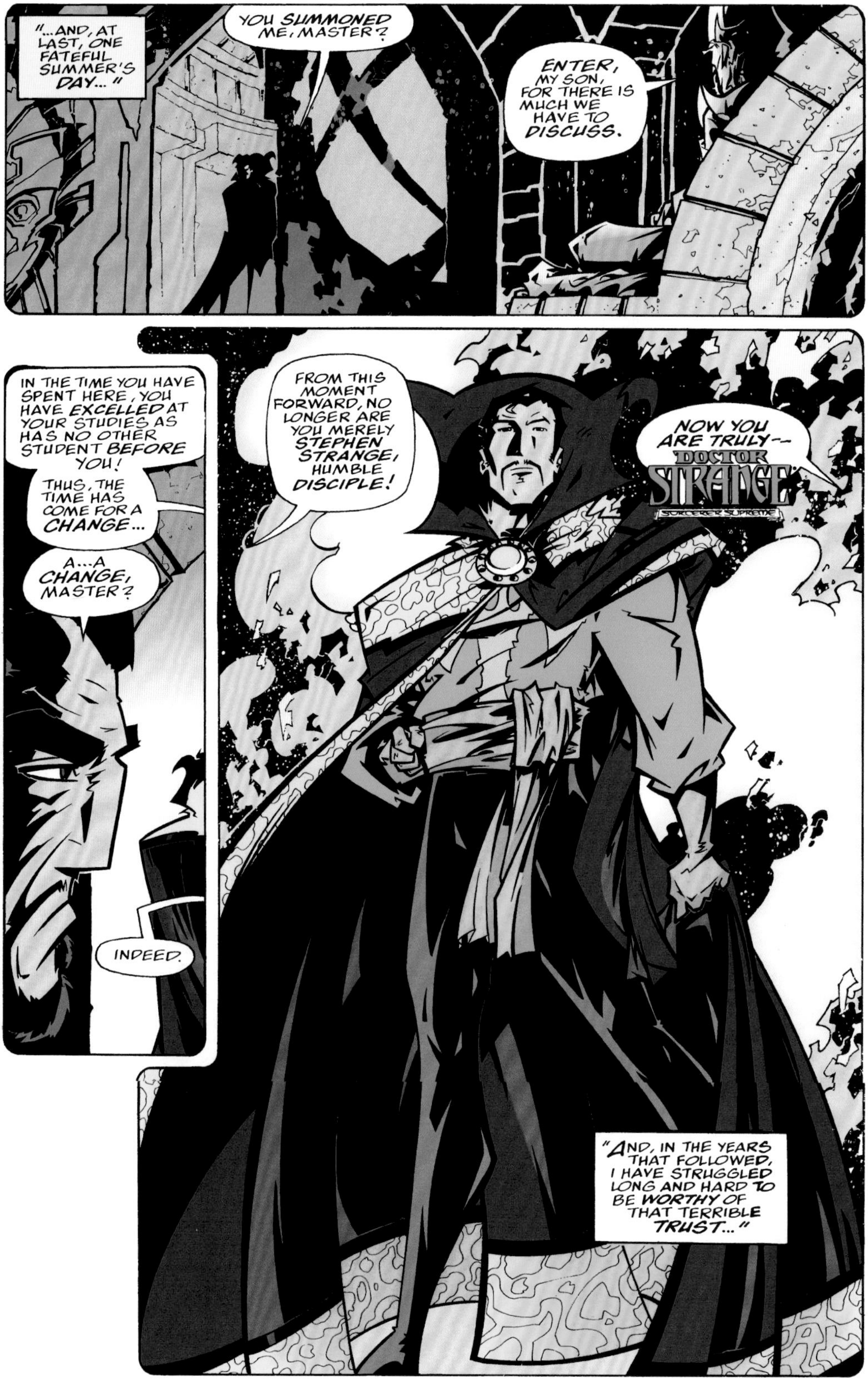
"...AND, AT LAST, ONE FATEFUL SUMMER'S DAY..."
YOU SUMMONED ME, MASTER?
ENTER, MY SON, FOR THERE IS MUCH WE HAVE TO DISCUSS.
IN THE TIME YOU HAVE SPENT HERE, YOU HAVE EXCELLED AT YOUR STUDIES AS HAS NO OTHER STUDENT BEFORE YOU!
THUS, THE TIME HAS COME FOR A CHANGE...
A...A CHANGE, MASTER?
INDEED.
FROM THIS MOMENT FORWARD, NO LONGER ARE YOU MERELY STEPHEN STRANGE, HUMBLE DISCIPLE!
NOW YOU ARE TRULY--
DOCTOR STRANGE
SORCERER SUPREME
"AND, IN THE YEARS THAT FOLLOWED, I HAVE STRUGGLED LONG AND HARD TO BE WORTHY OF THAT TERRIBLE TRUST..."

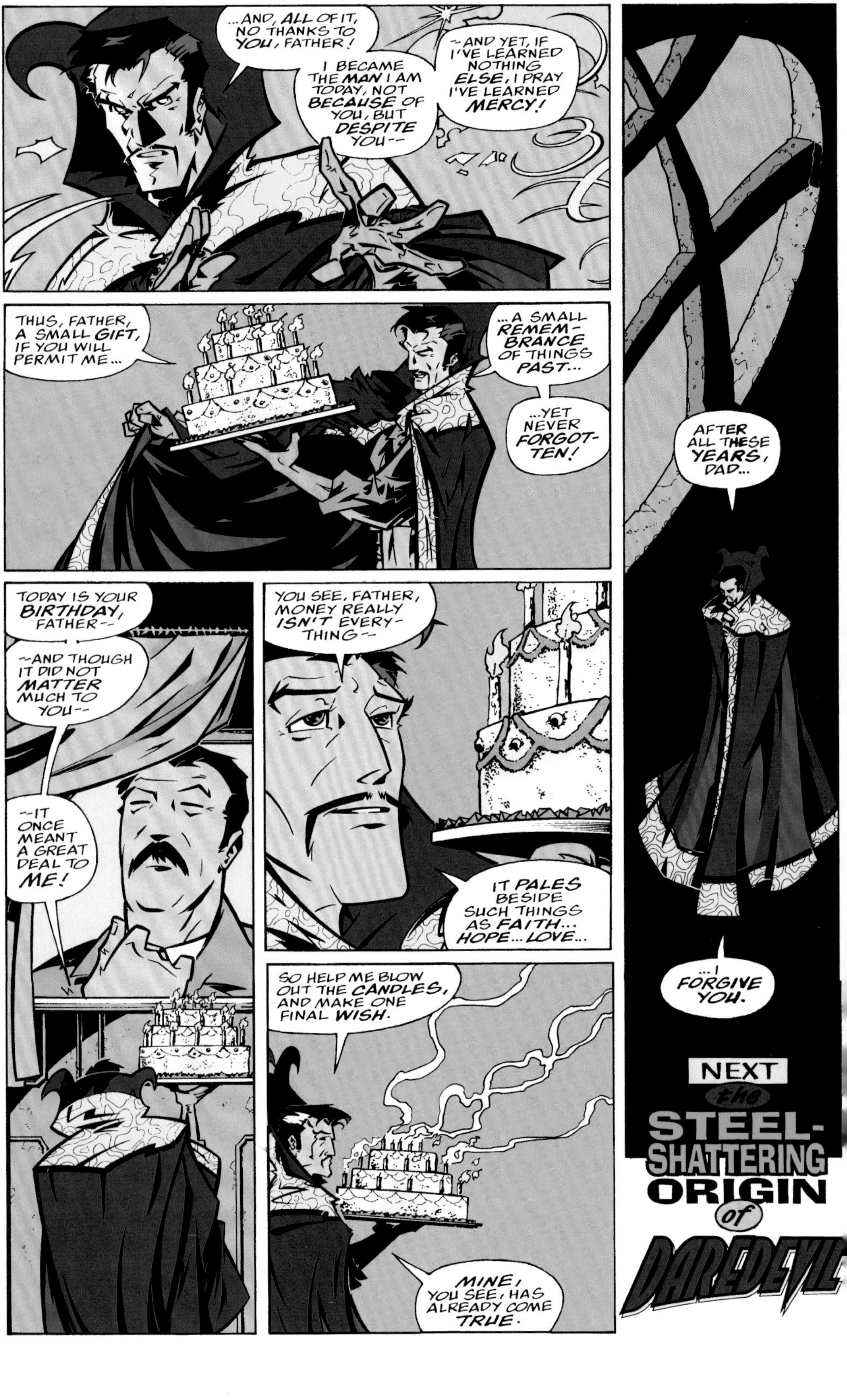
...AND, ALL OF IT, NO THANKS TO YOU, FATHER!
I BECAME THE MAN I AM TODAY, NOT BECAUSE OF YOU, BUT DESPITE YOU--
--AND YET, IF I'VE LEARNED NOTHING ELSE, I PRAY I'VE LEARNED MERCY!
THUS, FATHER, A SMALL GIFT, IF YOU WILL PERMIT ME...
...A SMALL REMEMBRANCE OF THINGS PAST...
...YET NEVER FORGOTTEN!
AFTER ALL THESE YEARS, DAD...
TODAY IS YOUR BIRTHDAY, FATHER--
--AND THOUGH IT DID NOT MATTER MUCH TO YOU--
--IT ONCE MEANT A GREAT DEAL TO ME!
YOU SEE, FATHER, MONEY REALLY ISN'T EVERYTHING--
IT PALES BESIDE SUCH THINGS AS FAITH... HOPE... LOVE...
SO HELP ME BLOW OUT THE CANDLES, AND MAKE ONE FINAL WISH.
MINE, YOU SEE, HAS ALREADY COME TRUE.
...I FORGIVE YOU.
NEXT
the
STEEL-SHATTERING ORIGIN of DAREDEVIL

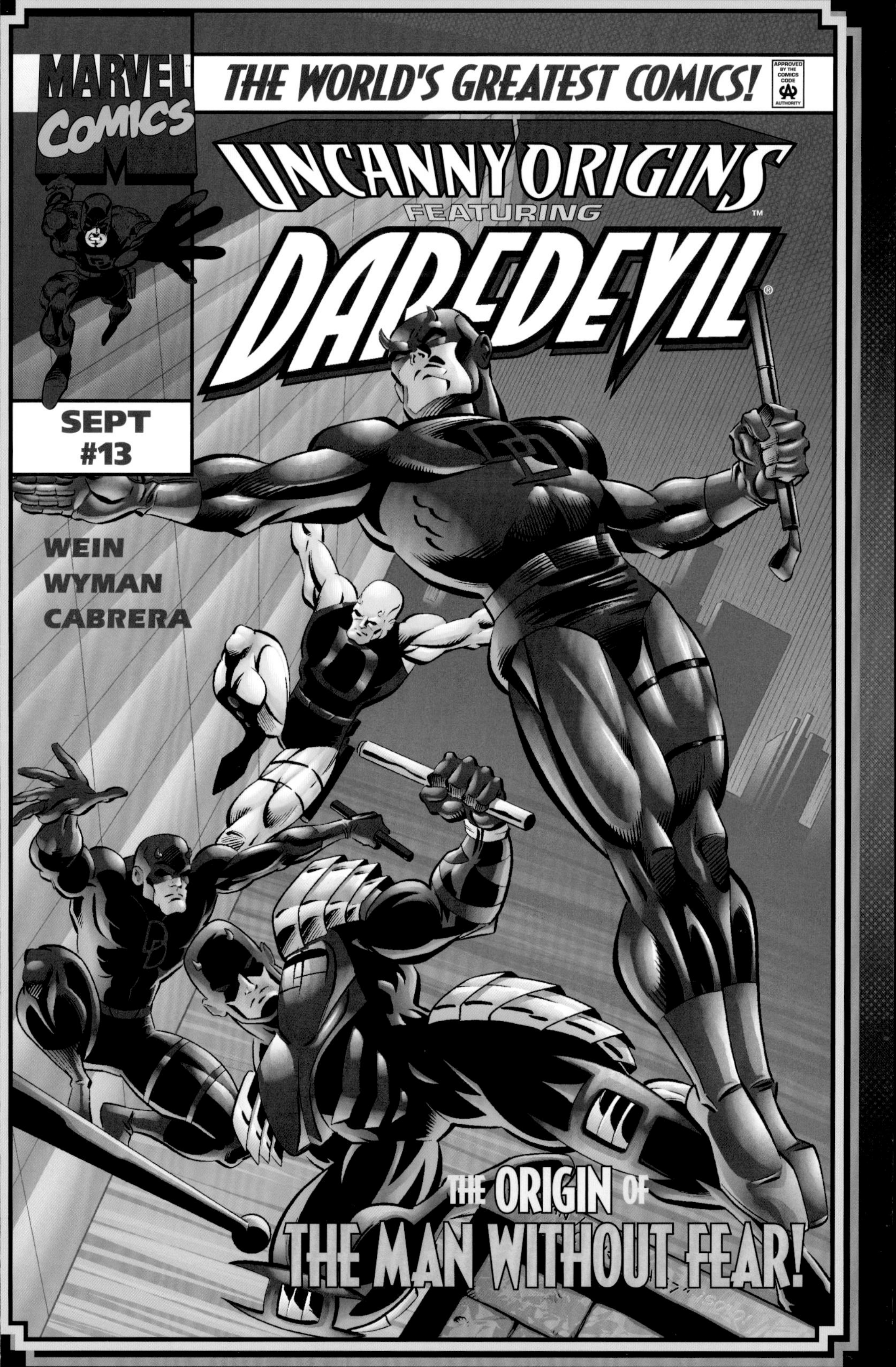
MARVEL COMICS
THE WORLD'S GREATEST COMICS!
APPROVED BY THE COMICS CODE AUTHORITY
UNCANNY ORIGINS
FEATURING
DAREDEVIL
SEPT
#13
WEIN
WYMAN
CABRERA
THE ORIGIN OF
THE MAN WITHOUT FEAR!

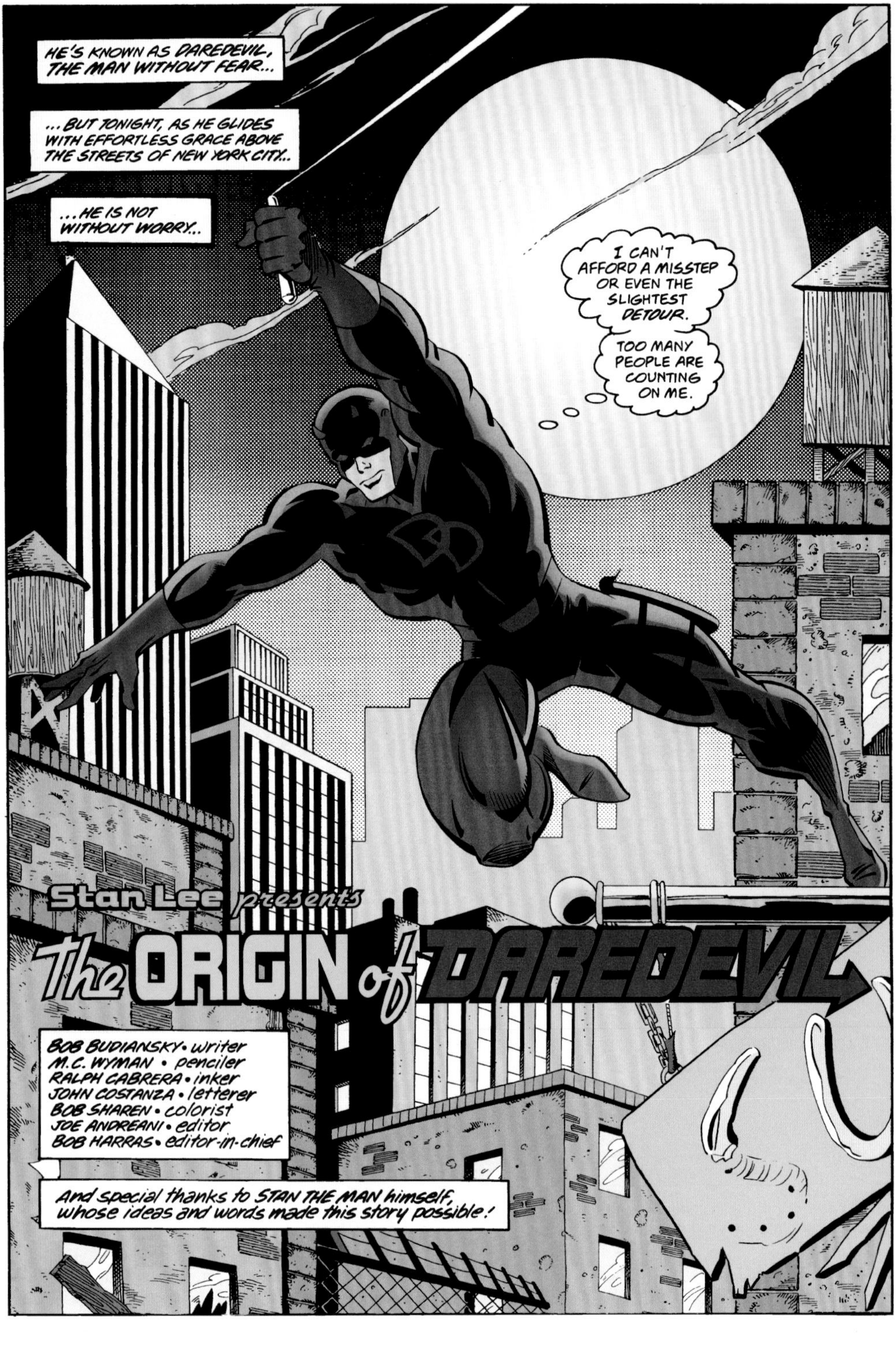
HE'S KNOWN AS DAREDEVIL, THE MAN WITHOUT FEAR...
...BUT TONIGHT, AS HE GLIDES WITH EFFORTLESS GRACE ABOVE THE STREETS OF NEW YORK CITY...
...HE IS NOT WITHOUT WORRY...
I CAN'T AFFORD A MISSTEP OR EVEN THE SLIGHTEST DETOUR.
TOO MANY PEOPLE ARE COUNTING ON ME.
Stan Lee presents
The ORIGIN of DAREDEVIL
BOB BUDIANSKY • writer
M.C. WYMAN • penciler
RALPH CABRERA • inker
JOHN COSTANZA • letterer
BOB SHAREN • colorist
JOE ANDREANI • editor
BOB HARRAS • editor-in-chief
And special thanks to STAN THE MAN himself, whose ideas and words made this story possible!

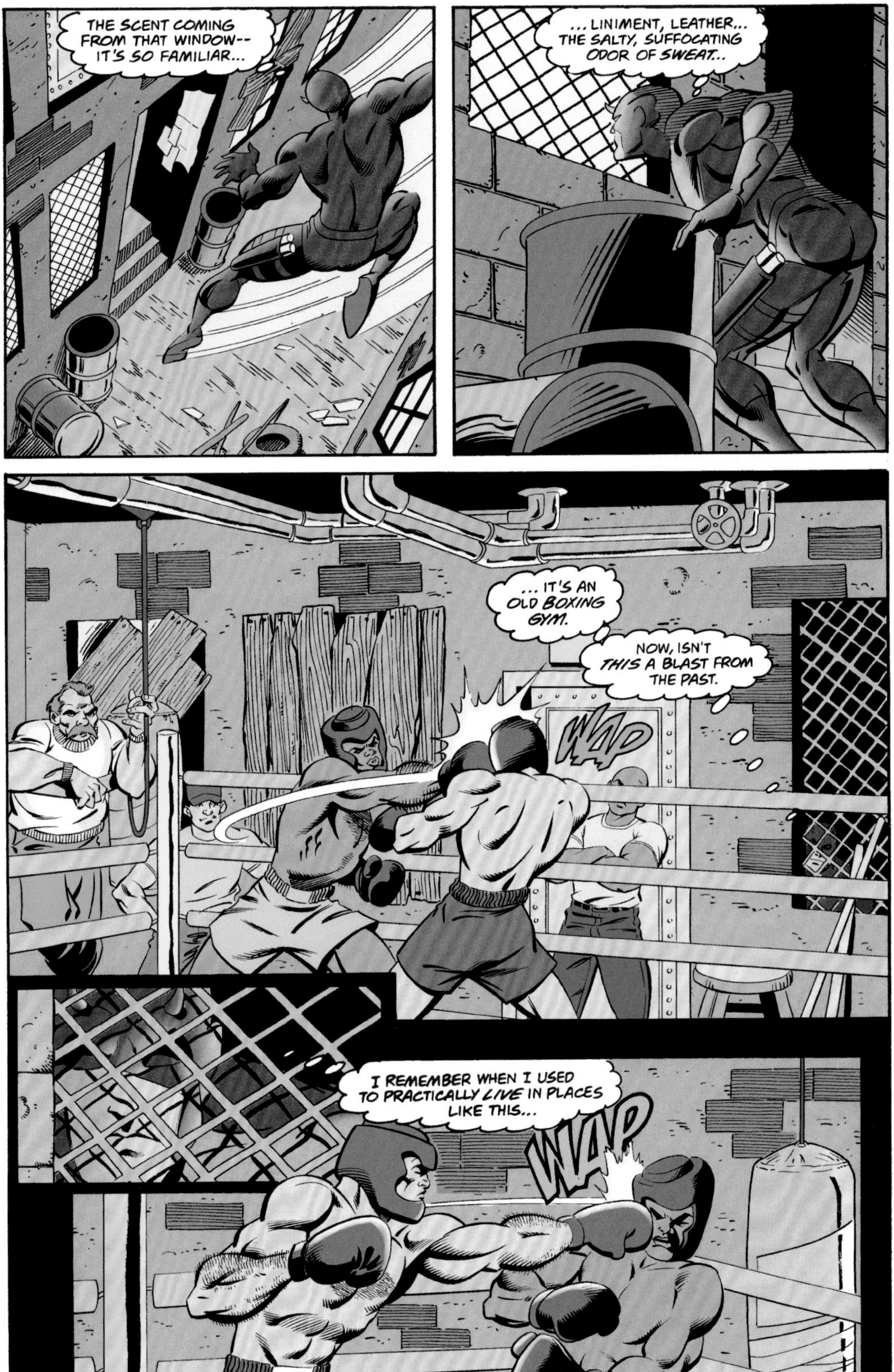
THE SCENT COMING FROM THAT WINDOW-- IT'S SO FAMILIAR...
...LINIMENT, LEATHER... THE SALTY, SUFFOCATING ODOR OF SWEAT...
...IT'S AN OLD BOXING GYM.
NOW, ISN'T THIS A BLAST FROM THE PAST.
WAP
I REMEMBER WHEN I USED TO PRACTICALLY LIVE IN PLACES LIKE THIS...
WAP

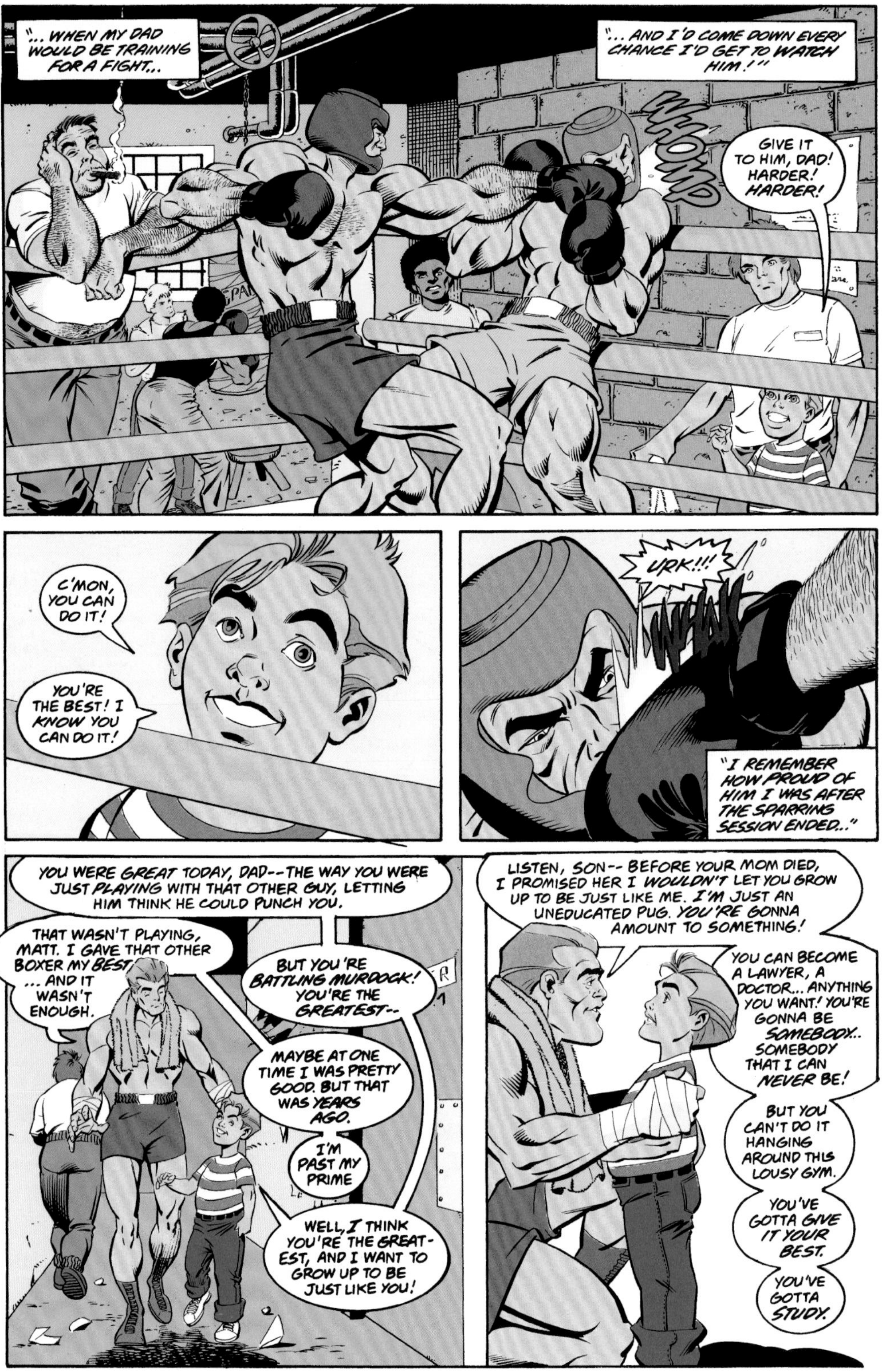
"... WHEN MY DAD WOULD BE TRAINING FOR A FIGHT...
"... AND I'D COME DOWN EVERY CHANCE I'D GET TO WATCH HIM!"
WHOMP
GIVE IT TO HIM, DAD! HARDER! HARDER!
C'MON, YOU CAN DO IT!
YOU'RE THE BEST! I KNOW YOU CAN DO IT!
URK!!!
WHAK
"I REMEMBER HOW PROUD OF HIM I WAS AFTER THE SPARRING SESSION ENDED..."
YOU WERE GREAT TODAY, DAD--THE WAY YOU WERE JUST PLAYING WITH THAT OTHER GUY, LETTING HIM THINK HE COULD PUNCH YOU.
THAT WASN'T PLAYING, MATT. I GAVE THAT OTHER BOXER MY BEST ... AND IT WASN'T ENOUGH.
BUT YOU'RE BATTLING MURDOCK! YOU'RE THE GREATEST--
MAYBE AT ONE TIME I WAS PRETTY GOOD. BUT THAT WAS YEARS AGO.
I'M PAST MY PRIME
WELL, I THINK YOU'RE THE GREATEST, AND I WANT TO GROW UP TO BE JUST LIKE YOU!
LISTEN, SON-- BEFORE YOUR MOM DIED, I PROMISED HER I WOULDN'T LET YOU GROW UP TO BE JUST LIKE ME. I'M JUST AN UNEDUCATED PUG. YOU'RE GONNA AMOUNT TO SOMETHING!
YOU CAN BECOME A LAWYER, A DOCTOR... ANYTHING YOU WANT! YOU'RE GONNA BE SOMEBODY... SOMEBODY THAT I CAN NEVER BE!
BUT YOU CAN'T DO IT HANGING AROUND THIS LOUSY GYM.
YOU'VE GOTTA GIVE IT YOUR BEST.
YOU'VE GOTTA STUDY.

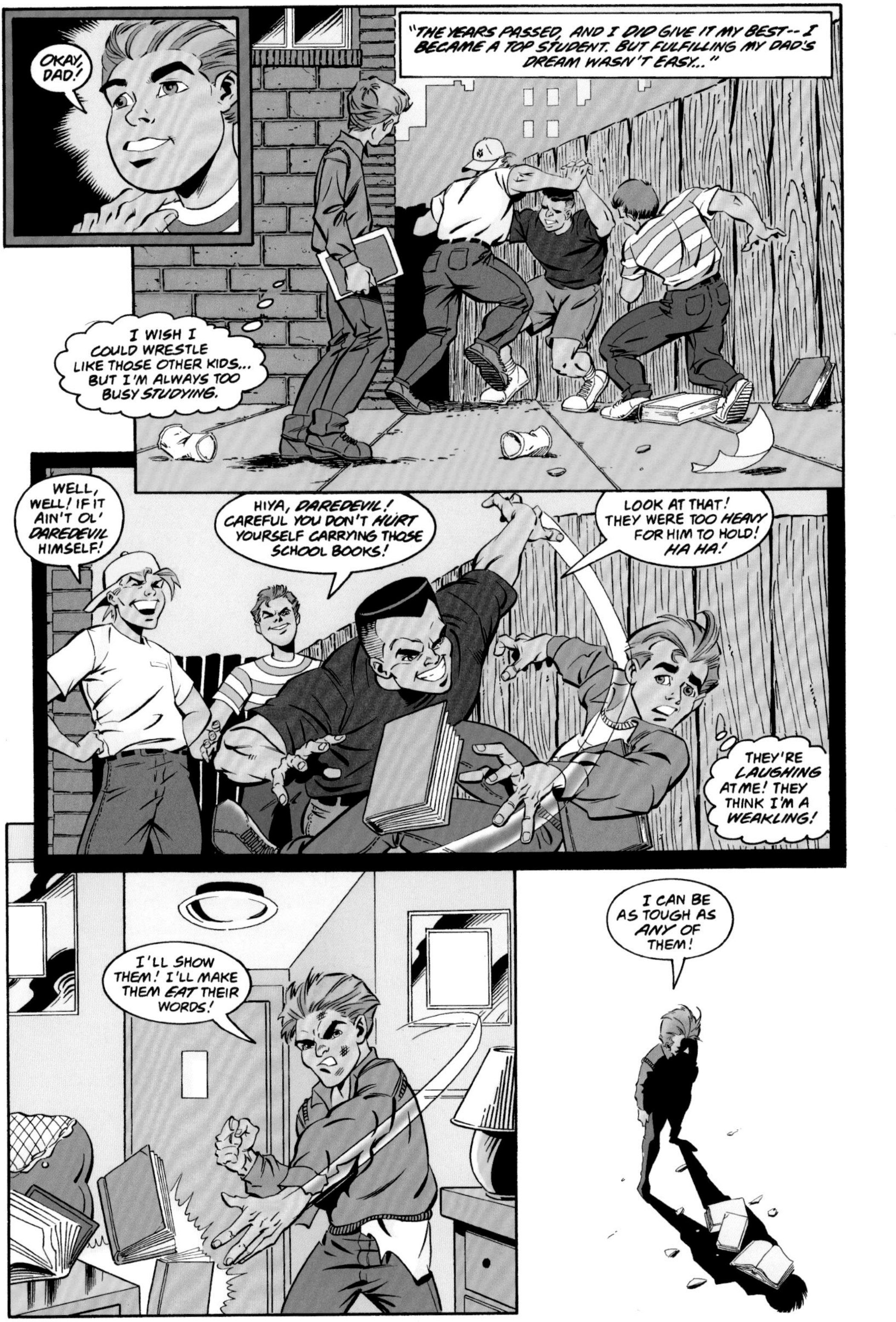
OKAY, DAD!
"THE YEARS PASSED, AND I DID GIVE IT MY BEST-- I BECAME A TOP STUDENT. BUT FULFILLING MY DAD'S DREAM WASN'T EASY..."
I WISH I COULD WRESTLE LIKE THOSE OTHER KIDS... BUT I'M ALWAYS TOO BUSY STUDYING.
WELL, WELL! IF IT AIN'T OL' DAREDEVIL HIMSELF!
HIYA, DAREDEVIL! CAREFUL YOU DON'T HURT YOURSELF CARRYING THOSE SCHOOL BOOKS!
LOOK AT THAT! THEY WERE TOO HEAVY FOR HIM TO HOLD! HA HA!
THEY'RE LAUGHING AT ME! THEY THINK I'M A WEAKLING!
I'LL SHOW THEM! I'LL MAKE THEM EAT THEIR WORDS!
I CAN BE AS TOUGH AS ANY OF THEM!

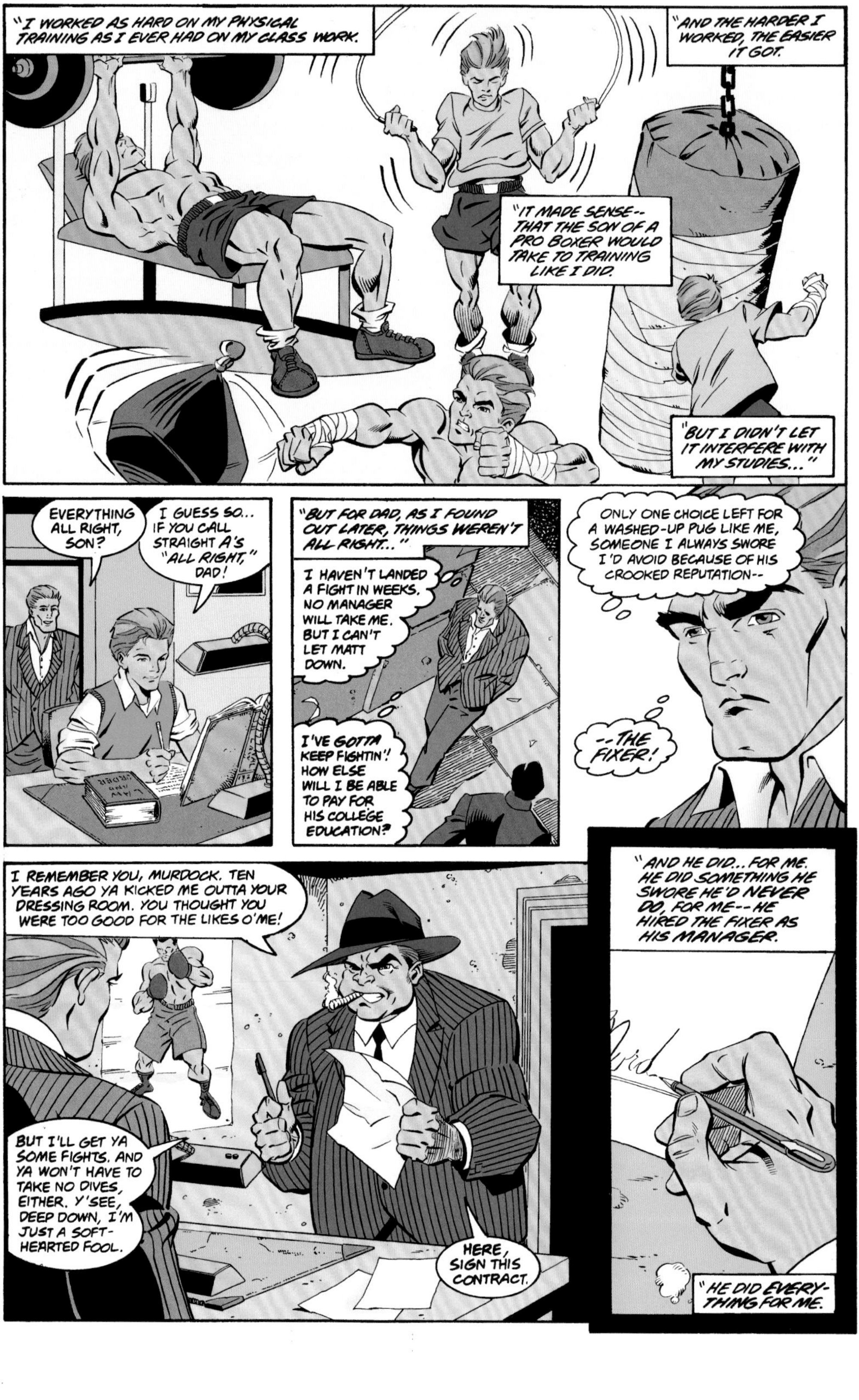
"I WORKED AS HARD ON MY PHYSICAL TRAINING AS I EVER HAD ON MY CLASS WORK.
"AND THE HARDER I WORKED, THE EASIER IT GOT.
"IT MADE SENSE-- THAT THE SON OF A PRO BOXER WOULD TAKE TO TRAINING LIKE I DID.
"BUT I DIDN'T LET IT INTERFERE WITH MY STUDIES..."
EVERYTHING ALL RIGHT, SON?
I GUESS SO... IF YOU CALL STRAIGHT A's "ALL RIGHT," DAD!
"BUT FOR DAD, AS I FOUND OUT LATER, THINGS WEREN'T ALL RIGHT..."
I HAVEN'T LANDED A FIGHT IN WEEKS. NO MANAGER WILL TAKE ME. BUT I CAN'T LET MATT DOWN.
I'VE GOTTA KEEP FIGHTIN'! HOW ELSE WILL I BE ABLE TO PAY FOR HIS COLLEGE EDUCATION?
ONLY ONE CHOICE LEFT FOR A WASHED-UP PUG LIKE ME, SOMEONE I ALWAYS SWORE I'D AVOID BECAUSE OF HIS CROOKED REPUTATION--
--THE FIXER!
I REMEMBER YOU, MURDOCK. TEN YEARS AGO YA KICKED ME OUTTA YOUR DRESSING ROOM. YOU THOUGHT YOU WERE TOO GOOD FOR THE LIKES O'ME!
BUT I'LL GET YA SOME FIGHTS. AND YA WON'T HAVE TO TAKE NO DIVES, EITHER. Y'SEE, DEEP DOWN, I'M JUST A SOFT-HEARTED FOOL.
HERE, SIGN THIS CONTRACT.
"AND HE DID... FOR ME. HE DID SOMETHING HE SWORE HE'D NEVER DO, FOR ME-- HE HIRED THE FIXER AS HIS MANAGER.
"HE DID EVERYTHING FOR ME.

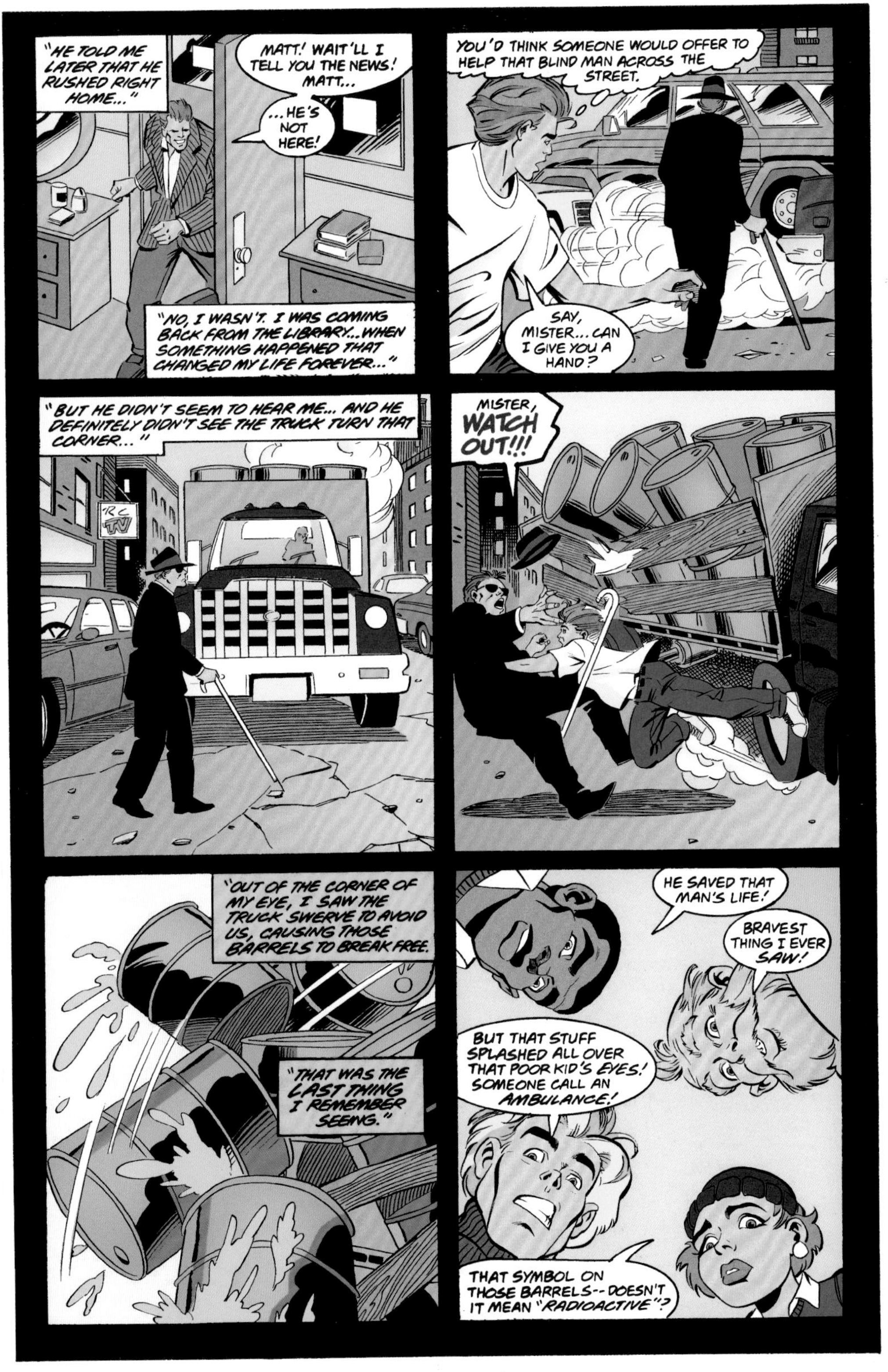
"HE TOLD ME LATER THAT HE RUSHED RIGHT HOME..."
MATT! WAIT'LL I TELL YOU THE NEWS! MATT...
...HE'S NOT HERE!
"NO, I WASN'T. I WAS COMING BACK FROM THE LIBRARY... WHEN SOMETHING HAPPENED THAT CHANGED MY LIFE FOREVER..."
YOU'D THINK SOMEONE WOULD OFFER TO HELP THAT BLIND MAN ACROSS THE STREET.
SAY, MISTER... CAN I GIVE YOU A HAND?
"BUT HE DIDN'T SEEM TO HEAR ME... AND HE DEFINITELY DIDN'T SEE THE TRUCK TURN THAT CORNER..."
RC TV
MISTER, WATCH OUT!!!
"OUT OF THE CORNER OF MY EYE, I SAW THE TRUCK SWERVE TO AVOID US, CAUSING THOSE BARRELS TO BREAK FREE.
"THAT WAS THE LAST THING I REMEMBER SEEING."
HE SAVED THAT MAN'S LIFE!
BRAVEST THING I EVER SAW!
BUT THAT STUFF SPLASHED ALL OVER THAT POOR KID'S EYES! SOMEONE CALL AN AMBULANCE!
THAT SYMBOL ON THOSE BARRELS--DOESN'T IT MEAN "RADIOACTIVE"?

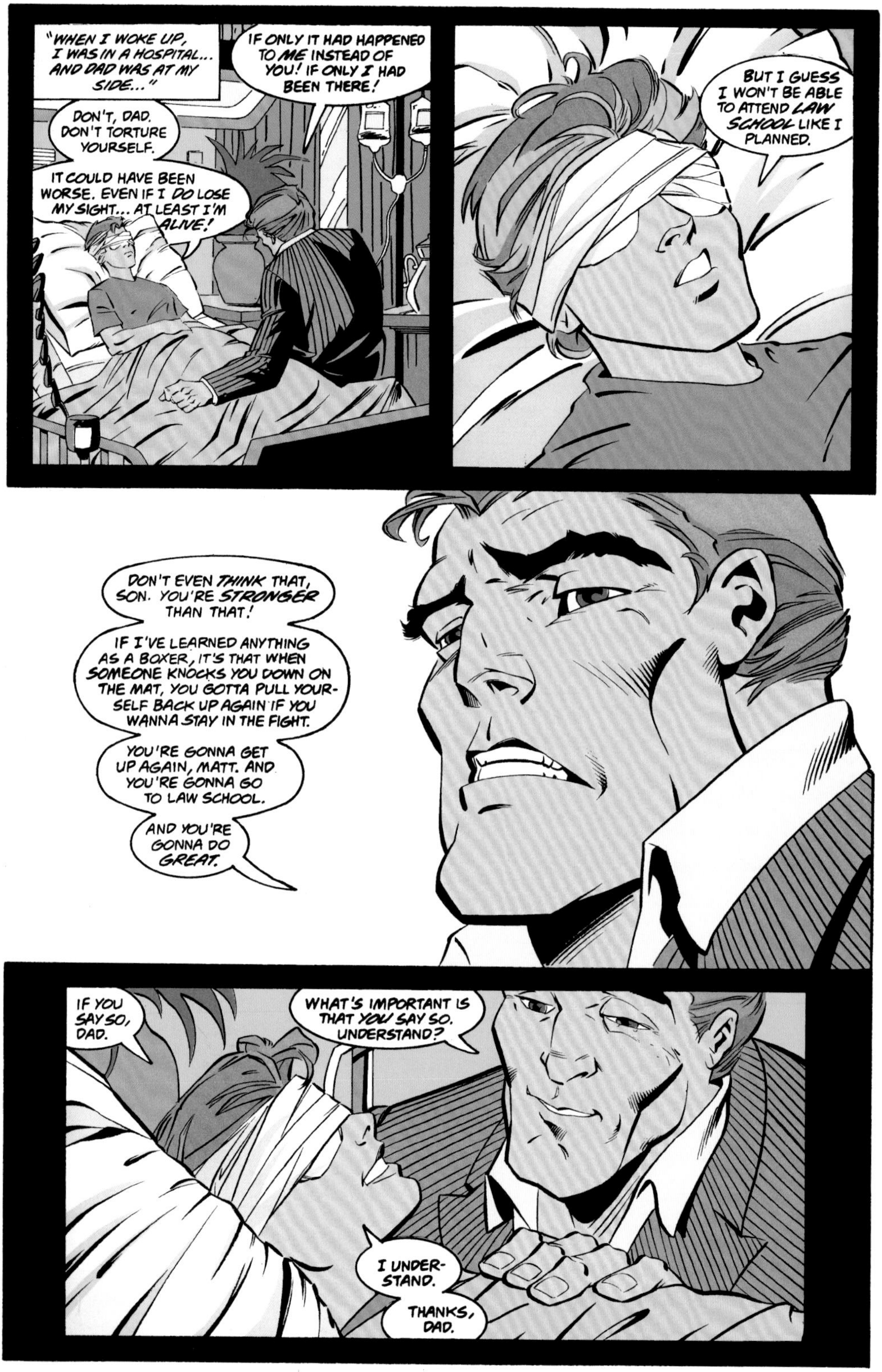
"WHEN I WOKE UP, I WAS IN A HOSPITAL... AND DAD WAS AT MY SIDE..."
IF ONLY IT HAD HAPPENED TO ME INSTEAD OF YOU! IF ONLY I HAD BEEN THERE!
DON'T, DAD. DON'T TORTURE YOURSELF.
IT COULD HAVE BEEN WORSE. EVEN IF I DO LOSE MY SIGHT... AT LEAST I'M ALIVE!
BUT I GUESS I WON'T BE ABLE TO ATTEND LAW SCHOOL LIKE I PLANNED.
DON'T EVEN THINK THAT, SON. YOU'RE STRONGER THAN THAT!
IF I'VE LEARNED ANYTHING AS A BOXER, IT'S THAT WHEN SOMEONE KNOCKS YOU DOWN ON THE MAT, YOU GOTTA PULL YOURSELF BACK UP AGAIN IF YOU WANNA STAY IN THE FIGHT.
YOU'RE GONNA GET UP AGAIN, MATT. AND YOU'RE GONNA GO TO LAW SCHOOL.
AND YOU'RE GONNA DO GREAT.
IF YOU SAY SO, DAD.
WHAT'S IMPORTANT IS THAT YOU SAY SO. UNDERSTAND?
I UNDERSTAND.
THANKS, DAD.

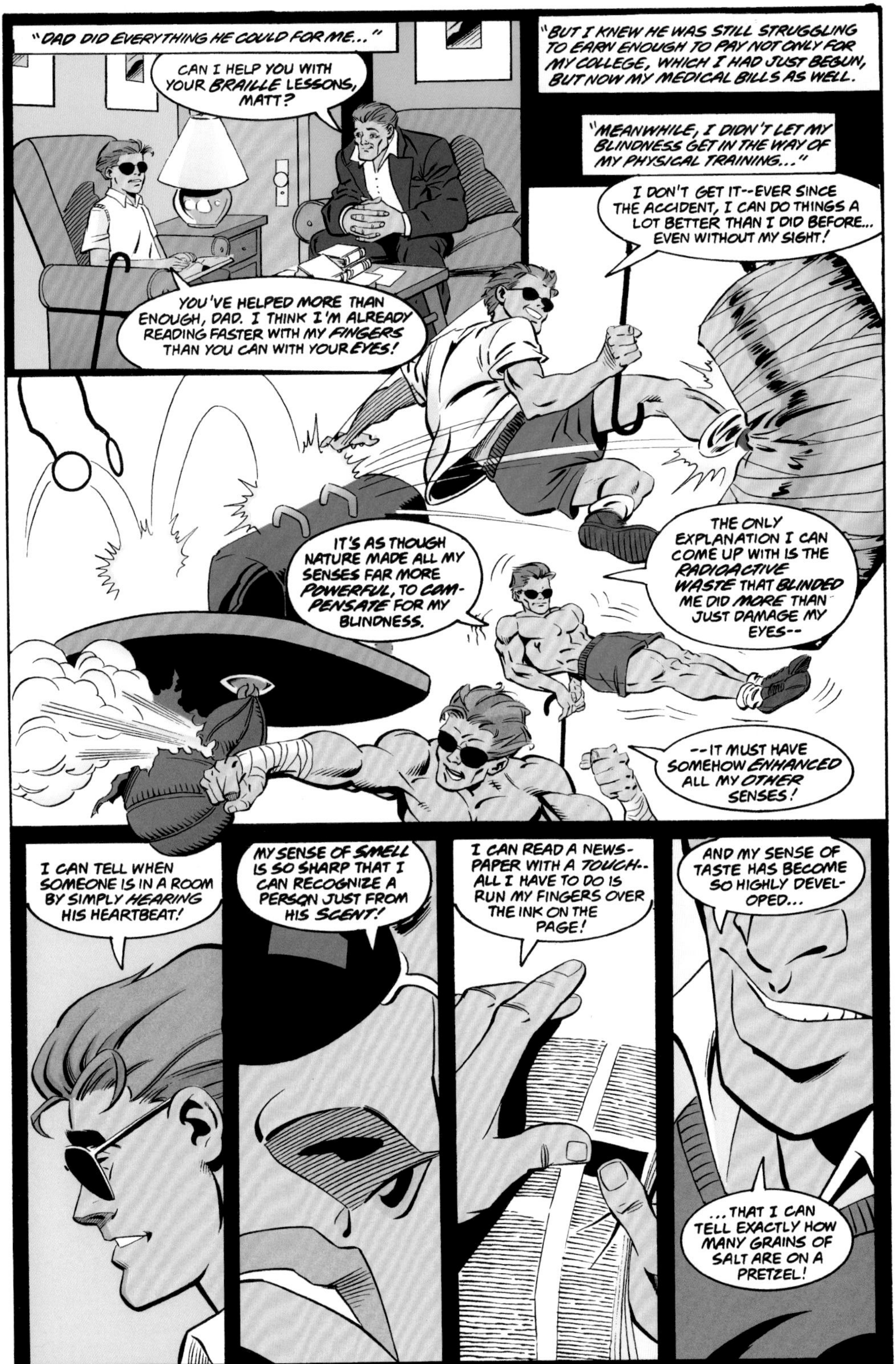
"DAD DID EVERYTHING HE COULD FOR ME..."
CAN I HELP YOU WITH YOUR BRAILLE LESSONS, MATT?
YOU'VE HELPED MORE THAN ENOUGH, DAD. I THINK I'M ALREADY READING FASTER WITH MY FINGERS THAN YOU CAN WITH YOUR EYES!
"BUT I KNEW HE WAS STILL STRUGGLING TO EARN ENOUGH TO PAY NOT ONLY FOR MY COLLEGE, WHICH I HAD JUST BEGUN, BUT NOW MY MEDICAL BILLS AS WELL.
"MEANWHILE, I DIDN'T LET MY BLINDNESS GET IN THE WAY OF MY PHYSICAL TRAINING..."
I DON'T GET IT--EVER SINCE THE ACCIDENT, I CAN DO THINGS A LOT BETTER THAN I DID BEFORE... EVEN WITHOUT MY SIGHT!
IT'S AS THOUGH NATURE MADE ALL MY SENSES FAR MORE POWERFUL, TO COMPENSATE FOR MY BLINDNESS.
THE ONLY EXPLANATION I CAN COME UP WITH IS THE RADIOACTIVE WASTE THAT BLINDED ME DID MORE THAN JUST DAMAGE MY EYES--
--IT MUST HAVE SOMEHOW ENHANCED ALL MY OTHER SENSES!
I CAN TELL WHEN SOMEONE IS IN A ROOM BY SIMPLY HEARING HIS HEARTBEAT!
MY SENSE OF SMELL IS SO SHARP THAT I CAN RECOGNIZE A PERSON JUST FROM HIS SCENT!
I CAN READ A NEWSPAPER WITH A TOUCH-- ALL I HAVE TO DO IS RUN MY FINGERS OVER THE INK ON THE PAGE!
AND MY SENSE OF TASTE HAS BECOME SO HIGHLY DEVELOPED...
...THAT I CAN TELL EXACTLY HOW MANY GRAINS OF SALT ARE ON A PRETZEL!

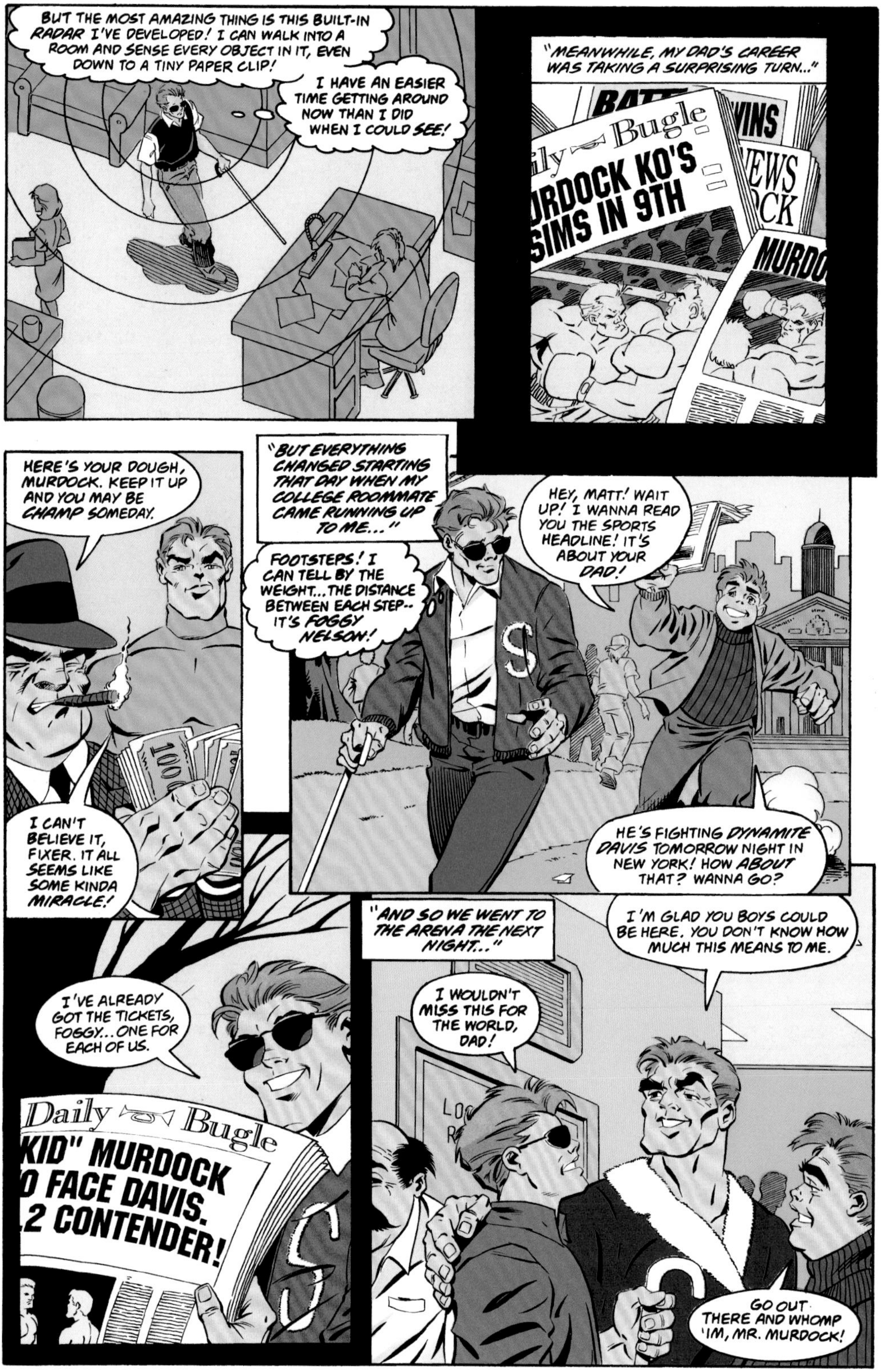
BUT THE MOST AMAZING THING IS THIS BUILT-IN RADAR I'VE DEVELOPED! I CAN WALK INTO A ROOM AND SENSE EVERY OBJECT IN IT, EVEN DOWN TO A TINY PAPER CLIP!
I HAVE AN EASIER TIME GETTING AROUND NOW THAN I DID WHEN I COULD SEE!
"MEANWHILE, MY DAD'S CAREER WAS TAKING A SURPRISING TURN..."
Daily Bugle
MURDOCK KO'S SIMS IN 9TH
MURDO
HERE'S YOUR DOUGH, MURDOCK. KEEP IT UP AND YOU MAY BE CHAMP SOMEDAY.
I CAN'T BELIEVE IT, FIXER. IT ALL SEEMS LIKE SOME KINDA MIRACLE!
"BUT EVERYTHING CHANGED STARTING THAT DAY WHEN MY COLLEGE ROOMMATE CAME RUNNING UP TO ME..."
FOOTSTEPS! I CAN TELL BY THE WEIGHT...THE DISTANCE BETWEEN EACH STEP.. IT'S FOGGY NELSON!
HEY, MATT! WAIT UP! I WANNA READ YOU THE SPORTS HEADLINE! IT'S ABOUT YOUR DAD!
HE'S FIGHTING DYNAMITE DAVIS TOMORROW NIGHT IN NEW YORK! HOW ABOUT THAT? WANNA GO?
I'VE ALREADY GOT THE TICKETS, FOGGY...ONE FOR EACH OF US.
Daily Bugle
"KID" MURDOCK TO FACE DAVIS. 2 CONTENDER!
"AND SO WE WENT TO THE ARENA THE NEXT NIGHT..."
I'M GLAD YOU BOYS COULD BE HERE. YOU DON'T KNOW HOW MUCH THIS MEANS TO ME.
I WOULDN'T MISS THIS FOR THE WORLD, DAD!
GO OUT THERE AND WHOMP 'IM, MR. MURDOCK!

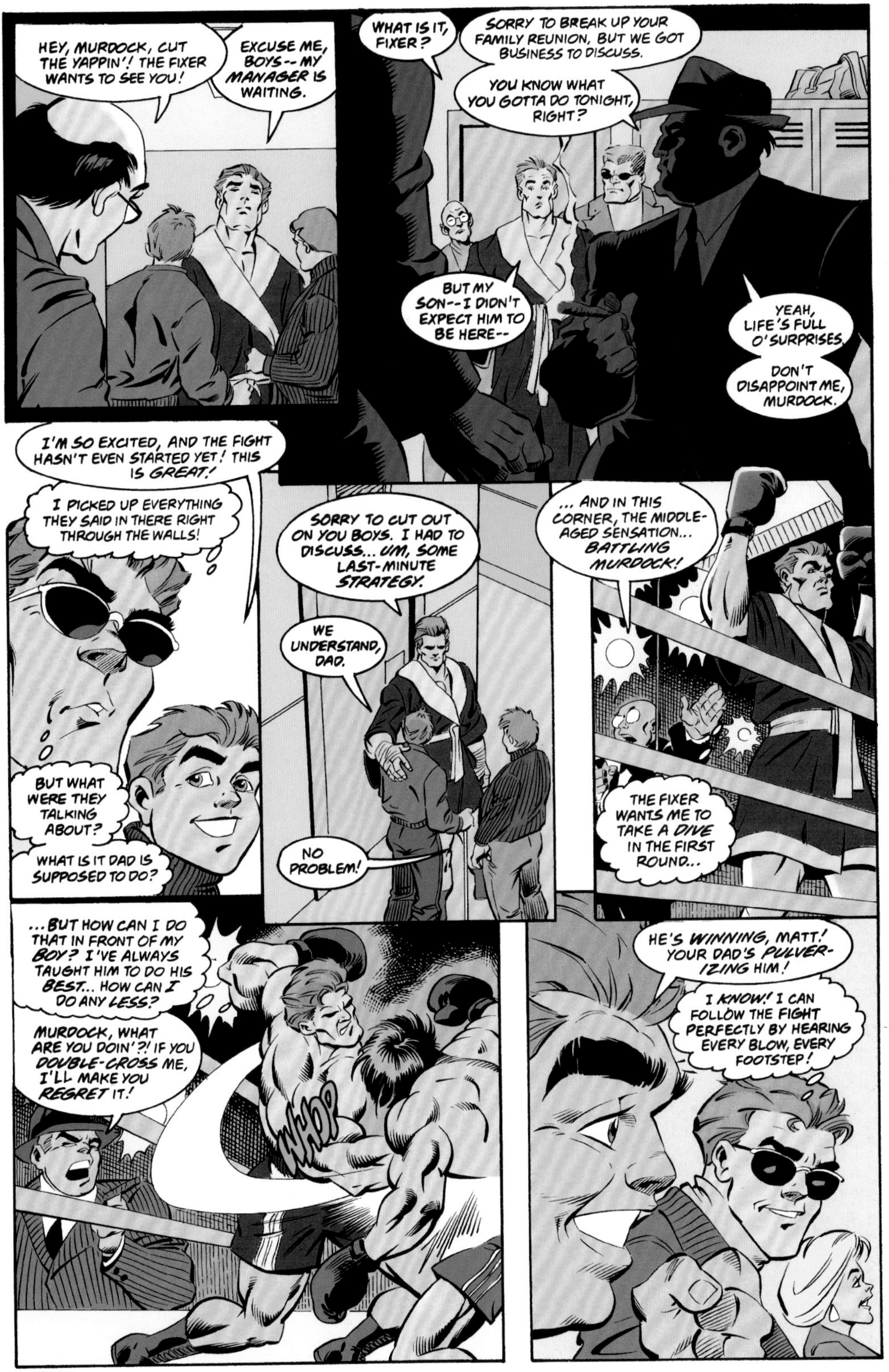
HEY, MURDOCK, CUT THE YAPPIN'! THE FIXER WANTS TO SEE YOU!
EXCUSE ME, BOYS--MY MANAGER IS WAITING.
WHAT IS IT, FIXER?
SORRY TO BREAK UP YOUR FAMILY REUNION, BUT WE GOT BUSINESS TO DISCUSS.
YOU KNOW WHAT YOU GOTTA DO TONIGHT, RIGHT?
BUT MY SON--I DIDN'T EXPECT HIM TO BE HERE--
YEAH, LIFE'S FULL O' SURPRISES.
DON'T DISAPPOINT ME, MURDOCK.
I'M SO EXCITED, AND THE FIGHT HASN'T EVEN STARTED YET! THIS IS GREAT!
I PICKED UP EVERYTHING THEY SAID IN THERE RIGHT THROUGH THE WALLS!
BUT WHAT WERE THEY TALKING ABOUT?
WHAT IS IT DAD IS SUPPOSED TO DO?
SORRY TO CUT OUT ON YOU BOYS. I HAD TO DISCUSS... UM, SOME LAST-MINUTE STRATEGY.
WE UNDERSTAND, DAD.
NO PROBLEM!
... AND IN THIS CORNER, THE MIDDLE-AGED SENSATION... BATTLING MURDOCK!
THE FIXER WANTS ME TO TAKE A DIVE IN THE FIRST ROUND...
... BUT HOW CAN I DO THAT IN FRONT OF MY BOY? I'VE ALWAYS TAUGHT HIM TO DO HIS BEST... HOW CAN I DO ANY LESS?
MURDOCK, WHAT ARE YOU DOIN'?! IF YOU DOUBLE-CROSS ME, I'LL MAKE YOU REGRET IT!
WHOP
HE'S WINNING, MATT! YOUR DAD'S PULVERIZING HIM!
I KNOW! I CAN FOLLOW THE FIGHT PERFECTLY BY HEARING EVERY BLOW, EVERY FOOTSTEP!

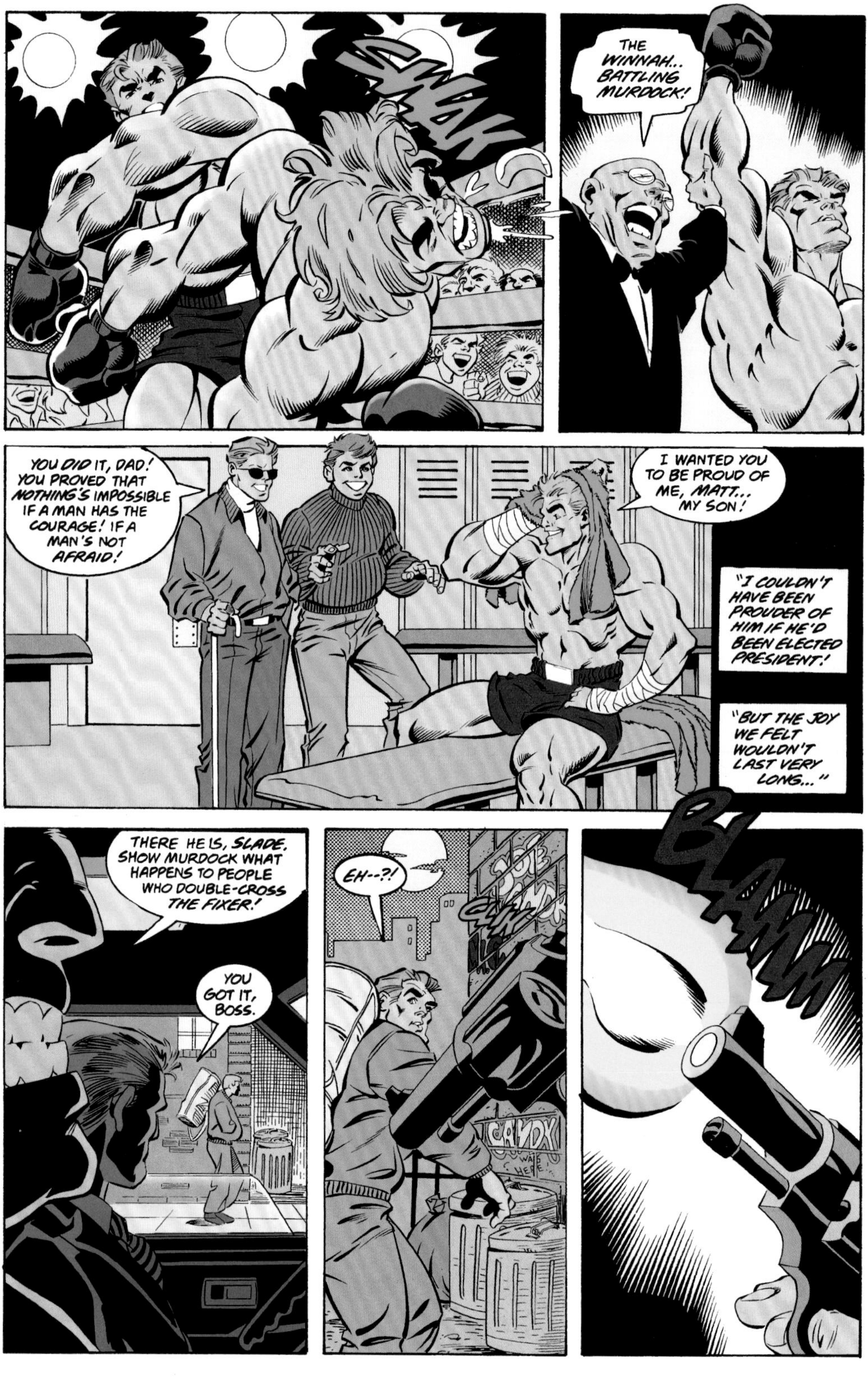
SMAK
THE WINNAH... BATTLING MURDOCK!
YOU DID IT, DAD! YOU PROVED THAT NOTHING'S IMPOSSIBLE IF A MAN HAS THE COURAGE! IF A MAN'S NOT AFRAID!
I WANTED YOU TO BE PROUD OF ME, MATT... MY SON!
"I COULDN'T HAVE BEEN PROUDER OF HIM IF HE'D BEEN ELECTED PRESIDENT!
"BUT THE JOY WE FELT WOULDN'T LAST VERY LONG..."
THERE HE IS, SLADE. SHOW MURDOCK WHAT HAPPENS TO PEOPLE WHO DOUBLE-CROSS THE FIXER!
YOU GOT IT, BOSS.
EH--?!
CANDY
BLAMM

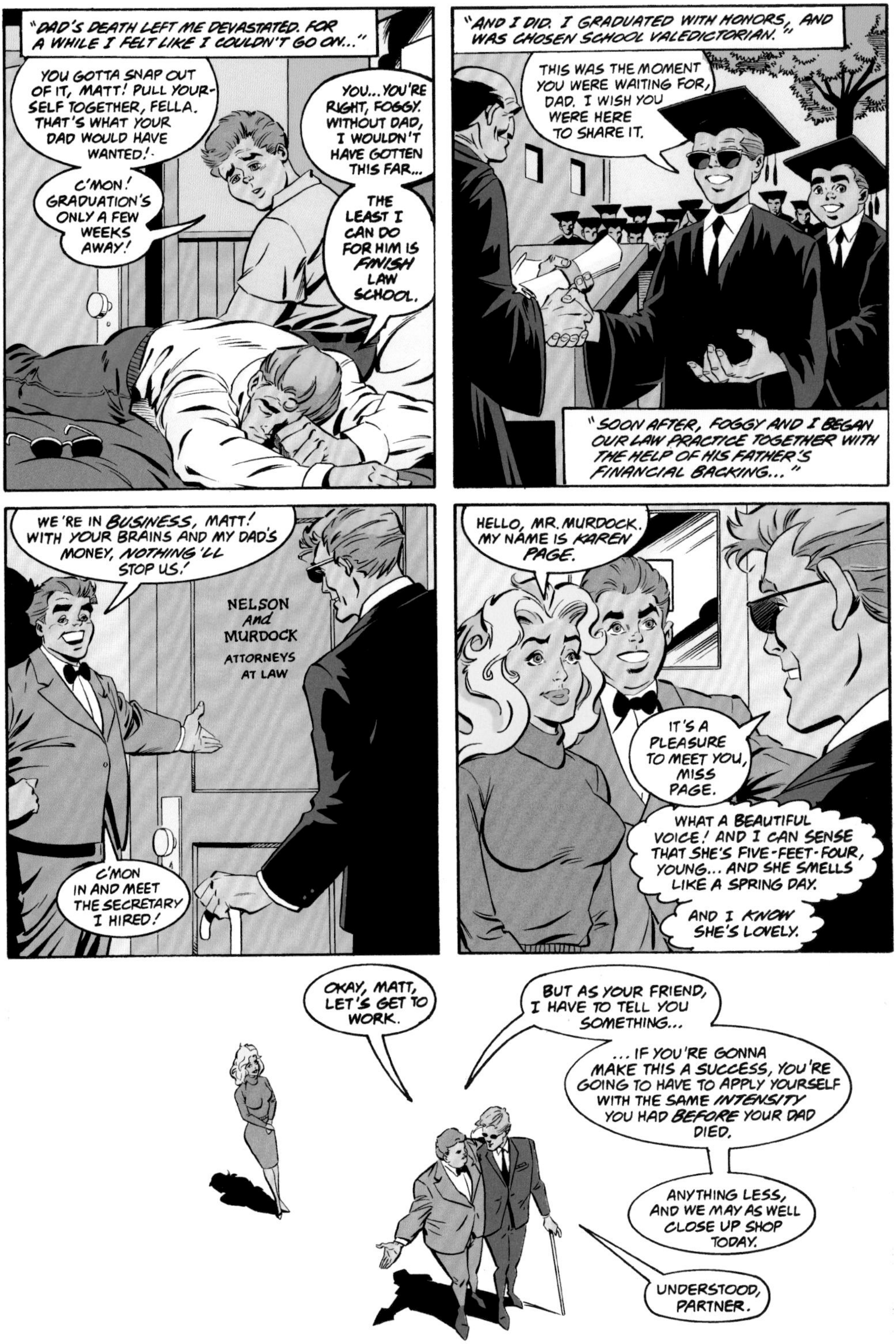
"DAD'S DEATH LEFT ME DEVASTATED. FOR A WHILE I FELT LIKE I COULDN'T GO ON..."
YOU GOTTA SNAP OUT OF IT, MATT! PULL YOURSELF TOGETHER, FELLA. THAT'S WHAT YOUR DAD WOULD HAVE WANTED!
C'MON! GRADUATION'S ONLY A FEW WEEKS AWAY!
YOU...YOU'RE RIGHT, FOGGY. WITHOUT DAD, I WOULDN'T HAVE GOTTEN THIS FAR...
THE LEAST I CAN DO FOR HIM IS FINISH LAW SCHOOL.
"AND I DID. I GRADUATED WITH HONORS, AND WAS CHOSEN SCHOOL VALEDICTORIAN."
THIS WAS THE MOMENT YOU WERE WAITING FOR, DAD. I WISH YOU WERE HERE TO SHARE IT.
"SOON AFTER, FOGGY AND I BEGAN OUR LAW PRACTICE TOGETHER WITH THE HELP OF HIS FATHER'S FINANCIAL BACKING..."
WE'RE IN BUSINESS, MATT! WITH YOUR BRAINS AND MY DAD'S MONEY, NOTHING'LL STOP US!
NELSON and MURDOCK ATTORNEYS AT LAW
C'MON IN AND MEET THE SECRETARY I HIRED!
HELLO, MR. MURDOCK. MY NAME IS KAREN PAGE.
IT'S A PLEASURE TO MEET YOU, MISS PAGE.
WHAT A BEAUTIFUL VOICE! AND I CAN SENSE THAT SHE'S FIVE-FEET-FOUR, YOUNG... AND SHE SMELLS LIKE A SPRING DAY.
AND I KNOW SHE'S LOVELY.
OKAY, MATT, LET'S GET TO WORK.
BUT AS YOUR FRIEND, I HAVE TO TELL YOU SOMETHING...
... IF YOU'RE GONNA MAKE THIS A SUCCESS, YOU'RE GOING TO HAVE TO APPLY YOURSELF WITH THE SAME INTENSITY YOU HAD BEFORE YOUR DAD DIED.
ANYTHING LESS, AND WE MAY AS WELL CLOSE UP SHOP TODAY.
UNDERSTOOD, PARTNER.

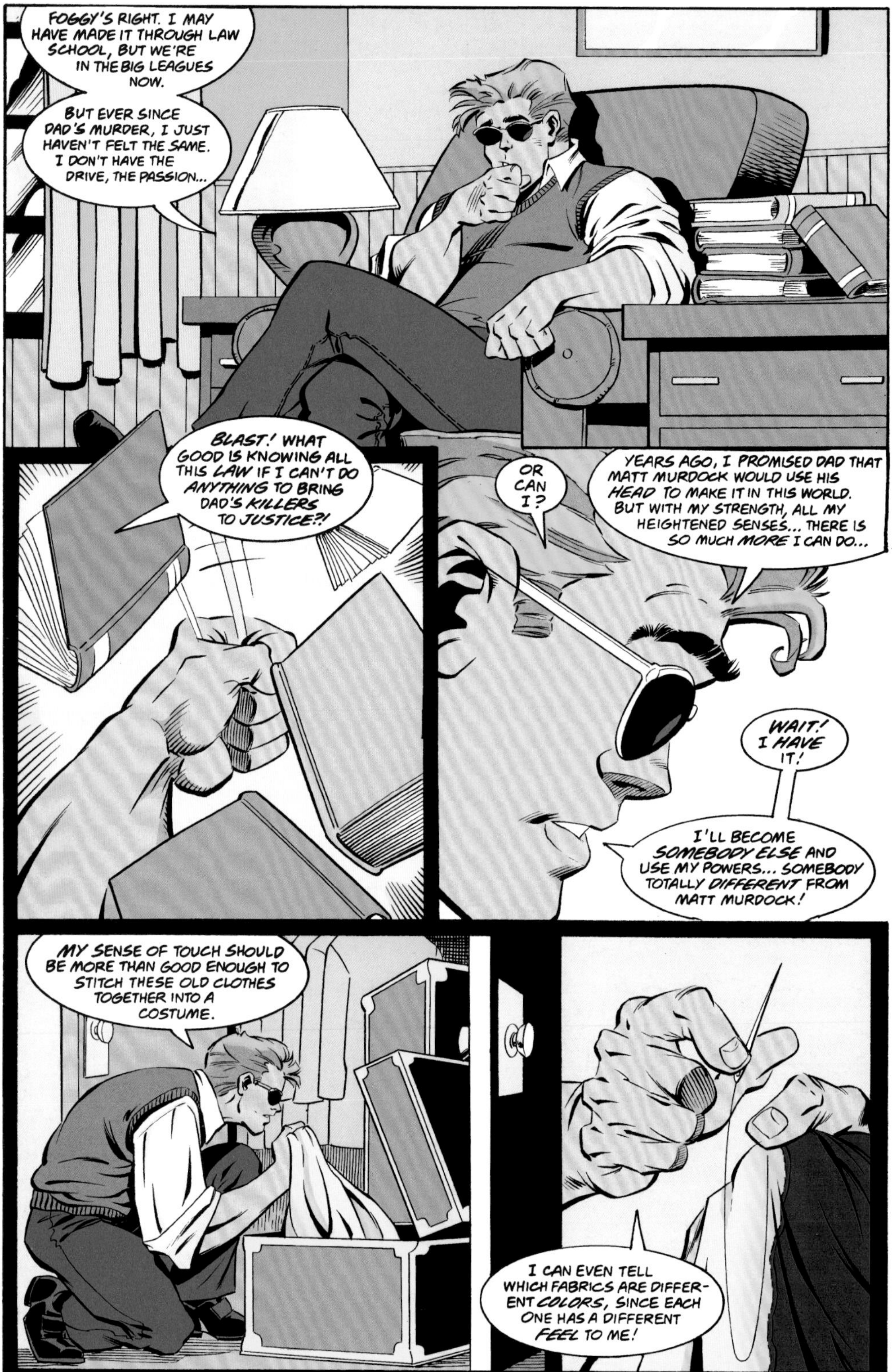
FOGGY'S RIGHT. I MAY HAVE MADE IT THROUGH LAW SCHOOL, BUT WE'RE IN THE BIG LEAGUES NOW.
BUT EVER SINCE DAD'S MURDER, I JUST HAVEN'T FELT THE SAME. I DON'T HAVE THE DRIVE, THE PASSION...
BLAST! WHAT GOOD IS KNOWING ALL THIS LAW IF I CAN'T DO ANYTHING TO BRING DAD'S KILLERS TO JUSTICE?!
OR CAN I?
YEARS AGO, I PROMISED DAD THAT MATT MURDOCK WOULD USE HIS HEAD TO MAKE IT IN THIS WORLD. BUT WITH MY STRENGTH, ALL MY HEIGHTENED SENSES... THERE IS SO MUCH MORE I CAN DO...
WAIT! I HAVE IT!
I'LL BECOME SOMEBODY ELSE AND USE MY POWERS... SOMEBODY TOTALLY DIFFERENT FROM MATT MURDOCK!
MY SENSE OF TOUCH SHOULD BE MORE THAN GOOD ENOUGH TO STITCH THESE OLD CLOTHES TOGETHER INTO A COSTUME.
I CAN EVEN TELL WHICH FABRICS ARE DIFFERENT COLORS, SINCE EACH ONE HAS A DIFFERENT FEEL TO ME!

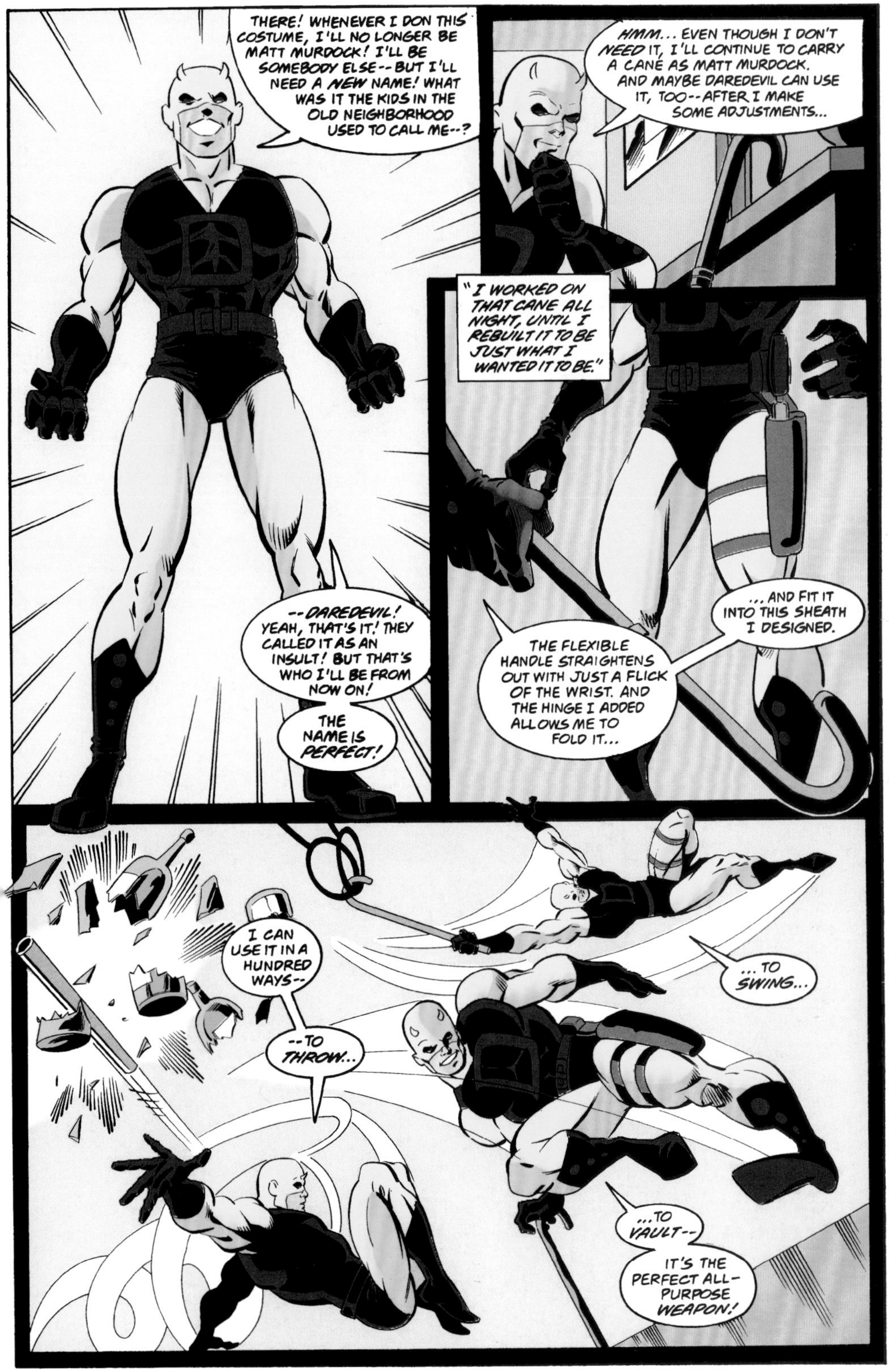
THERE! WHENEVER I DON THIS COSTUME, I'LL NO LONGER BE MATT MURDOCK! I'LL BE SOMEBODY ELSE--BUT I'LL NEED A NEW NAME! WHAT WAS IT THE KIDS IN THE OLD NEIGHBORHOOD USED TO CALL ME--?
--DAREDEVIL! YEAH, THAT'S IT! THEY CALLED IT AS AN INSULT! BUT THAT'S WHO I'LL BE FROM NOW ON!
THE NAME IS PERFECT!
HMM... EVEN THOUGH I DON'T NEED IT, I'LL CONTINUE TO CARRY A CANE AS MATT MURDOCK. AND MAYBE DAREDEVIL CAN USE IT, TOO--AFTER I MAKE SOME ADJUSTMENTS...
"I WORKED ON THAT CANE ALL NIGHT, UNTIL I REBUILT IT TO BE JUST WHAT I WANTED IT TO BE."
THE FLEXIBLE HANDLE STRAIGHTENS OUT WITH JUST A FLICK OF THE WRIST. AND THE HINGE I ADDED ALLOWS ME TO FOLD IT...
...AND FIT IT INTO THIS SHEATH I DESIGNED.
I CAN USE IT IN A HUNDRED WAYS--
--TO THROW...
...TO SWING...
...TO VAULT--
IT'S THE PERFECT ALL-PURPOSE WEAPON!

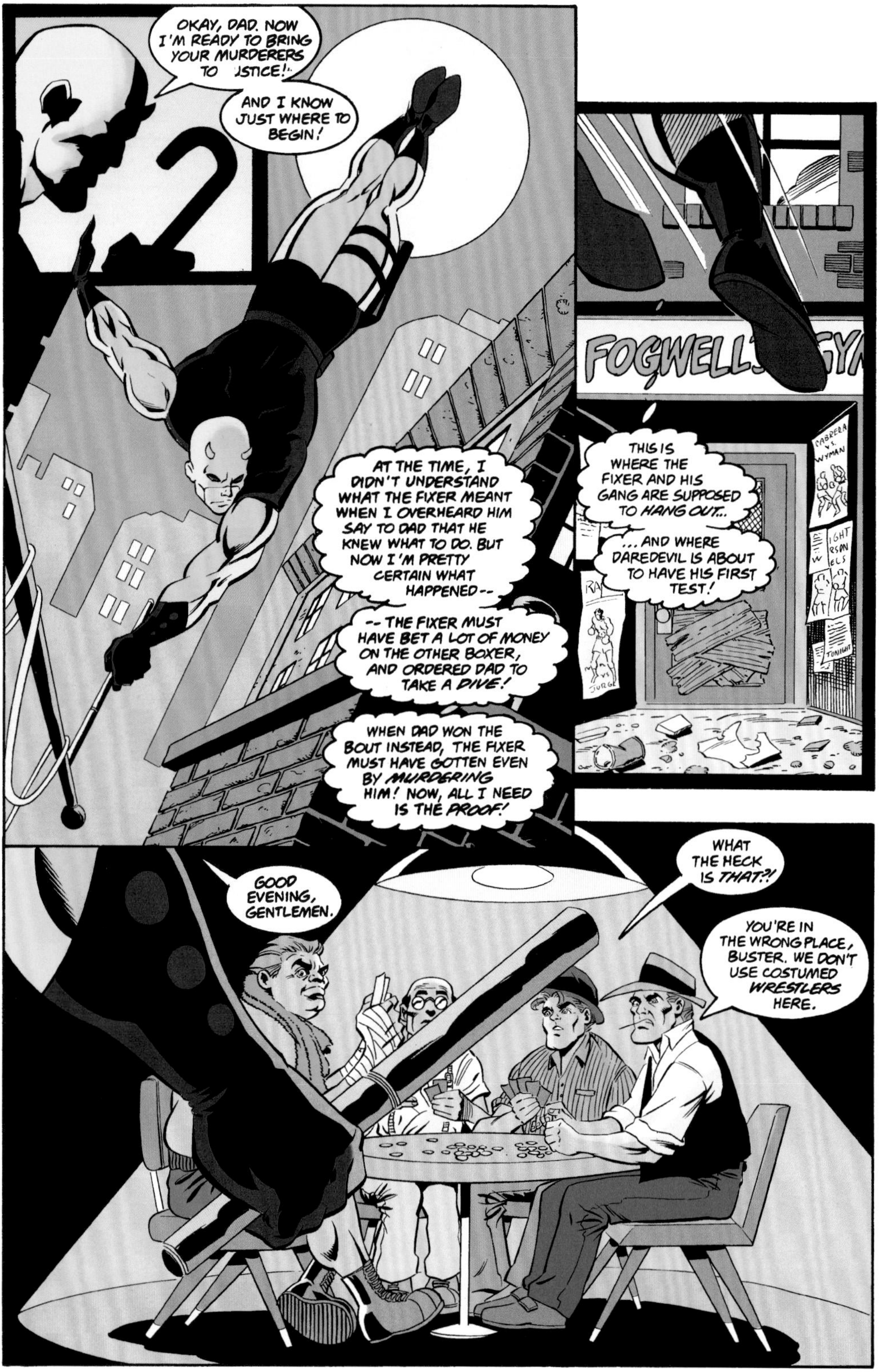
OKAY, DAD. NOW I'M READY TO BRING YOUR MURDERERS TO JUSTICE!
AND I KNOW JUST WHERE TO BEGIN!
AT THE TIME, I DIDN'T UNDERSTAND WHAT THE FIXER MEANT WHEN I OVERHEARD HIM SAY TO DAD THAT HE KNEW WHAT TO DO. BUT NOW I'M PRETTY CERTAIN WHAT HAPPENED--
--THE FIXER MUST HAVE BET A LOT OF MONEY ON THE OTHER BOXER, AND ORDERED DAD TO TAKE A DIVE!
WHEN DAD WON THE BOUT INSTEAD, THE FIXER MUST HAVE GOTTEN EVEN BY MURDERING HIM! NOW, ALL I NEED IS THE PROOF!
FOGWELL'S GYM
CABRERA VS. WYMAN
TONIGHT
THIS IS WHERE THE FIXER AND HIS GANG ARE SUPPOSED TO HANG OUT...
...AND WHERE DAREDEVIL IS ABOUT TO HAVE HIS FIRST TEST!
GOOD EVENING, GENTLEMEN.
WHAT THE HECK IS THAT?!
YOU'RE IN THE WRONG PLACE, BUSTER. WE DON'T USE COSTUMED WRESTLERS HERE.

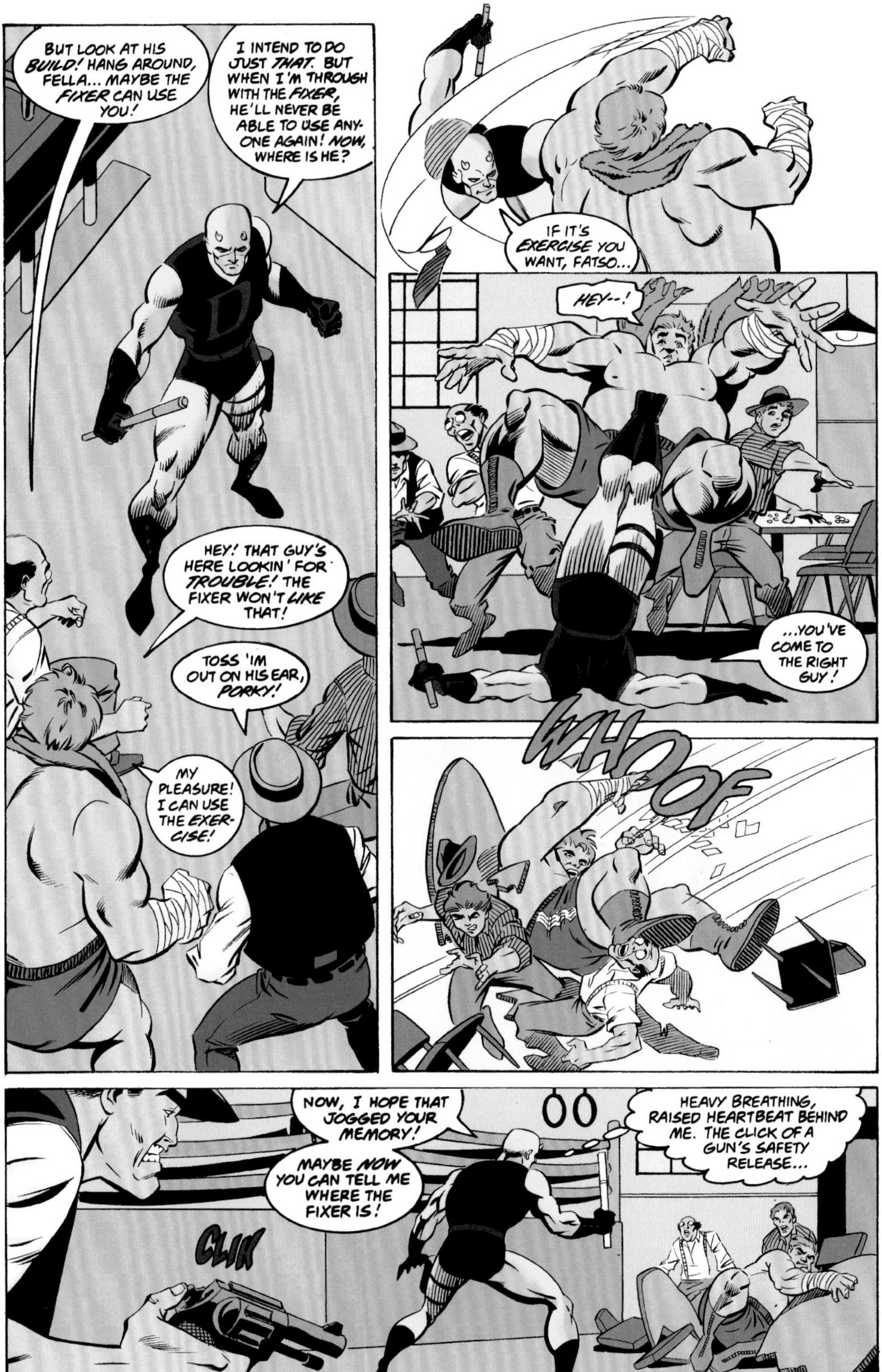
BUT LOOK AT HIS BUILD! HANG AROUND, FELLA... MAYBE THE FIXER CAN USE YOU!
I INTEND TO DO JUST THAT. BUT WHEN I'M THROUGH WITH THE FIXER, HE'LL NEVER BE ABLE TO USE ANYONE AGAIN! NOW, WHERE IS HE?
HEY! THAT GUY'S HERE LOOKIN' FOR TROUBLE! THE FIXER WON'T LIKE THAT!
TOSS 'IM OUT ON HIS EAR, PORKY!
MY PLEASURE! I CAN USE THE EXERCISE!
IF IT'S EXERCISE YOU WANT, FATSO...
HEY--!
...YOU'VE COME TO THE RIGHT GUY!
WHOOF
NOW, I HOPE THAT JOGGED YOUR MEMORY!
MAYBE NOW YOU CAN TELL ME WHERE THE FIXER IS!
HEAVY BREATHING, RAISED HEARTBEAT BEHIND ME. THE CLICK OF A GUN'S SAFETY RELEASE...
CLIK

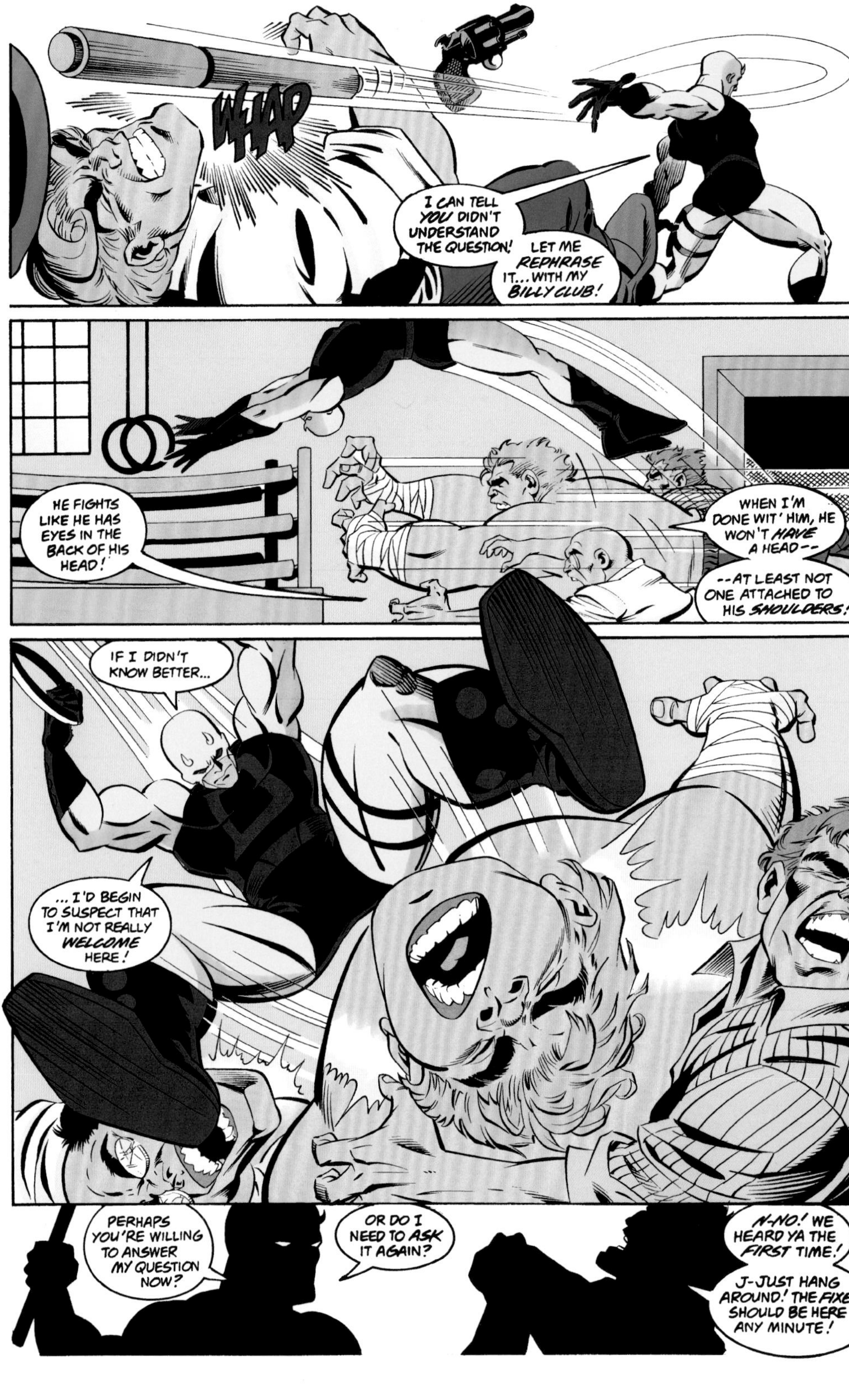
WHAP
I CAN TELL YOU DIDN'T UNDERSTAND THE QUESTION!
LET ME REPHRASE IT... WITH MY BILLY CLUB!
HE FIGHTS LIKE HE HAS EYES IN THE BACK OF HIS HEAD!
WHEN I'M DONE WIT' HIM, HE WON'T HAVE A HEAD--
--AT LEAST NOT ONE ATTACHED TO HIS SHOULDERS!
IF I DIDN'T KNOW BETTER...
...I'D BEGIN TO SUSPECT THAT I'M NOT REALLY WELCOME HERE!
PERHAPS YOU'RE WILLING TO ANSWER MY QUESTION NOW?
OR DO I NEED TO ASK IT AGAIN?
N-NO! WE HEARD YA THE FIRST TIME!
J-JUST HANG AROUND! THE FIXER SHOULD BE HERE ANY MINUTE!

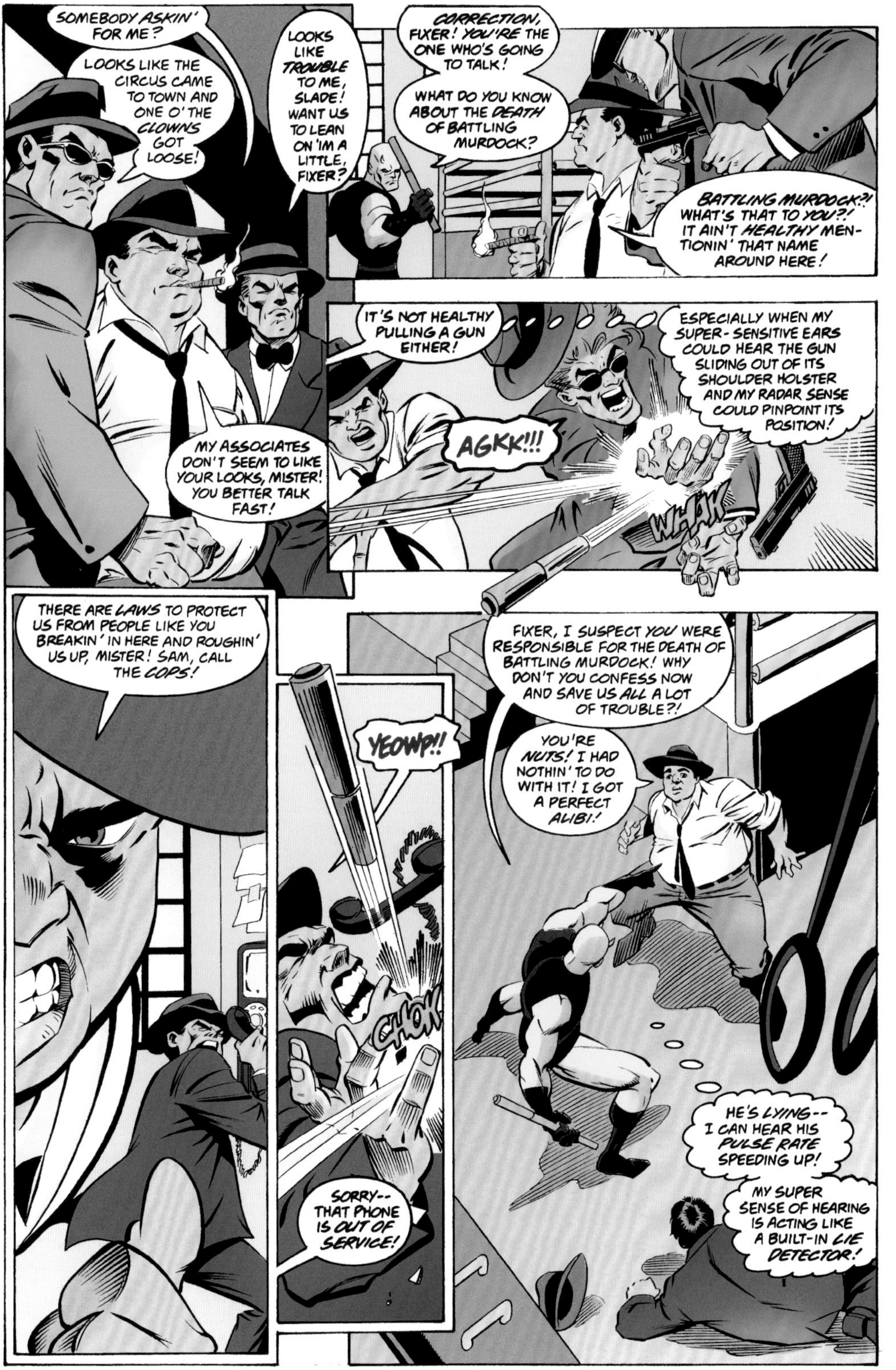
SOMEBODY ASKIN' FOR ME?
LOOKS LIKE THE CIRCUS CAME TO TOWN AND ONE O' THE CLOWNS GOT LOOSE!
MY ASSOCIATES DON'T SEEM TO LIKE YOUR LOOKS, MISTER! YOU BETTER TALK FAST!
LOOKS LIKE TROUBLE TO ME, SLADE! WANT US TO LEAN ON 'IM A LITTLE, FIXER?
CORRECTION, FIXER! YOU'RE THE ONE WHO'S GOING TO TALK!
WHAT DO YOU KNOW ABOUT THE DEATH OF BATTLING MURDOCK?
BATTLING MURDOCK?! WHAT'S THAT TO YOU?! IT AIN'T HEALTHY MEN-TIONIN' THAT NAME AROUND HERE!
IT'S NOT HEALTHY PULLING A GUN EITHER!
ESPECIALLY WHEN MY SUPER-SENSITIVE EARS COULD HEAR THE GUN SLIDING OUT OF ITS SHOULDER HOLSTER AND MY RADAR SENSE COULD PINPOINT ITS POSITION!
AGKK!!!
WHAK
THERE ARE LAWS TO PROTECT US FROM PEOPLE LIKE YOU BREAKIN' IN HERE AND ROUGHIN' US UP, MISTER! SAM, CALL THE COPS!
YEOWP!!
CHOK
SORRY-- THAT PHONE IS OUT OF SERVICE!
FIXER, I SUSPECT YOU WERE RESPONSIBLE FOR THE DEATH OF BATTLING MURDOCK! WHY DON'T YOU CONFESS NOW AND SAVE US ALL A LOT OF TROUBLE?!
YOU'RE NUTS! I HAD NOTHIN' TO DO WITH IT! I GOT A PERFECT ALIBI!
HE'S LYING-- I CAN HEAR HIS PULSE RATE SPEEDING UP!
MY SUPER SENSE OF HEARING IS ACTING LIKE A BUILT-IN LIE DETECTOR!

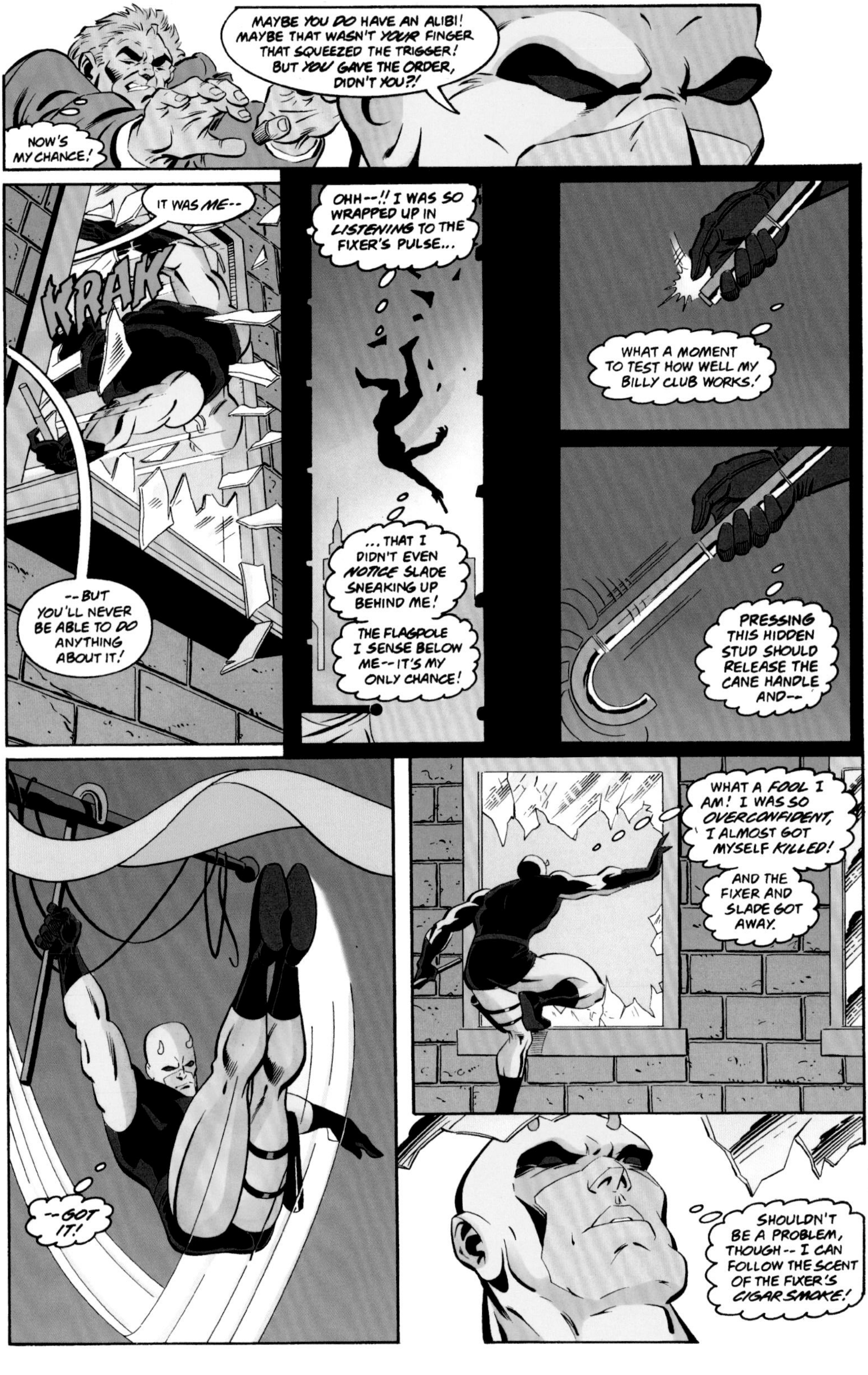
MAYBE YOU DO HAVE AN ALIBI! MAYBE THAT WASN'T YOUR FINGER THAT SQUEEZED THE TRIGGER! BUT YOU GAVE THE ORDER, DIDN'T YOU?!
NOW'S MY CHANCE!
IT WAS ME--
KRAK
--BUT YOU'LL NEVER BE ABLE TO DO ANYTHING ABOUT IT!
OHH--!! I WAS SO WRAPPED UP IN LISTENING TO THE FIXER'S PULSE...
...THAT I DIDN'T EVEN NOTICE SLADE SNEAKING UP BEHIND ME!
THE FLAGPOLE I SENSE BELOW ME--IT'S MY ONLY CHANCE!
WHAT A MOMENT TO TEST HOW WELL MY BILLY CLUB WORKS!
PRESSING THIS HIDDEN STUD SHOULD RELEASE THE CANE HANDLE AND--
--GOT IT!
WHAT A FOOL I AM! I WAS SO OVERCONFIDENT, I ALMOST GOT MYSELF KILLED!
AND THE FIXER AND SLADE GOT AWAY.
SHOULDN'T BE A PROBLEM, THOUGH--I CAN FOLLOW THE SCENT OF THE FIXER'S CIGAR SMOKE!

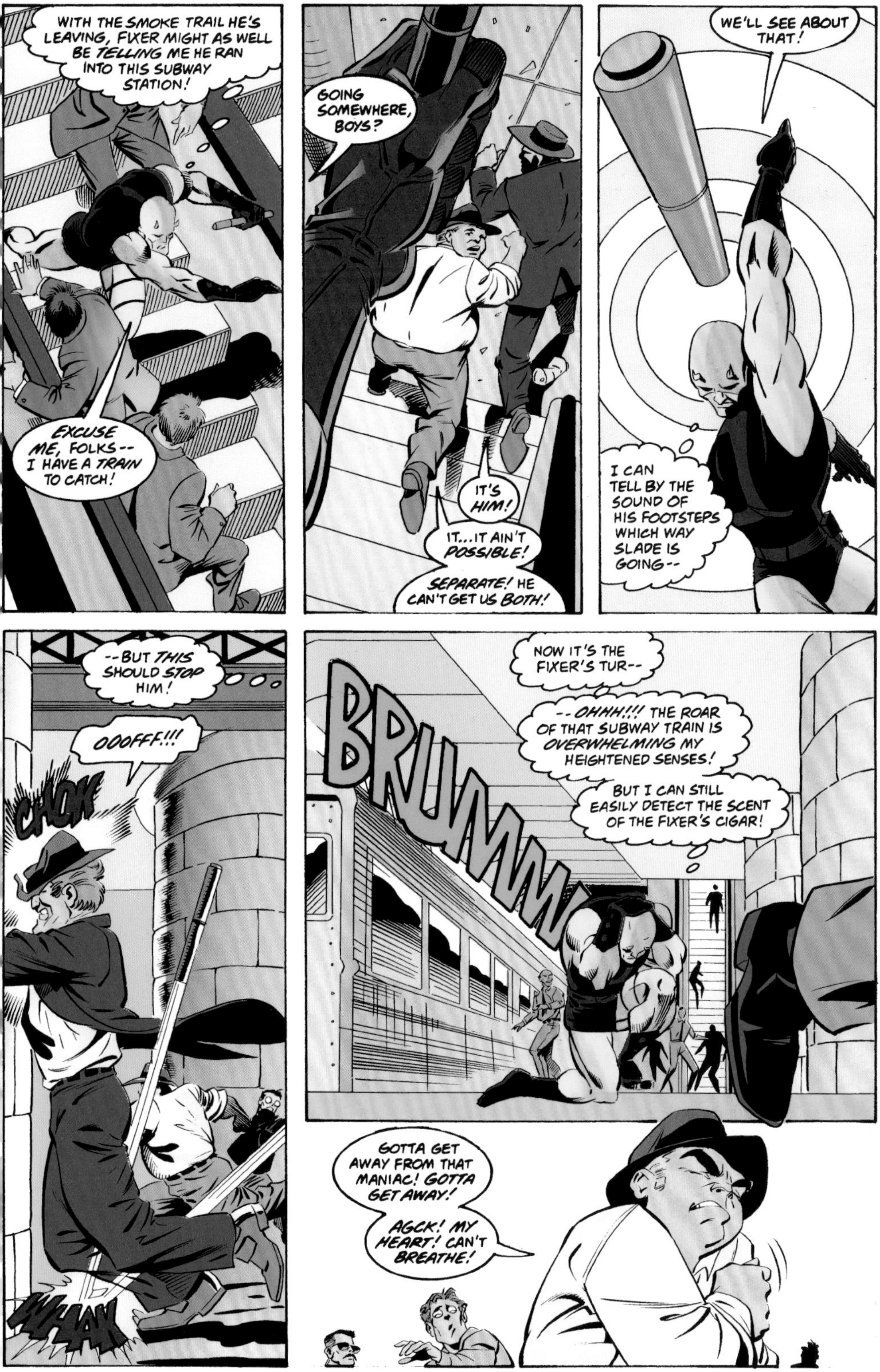
WITH THE SMOKE TRAIL HE'S LEAVING, FIXER MIGHT AS WELL BE TELLING ME HE RAN INTO THIS SUBWAY STATION!
EXCUSE ME, FOLKS-- I HAVE A TRAIN TO CATCH!
GOING SOMEWHERE, BOYS?
IT'S HIM!
IT...IT AIN'T POSSIBLE!
SEPARATE! HE CAN'T GET US BOTH!
WE'LL SEE ABOUT THAT!
I CAN TELL BY THE SOUND OF HIS FOOTSTEPS WHICH WAY SLADE IS GOING--
--BUT THIS SHOULD STOP HIM!
OOOFFF!!!
CHOK
WHAK
NOW IT'S THE FIXER'S TUR--
BRUMMM
--OHHH!!! THE ROAR OF THAT SUBWAY TRAIN IS OVERWHELMING MY HEIGHTENED SENSES!
BUT I CAN STILL EASILY DETECT THE SCENT OF THE FIXER'S CIGAR!
GOTTA GET AWAY FROM THAT MANIAC! GOTTA GET AWAY!
AGCK! MY HEART! CAN'T BREATHE!

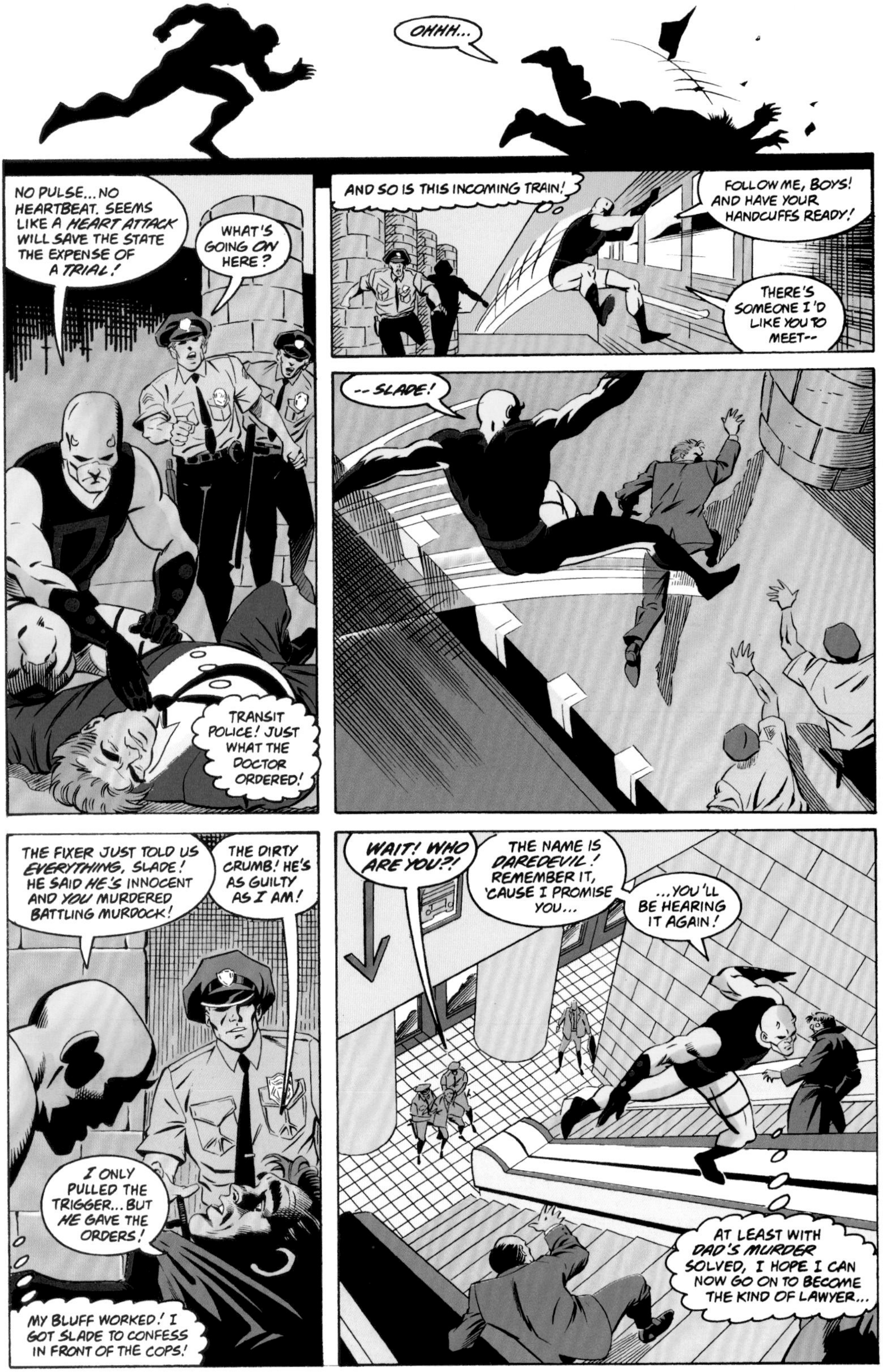

OHHH...
NO PULSE... NO HEARTBEAT. SEEMS LIKE A HEART ATTACK WILL SAVE THE STATE THE EXPENSE OF A TRIAL!
WHAT'S GOING ON HERE?
TRANSIT POLICE! JUST WHAT THE DOCTOR ORDERED!
AND SO IS THIS INCOMING TRAIN!
FOLLOW ME, BOYS! AND HAVE YOUR HANDCUFFS READY!
THERE'S SOMEONE I'D LIKE YOU TO MEET--
--SLADE!
THE FIXER JUST TOLD US EVERYTHING, SLADE! HE SAID HE'S INNOCENT AND YOU MURDERED BATTLING MURDOCK!
THE DIRTY CRUMB! HE'S AS GUILTY AS I AM!
I ONLY PULLED THE TRIGGER... BUT HE GAVE THE ORDERS!
MY BLUFF WORKED! I GOT SLADE TO CONFESS IN FRONT OF THE COPS!
WAIT! WHO ARE YOU?!
THE NAME IS DAREDEVIL! REMEMBER IT, 'CAUSE I PROMISE YOU...
...YOU'LL BE HEARING IT AGAIN!
AT LEAST WITH DAD'S MURDER SOLVED, I HOPE I CAN NOW GO ON TO BECOME THE KIND OF LAWYER...

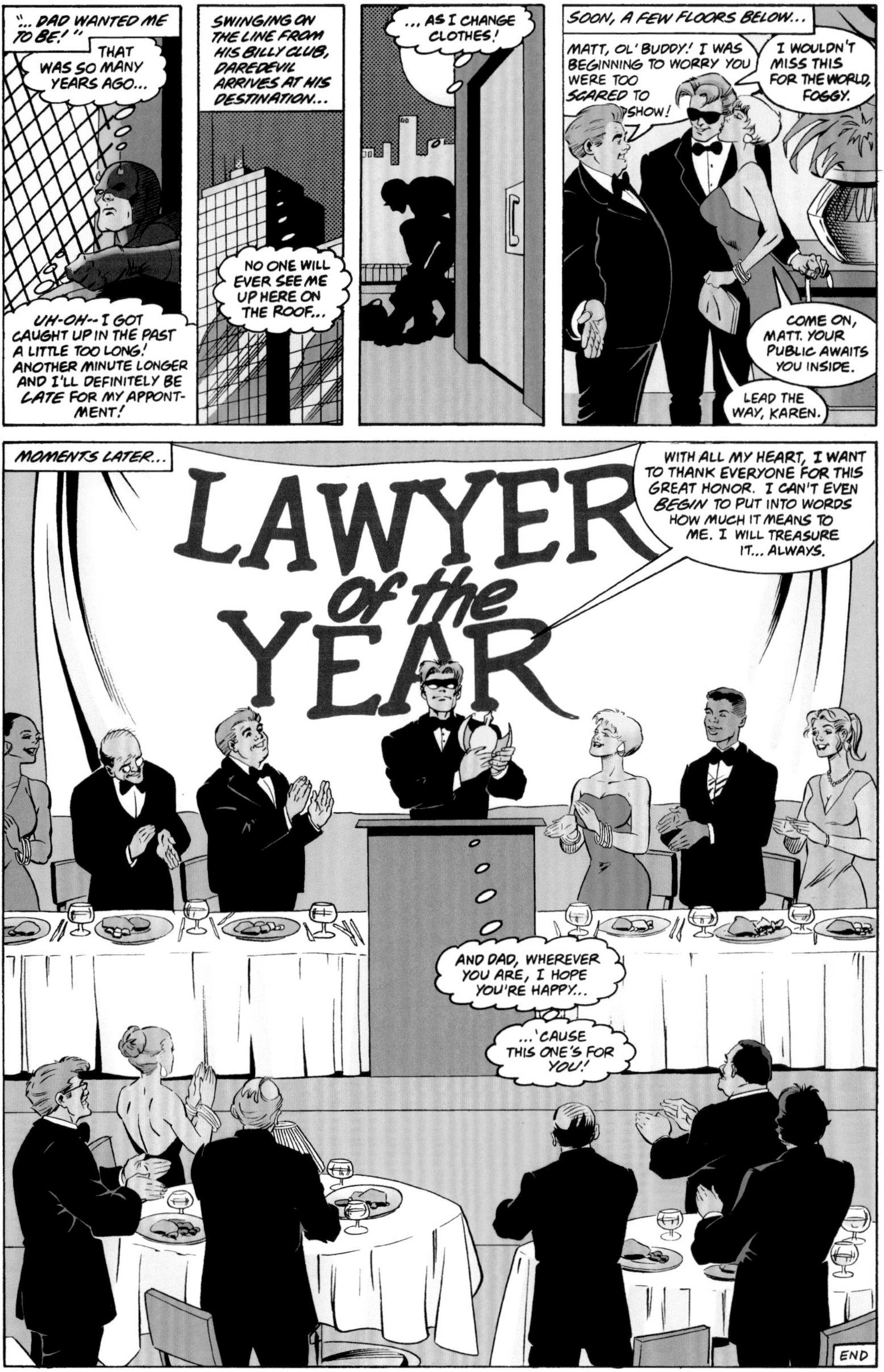
"... DAD WANTED ME TO BE!"
THAT WAS SO MANY YEARS AGO...
UH-OH-- I GOT CAUGHT UP IN THE PAST A LITTLE TOO LONG! ANOTHER MINUTE LONGER AND I'LL DEFINITELY BE LATE FOR MY APPOINT-MENT!
SWINGING ON THE LINE FROM HIS BILLY CLUB, DAREDEVIL ARRIVES AT HIS DESTINATION...
NO ONE WILL EVER SEE ME UP HERE ON THE ROOF...
... AS I CHANGE CLOTHES!
SOON, A FEW FLOORS BELOW...
MATT, OL' BUDDY! I WAS BEGINNING TO WORRY YOU WERE TOO SCARED TO
SHOW!
I WOULDN'T MISS THIS FOR THE WORLD, FOGGY.
COME ON, MATT. YOUR PUBLIC AWAITS YOU INSIDE.
LEAD THE WAY, KAREN.
MOMENTS LATER...
LAWYER of the YEAR
WITH ALL MY HEART, I WANT TO THANK EVERYONE FOR THIS GREAT HONOR. I CAN'T EVEN BEGIN TO PUT INTO WORDS HOW MUCH IT MEANS TO ME. I WILL TREASURE IT... ALWAYS.
AND DAD, WHEREVER YOU ARE, I HOPE YOU'RE HAPPY...
... 'CAUSE THIS ONE'S FOR YOU!
END

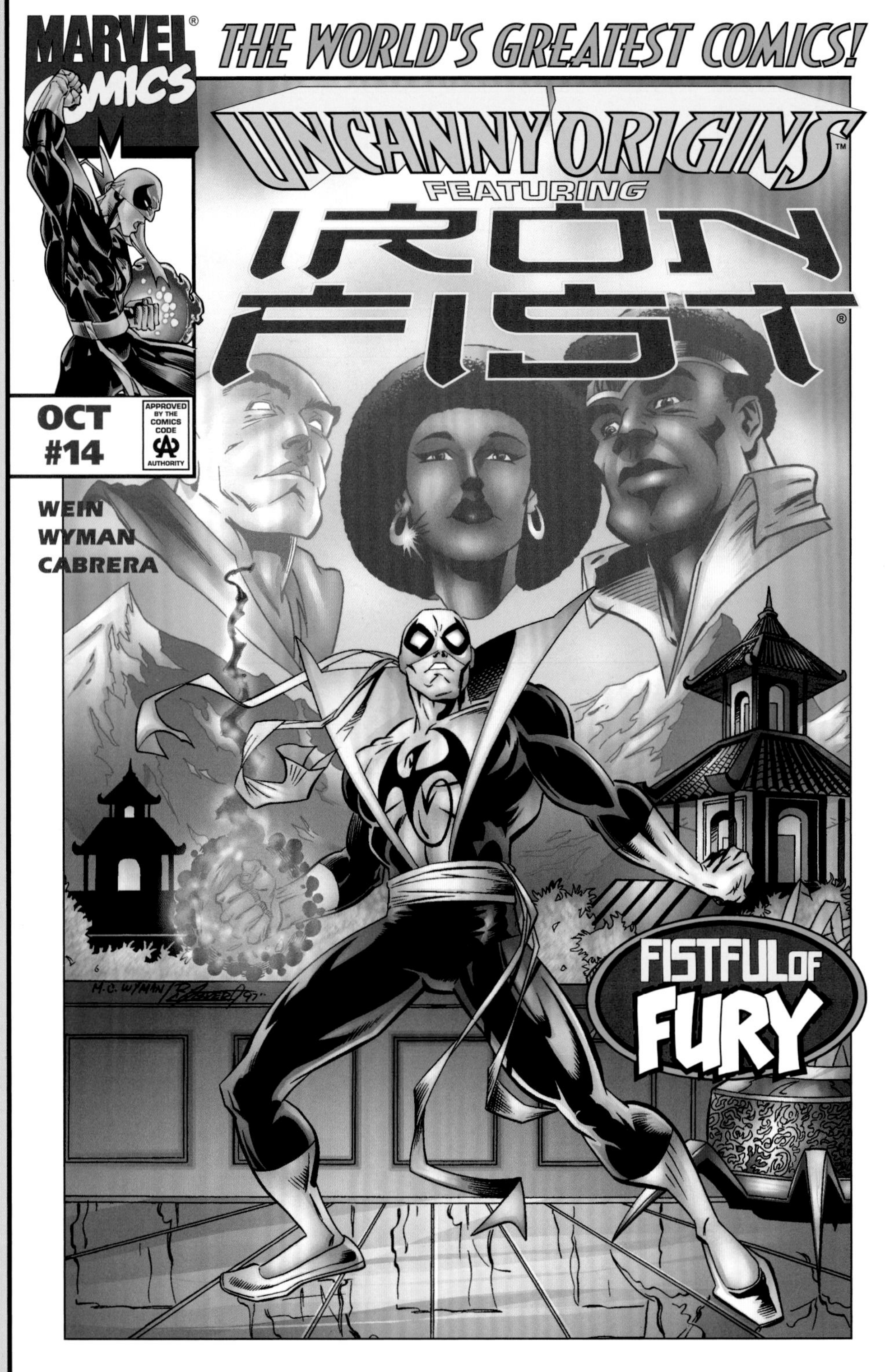
MARVEL COMICS
THE WORLD'S GREATEST COMICS!
UNCANNY ORIGINS
FEATURING
IRON FIST
OCT
#14
APPROVED BY THE COMICS CODE AUTHORITY
WEIN
WYMAN
CABRERA
FISTFUL OF FURY

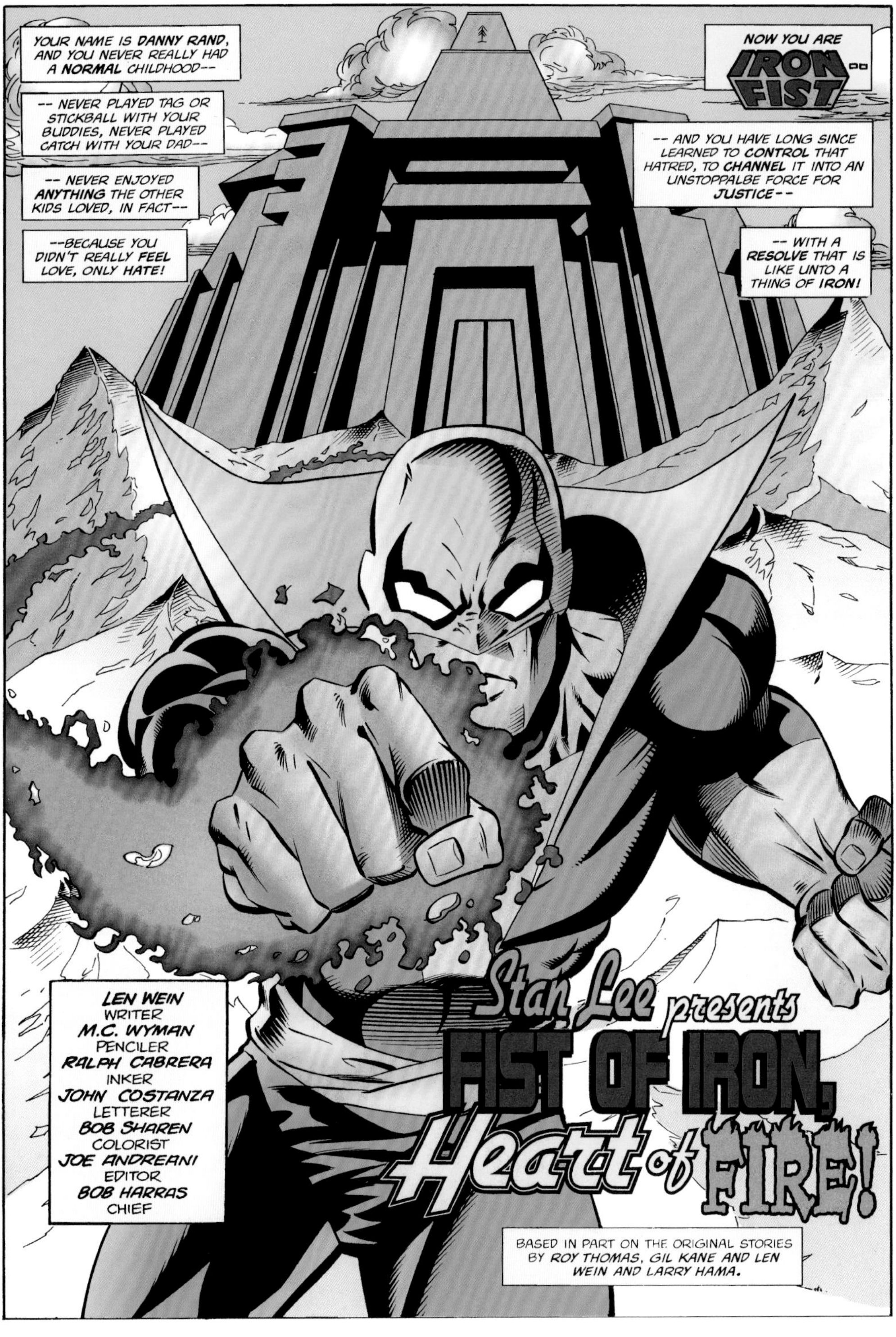

YOUR NAME IS DANNY RAND, AND YOU NEVER REALLY HAD A NORMAL CHILDHOOD--
-- NEVER PLAYED TAG OR STICKBALL WITH YOUR BUDDIES, NEVER PLAYED CATCH WITH YOUR DAD--
-- NEVER ENJOYED ANYTHING THE OTHER KIDS LOVED, IN FACT--
--BECAUSE YOU DIDN'T REALLY FEEL LOVE, ONLY HATE!
NOW YOU ARE IRON FIST..
-- AND YOU HAVE LONG SINCE LEARNED TO CONTROL THAT HATRED, TO CHANNEL IT INTO AN UNSTOPPALBE FORCE FOR JUSTICE--
-- WITH A RESOLVE THAT IS LIKE UNTO A THING OF IRON!
LEN WEIN WRITER
M.C. WYMAN PENCILER
RALPH CABRERA INKER
JOHN COSTANZA LETTERER
BOB SHAREN COLORIST
JOE ANDREANI EDITOR
BOB HARRAS CHIEF
Stan Lee presents
FIST OF IRON, Heart of FIRE!
BASED IN PART ON THE ORIGINAL STORIES BY ROY THOMAS, GIL KANE AND LEN WEIN AND LARRY HAMA.

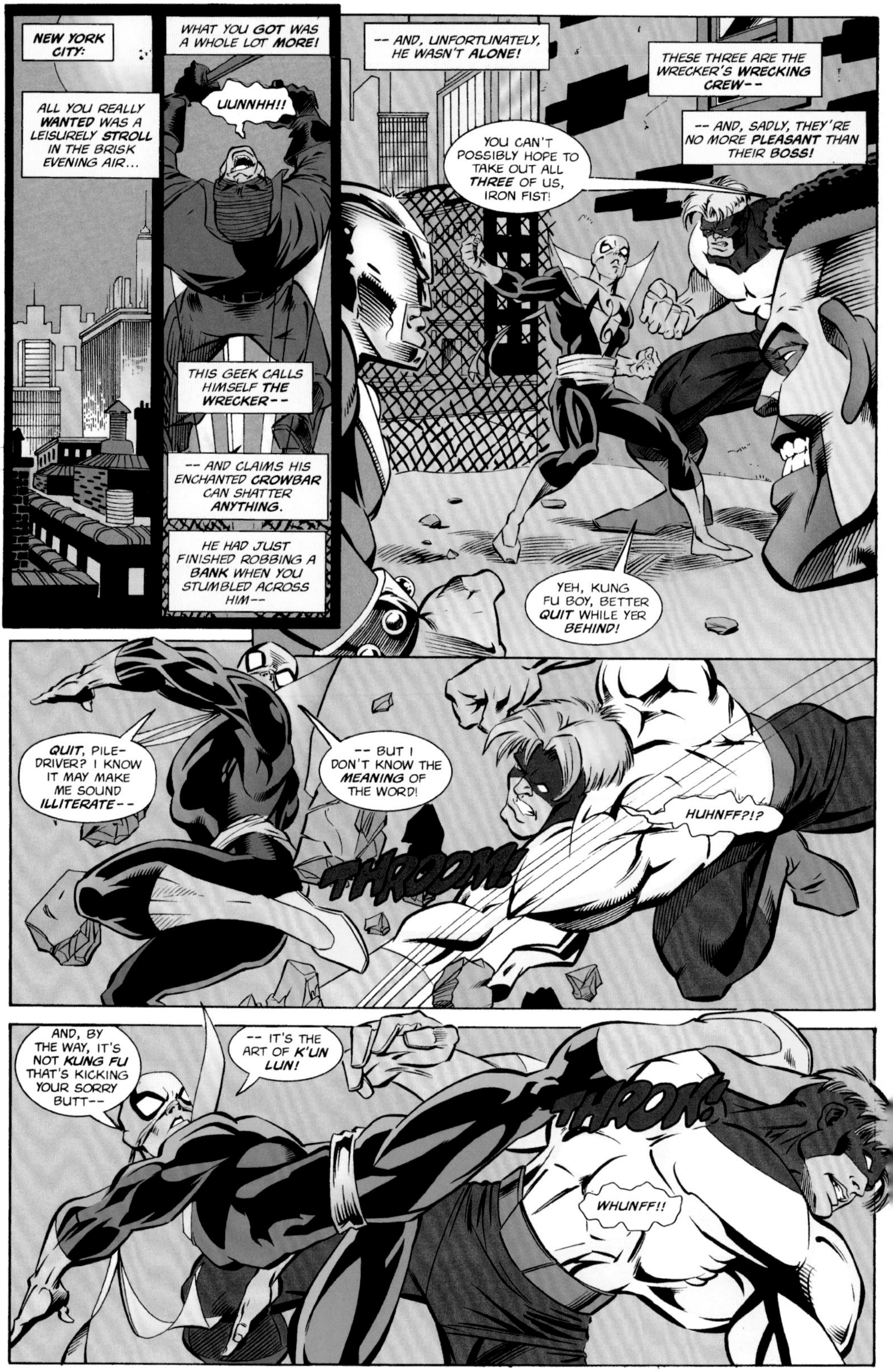
NEW YORK CITY:
ALL YOU REALLY WANTED WAS A LEISURELY STROLL IN THE BRISK EVENING AIR...
WHAT YOU GOT WAS A WHOLE LOT MORE!
UUNNHH!!
THIS GEEK CALLS HIMSELF THE WRECKER--
-- AND CLAIMS HIS ENCHANTED CROWBAR CAN SHATTER ANYTHING.
HE HAD JUST FINISHED ROBBING A BANK WHEN YOU STUMBLED ACROSS HIM--
-- AND, UNFORTUNATELY, HE WASN'T ALONE!
THESE THREE ARE THE WRECKER'S WRECKING CREW--
-- AND, SADLY, THEY'RE NO MORE PLEASANT THAN THEIR BOSS!
YOU CAN'T POSSIBLY HOPE TO TAKE OUT ALL THREE OF US, IRON FIST!
YEH, KUNG FU BOY, BETTER QUIT WHILE YER BEHIND!
QUIT, PILE-DRIVER? I KNOW IT MAY MAKE ME SOUND ILLITERATE--
-- BUT I DON'T KNOW THE MEANING OF THE WORD!
HUHNFF?!?
THROOM!
AND, BY THE WAY, IT'S NOT KUNG FU THAT'S KICKING YOUR SORRY BUTT--
-- IT'S THE ART OF K'UN LUN!
THROOM!
WHUNFF!!

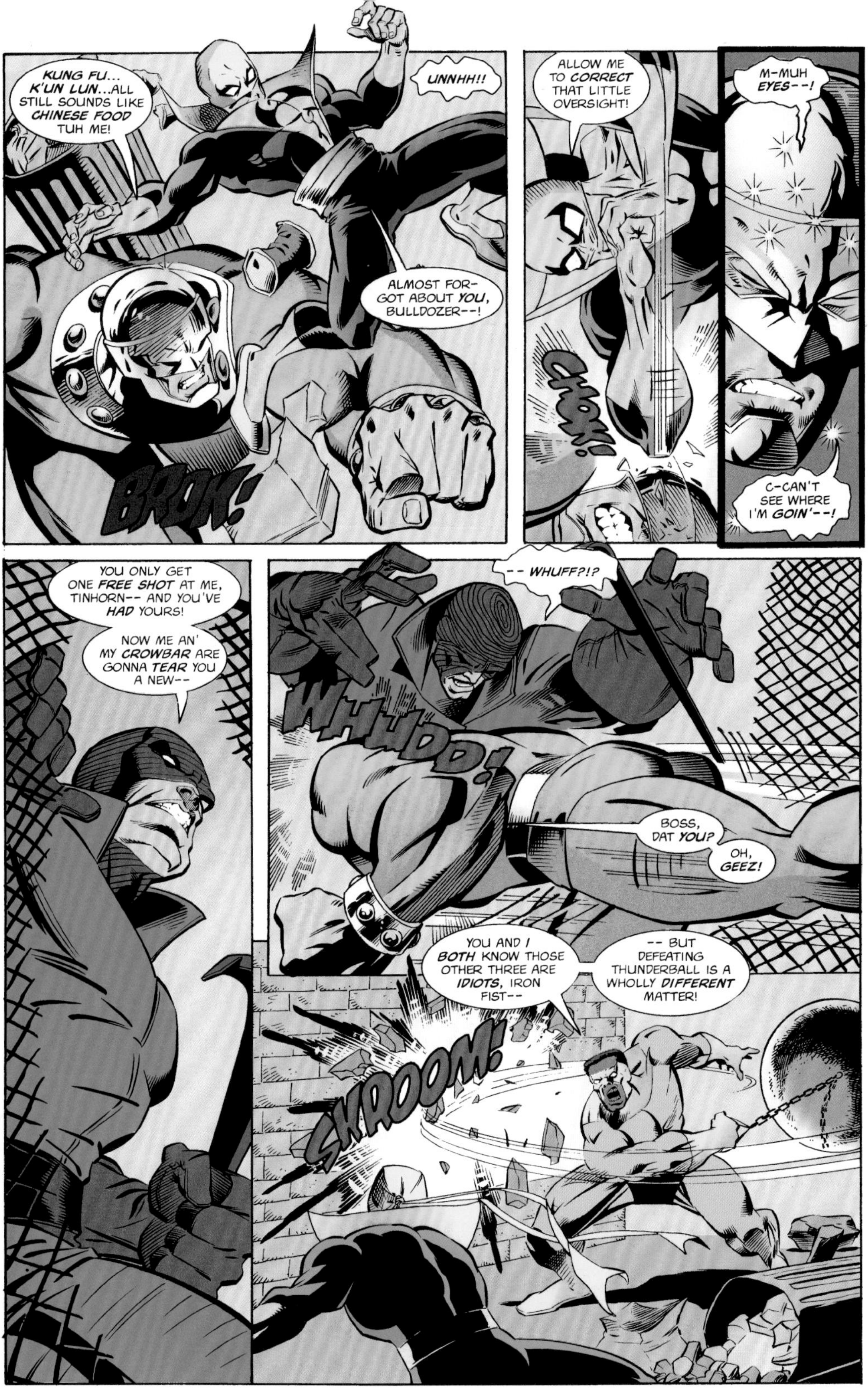
KUNG FU... K'UN LUN...ALL STILL SOUNDS LIKE CHINESE FOOD TUH ME!
UNNHH!!
ALMOST FOR-GOT ABOUT YOU, BULLDOZER--!
BRAK!
ALLOW ME TO CORRECT THAT LITTLE OVERSIGHT!
CHOK!
M-MUH EYES--!
C-CAN'T SEE WHERE I'M GOIN'--!
YOU ONLY GET ONE FREE SHOT AT ME, TINHORN-- AND YOU'VE HAD YOURS!
NOW ME AN' MY CROWBAR ARE GONNA TEAR YOU A NEW--
--WHUFF?!?
WHUDD!
BOSS, DAT YOU?
OH, GEEZ!
YOU AND I BOTH KNOW THOSE OTHER THREE ARE IDIOTS, IRON FIST--
-- BUT DEFEATING THUNDERBALL IS A WHOLLY DIFFERENT MATTER!
SKROOM!

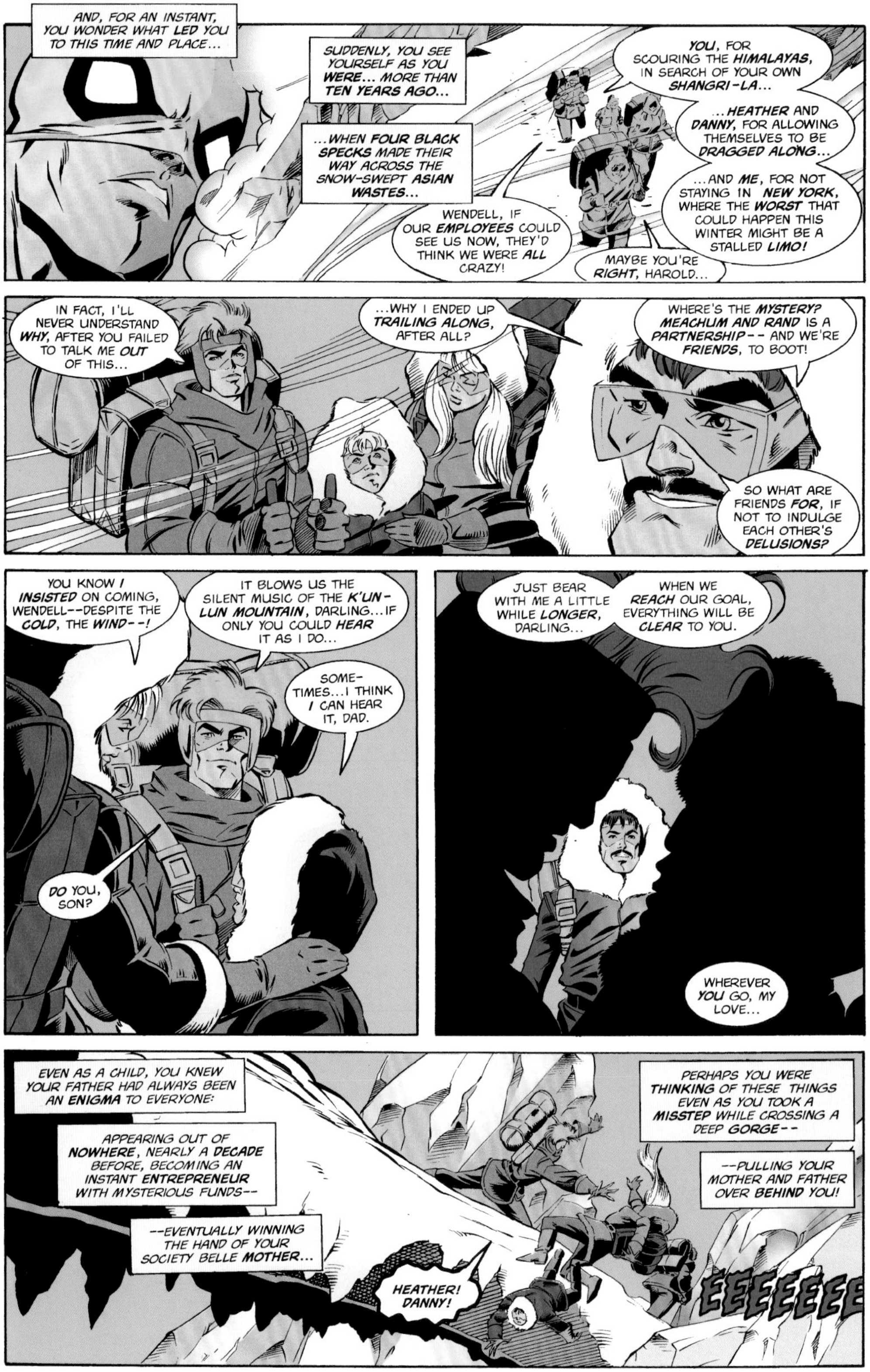
AND, FOR AN INSTANT, YOU WONDER WHAT LED YOU TO THIS TIME AND PLACE...
SUDDENLY, YOU SEE YOURSELF AS YOU WERE... MORE THAN TEN YEARS AGO...
...WHEN FOUR BLACK SPECKS MADE THEIR WAY ACROSS THE SNOW-SWEPT ASIAN WASTES...
YOU, FOR SCOURING THE HIMALAYAS, IN SEARCH OF YOUR OWN SHANGRI-LA...
...HEATHER AND DANNY, FOR ALLOWING THEMSELVES TO BE DRAGGED ALONG...
...AND ME, FOR NOT STAYING IN NEW YORK, WHERE THE WORST THAT COULD HAPPEN THIS WINTER MIGHT BE A STALLED LIMO!
WENDELL, IF OUR EMPLOYEES COULD SEE US NOW, THEY'D THINK WE WERE ALL CRAZY!
MAYBE YOU'RE RIGHT, HAROLD...
IN FACT, I'LL NEVER UNDERSTAND WHY, AFTER YOU FAILED TO TALK ME OUT OF THIS...
...WHY I ENDED UP TRAILING ALONG, AFTER ALL?
WHERE'S THE MYSTERY? MEACHUM AND RAND IS A PARTNERSHIP-- AND WE'RE FRIENDS, TO BOOT!
SO WHAT ARE FRIENDS FOR, IF NOT TO INDULGE EACH OTHER'S DELUSIONS?
YOU KNOW I INSISTED ON COMING, WENDELL--DESPITE THE COLD, THE WIND--!
IT BLOWS US THE SILENT MUSIC OF THE K'UN-LUN MOUNTAIN, DARLING...IF ONLY YOU COULD HEAR IT AS I DO...
SOME-TIMES...I THINK I CAN HEAR IT, DAD.
DO YOU, SON?
JUST BEAR WITH ME A LITTLE WHILE LONGER, DARLING...
WHEN WE REACH OUR GOAL, EVERYTHING WILL BE CLEAR TO YOU.
WHEREVER YOU GO, MY LOVE...
EVEN AS A CHILD, YOU KNEW YOUR FATHER HAD ALWAYS BEEN AN ENIGMA TO EVERYONE:
APPEARING OUT OF NOWHERE, NEARLY A DECADE BEFORE, BECOMING AN INSTANT ENTREPRENEUR WITH MYSTERIOUS FUNDS--
--EVENTUALLY WINNING THE HAND OF YOUR SOCIETY BELLE MOTHER...
PERHAPS YOU WERE THINKING OF THESE THINGS EVEN AS YOU TOOK A MISSTEP WHILE CROSSING A DEEP GORGE--
--PULLING YOUR MOTHER AND FATHER OVER BEHIND YOU!
HEATHER! DANNY!
EEEEEEE

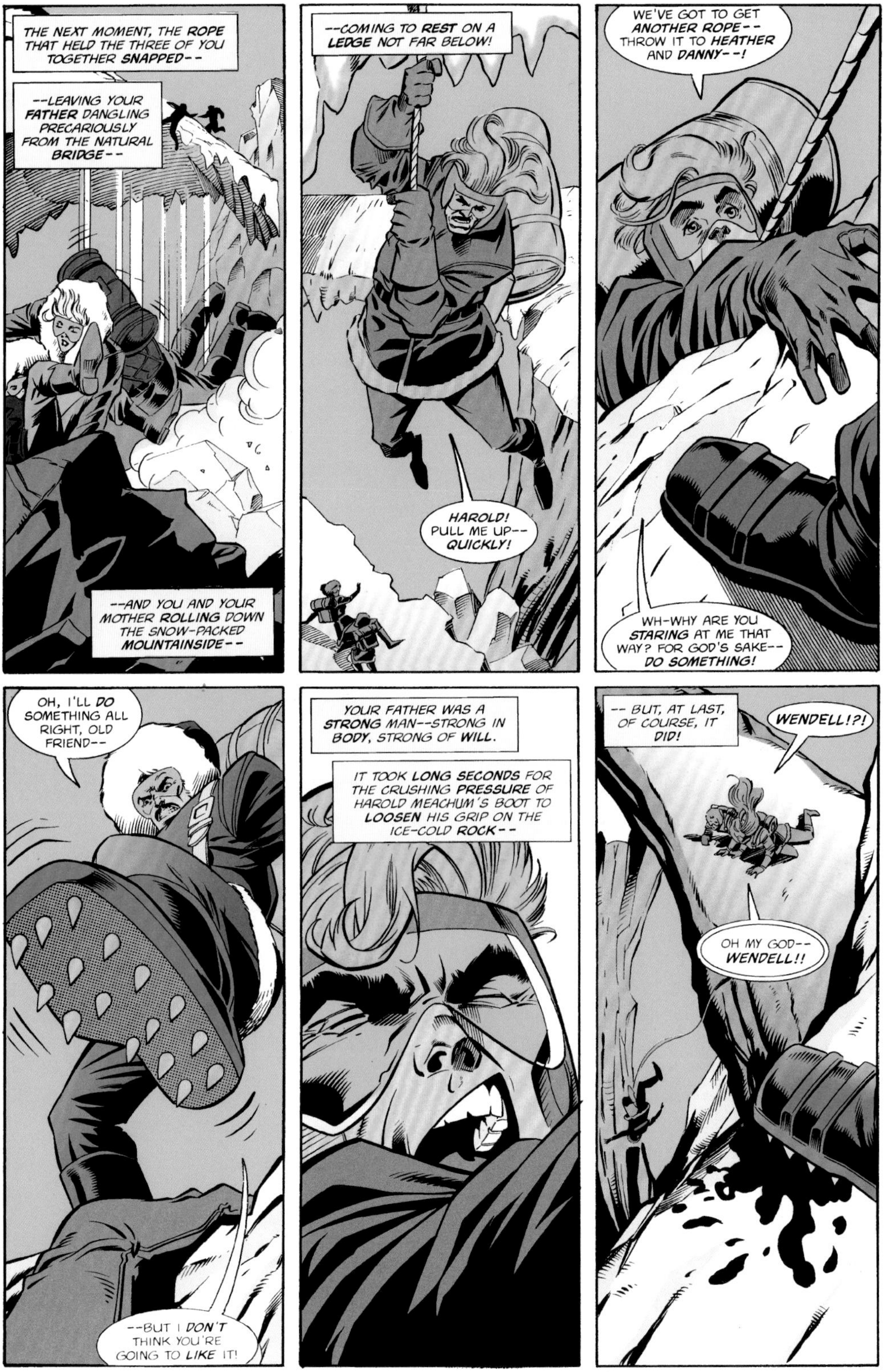
THE NEXT MOMENT, THE ROPE THAT HELD THE THREE OF YOU TOGETHER SNAPPED--
--LEAVING YOUR FATHER DANGLING PRECARIOUSLY FROM THE NATURAL BRIDGE--
--AND YOU AND YOUR MOTHER ROLLING DOWN THE SNOW-PACKED MOUNTAINSIDE--
--COMING TO REST ON A LEDGE NOT FAR BELOW!
HAROLD! PULL ME UP-- QUICKLY!
WE'VE GOT TO GET ANOTHER ROPE-- THROW IT TO HEATHER AND DANNY--!
WH-WHY ARE YOU STARING AT ME THAT WAY? FOR GOD'S SAKE-- DO SOMETHING!
OH, I'LL DO SOMETHING ALL RIGHT, OLD FRIEND--
--BUT I DON'T THINK YOU'RE GOING TO LIKE IT!
YOUR FATHER WAS A STRONG MAN--STRONG IN BODY, STRONG OF WILL.
IT TOOK LONG SECONDS FOR THE CRUSHING PRESSURE OF HAROLD MEACHUM'S BOOT TO LOOSEN HIS GRIP ON THE ICE-COLD ROCK--
-- BUT, AT LAST, OF COURSE, IT DID!
WENDELL!?!
OH MY GOD-- WENDELL!!

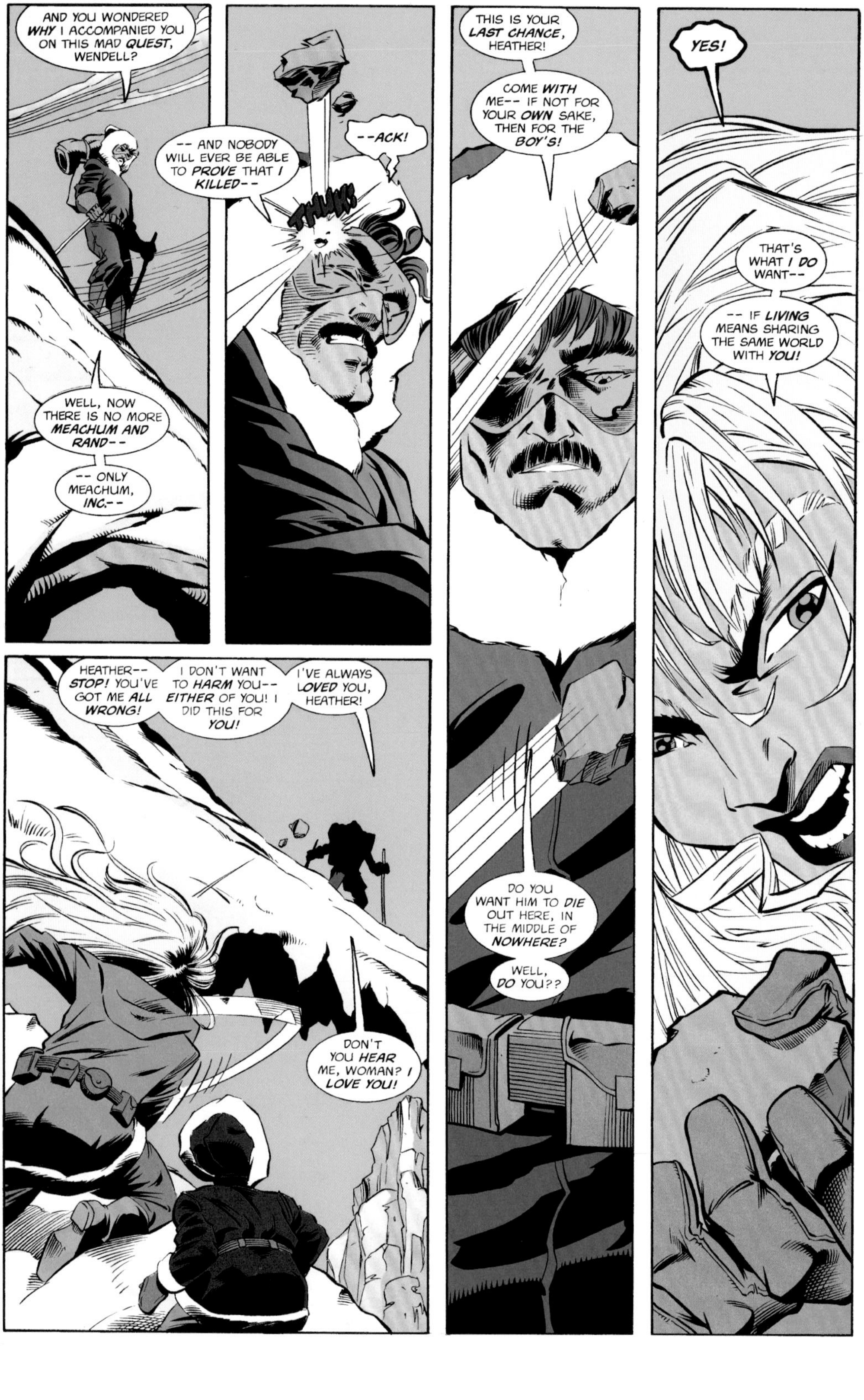
AND YOU WONDERED WHY I ACCOMPANIED YOU ON THIS MAD QUEST, WENDELL?
WELL, NOW THERE IS NO MORE MEACHUM AND RAND--
-- ONLY MEACHUM, INC.--
-- AND NOBODY WILL EVER BE ABLE TO PROVE THAT I KILLED--
--ACK!
THUKK
HEATHER-- STOP! YOU'VE GOT ME ALL WRONG!
I DON'T WANT TO HARM YOU-- EITHER OF YOU! I DID THIS FOR YOU!
I'VE ALWAYS LOVED YOU, HEATHER!
DON'T YOU HEAR ME, WOMAN? I LOVE YOU!
THIS IS YOUR LAST CHANCE, HEATHER!
COME WITH ME-- IF NOT FOR YOUR OWN SAKE, THEN FOR THE BOY'S!
DO YOU WANT HIM TO DIE OUT HERE, IN THE MIDDLE OF NOWHERE?
WELL, DO YOU??
YES!
THAT'S WHAT I DO WANT--
-- IF LIVING MEANS SHARING THE SAME WORLD WITH YOU!

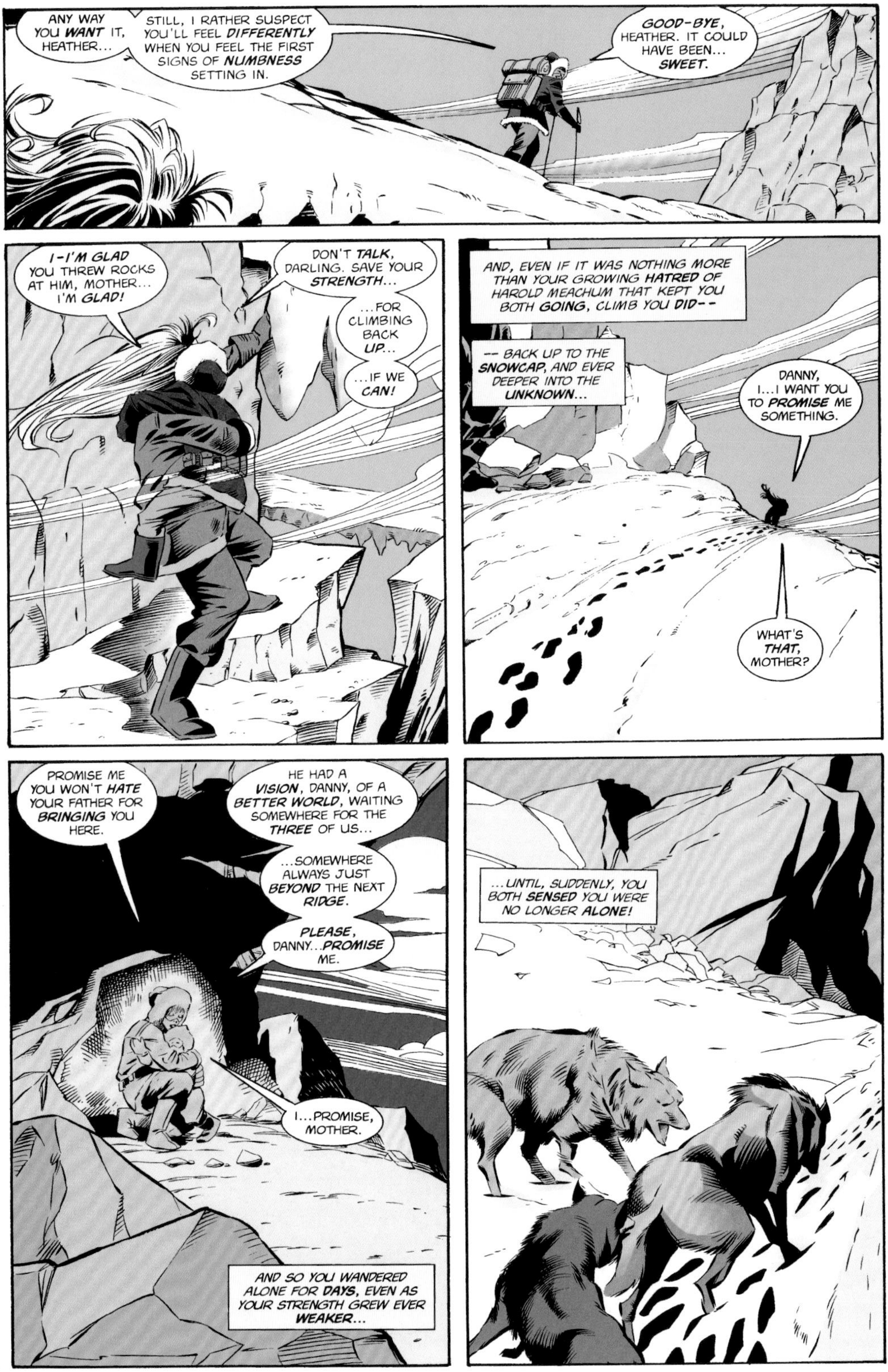
ANY WAY YOU WANT IT, HEATHER...
STILL, I RATHER SUSPECT YOU'LL FEEL DIFFERENTLY WHEN YOU FEEL THE FIRST SIGNS OF NUMBNESS SETTING IN.
GOOD-BYE, HEATHER. IT COULD HAVE BEEN... SWEET.
I-I'M GLAD YOU THREW ROCKS AT HIM, MOTHER... I'M GLAD!
DON'T TALK, DARLING. SAVE YOUR STRENGTH...
...FOR CLIMBING BACK UP...
...IF WE CAN!
AND, EVEN IF IT WAS NOTHING MORE THAN YOUR GROWING HATRED OF HAROLD MEACHUM THAT KEPT YOU BOTH GOING, CLIMB YOU DID--
-- BACK UP TO THE SNOWCAP, AND EVER DEEPER INTO THE UNKNOWN...
DANNY, I...I WANT YOU TO PROMISE ME SOMETHING.
WHAT'S THAT, MOTHER?
PROMISE ME YOU WON'T HATE YOUR FATHER FOR BRINGING YOU HERE.
HE HAD A VISION, DANNY, OF A BETTER WORLD, WAITING SOMEWHERE FOR THE THREE OF US...
...SOMEWHERE ALWAYS JUST BEYOND THE NEXT RIDGE.
PLEASE, DANNY...PROMISE ME.
I...PROMISE, MOTHER.
AND SO YOU WANDERED ALONE FOR DAYS, EVEN AS YOUR STRENGTH GREW EVER WEAKER...
...UNTIL, SUDDENLY, YOU BOTH SENSED YOU WERE NO LONGER ALONE!

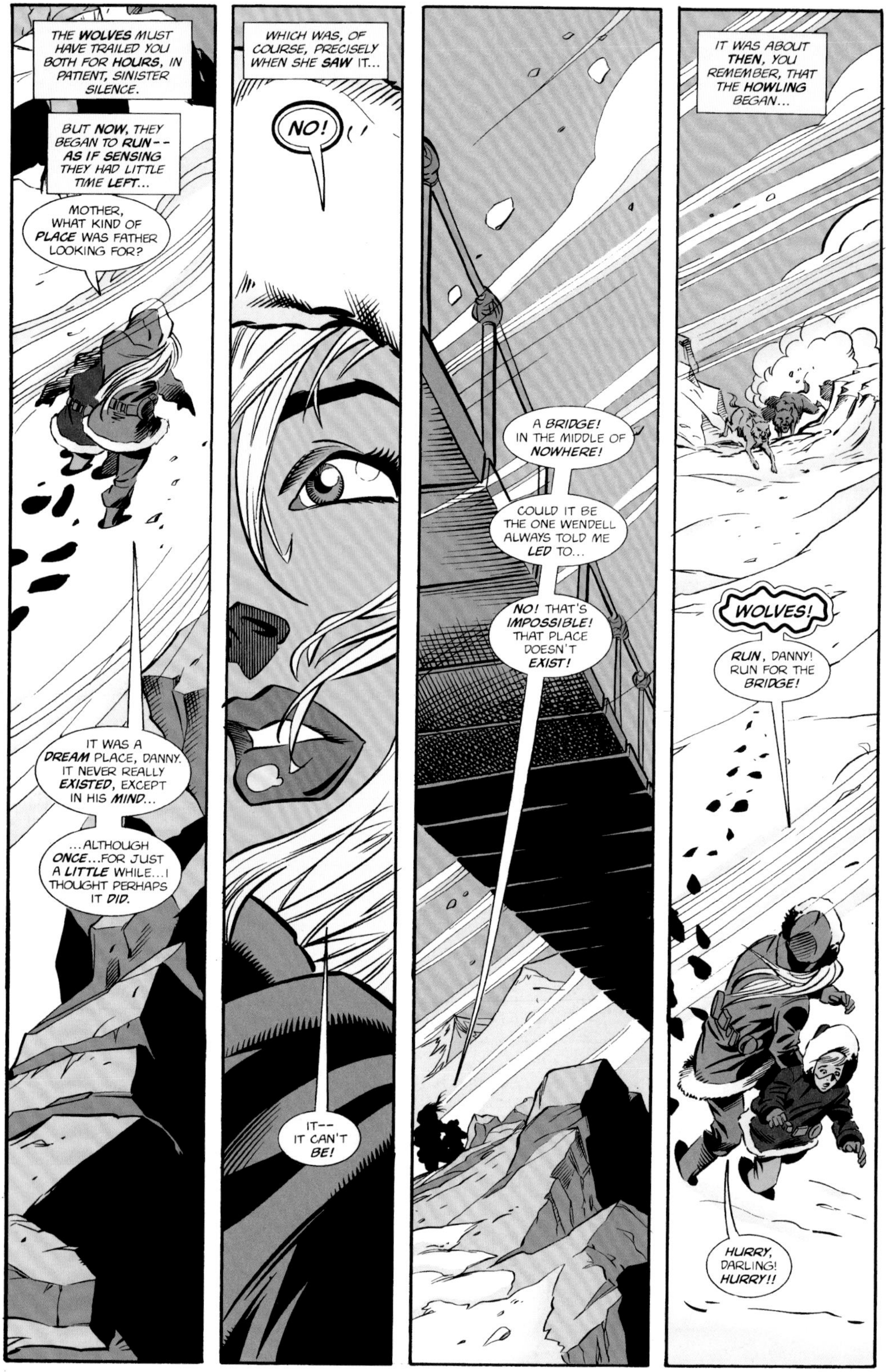
THE WOLVES MUST HAVE TRAILED YOU BOTH FOR HOURS, IN PATIENT, SINISTER SILENCE.
BUT NOW, THEY BEGAN TO RUN--AS IF SENSING THEY HAD LITTLE TIME LEFT...
MOTHER, WHAT KIND OF PLACE WAS FATHER LOOKING FOR?
IT WAS A DREAM PLACE, DANNY. IT NEVER REALLY EXISTED, EXCEPT IN HIS MIND...
...ALTHOUGH ONCE...FOR JUST A LITTLE WHILE...I THOUGHT PERHAPS IT DID.
WHICH WAS, OF COURSE, PRECISELY WHEN SHE SAW IT...
NO!
IT--IT CAN'T BE!
A BRIDGE! IN THE MIDDLE OF NOWHERE!
COULD IT BE THE ONE WENDELL ALWAYS TOLD ME LED TO...
NO! THAT'S IMPOSSIBLE! THAT PLACE DOESN'T EXIST!
IT WAS ABOUT THEN, YOU REMEMBER, THAT THE HOWLING BEGAN...
WOLVES!
RUN, DANNY! RUN FOR THE BRIDGE!
HURRY, DARLING! HURRY!!

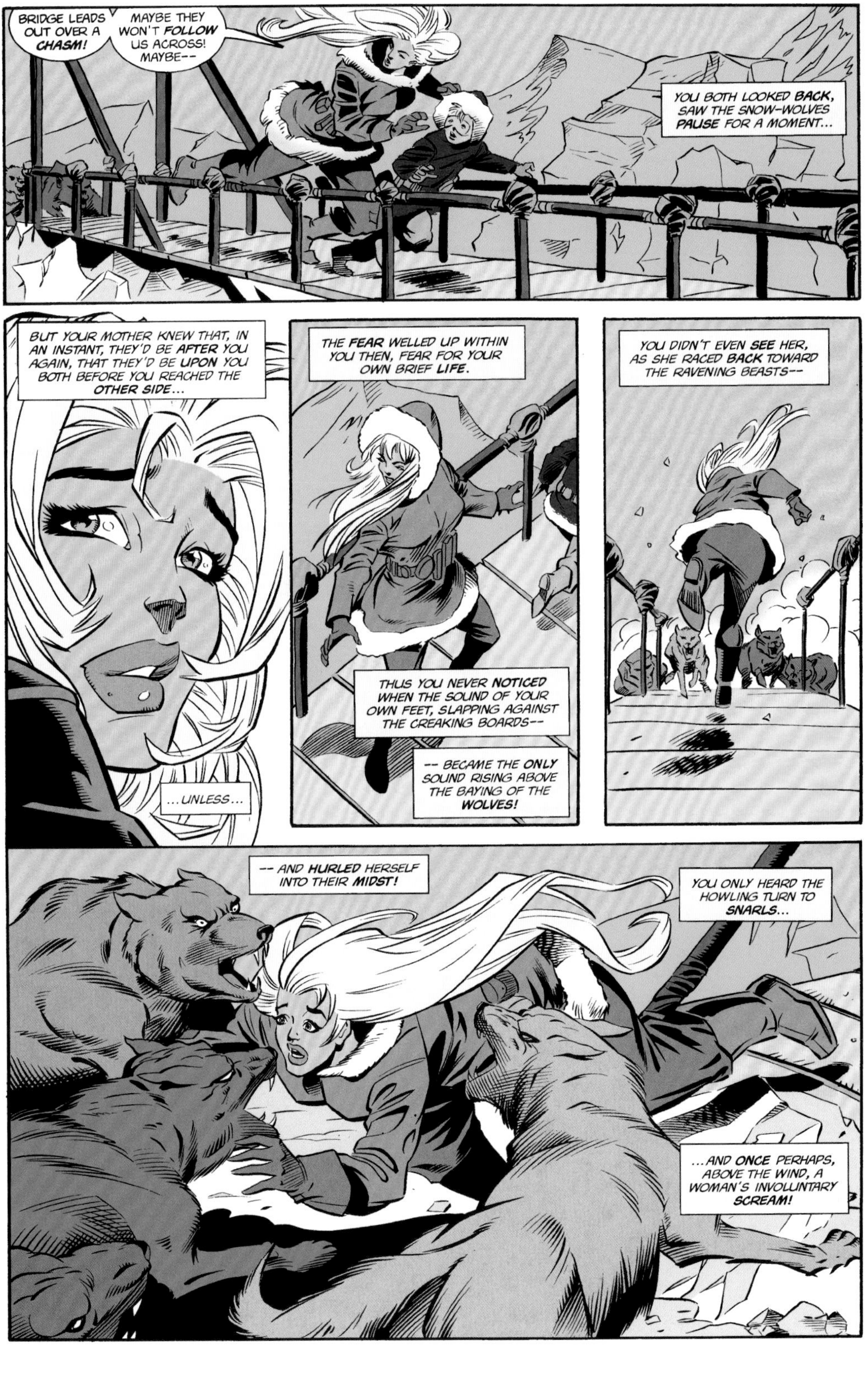
BRIDGE LEADS OUT OVER A CHASM!
MAYBE THEY WON'T FOLLOW US ACROSS! MAYBE--
YOU BOTH LOOKED BACK, SAW THE SNOW-WOLVES PAUSE FOR A MOMENT...
BUT YOUR MOTHER KNEW THAT, IN AN INSTANT, THEY'D BE AFTER YOU AGAIN, THAT THEY'D BE UPON YOU BOTH BEFORE YOU REACHED THE OTHER SIDE...
...UNLESS...
THE FEAR WELLED UP WITHIN YOU THEN, FEAR FOR YOUR OWN BRIEF LIFE.
THUS YOU NEVER NOTICED WHEN THE SOUND OF YOUR OWN FEET, SLAPPING AGAINST THE CREAKING BOARDS--
-- BECAME THE ONLY SOUND RISING ABOVE THE BAYING OF THE WOLVES!
YOU DIDN'T EVEN SEE HER, AS SHE RACED BACK TOWARD THE RAVENING BEASTS--
-- AND HURLED HERSELF INTO THEIR MIDST!
YOU ONLY HEARD THE HOWLING TURN TO SNARLS...
...AND ONCE PERHAPS, ABOVE THE WIND, A WOMAN'S INVOLUNTARY SCREAM!

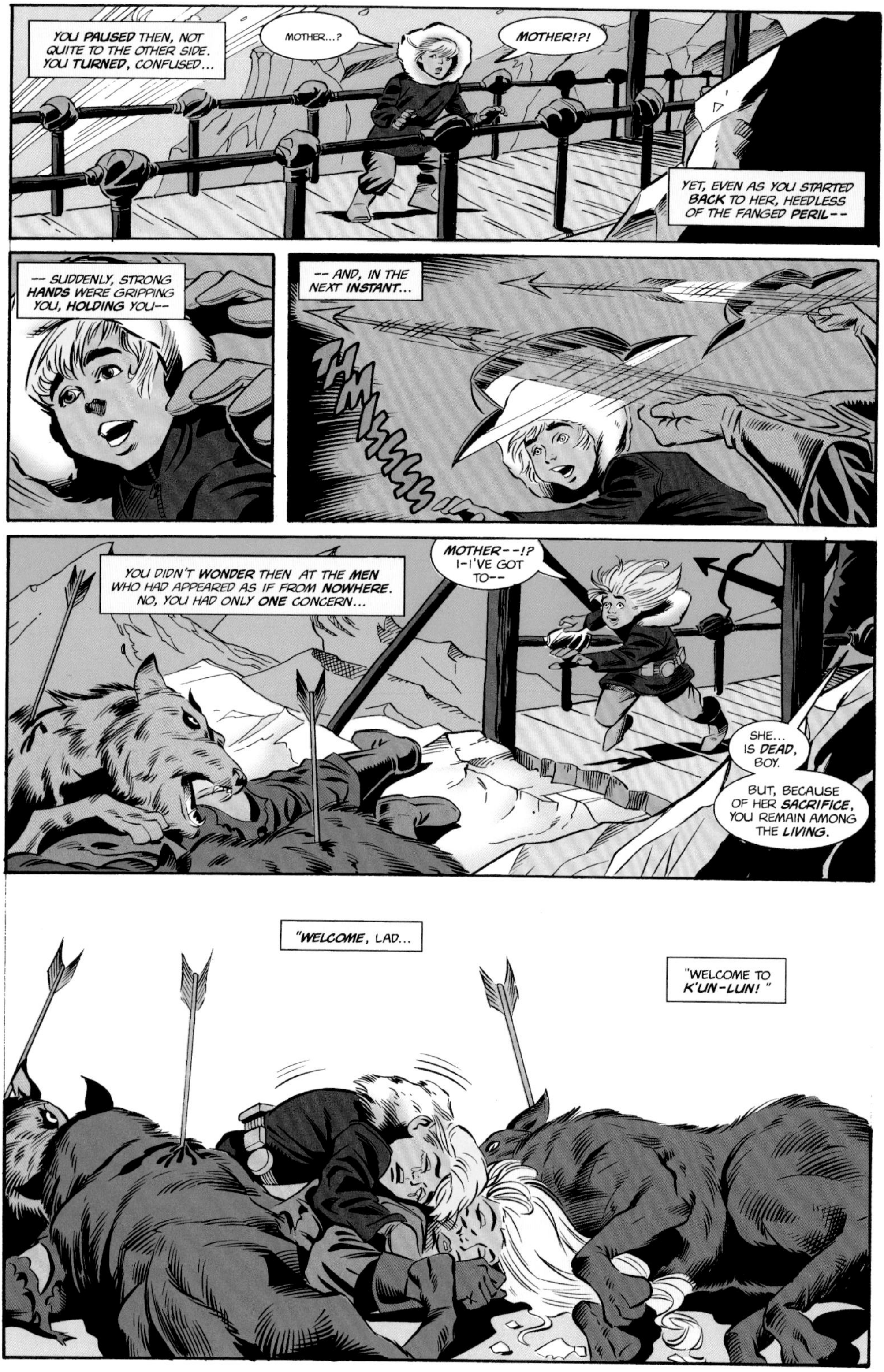
YOU PAUSED THEN, NOT QUITE TO THE OTHER SIDE. YOU TURNED, CONFUSED...
MOTHER...?
MOTHER!?!
YET, EVEN AS YOU STARTED BACK TO HER, HEEDLESS OF THE FANGED PERIL--
-- SUDDENLY, STRONG HANDS WERE GRIPPING YOU, HOLDING YOU--
-- AND, IN THE NEXT INSTANT...
THWISSSS
YOU DIDN'T WONDER THEN AT THE MEN WHO HAD APPEARED AS IF FROM NOWHERE. NO, YOU HAD ONLY ONE CONCERN...
MOTHER--!? I-I'VE GOT TO--
SHE... IS DEAD, BOY.
BUT, BECAUSE OF HER SACRIFICE, YOU REMAIN AMONG THE LIVING.
"WELCOME, LAD...
"WELCOME TO K'UN-LUN!"

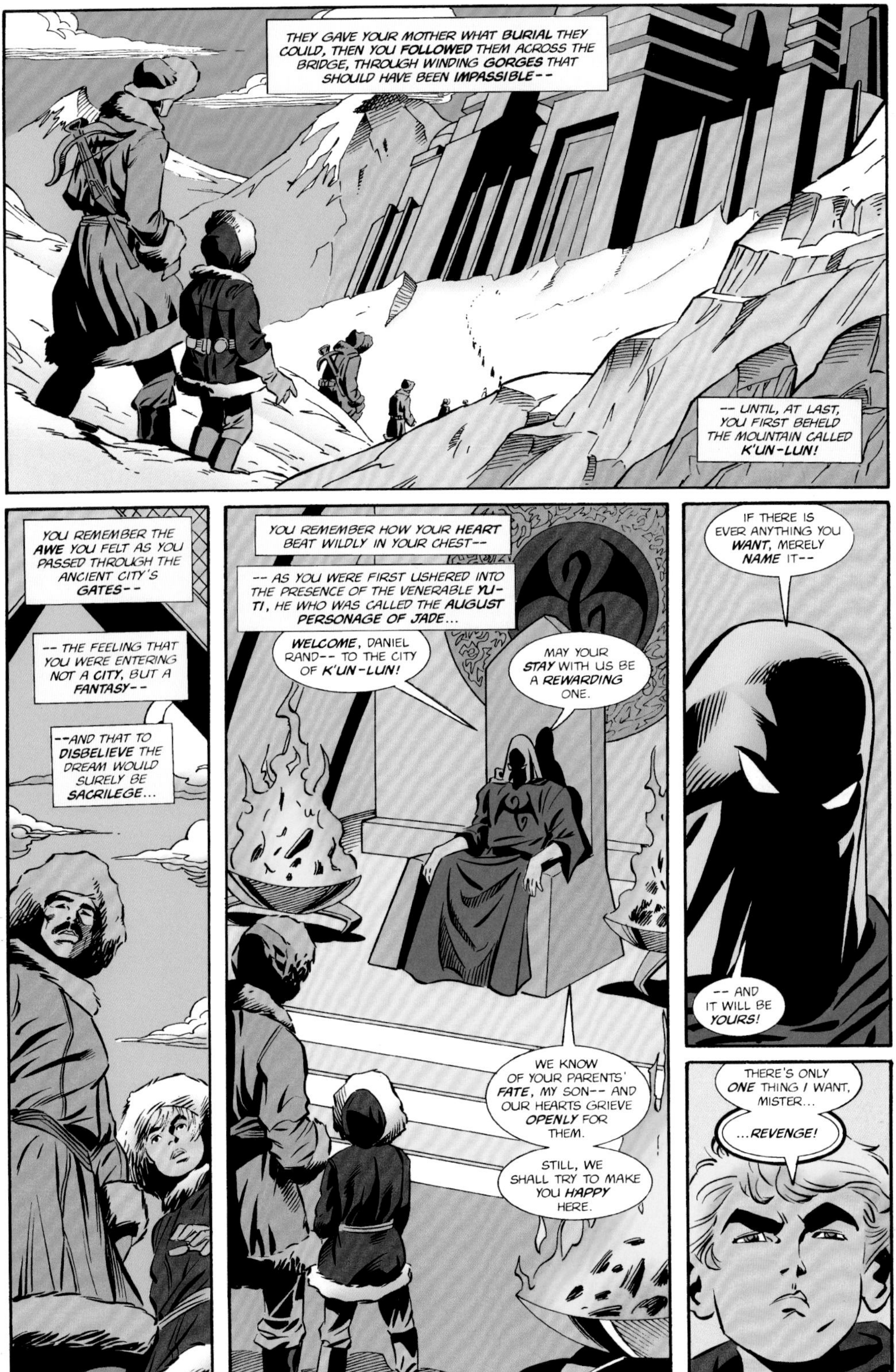
THEY GAVE YOUR MOTHER WHAT BURIAL THEY COULD, THEN YOU FOLLOWED THEM ACROSS THE BRIDGE, THROUGH WINDING GORGES THAT SHOULD HAVE BEEN IMPASSIBLE--
-- UNTIL, AT LAST, YOU FIRST BEHELD THE MOUNTAIN CALLED K'UN-LUN!
YOU REMEMBER THE AWE YOU FELT AS YOU PASSED THROUGH THE ANCIENT CITY'S GATES--
-- THE FEELING THAT YOU WERE ENTERING NOT A CITY, BUT A FANTASY--
--AND THAT TO DISBELIEVE THE DREAM WOULD SURELY BE SACRILEGE...
YOU REMEMBER HOW YOUR HEART BEAT WILDLY IN YOUR CHEST--
-- AS YOU WERE FIRST USHERED INTO THE PRESENCE OF THE VENERABLE YU-TI, HE WHO WAS CALLED THE AUGUST PERSONAGE OF JADE...
WELCOME, DANIEL RAND-- TO THE CITY OF K'UN-LUN!
MAY YOUR STAY WITH US BE A REWARDING ONE.
WE KNOW OF YOUR PARENTS' FATE, MY SON-- AND OUR HEARTS GRIEVE OPENLY FOR THEM.
STILL, WE SHALL TRY TO MAKE YOU HAPPY HERE.
IF THERE IS EVER ANYTHING YOU WANT, MERELY NAME IT--
-- AND IT WILL BE YOURS!
THERE'S ONLY ONE THING I WANT, MISTER...
...REVENGE!

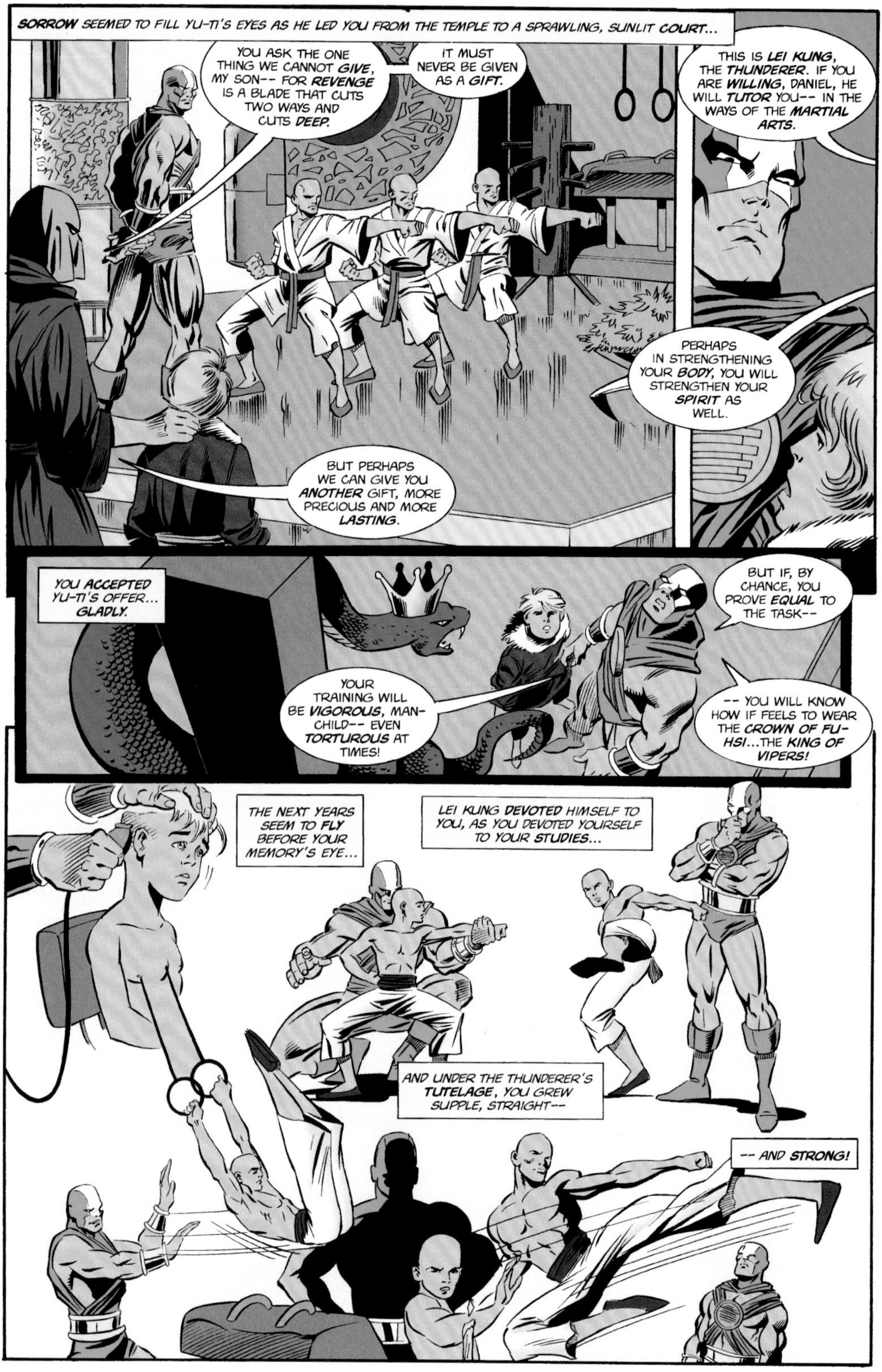
SORROW SEEMED TO FILL YU-TI'S EYES AS HE LED YOU FROM THE TEMPLE TO A SPRAWLING, SUNLIT COURT...
YOU ASK THE ONE THING WE CANNOT GIVE, MY SON-- FOR REVENGE IS A BLADE THAT CUTS TWO WAYS AND CUTS DEEP.
IT MUST NEVER BE GIVEN AS A GIFT.
BUT PERHAPS WE CAN GIVE YOU ANOTHER GIFT, MORE PRECIOUS AND MORE LASTING.
THIS IS LEI KUNG, THE THUNDERER. IF YOU ARE WILLING, DANIEL, HE WILL TUTOR YOU-- IN THE WAYS OF THE MARTIAL ARTS.
PERHAPS IN STRENGTHENING YOUR BODY, YOU WILL STRENGTHEN YOUR SPIRIT AS WELL.
YOU ACCEPTED YU-TI'S OFFER... GLADLY.
YOUR TRAINING WILL BE VIGOROUS, MAN-CHILD-- EVEN TORTUROUS AT TIMES!
BUT IF, BY CHANCE, YOU PROVE EQUAL TO THE TASK--
-- YOU WILL KNOW HOW IF FEELS TO WEAR THE CROWN OF FU-HSI...THE KING OF VIPERS!
THE NEXT YEARS SEEM TO FLY BEFORE YOUR MEMORY'S EYE...
LEI KUNG DEVOTED HIMSELF TO YOU, AS YOU DEVOTED YOURSELF TO YOUR STUDIES...
AND UNDER THE THUNDERER'S TUTELAGE, YOU GREW SUPPLE, STRAIGHT--
-- AND STRONG!

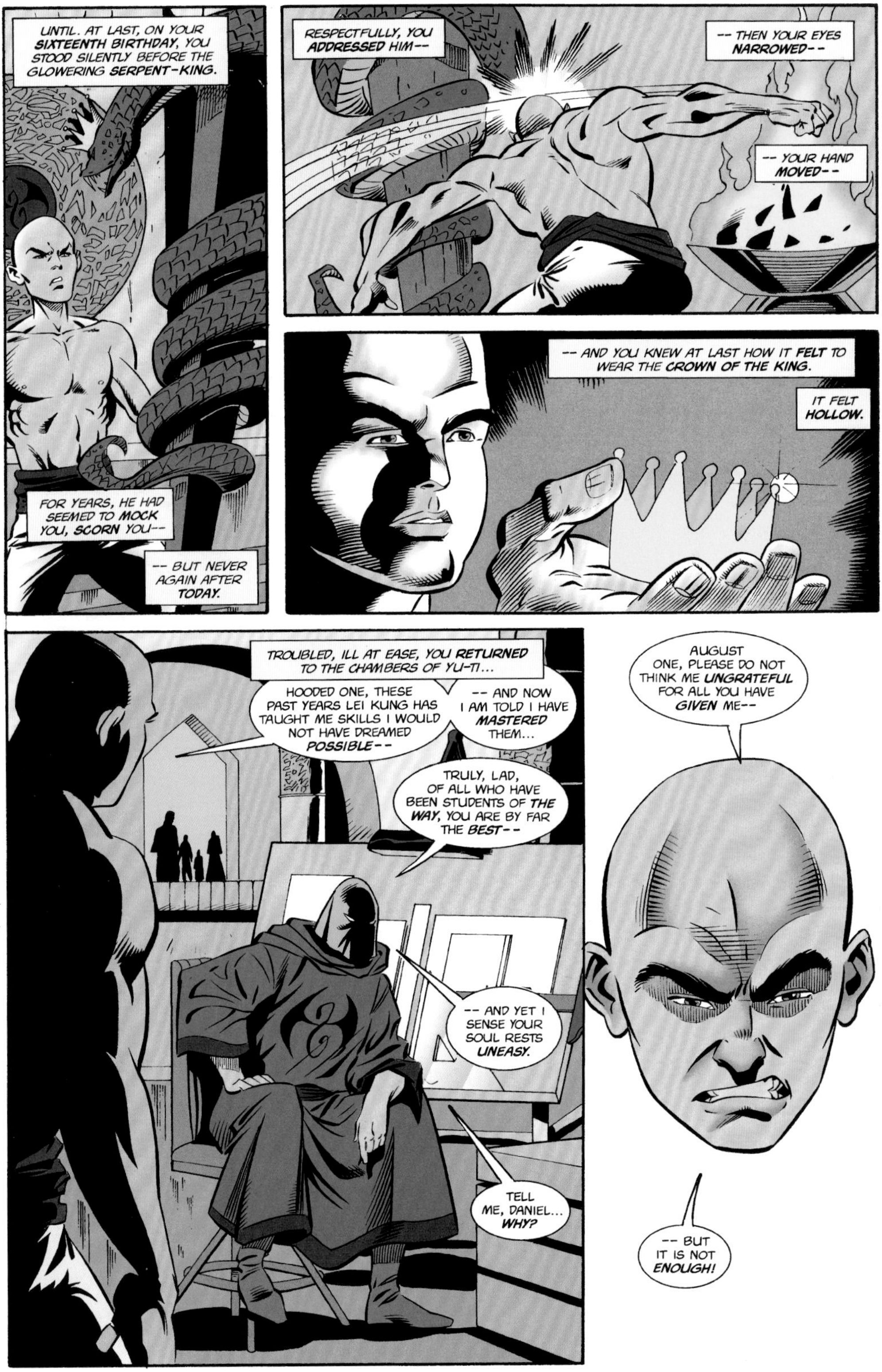
UNTIL. AT LAST, ON YOUR SIXTEENTH BIRTHDAY, YOU STOOD SILENTLY BEFORE THE GLOWERING SERPENT-KING.
FOR YEARS, HE HAD SEEMED TO MOCK YOU, SCORN YOU--
-- BUT NEVER AGAIN AFTER TODAY.
RESPECTFULLY, YOU ADDRESSED HIM--
-- THEN YOUR EYES NARROWED--
-- YOUR HAND MOVED--
-- AND YOU KNEW AT LAST HOW IT FELT TO WEAR THE CROWN OF THE KING.
IT FELT HOLLOW.
TROUBLED, ILL AT EASE, YOU RETURNED TO THE CHAMBERS OF YU-TI...
HOODED ONE, THESE PAST YEARS LEI KUNG HAS TAUGHT ME SKILLS I WOULD NOT HAVE DREAMED POSSIBLE--
-- AND NOW I AM TOLD I HAVE MASTERED THEM...
TRULY, LAD, OF ALL WHO HAVE BEEN STUDENTS OF THE WAY, YOU ARE BY FAR THE BEST--
-- AND YET I SENSE YOUR SOUL RESTS UNEASY.
TELL ME, DANIEL... WHY?
AUGUST ONE, PLEASE DO NOT THINK ME UNGRATEFUL FOR ALL YOU HAVE GIVEN ME--
-- BUT IT IS NOT ENOUGH!

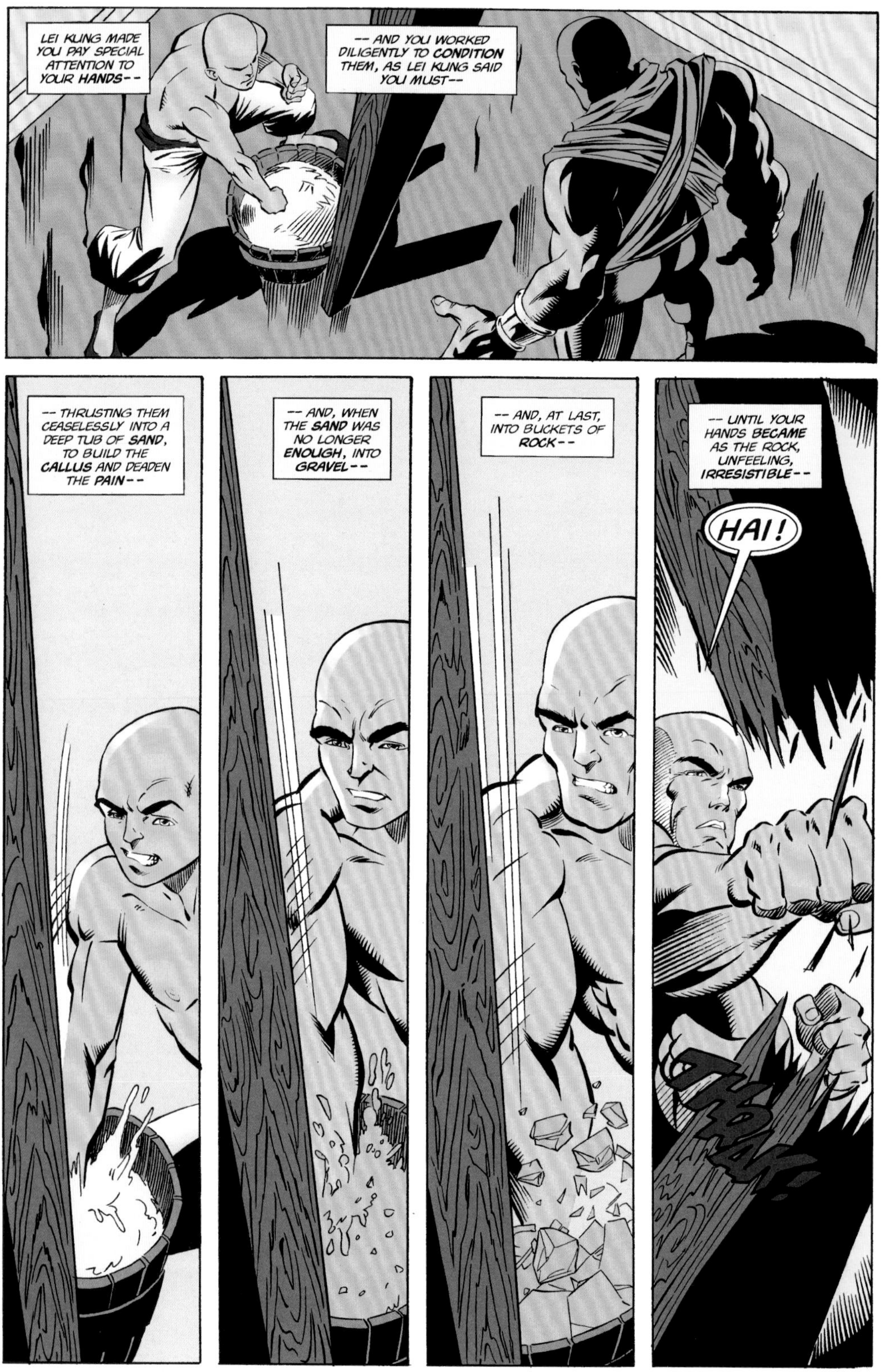
LEI KUNG MADE YOU PAY SPECIAL ATTENTION TO YOUR HANDS--
-- AND YOU WORKED DILIGENTLY TO CONDITION THEM, AS LEI KUNG SAID YOU MUST--
-- THRUSTING THEM CEASELESSLY INTO A DEEP TUB OF SAND, TO BUILD THE CALLUS AND DEADEN THE PAIN--
-- AND, WHEN THE SAND WAS NO LONGER ENOUGH, INTO GRAVEL--
-- AND, AT LAST, INTO BUCKETS OF ROCK--
-- UNTIL YOUR HANDS BECAME AS THE ROCK, UNFEELING, IRRESISTIBLE--
HAI!
THAAK!

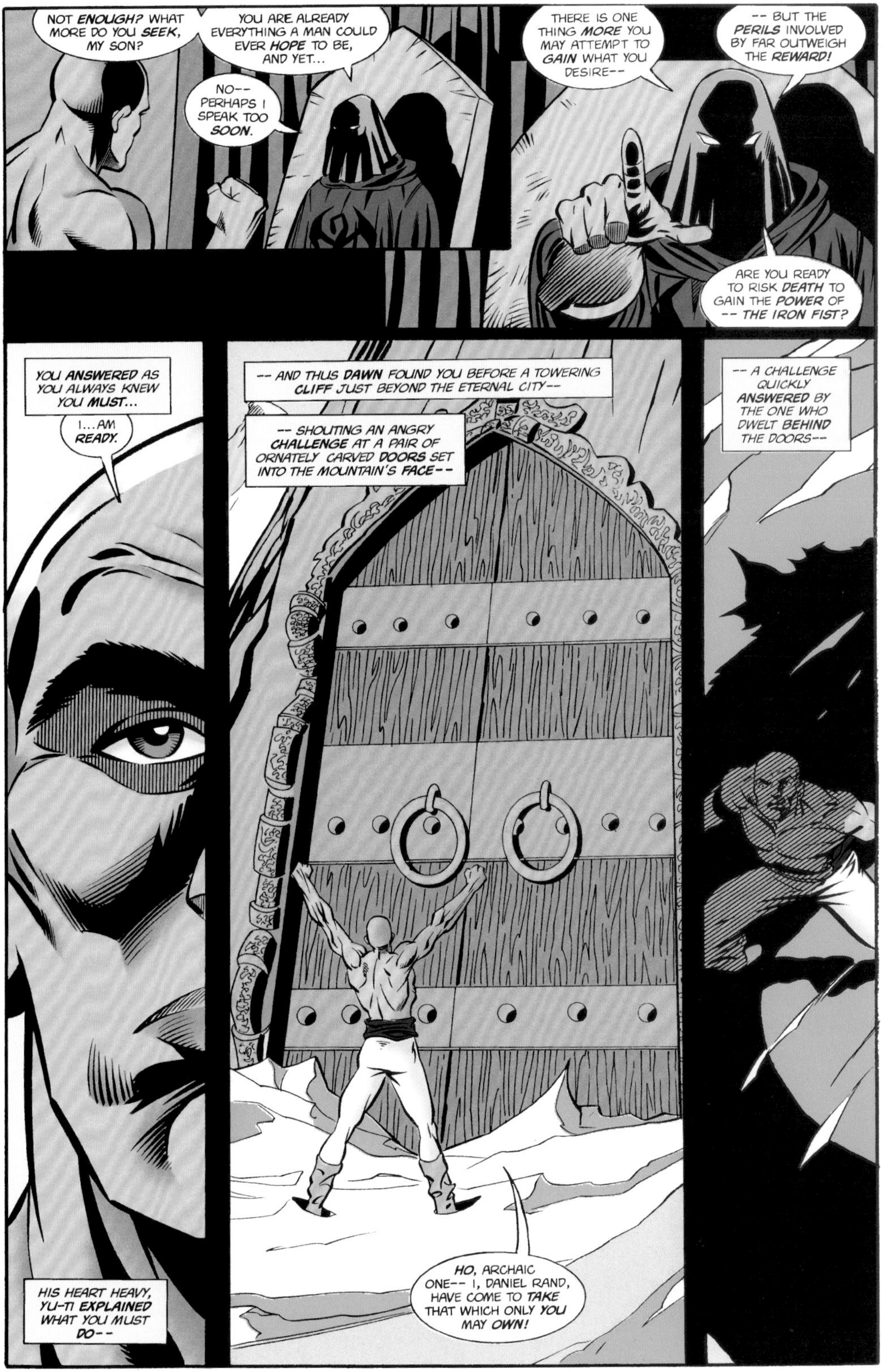

NOT ENOUGH? WHAT MORE DO YOU SEEK, MY SON?
YOU ARE ALREADY EVERYTHING A MAN COULD EVER HOPE TO BE, AND YET...
NO-- PERHAPS I SPEAK TOO SOON.
THERE IS ONE THING MORE YOU MAY ATTEMPT TO GAIN WHAT YOU DESIRE--
-- BUT THE PERILS INVOLVED BY FAR OUTWEIGH THE REWARD!
ARE YOU READY TO RISK DEATH TO GAIN THE POWER OF -- THE IRON FIST?
YOU ANSWERED AS YOU ALWAYS KNEW YOU MUST...
I...AM READY.
HIS HEART HEAVY, YU-TI EXPLAINED WHAT YOU MUST DO--
-- AND THUS DAWN FOUND YOU BEFORE A TOWERING CLIFF JUST BEYOND THE ETERNAL CITY--
-- SHOUTING AN ANGRY CHALLENGE AT A PAIR OF ORNATELY CARVED DOORS SET INTO THE MOUNTAIN'S FACE--
HO, ARCHAIC ONE-- I, DANIEL RAND, HAVE COME TO TAKE THAT WHICH ONLY YOU MAY OWN!
-- A CHALLENGE QUICKLY ANSWERED BY THE ONE WHO DWELT BEHIND THE DOORS--

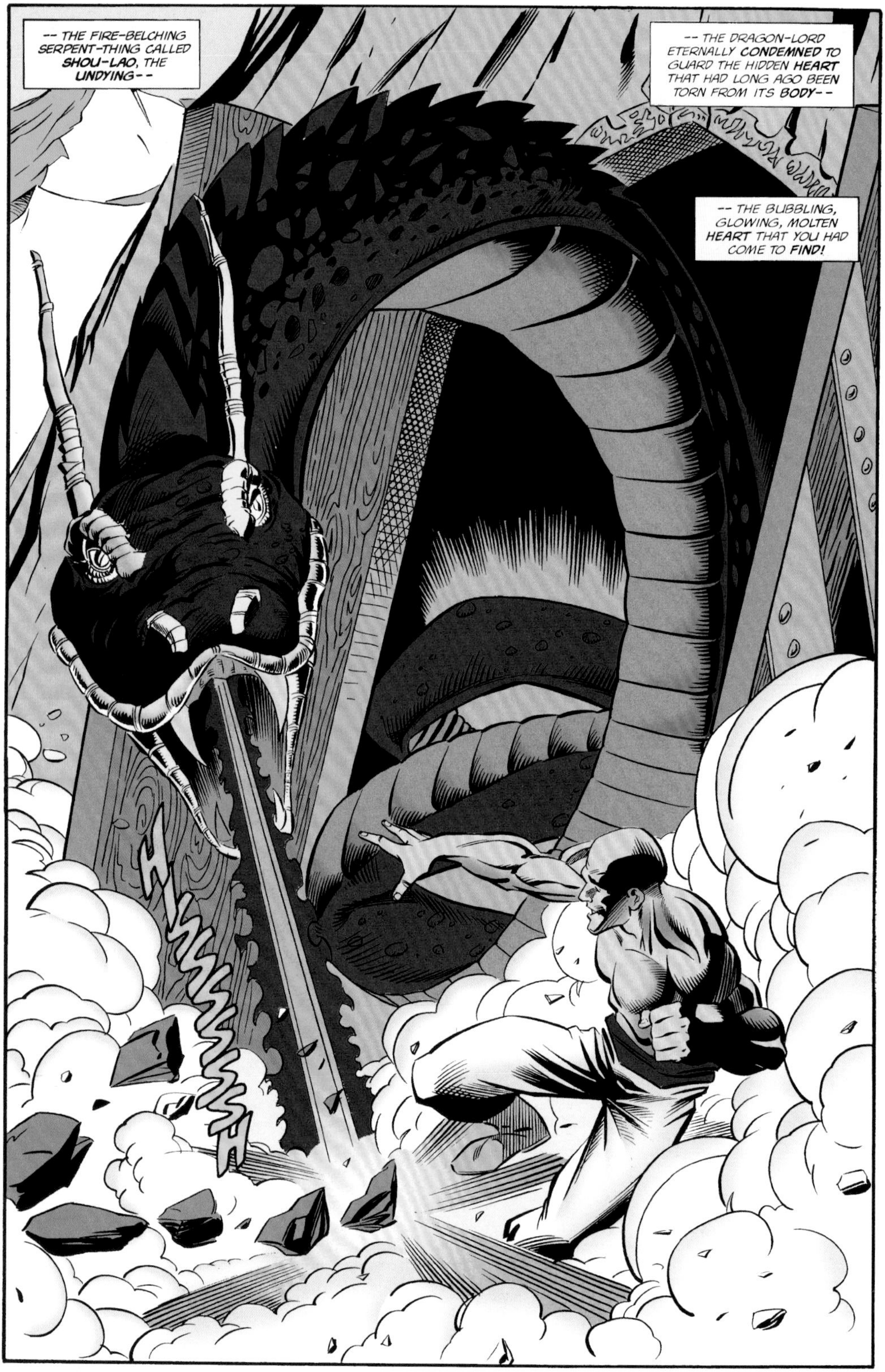
-- THE FIRE-BELCHING SERPENT-THING CALLED **SHOU-LAO**, THE **UNDYING**--
-- THE DRAGON-LORD ETERNALLY **CONDEMNED** TO GUARD THE HIDDEN **HEART** THAT HAD LONG AGO BEEN TORN FROM ITS **BODY**--
-- THE BUBBLING, GLOWING, MOLTEN **HEART** THAT YOU HAD COME TO **FIND!**

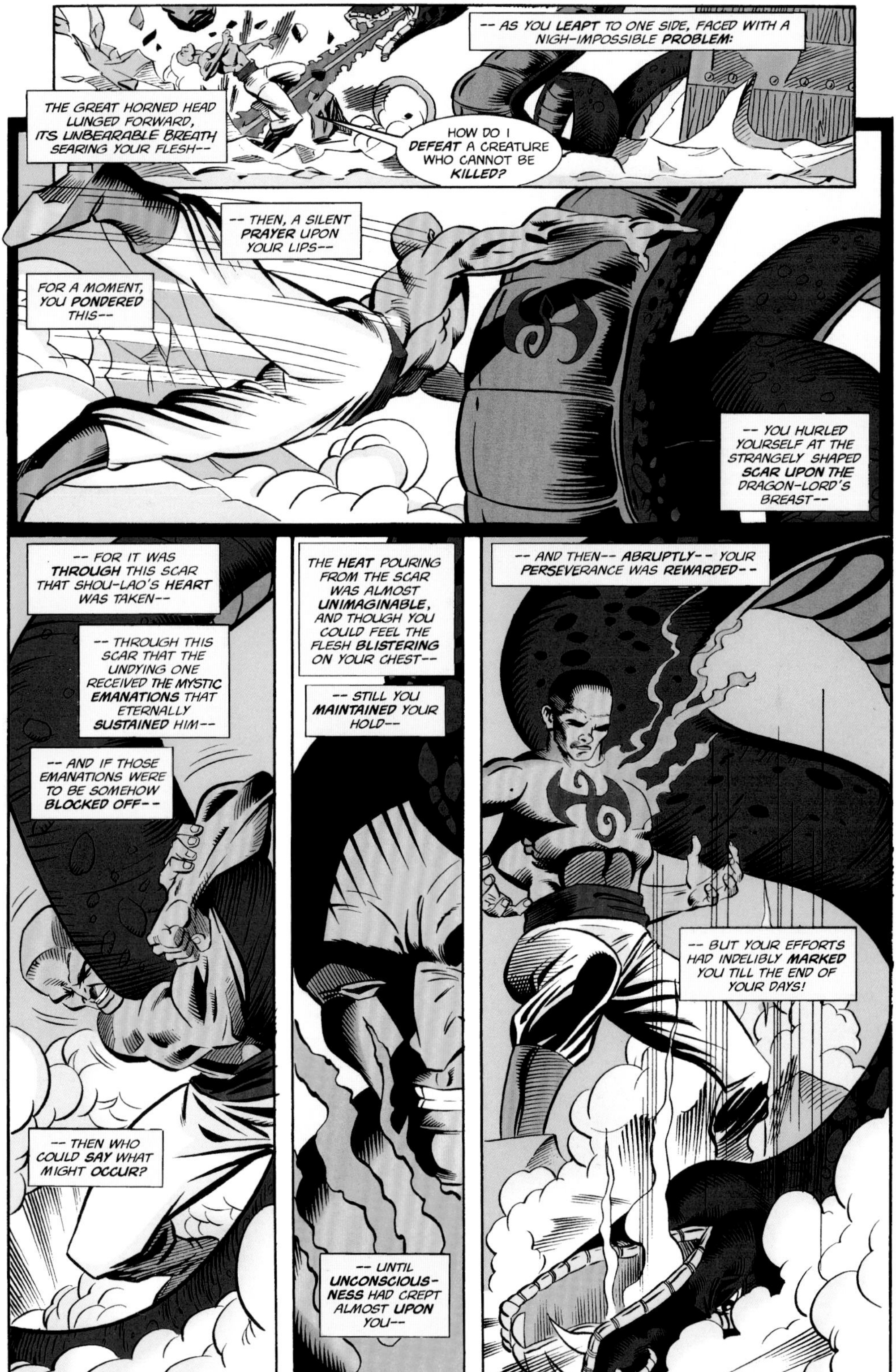
-- AS YOU LEAPT TO ONE SIDE, FACED WITH A NIGH-IMPOSSIBLE PROBLEM:
THE GREAT HORNED HEAD LUNGED FORWARD, ITS UNBEARABLE BREATH SEARING YOUR FLESH--
HOW DO I DEFEAT A CREATURE WHO CANNOT BE KILLED?
FOR A MOMENT, YOU PONDERED THIS--
-- THEN, A SILENT PRAYER UPON YOUR LIPS--
-- YOU HURLED YOURSELF AT THE STRANGELY SHAPED SCAR UPON THE DRAGON-LORD'S BREAST--
-- FOR IT WAS THROUGH THIS SCAR THAT SHOU-LAO'S HEART WAS TAKEN--
-- THROUGH THIS SCAR THAT THE UNDYING ONE RECEIVED THE MYSTIC EMANATIONS THAT ETERNALLY SUSTAINED HIM--
-- AND IF THOSE EMANATIONS WERE TO BE SOMEHOW BLOCKED OFF--
-- THEN WHO COULD SAY WHAT MIGHT OCCUR?
THE HEAT POURING FROM THE SCAR WAS ALMOST UNIMAGINABLE, AND THOUGH YOU COULD FEEL THE FLESH BLISTERING ON YOUR CHEST--
-- STILL YOU MAINTAINED YOUR HOLD--
-- UNTIL UNCONSCIOUS-NESS HAD CREPT ALMOST UPON YOU--
-- AND THEN-- ABRUPTLY-- YOUR PERSEVERANCE WAS REWARDED--
-- BUT YOUR EFFORTS HAD INDELIBLY MARKED YOU TILL THE END OF YOUR DAYS!

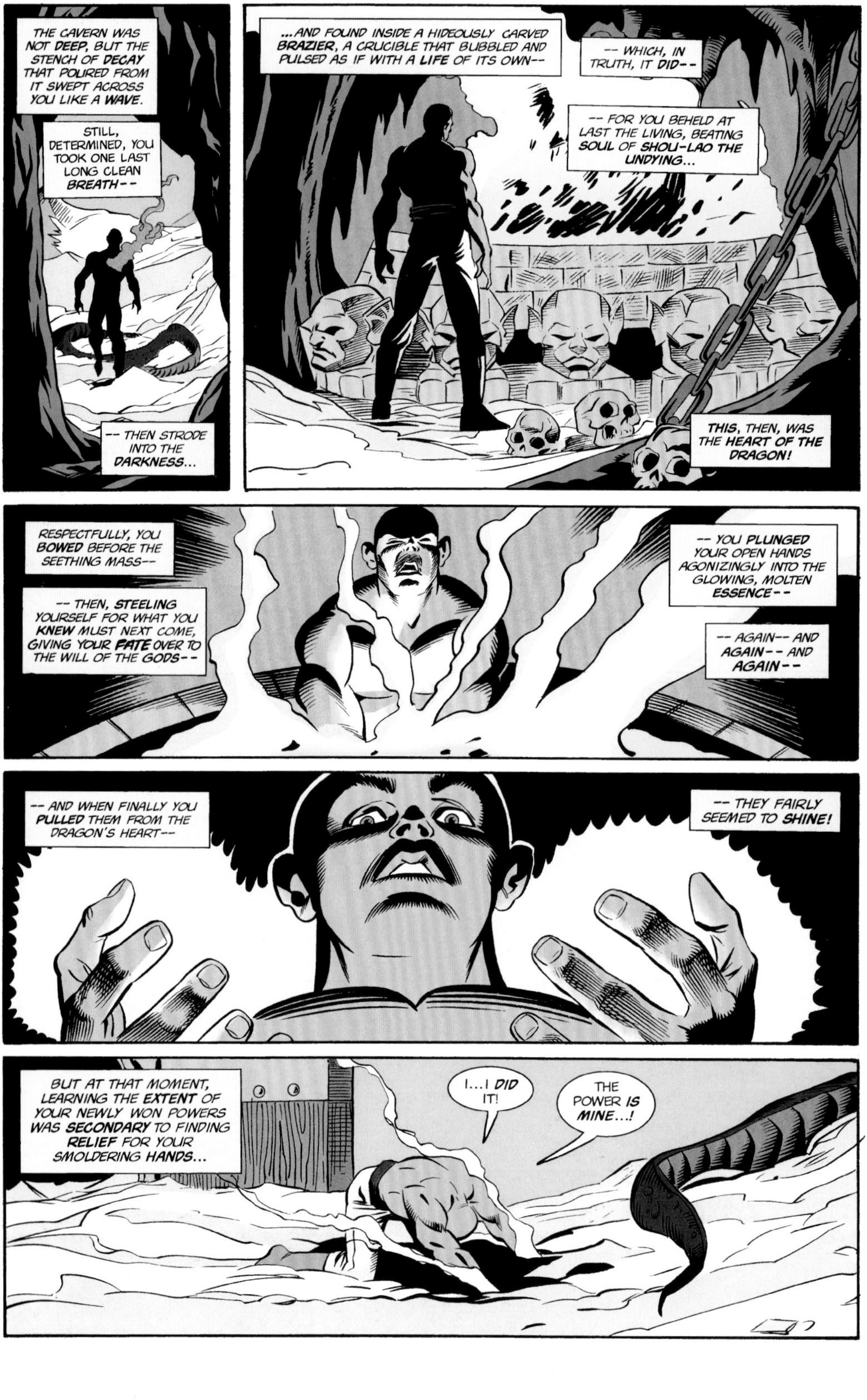
THE CAVERN WAS NOT DEEP, BUT THE STENCH OF DECAY THAT POURED FROM IT SWEPT ACROSS YOU LIKE A WAVE.
STILL, DETERMINED, YOU TOOK ONE LAST LONG CLEAN BREATH--
-- THEN STRODE INTO THE DARKNESS...
...AND FOUND INSIDE A HIDEOUSLY CARVED BRAZIER, A CRUCIBLE THAT BUBBLED AND PULSED AS IF WITH A LIFE OF ITS OWN--
-- WHICH, IN TRUTH, IT DID--
-- FOR YOU BEHELD AT LAST THE LIVING, BEATING SOUL OF SHOU-LAO THE UNDYING...
THIS, THEN, WAS THE HEART OF THE DRAGON!
RESPECTFULLY, YOU BOWED BEFORE THE SEETHING MASS--
-- THEN, STEELING YOURSELF FOR WHAT YOU KNEW MUST NEXT COME, GIVING YOUR FATE OVER TO THE WILL OF THE GODS--
-- YOU PLUNGED YOUR OPEN HANDS AGONIZINGLY INTO THE GLOWING, MOLTEN ESSENCE--
-- AGAIN-- AND AGAIN-- AND AGAIN--
-- AND WHEN FINALLY YOU PULLED THEM FROM THE DRAGON'S HEART--
-- THEY FAIRLY SEEMED TO SHINE!
BUT AT THAT MOMENT, LEARNING THE EXTENT OF YOUR NEWLY WON POWERS WAS SECONDARY TO FINDING RELIEF FOR YOUR SMOLDERING HANDS...
I...I DID IT!
THE POWER IS MINE...!

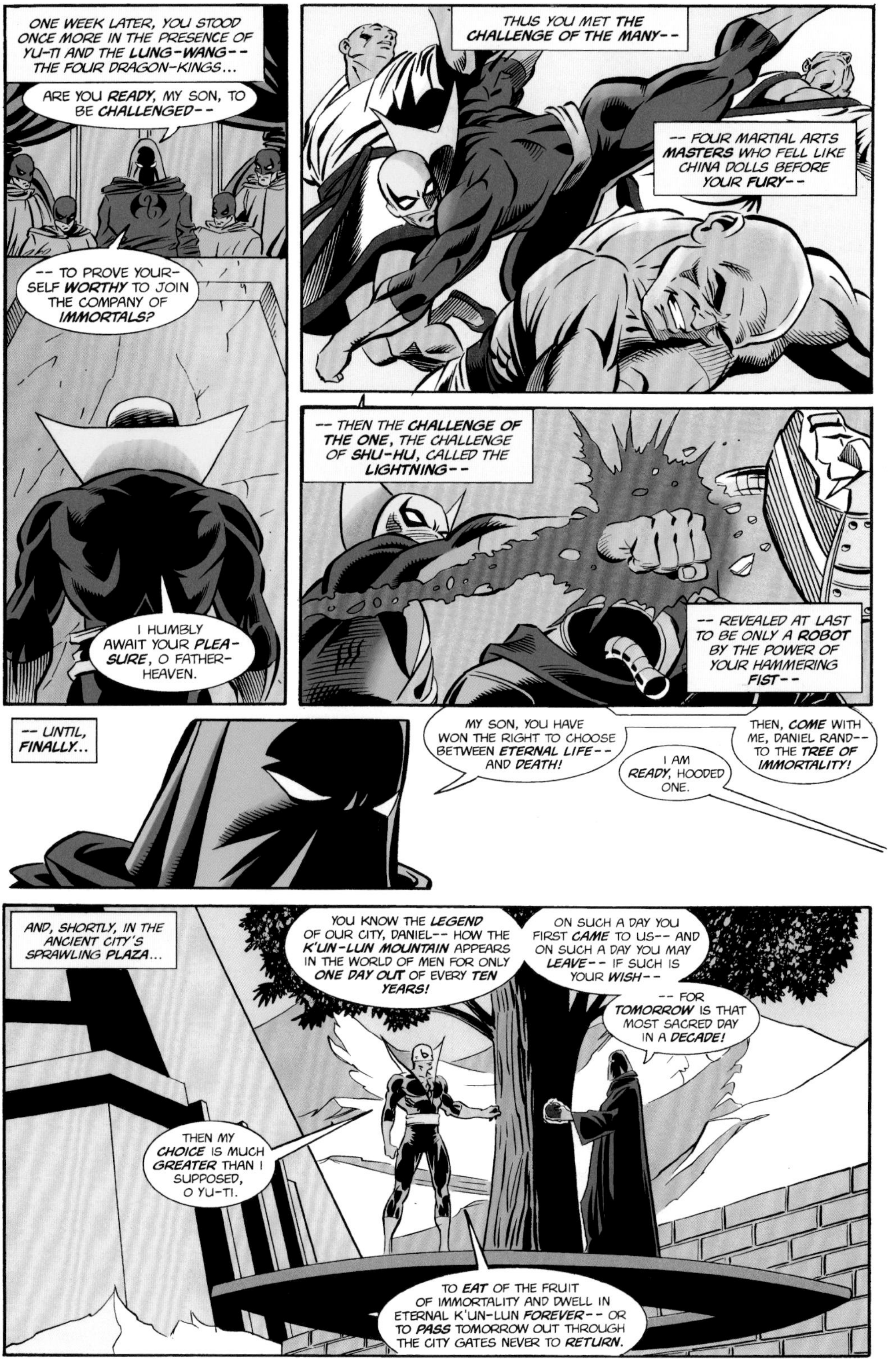
ONE WEEK LATER, YOU STOOD ONCE MORE IN THE PRESENCE OF YU-TI AND THE LUNG-WANG-- THE FOUR DRAGON-KINGS...
ARE YOU READY, MY SON, TO BE CHALLENGED--
-- TO PROVE YOURSELF WORTHY TO JOIN THE COMPANY OF IMMORTALS?
I HUMBLY AWAIT YOUR PLEASURE, O FATHER-HEAVEN.
THUS YOU MET THE CHALLENGE OF THE MANY--
-- FOUR MARTIAL ARTS MASTERS WHO FELL LIKE CHINA DOLLS BEFORE YOUR FURY--
-- THEN THE CHALLENGE OF THE ONE, THE CHALLENGE OF SHU-HU, CALLED THE LIGHTNING--
-- REVEALED AT LAST TO BE ONLY A ROBOT BY THE POWER OF YOUR HAMMERING FIST--
-- UNTIL, FINALLY...
MY SON, YOU HAVE WON THE RIGHT TO CHOOSE BETWEEN ETERNAL LIFE-- AND DEATH!
I AM READY, HOODED ONE.
THEN, COME WITH ME, DANIEL RAND-- TO THE TREE OF IMMORTALITY!
AND, SHORTLY, IN THE ANCIENT CITY'S SPRAWLING PLAZA...
YOU KNOW THE LEGEND OF OUR CITY, DANIEL-- HOW THE K'UN-LUN MOUNTAIN APPEARS IN THE WORLD OF MEN FOR ONLY ONE DAY OUT OF EVERY TEN YEARS!
ON SUCH A DAY YOU FIRST CAME TO US-- AND ON SUCH A DAY YOU MAY LEAVE-- IF SUCH IS YOUR WISH--
-- FOR TOMORROW IS THAT MOST SACRED DAY IN A DECADE!
THEN MY CHOICE IS MUCH GREATER THAN I SUPPOSED, O YU-TI.
TO EAT OF THE FRUIT OF IMMORTALITY AND DWELL IN ETERNAL K'UN-LUN FOREVER-- OR TO PASS TOMORROW OUT THROUGH THE CITY GATES NEVER TO RETURN.

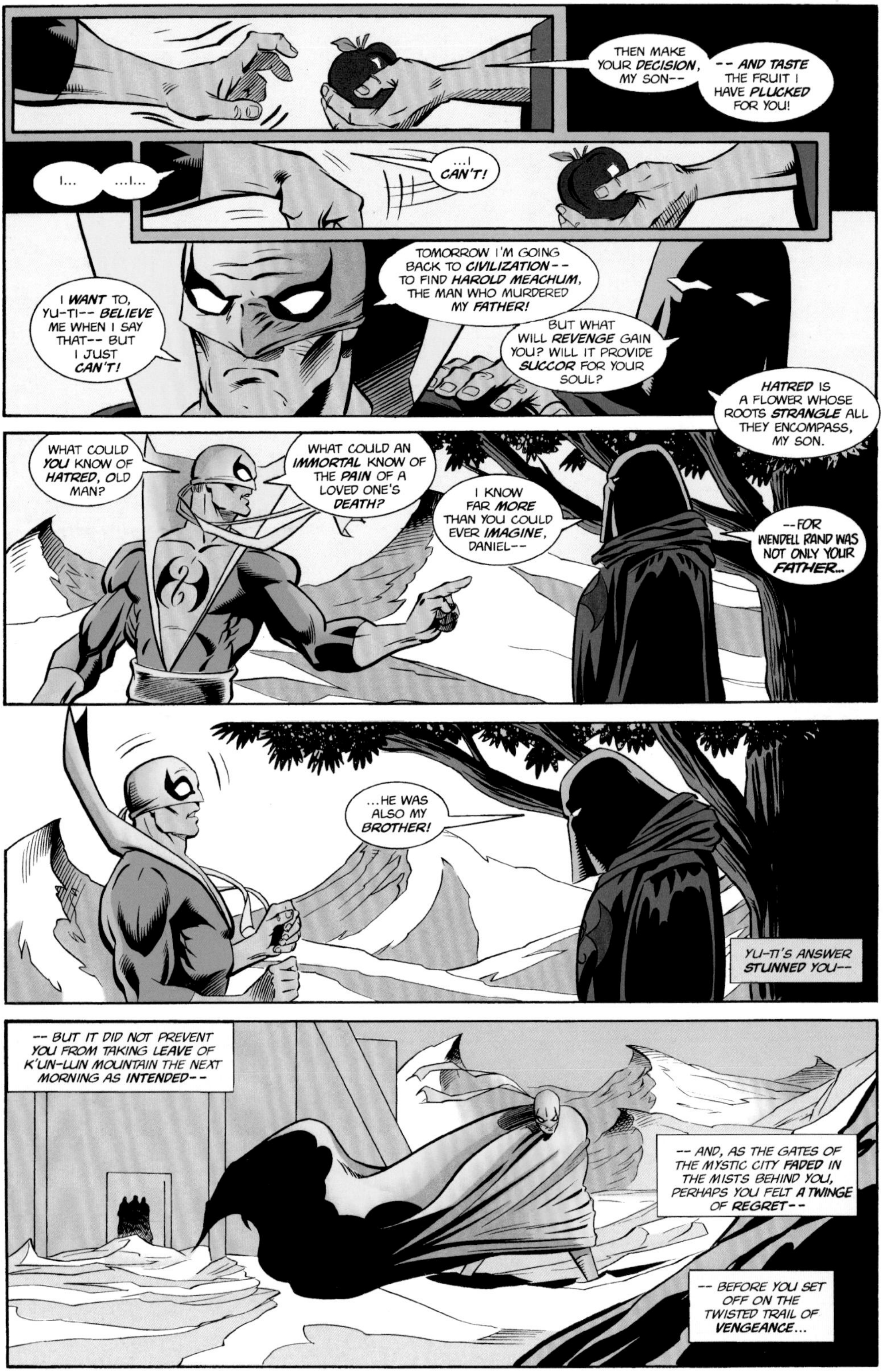

THEN MAKE YOUR DECISION, MY SON--
-- AND TASTE THE FRUIT I HAVE PLUCKED FOR YOU!
I...
...I...
...I CAN'T!
I WANT TO, YU-TI-- BELIEVE ME WHEN I SAY THAT-- BUT I JUST CAN'T!
TOMORROW I'M GOING BACK TO CIVILIZATION-- TO FIND HAROLD MEACHUM, THE MAN WHO MURDERED MY FATHER!
BUT WHAT WILL REVENGE GAIN YOU? WILL IT PROVIDE SUCCOR FOR YOUR SOUL?
HATRED IS A FLOWER WHOSE ROOTS STRANGLE ALL THEY ENCOMPASS, MY SON.
WHAT COULD YOU KNOW OF HATRED, OLD MAN?
WHAT COULD AN IMMORTAL KNOW OF THE PAIN OF A LOVED ONE'S DEATH?
I KNOW FAR MORE THAN YOU COULD EVER IMAGINE, DANIEL--
--FOR WENDELL RAND WAS NOT ONLY YOUR FATHER...
...HE WAS ALSO MY BROTHER!
YU-TI'S ANSWER STUNNED YOU--
-- BUT IT DID NOT PREVENT YOU FROM TAKING LEAVE OF K'UN-LUN MOUNTAIN THE NEXT MORNING AS INTENDED--
-- AND, AS THE GATES OF THE MYSTIC CITY FADED IN THE MISTS BEHIND YOU, PERHAPS YOU FELT A TWINGE OF REGRET--
-- BEFORE YOU SET OFF ON THE TWISTED TRAIL OF VENGEANCE...

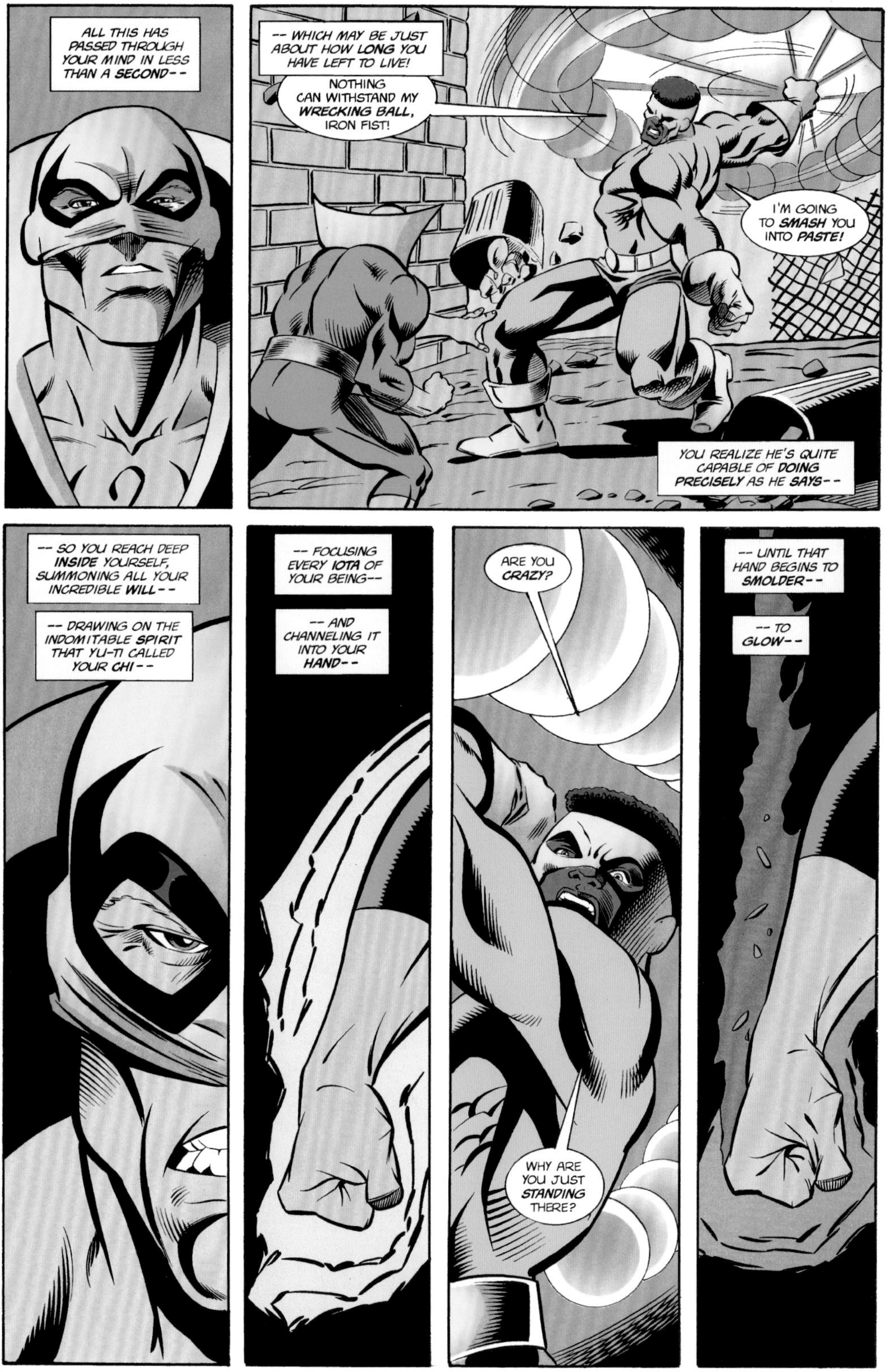
ALL THIS HAS PASSED THROUGH YOUR MIND IN LESS THAN A SECOND--
-- WHICH MAY BE JUST ABOUT HOW LONG YOU HAVE LEFT TO LIVE!
NOTHING CAN WITHSTAND MY WRECKING BALL, IRON FIST!
I'M GOING TO SMASH YOU INTO PASTE!
YOU REALIZE HE'S QUITE CAPABLE OF DOING PRECISELY AS HE SAYS--
-- SO YOU REACH DEEP INSIDE YOURSELF, SUMMONING ALL YOUR INCREDIBLE WILL--
-- DRAWING ON THE INDOMITABLE SPIRIT THAT YU-TI CALLED YOUR CHI--
-- FOCUSING EVERY IOTA OF YOUR BEING--
-- AND CHANNELING IT INTO YOUR HAND--
ARE YOU CRAZY?
WHY ARE YOU JUST STANDING THERE?
-- UNTIL THAT HAND BEGINS TO SMOLDER--
-- TO GLOW--

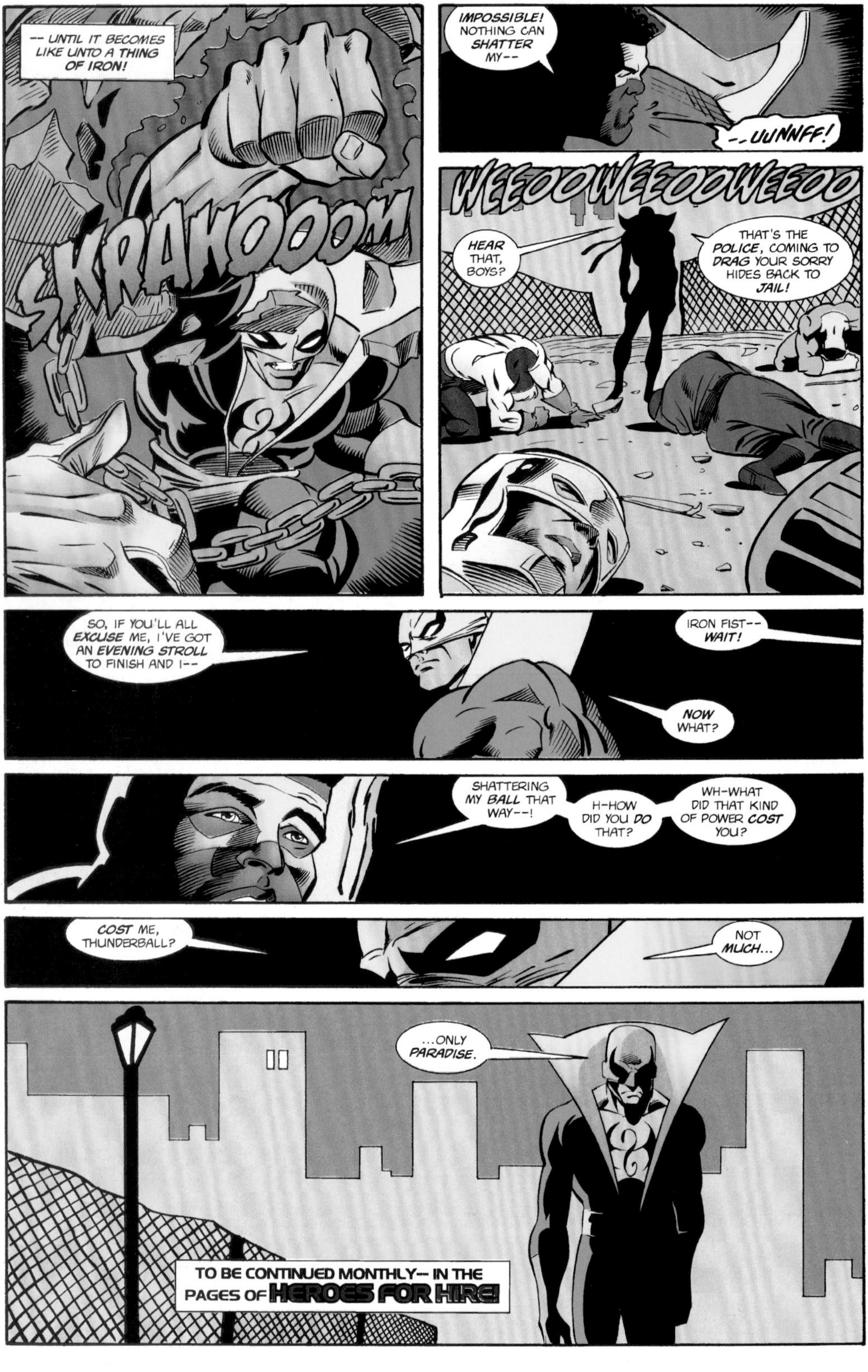
-- UNTIL IT BECOMES LIKE UNTO A THING OF IRON!
SKRAKOOOM
IMPOSSIBLE! NOTHING CAN SHATTER MY--
--UUNNFF!
WEEOOWEEOOWEEOO
HEAR THAT, BOYS?
THAT'S THE POLICE, COMING TO DRAG YOUR SORRY HIDES BACK TO JAIL!
SO, IF YOU'LL ALL EXCUSE ME, I'VE GOT AN EVENING STROLL TO FINISH AND I--
IRON FIST-- WAIT!
NOW WHAT?
SHATTERING MY BALL THAT WAY--!
H-HOW DID YOU DO THAT?
WH-WHAT DID THAT KIND OF POWER COST YOU?
COST ME, THUNDERBALL?
NOT MUCH...
...ONLY PARADISE.
TO BE CONTINUED MONTHLY-- IN THE PAGES OF HEROES FOR HIRE!

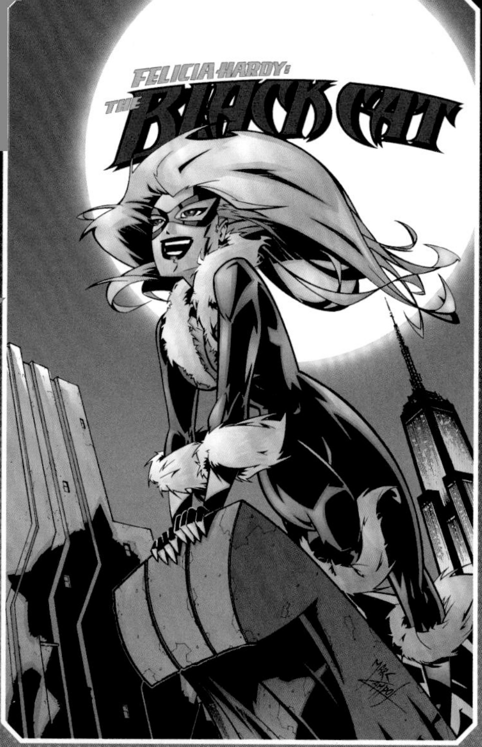
FELICIA HARDY:
THE BLACK CAT

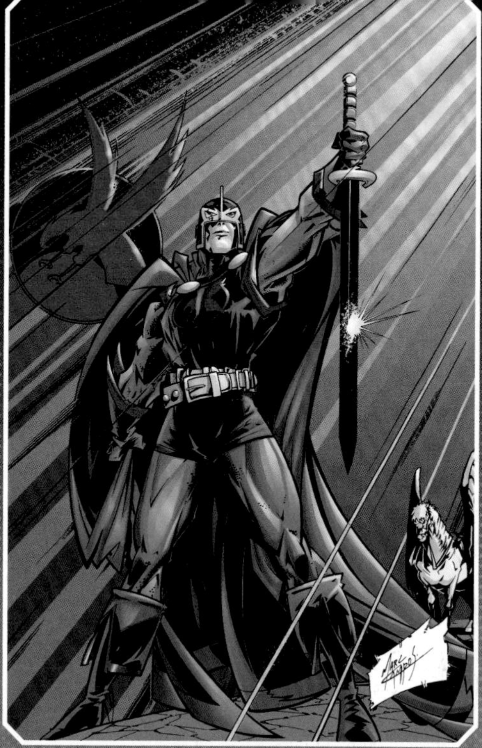

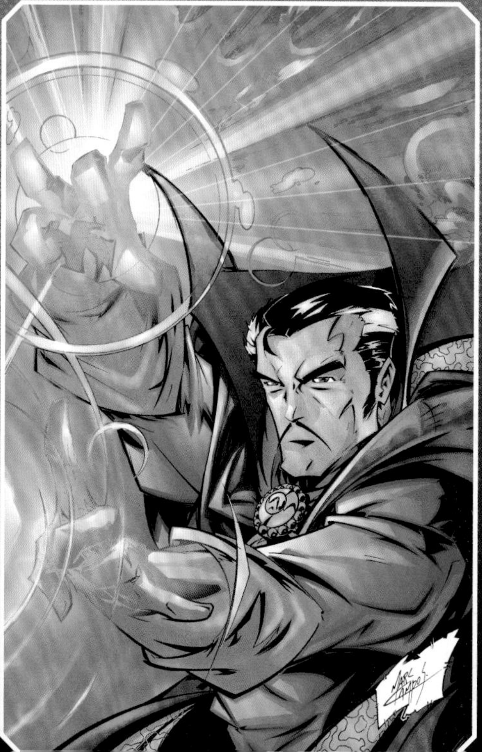

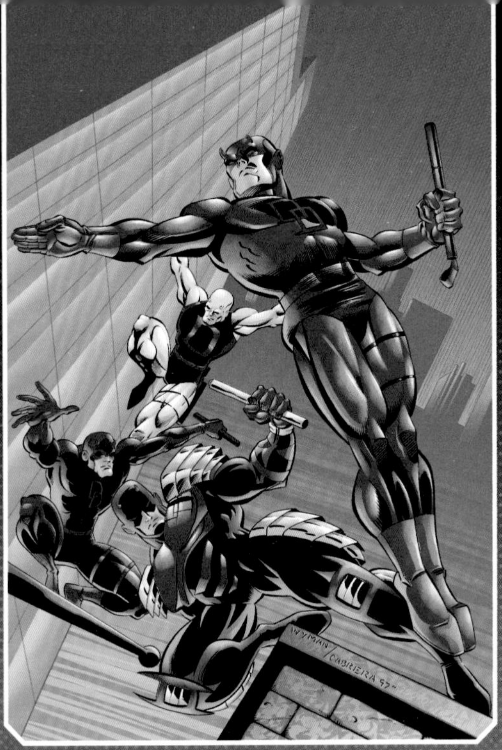
WYMAN/CABRERA '97

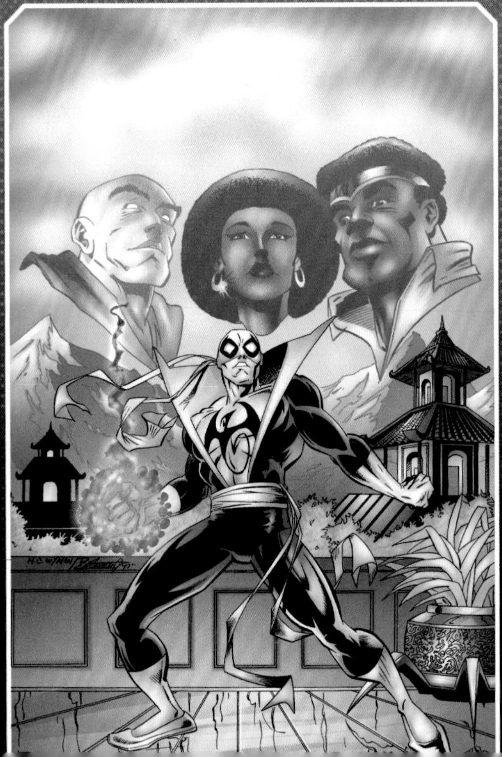